I0590086

J.K. ROSS

A Throne in Bloom

The Thorned Sigil Book 1

First published by Lark and Lore Press 2026

Copyright © 2026 by J.K. Ross

All rights reserved. No part of this publication may be reproduced, stored or transmitted in any form or by any means, electronic, mechanical, photocopying, recording, scanning, or otherwise without written permission from the publisher. It is illegal to copy this book, post it to a website, or distribute it by any other means without permission.

This novel is entirely a work of fiction. The names, characters and incidents portrayed in it are the work of the author's imagination. Any resemblance to actual persons, living or dead, events or localities is entirely coincidental.

J.K. Ross asserts the moral right to be identified as the author of this work.

J.K. Ross has no responsibility for the persistence or accuracy of URLs for external or third-party Internet Websites referred to in this publication and does not guarantee that any content on such Websites is, or will remain, accurate or appropriate.

Designations used by companies to distinguish their products are often claimed as trademarks. All brand names and product names used in this book and on its cover are trade names, service marks, trademarks and registered trademarks of their respective owners. The publishers and the book are not associated with any product or vendor mentioned in this book. None of the companies referenced within the book have endorsed the book.

ISBNs

Paperback Edition: 979-8-9937037-0-1

Special Edition Paperback: 979-8-9937037-2-5

Ebook / Kindle Edition: 979-8-9937037-1-8

First edition

ISBN: 979-8-9937037-0-1

Editing by Laura Dugan
Cover art by Selkkie Designs

This book was professionally typeset on Reedsy.
Find out more at reedsy.com

For my grandmother, who taught me that gardens and stories grow the same way—with patience, love, and a little bit of magic.

Contents

Acknowledgments

This book has lived in my heart since elementary school, when I made and illustrated stories every chance I got. These pages hold a lifetime of dreaming and a year of grief transformed into words.

To my grandmother, who read every day of her life and taught me that books are how we carry each other through time: You were right about everything. Your home was pure magic—a botanical garden that bloomed with the same life and color you brought to every story we shared. You tended words the way you tended flowers, with a green thumb that made everything flourish. Every happy memory I have of growing up happened in the world you created. When we lost you last year, I knew it was time. These words are how I've learned to let you go while keeping you close. Thank you for my love of books and for giving me stories to last a lifetime. Now your memory sits on shelves around the world, exactly where you always wanted to be—deep inside a story.

To AJ, my husband, who is every book boyfriend come to life: You've supported every hair-brained idea I've ever had and never once tried to clip my wings. Thank you for letting me fly.

To my kids, for bringing fun and wild moments that keep every day interesting and every story alive.

To Laura, for being both my best friend and my editor—I know you'll pick me up after you rip my pages apart.

To Melanie, Joscelyn, and Tori, who love reading as fiercely as I do and have been ridiculously excited through this entire journey. To Allison, my lifetime friend who has stood with me through every season and cheered me toward every goal. I love you all.

To Jayet Abdul (@madewithlovx) for the beautiful character art and

@selkkiedesigns for bringing the cover of my dreams to life—your talent is a gift I'm blessed to be associated with.

To my beta readers, who gave their precious time and left heartfelt, constructive feedback that elevated this novel beyond what I could have achieved alone. I am humbled by your generosity.

To my amazing street team, The Peebles. The most amazing hype squad I could have ever asked for. You have made this journey fun, and very fulfilling!

And finally, to you, my readers and followers: Thank you for helping me carry my grandmother forward through these words. Because of you, she lives on in the only place she ever wanted to be.

* * *

Professional Credits

Editorial Services — www.howyoudugan.com

Cover Design — www.selkkiedesigns.com

Publisher — www.larkandlore.press

THE THORNED SIGIL
BOOK 1

A THRONE IN BLOOM

J.K. ROSS

Content Warnings

This book contains themes and scenes that may be triggering for some readers. Please take care of yourself while reading.

Major content warnings include:

- Death of a loved one/grief processing (grandmother, off-page)
- Violence and battle scenes with injury descriptions
- Blood and gore in combat situations
- Body horror/transformation scenes
- Torture (physical and psychological)
- Captivity and restraints
- Power imbalances and coercion
- Systemic oppression and classism
- Magical corruption affecting the body
- Kidnapping/abduction
- Death of secondary characters
- Emotional manipulation
- Threats of violence against innocents
- Explicit sexual content (consensual, detailed)
- Sexual situations involving magical influence (aphrodisiac pollen, enchanted vines)
- Light bondage and restraint during sexual scenes (consensual)
- Dream / fantasy sexual encounter with blurred reality

Additional content that may be sensitive:

- Toxic family dynamics
- Past relationship betrayal (infidelity mentioned)
- Alcohol consumption
- Mild language/profanity
- Insects (magical bees feature prominently)
- Environmental decay/destruction

This is an adult fantasy romance with dark and explicit sexual themes. While there is love and hope throughout, the journey includes moments of peril, trauma, and moral complexity.

If you need to skip certain scenes, please know the story's heart is about finding light in darkness and love that transcends impossible circumstances.

For specific scene guidance or questions about content, readers are welcome to reach out via authorjkross.com.

Illustration by Jayet Abdul

1

Elle

The house exhaled when I crossed the threshold—a long, patient breath that smelled of lavender, old books, and something green I couldn't name. Like it had been holding its breath for sixty years, waiting for someone to finally come home.

"Just dump them wherever, Leo," I said, swiping sweat off my forehead with the back of my hand. August in Arkansas was hellish enough without hauling boxes up narrow Victorian stairs that creaked ominously with every step. "The dining room's already a disaster anyway."

The living room looked like a storage unit had exploded. Boxes stacked in precarious towers, furniture wrapped in dusty sheets that probably hadn't been removed in years, and at least seventeen lamps—I'd counted—that I'm pretty sure nobody had ever plugged in, let alone liked.

Grandma Jo had been many things, but a minimalist wasn't one of them. Every surface held something: porcelain birds, crystal bowls, those creepy dolls with eyes that followed you around the room. It was like she'd been afraid of empty spaces—like she needed to fill every corner with proof that she'd lived.

"That's the last of it," Leo declared, dropping a box marked 'FRAGILE' with absolutely zero regard for the label. He rubbed the back of his neck, his hair sticking up in twelve different directions—half from the humidity, half from pure exhaustion. "And before you ask, yes, I know it says fragile.

1

No, I don't care. Whatever's in there survived the drive from Little Rock, it can survive being set down with emphasis."

"My hero," I said dryly, pulling a warm Dr Pepper from the cooler we'd brought. The carbonation hissed as I cracked it open, and I took a long drink despite it being the temperature of bathwater. "Want one?"

"I still can't believe you drink those warm." Leo made a face like I'd offered him poison. "That's serial killer behavior, Elle."

"It's efficient behavior. No ice needed, no condensation ruining my sketches." I took another deliberate sip, maintaining eye contact just to watch him shudder. "Besides, you put ketchup on mac and cheese. You don't get to judge anyone's food choices."

"That's different. That's flavor enhancement."

"That's an abomination before God and man."

He laughed, the sound bouncing off the high ceilings and making the empty house feel less hollow for a moment. Leo and I had been doing this dance since we were kids—he the golden boy athlete with the easy smile, me the weird art kid who preferred fictional worlds to real ones. Cousins by blood, friends by choice, though lately, it felt like we were the only family each other had left.

His phone buzzed, and his expression shifted from amused to concerned in about two seconds flat. "Shit. Mom's having another episode with the neighbors. Something about their fence being two inches over the property line." He looked genuinely torn. "I should probably—"

"Go," I said, waving him off. "Aunt Sharon needs you more than I need help organizing Grandma's extensive collection of decorative spoons."

"You sure? I know this is..." He gestured vaguely at the chaos around us, but we both knew he meant more than just the boxes. This was Grandma Jo's house, and Grandma Jo was gone. Had been for three weeks now, though it still didn't feel real.

"I'm sure. I've got enough Dr Pepper to last me through the apocalypse, and the pizza place delivers until midnight." I forced a smile that probably looked more like a grimace. "Besides, I need to start going through her things. Figure out what to keep, what to donate, what to burn in a cleansing

2

ritual to appease whatever spirits she accidentally trapped in those creepy dolls."

Leo pulled me into a quick hug, the kind that said everything we couldn't put into words. His shirt smelled like sweat and that ridiculous body spray he'd been using since high school. "Call if you need anything. Even if it's just to complain about the dolls watching you."

"They are definitely watching me."

"They're definitely watching everyone. I'm pretty sure Grandma enchanted them." He paused at the door, looking back. "Hey, Elle? She'd be proud of you. Moving here, taking care of the house. She always said you were the only one who understood."

"Understood what?"

But he was already gone, the screen door banging shut behind him with a finality that made my chest tight. The sound of his truck starting up, gravel crunching under tires, then nothing. Just me and the house and seventeen unused lamps and whatever the hell Grandma Jo thought I understood.

I stood in the sudden silence, Dr Pepper in hand, and tried to feel something other than overwhelmed. The afternoon light slanted through the windows, catching dust motes that danced like tiny ghosts. Everything smelled old—not bad old, just old. Like pressed flowers and furniture polish and that particular scent that clings to houses where someone elderly lived alone for too long.

My car keys sat on the entry table next to a note Leo had left: "Your car's in the garage. Don't forget to drive it occasionally so the battery doesn't die. Again. -L"

Right. I had a car. A perfectly functional Honda that I'd driven exactly three times since moving here from Little Rock. Walking everywhere in a small town was one thing; forgetting you owned a vehicle was another level of—

The locket around my neck grew suddenly heavy, pulling my attention away from spiraling thoughts about my various dysfunctions. It pressed against my sternum, warm and insistent, like it was trying to tell me something.".

3

"It was my mother's," she'd said, her eyes fever-bright with whatever was killing her. "And her mother's before that. It goes to you now. When the time comes, you'll know what to do with it."

"'What time, Jo?' I'd asked, but she was already fading, morphine pulling her under. The cancer had come fast—too fast, the doctors said, surprised by how aggressive it was in someone who'd seemed so vital just months before."

Now it hung around my neck like a question I didn't have an answer to. Inside was a portrait of a woman who looked like Jo but wasn't—someone from before, from the old country, she'd always said, though she'd never specified which old country that was. The woman in the portrait had red hair like mine, like Jo's before it went silver, and eyes that seemed to know things. Secret things. Dangerous things.

I shook off the feeling and headed to the kitchen, weaving between boxes and trying not to trip over the truly impressive collection of extension cords Grandma had apparently been hoarding. The kitchen, at least, was mostly functional. Old appliances that probably qualified as antiques, but they worked. The refrigerator hummed like it was considering retirement but hadn't quite committed yet.

The afternoon stretched ahead, empty and daunting. I should unpack. Should start sorting. Should do literally anything productive. Instead, I found myself wandering, Dr Pepper in hand, reacquainting myself with the house I'd visited every summer as a kid.

The library was exactly as I remembered—floor-to-ceiling shelves crammed with everything from ancient encyclopedias to romance novels with absolutely scandalous covers. This was where I'd spent most of my summers, curled up in the window seat with a book while Grandma Jo worked in her garden. She'd bring me sandwiches and Dr Pepper—always Dr Pepper, never Coke, never coffee, like it was some sort of family tradition—and we'd eat in comfortable silence, surrounded by stories.

The window seat was still there, faded cushion and all. I sat down, muscle memory taking over, and looked out at the garden.

Or what was left of it.

Three weeks of neglect in August had not been kind. The lawn was more brown than green, and the flower beds looked like they were staging a botanical coup. Roses grew in wild tangles, their thorns catching the light like tiny daggers. The vegetable garden had gone completely feral—tomatoes rotting on the vine, squash plants attempting world domination, and something that might have been lettuce but now looked like it was planning to evolve consciousness.

But there, in the center of it all, stood Grandma Jo's pride and joy: an elm tree that had to be older than the house itself. Its branches spread wide, creating a pool of shade where the grass remained stubbornly, impossibly green—untouched by the drought that had killed everything else. I'd forgotten about that. How the grass under that tree never died, no matter what.

That tree had always been weird. Even as a kid, I'd felt it—like it was watching, waiting, keeping secrets Grandma Jo never talked about. She'd tend to everything else in the garden, but that tree she'd just stare at sometimes, her expression unreadable.

My phone buzzed. A text from my best friend Kya back in Little Rock: "How's the haunted house? Find any skeleton keys or mysterious journals yet?"

"Just a dozen lamps and a collection of dolls that definitely have souls trapped in them," I texted back.

"Burn them with fire."

"The dolls or the lamps?"

"Yes."

I smiled despite myself. Kya had wanted me to stay in Little Rock, get therapy, not isolate myself in my dead grandmother's house two hours away from civilization. She wasn't wrong, but she wasn't right either. I needed this—the space, the silence, the chance to figure out who I was when I wasn't someone's girlfriend, someone's daughter, someone's anything.

My last relationship had ended with me finding my fiancé in our bed with my supposed friend. Classic, really. So cliché it was almost funny, except for the part where it shattered my ability to trust anyone including myself.

How had I not seen it? How had I been so blind?

Julian had been perfect on paper—successful lawyer, came from a good family, treated me well in public. Behind closed doors, he'd been slowly shrinking my world, commenting on my art ("It's a nice hobby, but you can't expect to make a living from it"), my friends ("Kya's kind of trashy, don't you think?"), my dreams ("Romance novel covers? Really, Elle? You're better than that.").

I'd been disappearing piece by piece, and I hadn't even noticed until I walked in on him with Melissa and felt, beneath the hurt and rage, relief. Like I'd been holding my breath for two years and could finally exhale.

The locket grew warm against my skin, pulling me out of my spiral. I touched it absently, and for a second, I could swear I smelled roses. Not the dying ones in the garden, but fresh ones, impossibly fragrant, like summer concentrated into a single breath.

"I'm losing it," I said to the empty room. "Three weeks of grief and I'm having olfactory hallucinations."

But the smell lingered, and when I looked back at the garden, the elm tree's leaves were moving despite there being no wind. They fluttered in patterns that almost looked deliberate, like sign language made of chlorophyll and shadow.

I stood up so fast I nearly dropped my Dr Pepper. "Nope. Not today, tree. I've got enough problems without adding 'possibly sentient plant life' to the list."

The leaves stopped moving.

I stared at the tree. The tree, presumably, stared back.

"I'm talking to a tree," I said slowly. "I'm standing in my dead grandmother's library, drinking warm Dr Pepper, and talking to a tree."

The house creaked around me, settling in the heat, but it sounded almost like laughter. Fond laughter, the kind Grandma Jo used to make when I'd say something that reminded her of my mother. My mother, who'd died when I was two. My mother, who Grandma Jo said had been special, though she'd never elaborated on what kind of special she meant.

My phone rang, startling me out of my staring contest with the elm. Dad.

I let it go to voicemail. He'd been calling daily since the funeral, making sure I was "handling things," which was his way of asking if I'd finally snapped without actually having to deal with the heavy lifting if I said yes.

Dad meant well, but he'd checked out emotionally when Mom died. He went through the motions—parent-teacher conferences, birthday presents, college tuition—but there was always this distance, like he was afraid to get too close. Like he was afraid I'd disappear too.

Maybe that's why I'd stayed with Julian so long. I was used to loving people who kept me at arm's length.

The sun was starting to set, painting the library in shades of gold and amber. The dolls watched from their shelf, glassy eyes reflecting the light in ways that definitely weren't natural. One of them, a Victorian china doll in a blue dress, seemed to have turned its head slightly since this morning.

"If you're haunted, at least have the decency to be helpful," I told it. "Maybe do some unpacking while I sleep. Organize the kitchen. Something productive."

The doll, unsurprisingly, didn't respond.

I finished my Dr Pepper and headed back to the kitchen for another. That's when I noticed the back door was open. Not wide open, just cracked, like someone had forgotten to latch it properly. Except I distinctly remembered checking all the locks after Leo left.

The rational part of my brain said old house, settling wood, probably just popped open. The part of my brain that had watched too many horror movies said to grab a knife and call 911.

I grabbed a second Dr Pepper instead and approached the door cautiously. The elm tree stood in silhouette, its branches reaching toward the house like it wanted to come in.

I pushed the door open wider and stepped onto the back porch. The air was thick with humidity and the smell of growing things. Not dead things—the garden looked different somehow. Greener. The roses that had been brown and withered this afternoon showed hints of new growth. The vegetable garden looked less like a botanical battlefield and more like it was just enthusiastically overgrown.

"What the hell?"

I walked down the porch steps, drawn by something I couldn't name. The grass was cool under my bare feet, and definitely green. Not brown like it had been hours ago. Green and soft and very much alive.

The elm tree loomed ahead, and as I got closer, I could see something carved into its trunk. Letters, old and worn but still visible. They weren't in English—weren't in any language I recognized. They seemed to shift when I wasn't looking directly at them, rearranging themselves into almost-familiar patterns before scrambling back to nonsense.

I reached out to touch them, and the locket at my throat turned ice cold.

"Don't," a voice said, and I nearly jumped out of my skin.

But there was no one there. Just me and the tree and the garden that was definitely not the same garden it had been this afternoon.

"I need more Dr Pepper," I said to no one. "Or less. Or therapy. Definitely therapy."

I backed away from the tree, and the carved letters seemed to fade, becoming just random marks in the bark. The locket warmed again, settling back to normal body temperature. The garden looked overgrown but mundane.

"Stress," I told myself firmly. "It's just stress and grief and too much caffeine on an empty stomach."

I headed back to the house, but at the threshold, I turned back. The elm tree stood sentinel in the dying light, and for just a second, I could have sworn I saw a figure standing beneath it. Tall, made of shadows and starlight, there and gone before I could properly focus.

"Nope," I said, and went inside, closing and locking the door firmly behind me.

But even inside, even surrounded by boxes and dolls and an unhealthy amount of lamps, I could feel it. Something had changed. Something had begun. The house that had been holding its breath was starting to exhale, and I had the unsettling feeling that it was waiting for me to breathe with it.

I ordered pizza, unpacked exactly one box (books, because priorities), and studiously ignored the way shadows seemed to gather in corners where shadows shouldn't be. By the time I went to bed, in Grandma Jo's room because mine was still full of boxes, I'd almost convinced myself I'd imagined everything.

Almost.

The locket sat warm against my skin as I lay in the dark, and somewhere in the walls, the house sighed. It sounded like contentment. It sounded like finality.

It sounded like soon.

2

Elle

I woke to the sound of thunder that wasn't thunder.

The house shook—not violently, more like it was shivering. Picture frames rattled on the walls, and somewhere in the kitchen, something fell and shattered. The sound was sharp, followed by a silence so complete I could hear my own heartbeat.

3:17 AM, according to the old digital clock on the nightstand, its red numbers the only light in the room.

The not-thunder came again, rolling through the walls like the house was a drum and something massive had just struck it. This time, the lights flickered once, twice, then died completely, plunging the room into darkness broken only by the clock's dim red glow. But when I looked out the window, the night was clear. Stars scattered across the sky like spilled salt, no clouds in sight.

"Old house," I whispered to myself. "Old pipes. Old... something."

But I was already getting up, bare feet finding the cold wooden floor, because that wasn't the sound of settling wood or temperamental plumbing. That was something else. Something that made the locket around my neck turn cold enough to burn.

I pulled on the ratty oversized t-shirt I'd thrown over a chair—one of Julian's old shirts I'd kept out of spite more than sentiment—and padded toward the door. The hallway beyond was dark, but not normal dark. This was the kind of dark that had weight, that pressed against your skin like velvet made of shadow.

The emergency flashlight I'd left on the dresser clicked on with reassuring brightness, cutting through the unnatural darkness. The beam showed nothing unusual—just the familiar hallway with its faded wallpaper and creaky floorboards. But the shadows seemed to recoil from the light, pulling back into corners with something that looked almost like disappointment.

Another crash from downstairs, this one definitely from the kitchen.

"If this is a burglar, you picked the wrong house," I called out, trying to sound braver than I felt. "I have nothing worth stealing unless you're really into vintage lamps and creepy dolls."

No response. Just a sound like wind chimes, if wind chimes were made of glass and pain.

I made my way downstairs, each step creaking in a different key, creating a discordant melody that made my teeth ache. The air got thicker as I descended, like walking through invisible soup. It tasted purple—not smelled, tasted—and that's when I knew I was either still dreaming or something was very, very wrong.

The kitchen was a disaster. Every cabinet door hung open, contents scattered across the counters and floor. The ancient refrigerator hummed in three-part harmony with itself, and the sink was running, water overflowing onto the floor in patterns that defied physics—spiraling up before falling down, creating impossible geometries in the air.

But that wasn't the weirdest part.

The weirdest part was the beetle.

It sat on the kitchen table, was about the size of my thumb, and was definitely looking at me. Not in the way insects sometimes seem to look at you, but actually looking. With intent. With intelligence. With what I could only describe as impatience.

Its shell gleamed iridescent in the flashlight beam, colors rippling across its surface in impossible ways—purple so vivid it seemed to make a sound, bronze that gave me vertigo just looking at it. When it moved, it left tiny trails of light that faded slowly, like bioluminescent breadcrumbs.

"Finally," it said, and I dropped the flashlight.

The kitchen plunged into darkness, but not completely. The beetle glowed softly, casting shadows that moved independently of the light it produced.

"Did you just—" I started.

"Talk? Yes. Pick up the light, would you? This is difficult enough without you having hysterics in the dark."

I fumbled for the flashlight, fingers shaking. "Beetles don't talk."

"This one does." It cleaned its antennae with its front legs, a gesture that somehow managed to convey annoyance. "I'm Peeble, by the way. And before you ask—no, I'm not a hallucination. No, you're not dreaming. And no, this isn't a brain tumor, though that was a creative theory."

"Peeble?" I stared at the beetle. "And what the hell kind of name is Peeble? What does that even stand for? 'Probably evil beetle?'"

"It's a perfectly respectable name, thank you very much. And I hear everything you say near the tree. Have for years. Your grandmother and I had lovely conversations. She was much quicker on the uptake."

"Jo knew about you?"

"Knew about me? Child, she fed me sugar water every Tuesday and told me about her week. Lovely woman. Terrible at keeping plants alive, ironically, but lovely nonetheless."

I sank into a kitchen chair, the wood creaking ominously. "I need a Dr Pepper."

"Bottom shelf of the fridge, behind the pickles. Jo kept them there specifically for you."

I looked at the beetle—Peeble—then at the overflowing sink with its impossible water patterns, then back at the beetle. "How do you know that?"

"I told you, I hear everything near the tree. Also, I have compound eyes. Do you have any idea how much compound eyes can see? It's frankly overwhelming."

I got up and checked the fridge. Sure enough, behind an ancient jar of pickles that probably qualified as a bioweapon, sat a six-pack of Dr Pepper in glass bottles—the fancy kind Jo always splurged on for my visits.

"She knew I'd come here," I said, pulling one out. The cap popped off with a satisfying hiss. "She knew I'd inherit the house."

"She knew a lot of things," Peeble said, and for the first time, the sarcasm faded from its—their?—voice. "More than she ever told you. More than she could tell you, bound as she was."

"Bound by what?"

Before Peeble could answer, the not-thunder came again, so strong this time that the Dr Pepper in my hand rippled in patterns that reminded me of the water in the sink. The house didn't just shake—it groaned, like something enormous was pressing against it from all sides.

"Oh, bollocks," Peeble muttered. "It's starting already. I told her three weeks wasn't enough time. I told her you'd need preparation. But did she listen? 'The garden knows its own timing, Peeble.' Well, the garden's timing is shit, Jo!"

"What's starting?" I stood up, Dr Pepper forgotten. "What's happening to the house?"

"Not the house, dear. The boundary. It's... thinning." Peeble's antenna twitched. "Usually takes months, sometimes years, for it to get weak enough for a crossing. But something's changed. Something's pulling from the other side."

"The other side of what?"

Lightning flashed outside—real lightning this time—illuminating the kitchen in stark white. In that split second of brightness, I saw it. The kitchen wasn't just the kitchen. Overlaid on top of it, like a double exposure, was another room. Same layout, but different. Older. Grander. Walls covered in living vines, floor made of something that might have been marble or might have been compressed starlight.

Then darkness again, and just my grandmother's ordinary kitchen.

"The other side of here," Peeble said softly. "The place your grandmother fled. The place your mother died trying to protect you from. The place that's been calling to your bloodline for three generations."

The locket at my throat wasn't just cold now—it was burning, sending tendrils of ice and fire across my skin. When I looked down, it was glowing, soft golden light pulsing in time with my heartbeat.

"I need to leave," I said. "I need to get in my car and drive back to Little Rock and forget any of this happened."

"Too late for that." Peeble scuttled to the edge of the table, closer to me. "The moment you put on that locket, you accepted the inheritance. Not the house—anyone could inherit the house. The real inheritance. The one in your blood."

"I don't understand."

"Your grandmother was not from Arkansas, Elle. She wasn't even from Earth, not originally. She was nobility from a place where roses have eyes and trees speak in languages older than human speech. She fell in love with someone she shouldn't have, stole something precious, and ran here to hide."

"That's insane."

"Is it? You've been feeling it since you arrived. The garden growing back overnight. The tree watching you. The house breathing." Peeble's compound eyes reflected my face in a thousand tiny mirrors. "Your blood knows the truth even if your mind rejects it."

Another flash of lightning, and this time the overlay lasted longer. I could see through the walls to a garden that wasn't Jo's garden. Plants that glowed with their own light, flowers the size of dinner plates with petals that moved like they were underwater. And in the center, the elm tree shed its ordinary appearance like a mask, revealing what it had always been—something massive and beautiful and terrible, with bark like silver and leaves that burned without being consumed.

"The crossing is soon. Hours, maybe less. When it happens, you'll have a choice—let them drag you through on their terms, or step through on your own and discover what your grandmother spent sixty years protecting you from. But staying here safe and oblivious? That ship has sailed."

"What did she steal?" I asked, though I was afraid of the answer.

"A chance," Peeble said. "A possibility. A way to save both worlds from someone who would see them burn rather than lose control." They paused, and when they spoke again, their voice was older, sadder. "She stole you,

Elle. Or rather, the potential of you. The possibility that one day, someone of both bloodlines could return and finish what she started."

The house shook again, and this time, cracks appeared in the air itself. Not in the walls—in the actual air, like reality was a windshield and something had just thrown a stone at it. Through the cracks, I could see swirling colors that hurt to perceive, could hear music that was almost voices, could smell flowers that didn't exist.

"I'm not ready for this," I said, and hated how small my voice sounded.

"No one ever is," Peeble replied. "But ready or not, it's happening. The storm's not just weather, Elle. It's the boundary breaking down. And when it does, they'll come through."

"They?"

"The ones who've been hunting your bloodline for sixty years. The ones who want the locket and what it represents. The ones your grandmother fled from a lifetime ago—and the ones she's been hiding you from since the day you were born."

As if in response to Peeble's words, the boundary shuddered. What sounded like rain lashed against the windows—but when I glanced outside, there was nothing but clear night and impossible lightning. Wind that wasn't wind howled through the spaces between reality, carrying voices that might have been screaming or might have been singing.

I walked to the window, each step feeling like I was moving through molasses. Outside, the garden was transforming. With each lightning strike, I could see it more clearly—the overlay becoming more real than the reality. The dead grass was now silver moss that moved like water. The overgrown vegetables were glass-like structures that pulsed with inner light. And the elm tree...

The elm tree was opening like a door.

"It's beautiful," I whispered, and immediately felt guilty. This was terrifying. I should be running. Calling the police. Calling a psychiatrist. Something.

But it was beautiful. Heartbreakingly, impossibly beautiful.

"Beautiful things are often the most dangerous," Peeble said, now perched on my shoulder. I hadn't even noticed them move. "Your grandmother learned that the hard way."

"What happened to her? Really?"

"She loved a king. Bore his child—your mother. But the king already had a queen, and in that place, such things matter. The queen cursed your mother while she was still in the womb. 'May your bloodline forever be torn between worlds, never fully belonging to either.' Jo stole the locket—the key between worlds—and fled here, hoping distance would break the curse."

"Did it?"

"What do you think?" Peeble's legs tickled my neck. "Your mother died young, torn between two natures she couldn't reconcile. Jo spent sixty years in exile, trying to suppress the inheritance, hoping if your mother never crossed over—if you never knew, never crossed over—the curse would fade."

"But?"

"But blood calls to blood. Power calls to power. And the garden... the garden has been waiting for you since before you were born."

The crack in reality was spreading, spider-webbing across the kitchen like broken glass. Through it, I could see figures moving. Tall, impossible figures dressed in armor that might have been grown rather than forged. They carried weapons that looked shaped from radiant silver, and their faces...

Their faces were beautiful and terrible and utterly inhuman.

"The Rootguard," Peeble whispered. "The King's hunters. They've found you."

One of the figures turned toward the crack, and our eyes met across dimensions. His were silver, like mercury, like moonlight on water. His expression shifted from determination to something else—shock? Recognition? Hope?

He pressed his hand against the crack from his side, and I felt an insane urge to match the gesture. The locket burned against my skin, and suddenly I could hear Jo's voice, clear as if she stood beside me:

"Trust the Root, not the Bloom. The garden chooses its own."

"What does that mean?" I asked, but Jo's voice was gone.

The figure—the guard—was saying something, but I couldn't hear through the boundary. He looked frustrated, then afraid, then determined. He pulled out what looked like a blade made of condensed shadow and began cutting at the crack, widening it.

"He's trying to break through," I said, stumbling backward.

"No," Peeble said, sounding puzzled. "He's trying to... warn you? That's not right. The Rootguard don't warn. They hunt."

The guard's mouth moved urgently, and this time I could almost read his lips: Run. Hide. Now.

Then something hit him from behind—a blast of brilliant light that sent him flying out of view. Another figure stepped into frame, this one wearing a crown of thorns that writhed like living things. His smile was cold, perfect, and absolutely terrifying.

"Found you," he mouthed, and even through dimensions, I could feel the weight of his attention like hands around my throat.

The crack exploded outward, reality shattering like a mirror made of air. The overlay crashed into the real world, or maybe the real world crashed into the overlay. Either way, my grandmother's kitchen ceased to exist as a separate space.

I stood in a room that was both and neither, tiles shifting between linoleum and living wood, walls flickering between drywall and woven vines. The refrigerator grew roots that burrowed into the floor while simultaneously remaining a perfectly normal appliance.

And through what had been the kitchen's back door—not the tree, but a second breach in reality—stepped the crowned figure, his portal rimmed with thorns and starlight.

He was tall—impossibly tall, like perspective was just a suggestion he chose to ignore. His clothing seemed to be cut from the night sky, complete with slowly moving constellations. The crown of thorns on his head writhed and reached toward me with disturbing intent.

"Lady Elle," he said, and his voice was like honey poured over broken glass. "How delightful to finally make your acquaintance. I am Prince Auradelle, Regent of the Thornwood Realm, and I'm afraid you've inherited something that doesn't belong to you."

"The house is legally mine," I said, because apparently my panic response was sass. "I have the paperwork."

He laughed, and somewhere in the garden, flowers withered. "Not the house, dear child. The birthright. The blood. The binding." He stepped closer, and the temperature dropped twenty degrees. "Your grandmother stole more than just herself when she fled. She stole the future of our realm."

"People keep saying that, but I don't know what it means." I stepped back as he moved closer. "Peeble said Jo stole a 'possibility.' You're saying she stole a birthright. Which is it? What did she actually take?"

"No? Then why does the Root-mark bloom on your skin?"

I looked down. There, spreading across my collarbone like spilled ink, was a mark I hadn't had five minutes ago. It looked like vines, or veins, or maybe both—golden lines that pulsed with their own light, forming patterns that hurt to follow with my eyes.

"That's not possible," I whispered.

"Many things are possible when the blood runs true." Auradelle took another step closer. "You are the granddaughter of Josephine Thornweaver, daughter of Marielle the Lost, heir to magics you can't begin to comprehend. And I'm here to bring you home."

"This is my home."

"This?" He gestured dismissively, and the walls flickered more violently between realities. "This is a shadow. A refuge. A lie your grandmother told to keep you safe. But safety is an illusion, and lies have a way of coming undone."

He reached out, and I knew with absolute certainty that if he touched me, I would cease to exist in any meaningful way. I would become something else, something that served his will, something that—

A hand grabbed my arm and yanked me backward, through space that folded wrong, through air that tasted metallic with otherworldly glow. I tumbled through the ruins of my grandmother's kitchen and landed hard on moss that definitely hadn't been there before.

"Run," said a voice like distant thunder. "Now."

I looked up into silver eyes—the guard from before. Up close, he was even more inhuman. His features were sharp enough to cut, all angles and edges like someone had carved him from moonlight and shadow. Dark hair fell across his face, and there were markings on his skin too—but his were different. Darker. Carved rather than grown, silver-black lines that looked like scars lined with luminous silver.

"I said run!" He pulled me to my feet with strength that made my bones ache.

But there was nowhere to run to. We were caught between worlds—the kitchen floor beneath my feet one moment, soft moss the next. The house and garden had become the same confused space, realities merging and separating in waves that made me nauseous to watch. Earth plants fought for space with things that had no names in any human language, and the walls kept flickering in and out of existence.

"Who are you?" I gasped.

"Someone who doesn't want to see you become Auradelle's puppet. Now move!"

He dragged me toward the elm tree—or rather, toward what the elm tree had always truly been. The ancient door it had been masking. A door carved from wood that had never grown on Earth, standing free in space without frame or wall, opening onto darkness that had texture.

"I'm not going through that!"

"You are if you want to live."

Auradelle's voice echoed across the chaos: "Kaelren. I should have known you'd interfere. Still playing the hero, even after all these years?"

The guard—Kaelren—turned back with a smile that was all teeth and danger. "Still playing the tyrant, even after the Bloom rejected you?"

Auradelle's perfect face twisted with rage. "The Bloom chose patience. I chose action."

"You chose genocide."

"I chose survival."

They moved at the same time, faster than my eyes could follow, their battle tearing through the merged space around us. Darkness met light in an explosion that turned the air solid for a heartbeat. Kitchen cabinets shattered behind me—or were they trees? I couldn't tell anymore. I couldn't breathe, couldn't think, could only watch as they fought with magic that shouldn't exist.

Kaelren fought like a storm—all fury and chaos, shadows bending to his will like eager pets. Auradelle was precise, surgical, each gesture sending blades of light that cut through reality itself. Where their powers met, things unmade themselves, existed and didn't exist simultaneously.

"The door!" Peeble buzzed in my ear. "While they're distracted!"

But I couldn't move. The mark on my collarbone burned like molten gold pressed into flesh, the lines carving themselves deeper, solidifying. It felt like being rewritten from the inside out, like every cell was remembering something it had forgotten.

"I can't," I gasped.

"You can. You must. The door won't stay open much longer."

The door was flickering, its edges starting to fray. Through it, I could see glimpses of somewhere else—a forest that had never known axes, water that ran upward, stars that hung close enough to touch.

Kaelren went down, bright light wrapped around his throat like a noose. Auradelle stood over him, crown writhing with satisfaction.

"You always were too emotional," Auradelle said. "It made you weak."

"And you were always too cold," Kaelren gasped. "That's why you're alone."

Something in those words hit Auradelle like a physical blow. His perfect composure cracked for just a second, but a second was all Kaelren needed. Shadows exploded outward, sending the prince flying.

Kaelren rolled to his feet and looked at me with those impossible silver eyes. "Go! Now!"

"But—"

"GO!"

The mark on my skin flared, and suddenly I was moving without my permission. My body knew what my mind didn't—that this was flight or dissolution, escape or end. I ran toward the door as reality collapsed behind me, as two impossible beings tore the world apart with their war.

I reached the threshold and hesitated. Through the door was everything unknown, everything Jo had protected me from, everything my mother had died to keep me from becoming.

Behind me was everything falling apart, everything I'd known being unmade, everything human and normal and safe becoming anything but.

"Trust the Root," Peeble said, and I remembered Jo's voice, remembered the locket's warmth, remembered that sometimes the only choice is to choose the unknown over the unbearable.

I stepped through the door.

The last thing I heard was Kaelren shouting something in a language that sounded like breaking glass.

The last thing I saw was Auradelle's smile turning to rage.

The last thing I felt was the mark completing itself, spreading across my skin like roots, like wings, like coming home.

Then darkness, and falling, and the sound of roses laughing, whispering in a language older than words.

3

Kaelren

She fell through the door like debris—graceless, pathetic, wrong—and I threw myself after her, my shadows still coiling from Auradelle's last strike. The crossing burned. Every ward I'd carved into my skin screamed in rage as I tumbled through folded space. Every drop of corrupted magic in my veins recoiled in recognition and fury.

I hit the moss of the Thornwood hard, rolling to my feet with corruption already gathering in my hands. Where was he? Where was—

Auradelle's portal ripped open ten paces away, spilling golden light across the clearing. He stepped through with that insufferable grace, crown of thorns still writhing from battle-fury, not even winded. "Fascinating," he said, his eyes fixed on something behind me. "She survived the crossing. Most humans don't."

I spun.

The girl—Elle—was on her hands and knees in the moss, retching bile and what smelled like that insipid Earth drink. Dr Pepper. Pathetic. This was Josephine's precious cargo? This was what I'd sworn to protect?

But that wasn't what made my corruption flare with rage.

It was the marks.

The marks were choosing. After twenty years of nothing, of silence, of rejection—the marks were finally choosing.

And they were choosing her.

Golden lines spread across her collarbone, elegant and perfect and absolutely wrong. A human. A worthless, mewling human wearing marks that should have been mine.

Where her hands touched the moss, things grew—small shoots, barely visible, but the Root recognized her. Welcomed her. After all my sacrifices, all my bleeding, all my careful carving of marks that never quite fit—the Root welcomed her like she was coming home.

I wanted to kill her. The thought came so naturally, so easily, that I'd already taken a step forward before I caught myself.

Josephine's favor. I'd sworn. And I kept my word, even when it burned.

"Pity," I said flatly, meaning it. My hands were still clenched, corruption spreading up my wrists in response to my rage.

Auradelle's perfect eyebrow arched as he moved closer, his portal sealing behind him. "Such hostility, Kaelren. One might think you're... disappointed."

"One might think many things. Most would be right." I forced myself to step back, to put space between myself and the girl who was now muttering something about brain tumors. "This is what Josephine wanted protected? This weak, useless thing?"

Elle was pushing herself up now, that garish red hair matted with sweat and bile. At least she had some grasp of how wrong her presence here was.

"She has no idea what she is," Auradelle mused, his attention fixed on her with disturbing intensity. "Josephine kept her ignorant."

"Josephine was a fool." The words tasted like betrayal, but they were true. "She should have let the girl die human rather than become this... mockery."

"The marks chose her."

"The marks are wrong." My corruption flared, shadows gathering without conscious thought. "Twenty years, Auradelle. Twenty years I prepared. I bled. I carved these failures into my skin because the real marks wouldn't come. And now they choose her?"

"Jealousy is such an ugly emotion."

"It's not jealousy. It's rage."

He smiled that perfect smile, taking another step toward Elle. "Even uglier."

The girl—Elle—finally managed to stand, swaying like a newborn colt. When she saw us, her eyes went wide with the appropriate amount of terror. Good. She should be terrified.

"What—who are you?" she gasped.

"Your executioner, if I had my way," I said, and meant it.

Auradelle laughed. "Kaelren, always so dramatic. Ignore him, dear. He's having a bit of a crisis. You see, those marks you're wearing? They were meant for him."

Elle looked between us, then down at her skin where gilded vines spread from her collarbone. "I don't understand."

"Of course you don't," I snarled. "You understand nothing. You ARE nothing. A mistake. A cosmic joke at my expense."

"Kaelren—" Peeble started, materializing on the girl's shoulder.

"Don't." My voice could have frozen flame. "For years you whispered prophecies in my ear. Years of 'chosen one' and 'destiny' and 'patience.' And this is what you were waiting for?"

"The Root chooses—"

"The Root is senile." I moved closer, and Elle stumbled backward. Smart girl. "Or cruel. Or both."

"Now, now," Auradelle said, power gathering around him like silk. "We can't have you killing her before we understand what she represents."

"She represents nothing but theft."

"Perhaps. Or perhaps she represents opportunity." His crown writhed faster. "She needs training. Guidance. Protection."

"Then protect her yourself."

"Oh, I intend to."

That's when I understood. Auradelle didn't just want her for her marks— he wanted her to hurt me. To parade my replacement, my failure, in front of the entire realm. The girl would be his trophy, proof that the great Kaelren had been found wanting.

No.

I'd sworn to protect what came through the door. I hadn't sworn to do it nicely.

"She's mine," I said, the words tasting like ash.

"Yours?" Auradelle's amusement was nauseating. "You just said you wanted to kill her."

"I do. But Josephine asked me to protect her, and unlike you, I keep my word."

"Josephine is dead."

"And yet her debts remain." I grabbed Elle's arm, none too gently. She made a sound of protest that I ignored. "The girl comes with me."

"I think not."

Auradelle moved, faster than thought, and suddenly his hand was around my throat. Not squeezing—not yet—but present. A reminder of power disparities.

"You forget yourself, failed prince," he said softly. "You have no authority here. No right to claim anything."

My corruption responded to the threat, spreading faster, darker. The shadows around us writhed, and I felt that familiar edge where control became suggestion, where I could either direct the rot or become it.

"And you forget," I said, smiling with too many teeth, "that I have nothing left to lose."

I let the corruption explode outward.

The shadows hit Auradelle like a physical force, sending him stumbling back. His perfect composure cracked, and for a moment, I saw what he hid beneath—not beauty but hunger, not wisdom but desperation.

"You dare—"

"I dare everything," I snarled, corruption spreading up my jaw, across my temple. It hurt—God, it hurt—but pain was just currency now, and I was ready to spend. "You took everything from me. My parents. My future. My purpose. You will not take this too."

"This?" He laughed, power coalescing around his hands. "You mean this pathetic human girl who doesn't even know what she's carrying?"

"This debt." I moved between him and Elle, who was on her knees again, marks glowing wildly across her skin. "Josephine asked me to protect what

25

came through. I thought it would be an artifact. Maybe a weapon." I laughed, and it sounded like breaking things. "I didn't know it would be her. But a debt is a debt."

"You're protecting her out of obligation?"

"I'm protecting her out of spite." My corruption reached my eyes, and suddenly I could see everything—every thread of power, every weakness, every lie Auradelle told himself. "You want her. Therefore, you can't have her."

"Childish."

"Effective."

We moved at the same time. His light met my darkness with a sound like reality tearing. The Thornwood around us recoiled, ancient trees that had weathered centuries of storms bending away from our violence.

Auradelle fought with the precision of someone who'd been trained since birth—every gesture calculated, every attack measured. But I'd learned to fight in the spaces between civilization, where the only rule was survival.

I let the corruption guide me, became the rot that ate at the edges of his perfect light. Where he was form, I was chaos. Where he was beauty, I was the thing that made beauty decay.

His blade of condensed sunlight met my shadows, and the collision sent both of us flying. I hit a tree hard enough to crack the ancient bark, tasted blood and something worse. But I was up before he recovered, moving through darkness itself.

"You've gotten stronger," he said, wiping golden blood from his lip. "The corruption is consuming you faster than I thought."

"Good thing I don't plan to live long."

"And her? What happens to your precious debt when you're dead?"

I didn't answer. Couldn't. Because he was right—I was dying, had been dying since I carved the first mark. But I'd be damned if I died before I saw him lose something he wanted.

Behind us, Elle screamed. Not in pain this time—in fury. Golden light exploded outward from her marks, but it wasn't the gentle warmth of healing magic. This was Root-power in its rawest form, wild and angry and completely uncontrolled.

The ground beneath her feet cracked open.

Things pulled themselves out of the earth. Not plants—though they moved like growing things, fast and grasping. Wood twisted through bone, or bone calcified into bark—impossible to tell which came first. They were ancient things, remnants of the Thornwood's earliest days when it was still learning what it meant to be alive.

They surged toward Auradelle without strategy or intelligence, all grasping limbs and snapping joints, making sounds like trees breaking in a storm.

"Impossible," he breathed, actually taking a step back. "She hasn't been trained. She can't—"

"She's Josephine's blood," I said, understanding finally hitting. "Did you really think Jo would send her here defenseless?"

One of the creatures wrapped around Auradelle's ankle, wood splintering as it tried to pull him down. He destroyed it with a gesture, but three more erupted from the ground to take its place. They weren't strong— Elle didn't have the control for that—but they kept coming, wave after wave of mindless hunger.

"This isn't over," he snarled, portal already ripping open behind him. Light spilled through—wherever he was going, it wasn't anywhere near here.

"No," I agreed, grabbing Elle's arm and hauling her to her feet. "But it's a start. Now run."

I threw something at his portal—a shard of corrupted shadow that would twist his destination coordinates. He'd survive, probably. But he'd arrive somewhere... unpleasant. And it would buy us time.

Auradelle's eyes widened as he realized what I'd done. "You—"

The creatures swarmed him. Not strong enough to hold him, but enough to drag him backward through his own portal before he could stabilize it. The tear in reality snapped shut with a sound like the world hiccupping.

Silence fell.

"What—what did I—" Elle was staring at her hands, shaking. The things she'd summoned were already crumbling, breaking apart into soil and splinters. Within moments, there was no sign they'd existed except for the churned earth and the smell of disturbed ground.

"You defended yourself," I said, not gently. Gentleness wasn't what she needed. "Get used to it. This realm will require it of you daily."

"I don't understand—"

"You don't need to understand. You need to move. Now"

"But—"

"Go, or I leave you here for whatever comes investigating that light show."

She looked at me—really looked at me—and I saw Jo's steel in her spine. "You're not a good person."

"No. I'm not. I'm not even a particularly functional person. But I'm what you've got." I shoved her forward. "Josephine asked me to protect you. She didn't ask me to be nice about it."

"Why did she choose you?"

The question stopped me for a heartbeat. Why had Jo chosen me? The failed prince, the corrupted pretender, the walking cautionary tale?

"Because I have nothing left to lose," I said finally. "And people with nothing to lose are very good at keeping promises to the dead."

Elle stared at me, trembling. "This is insane."

"Yes. Welcome to your new life. It only gets worse from here."

She laughed—actually laughed—even as tears ran down her face. "Worse than this?"

"So much worse." I grabbed her arm and started pulling her through the trees. "But also more interesting. Now move."

"Wait—where are we—"

"Away from here. Auradelle won't stay gone long, and you just announced your presence to everything with power in a fifty-mile radius." I didn't slow down, half-dragging her through the underbrush. The Thornwood was dense here, ancient trees pressing close, but I knew these paths. Had walked them for twenty years.

Elle stumbled over roots, gasping for breath. Her body wasn't adapted to this realm yet—the air was thicker here, heavier with magic. Most humans couldn't breathe properly for days.

"I can't—I need to stop—"

"You can stop when you're dead. Which will be soon if you don't keep moving."

We ran for what must have been twenty minutes before she finally collapsed, rolling onto her side and vomiting into the moss. I kept watch while she heaved, scanning the forest for pursuit. Nothing yet. Good. My corruption trick should keep Auradelle occupied for at least an hour.

"I hate you," Elle gasped between heaves.

"Good. Hate will keep you sharp." I stood next to her, checking our surroundings. My crew should be close—I could feel Bryx's distinctive magical signature, like copper and ozone. "Can you walk?"

"Do I have a choice?"

"You always have a choice. It's just that most of them end with you dead."

She pushed herself up, swaying but standing. The marks on her skin had settled somewhat, forming elegant patterns across her collarbone. They were beautiful. I hated them.

"What happens now?" she asked.

"Now? Now we meet my crew. Try not to scream when you see Bryx—he's sensitive about his appearance."

"What's wrong with his appearance?"

"He's part insect. Compound eyes, antennae, the works."

"Of course he is." She laughed again, that broken sound that was becoming familiar. "Why wouldn't he be?"

I started walking, not waiting to see if she'd follow. She did—what else was she going to do?

"For what it's worth," I said, not looking back, "I'm sorry."

"For what?"

"For everything that's about to happen to you. For the marks choosing you. For Josephine not preparing you. For me being the one protecting you." I paused. "Mostly that last one."

"Are you really that bad?"

I turned to look at her, letting her see the corruption spreading across my face, the inked veins that pulsed with each heartbeat, the carved marks that were slowly killing me from the inside out.

"I'm worse," I said simply. "But I keep my word. Jo asked me to protect you, so I will. But don't mistake that for kindness. Or friendship. Or anything other than debt."

"I won't," she said, and there was steel in her voice now. Good. She'd need it.

The Thornwood opened before us, revealing a clearing where my crew waited. They looked up as we approached—Bryx with his compound eyes gleaming, Nimor materializing from mist, Eltrien glowing softly with healer's light, Vashael's pollen cloud shimmering gold, Sarnyx's thorns already extended.

"Boss," Bryx said, his antennae twitching. "You found—" He stopped, staring at Elle. They all did. "Holy shit. Those are the marks. The actual marks."

"Yes."

"The ones that were supposed to be—"

"Yes."

An awkward silence fell. Everyone knew my story. Everyone knew what the marks meant to me.

Elle looked between us, then squared her shoulders. "Hi. I'm Elle. Apparently, I'm wearing something that should belong to tall, dark, and furious over there. I have no idea what's happening, and I might vomit again. Fair warning."

Bryx laughed, a chittering sound that most humans found terrifying. Elle didn't even flinch. "I like her."

"You like everyone," Vashael said, her voice like wind through flowers.

"I like everyone interesting. She's definitely interesting."

"She's definitely going to get us killed," Sarnyx muttered.

"Probably," I agreed. "But we were heading that direction anyway."

Eltrien stepped forward, his pale features concerned. "Kaelren, your marks—"

"Are spreading. I know."

"The corruption is accelerating. That fight—"

"Was necessary." I cut him off. "Auradelle wanted her. Now he doesn't have her."

"And when he comes for her?"

"Then we'll deal with it." I turned to Elle. "These are the people who'll keep you alive. Maybe. If you don't do anything catastrophically stupid."

"Define catastrophically stupid."

"Trusting anyone. Including us." I started walking deeper into the forest. "Especially me."

Behind me, I heard Bryx whisper to Elle, "He's actually much worse than he seems."

"That's oddly reassuring," she replied, and despite everything, I almost smiled.

Almost.

4

Elle

"Camp," Kaelren said, the word sharp as broken glass. "Now."

We'd been walking for what felt like hours but was probably less—time moved weird here, stretching and compressing like it had its own agenda. The Thornwood, as they called it, around us had gradually thinned, opening into a clearing where several structures that might generously be called tents were already set up. They glowed faintly in the eternal twilight, made of something that definitely wasn't canvas—more like spider silk woven with moonlight.

"Inside," Kaelren ordered, grabbing my arm and steering me toward the largest tent. Not gently—his fingers pressed hard enough to bruise. "You need to be examined."

"I'm fine—"

"You're carrying marks that shouldn't exist, you've been conscious for less than six hours in this realm, and you just summoned things from the ground to attack someone. You're not fine."

He shoved me through the tent flap, and I stumbled inside, catching myself against something solid. The interior shimmered with its own faint luminescence, casting everything in a pale blue glow that made me feel like I was underwater.

Five members of his crew filed in behind us. I'd been introduced to them hours ago, but everything had been a blur of exhaustion and terror. Now, forced to be still in the tent's close quarters, my brain actually registered what I was looking at. They all moved with the predatory grace of things that knew exactly how dangerous they were.

The insect one—Bryx, I remembered—tilted his head, compound eyes reflecting my face in a thousand tiny mirrors. When he smiled, it was too wide, showing too many teeth.

"Human," he said, antennae twitching. "You smell like Earth. Like... what is that? Carbonated sugar water?"

"Dr Pepper," I said automatically, then wondered why the hell I was discussing soft drinks with a bug person.

He laughed, a chittering sound that raised every hair on my arms. "Dr Pepper! I knew someone who loved that stuff. Said it tasted like carbonated prune juice but somehow good."

"That's... actually not a bad description."

"I have my moments. Usually followed by much worse moments, but still."

"Stop scaring her," said another figure, and I had to look twice to make sure I was seeing correctly. This one seemed to be made partially of mist, his edges constantly shifting between solid and vapor. Patterns moved across his skin like living tattoos, and his eyes were the color of fog at dawn. His voice was quiet, barely above a whisper.

The third was easier to look at—pale as winter moonlight, tall and willowy, with softly glowing runes traced along his arms. He moved with a healer's careful grace, already pulling supplies from a pack that shouldn't have fit through the tent opening. When he looked at me, his eyes were kind despite being an unsettling shade of silver.

"You're wounded," he said.

The fourth made me sneeze. She was surrounded by a cloud of golden pollen that sparkled in the tent's strange light, her face hidden behind a veil that seemed to be made of flower petals. When she moved, it was with a deliberate sensuality that felt calculated, like she was always performing for an audience.

The fifth leaned against the tent wall, and I recognized her voice before her face—the one who'd muttered about me getting them killed. Sarnyx. She had thorns growing from her arms like they belonged there, and her eyes were the color of dried blood.

I looked down at myself, taking inventory of the damage I'd accumulated in just a few hours in this nightmare realm. My jeans were torn in three places, my t-shirt was more holes than fabric, and I was pretty sure I had moss in my hair. There were cuts I didn't remember getting, bruises already turning purple-green, and my collarbone where the mark spread was still burning with that radiant fire.

"I'm fine," I lied.

"You're not," Kaelren said flatly. "Eltrien, check her wounds. Vashael, find her appropriate clothing. Nimor, scout the perimeter. Bryx, watch for Crown scouts. Sarnyx, sharpen your thorns—we may need them before dawn."

"With pleasure," Sarnyx said, and the way she looked at me made it clear whose flesh she'd prefer to test them on.

They all moved with the efficiency of people who'd worked together for years. The healer—Eltrien—approached me slowly, hands visible, like I was a spooked animal.

"May I?" he asked, gesturing to a cut on my arm I hadn't noticed was bleeding.

I nodded, not trusting my voice. His touch was cool, clinical, but gentle. The runes on his arms glowed brighter, and I felt a tingling sensation where his fingers traced the wound. The pain faded, replaced by a weird itch as the skin began knitting itself back together.

"Healer," I said, not really a question.

"Among other things." He moved to the next wound with the same careful efficiency. "The marks on your collarbone—may I examine them?"

"Why?"

"Because they're spreading faster than they should. And that concerns me."

I glanced at Kaelren, who was conferring with the mist one—Nimor—in low tones. He caught my look and something flickered across his face. Not

34

concern. Never concern. More like... calculation.

"Fine," I said to Eltrien. "But if you try anything weird—"

"Define weird in a realm where normalcy doesn't exist," the one with the pollen—Vashael—said, pulling clothing from a pack that definitely violated several laws of physics with how much it held. "These should fit."

She held up what looked like armor made of leaves and leather, with accompanying pants that seemed to be woven from spider silk and boots that might have been carved from bark.

"I'm not wearing tree cosplay," I said.

"Cos... play?" she said, the unfamiliar word awkward in her mouth. 'It's not play. Your human clothing won't survive another day here. The realm itself will eat through it."

"The realm eats clothing?"

"The realm eats everything, eventually," Bryx said cheerfully. "But it starts with the foreign stuff. Like you!"

"That's not reassuring."

"Wasn't meant to be. Honesty is more useful than comfort here."

Eltrien's fingers paused on my collarbone, right where the mark was spreading. "Interesting," he murmured.

"What's interesting?" Kaelren was suddenly there, looming over Eltrien's shoulder. His carved marks were pulsing with that silver-black light, reaching toward my golden ones like magnets.

"The pattern. It's not following the usual progression." Eltrien traced the air above my skin, not quite touching. "Look—here, where it branches. That's not Root pattern. That's something older."

"Older than Root?" Nimor asked, his voice barely audible. "That's not possible."

"Many impossible things are proving possible lately," Eltrien said, stepping back. "She needs rest. Real rest, not the half-unconscious stumbling she's been doing."

"I'm right here," I said. "And I'm fine."

"You've said that several times," Kaelren observed. "You've been wrong every time."

"Well, excuse me for not having a perfect grasp on my wellbeing in bizarro world."

"Bizarro world?" Bryx perked up. "Is that what you call it? I like it!"

"We need to move at dawn," Kaelren said, ignoring the enthusiasm. "The Crown's scouts will have found our trail by now. We head to Vyn Hollow."

"How far is that?" I asked.

"Three days on foot through terrain where everything wants to kill you," Bryx said cheerfully. "Or half a day if we fly."

"Fly on what exactly?' I couldn't quite picture what he meant..

"You'll see in the morning," Kaelren said. "Better you don't spend all night imagining the worst."

"That's ominous."

"That's practical. Fear exhausts, and you need rest."

My head was spinning. Whatever they used for flying, marks that shouldn't exist, a realm that literally consumed foreign objects. And through it all, Kaelren watched me with those silver eyes, calculating, measuring, waiting for me to break.

"The clothing," he said abruptly. "Change. We leave before dawn."

"I'm not changing in front of—"

"We'll step out," Eltrien said gently. "But you need to change. Your current clothing is already beginning to degrade."

I looked down. He was right. The edges of my jeans were fraying in patterns that looked deliberate, like something was eating them in artistic spirals. My shirt was developing holes that definitely hadn't been there an hour ago.

"This place is literally eating my clothes?"

"The realm doesn't like foreign material," Nimor said quietly. "It's trying to make you match."

"Match what?"

"It," Kaelren said. "Change, or you'll be naked by morning. Your choice."

He turned and left the tent, the others following. Except Peeble, who materialized on my shoulder.

"You should know," the beetle said, "they're all terrified of you."

36

"They're terrified? I'm the one surrounded by bug people and mist men and whatever Vashael is under all that pollen."

"Exactly. You're human, wearing marks that shouldn't exist, bonded to their broken leader, and you haven't gone insane yet. That terrifies them."

"Bonded? What do you mean bonded?"

"Oh, didn't I mention that part? The marks recognize each other. His corruption reaches for your Root magic like—well, like magnets, as you might say. You're connected now, whether either of you likes it or not.

"Yet?"

"Everyone goes insane here eventually. It's just a matter of degree."

"Even you?"

"Oh, I went insane centuries ago. It's quite liberating once you get used to it."

I picked up the clothes Vashael had left. The leather was soft as butter, worked with patterns that seemed to shift when I wasn't looking directly at them. The leaf armor was surprisingly light, each piece overlapping like scales. The boots looked like they'd been grown rather than made.

"This is insane," I muttered, starting to change.

"Yes," Peeble agreed. "But it's insanely beautiful. That has to count for something."

The clothes fit perfectly, like they'd been made for me. Or grew for me. I didn't want to think too hard about it. The leaf armor adjusted itself as I moved, tightening where it needed support, loosening where I needed flexibility. The boots molded to my feet like second skin.

"How do I look?" I asked Peeble.

"Like you belong here. Which is either wonderful or terrible, depending on your perspective."

"What's your perspective?"

"That you were always meant to be here. The realm's been waiting for you since before you were born."

Before I could respond, Kaelren re-entered the tent. His eyes swept over me, and something flickered in their depths. Not approval. More like... recognition.

"Better," he said simply.

"I look like a walking bush."

"You look like Wynmire. That's what matters." He moved closer, and I caught that scent of pine and leather and danger. "Get some rest. Tomorrow, we fly to the Hollow. Try not to fall off."

"What if I can't sleep?"

"Then you'll be tired and terrified tomorrow instead of just terrified."

"Your bedside manner is terrible."

"I'm not a healer. I'm a killer who happens to be keeping you alive."

The distinction mattered to him, I could tell. He needed me to understand that he wasn't kind, wasn't good, wasn't anything but practical.

"Your marks," he said suddenly. "They're spreading."

I looked down. He was right. The vines had crept past my collarbone, starting to trace down my arm in delicate spirals.

"Is that bad?"

"I don't know." The admission seemed to cost him something. "Nothing about you follows the rules."

"Maybe the rules are wrong."

He looked at me then, really looked at me, and for a moment his guard dropped. I saw exhaustion, pain, and something else. Something that might have been hope if hope hadn't been beaten out of him years ago.

"Maybe," he said quietly. Then his walls slammed back up. "Rest. Tomorrow will be worse."

"You really need to work on your motivational speeches."

"I'm not trying to motivate you. I'm trying to prepare you."

"For what?"

"For Wynmire. For the Hollow. For the truth about what you are." He paused at the tent entrance. "The marks chose you for a reason. Tomorrow, we start finding out why."

"And if I don't like the answer?"

"Then you'll join a very long list of people disappointed by destiny."

He left, and I was alone with Peeble and the sound of the realm eating what was left of my human clothes. Outside, I could hear the crew setting up watches—Bryx's chittering laugh, Vashael humming a melody that made my teeth ache, Nimor's occasional whispered observations, Eltrien's gentle corrections, Sarnyx's thorns scraping against something metallic.

They were a family, I realized. Broken and strange and dangerous, but family nonetheless. And I was the outsider who'd disrupted their dynamic, wearing marks their leader had carved into his own flesh trying to claim.

"They'll warm up to you," Peeble said, reading my thoughts. "Or they'll try to kill you. Seventy-thirty odds in favor of warming up, though those aren't great odds when your life is on the line."

I lay down on the bedroll someone had left, probably Eltrien, since it smelled faintly of those healing herbs he carried. The material was soft, woven from something that felt like clouds and smelled like rain. Above me, the tent's luminescent fabric pulsed gently, creating patterns that almost looked like constellations if I squinted.

"Peeble?"

"Yes?"

"Is Kaelren going to die?"

The beetle was quiet for a long moment. "We're all going to die eventually."

"That's not an answer."

"It's the only answer I'm allowed to give."

"Allowed by who?"

But Peeble had vanished, leaving me alone with my spreading marks and the sound of the crew preparing for threats I couldn't imagine. Tomorrow, I'd apparently fly on something terrifying through a realm that wanted to eat me, heading toward a place called the Hollow to find answers I probably didn't want.

But tonight, I was just a woman in borrowed clothes that grew to fit me, in a fantasy tent, in a realm where nothing made sense except the certainty that tomorrow would be worse.

"I miss normal," I said to no one.

Outside, something that wasn't quite wind but wasn't quite not-wind rustled through the camp, carrying the scent of flowers that shouldn't exist and the promise of dangers I couldn't yet imagine.

I closed my eyes and tried not to think about how the marks on my skin pulsed in rhythm with my heartbeat, or how I could sense Kaelren's presence even through the tent walls—a cold fury wrapped around pain that never stopped.

Tomorrow would definitely be worse.

But at least I wouldn't be naked when it happened.

5

Elle

"Absolutely not."

I stood at the edge of the clearing, staring at twenty giant bees that stared back with compound eyes the size of dinner plates. They were massive—horse-sized—with wings that created wind gusts that flattened the grass with each lazy movement. Their fur looked soft but substantial, black and yellow stripes gleaming in the strange light of the Thornwood.

"It's perfectly safe," Bryx said, already approaching the largest bee, which had patches of electric blue among its black and yellow stripes. "Kevin here has only dropped two riders in the last year."

"Kevin?" I looked at the monstrous insect. "Your giant death bee is named Kevin?"

"All the best bees are named Kevin," Bryx said solemnly, patting the bee's fur with obvious affection.

"That makes no sense," Nimor said, materializing more fully from the morning mist. "You've only ever had one bee."

"Exactly. And he's the best. Therefore, all the best bees are named Kevin. Logic."

"That's not how logic works," Eltrien said mildly.

Kevin buzzed, a sound like a freight train made of vibration, and Bryx laughed. "See? Kevin agrees with me."

"The death bee is named Kevin," I repeated, because apparently my brain

41

was stuck on this point.

The morning had come too quickly. One moment I was fitfully sleeping, dreaming of roses with teeth and mirrors that led nowhere, and the next Vashael was shaking me awake with her pollen-covered hands, telling me it was time to fly.

The clothes they'd given me had adjusted overnight, fitting even better, like they'd been learning my body while I slept. Which was creepy, but less creepy than being naked because the realm ate my jeans, so I was calling it a win.

"You'll ride with me," Kaelren said, approaching one of the mid-sized bees. This one was darker than the others, with silver markings that reminded me of his carved marks.

"Why do I have to ride with you?"

"Because you'll fall off otherwise."

"Your confidence in me is overwhelming."

"Would you prefer false encouragement?"

"I'd prefer not riding a giant insect through the sky, but apparently that's not an option."

He mounted the bee with practiced ease, then held out a hand to me. I stared at it like it might bite.

"Today," he said. "The Crown scouts are less than an hour behind us."

That motivated me. I took his hand—his skin was warm, which surprised me—and let him pull me up. The ease with which he lifted me was startling; I'd forgotten how much taller he was than me, broad-shouldered and solidly built under all that leather and thorn-laced armor. The bee's fur was softer than I expected, like velvet made of sunshine. I could feel its breathing, slow and steady, and underneath that, a vibration that might have been contentment.

'Hold on,' Kaelren said.

'To what?'

He grabbed my arms and wrapped them around his waist. 'To me.'

I was suddenly very aware of everything about him—the solid muscle beneath the dark leathers, the thorn-reinforced armor that looked like it had been grown rather than forged, the way his dark hair was already wind-tossed even though we hadn't taken off yet. He smelled like pine and danger and something else, like storms about to break. This close, I could see the corruption spreading up his neck, silver-black veins pulsing with each heartbeat.

"This is awkward," I muttered against his back.

"It's necessary. Unless you'd prefer to fall a thousand feet?"

"How high are we going?"

"High enough that falling would give you time to think about all your life choices before you hit the ground."

"You're really bad at reassurance."

"I told you, I'm not trying to reassure you."

The bee's wings started moving, a sound like the world's largest hand fan. My stomach dropped as we lifted off, and I definitely didn't squeak and hold on tighter. Definitely not.

The ground fell away with alarming speed. The clearing became a speck, the forest became a carpet of green and shadow, and suddenly we were above the canopy, in a world I didn't know existed.

Wynmire from above was impossible.

The trees weren't just tall—they were monuments to growth itself, some reaching so high their tops disappeared into actual clouds. Bridges made of living vines connected them, creating highways in the sky where I could see tiny figures moving. There were structures built into the trees themselves, growing from the bark like architectural tumors, windows glowing with bioluminescent light even in the morning sun.

And the mushrooms. God, the mushrooms.

They grew from the sides of the trees, some small as dinner plates, others large enough to build houses on—which someone had, apparently. I could see entire communities built on fungal platforms, connected by stairs that looked like they were spun from gossamer threads.

"It's beautiful," I said without meaning to.

"It's dying," Kaelren replied, and I felt the tension in his body. "Look closer."

I did, and saw what he meant. There were patches of black rot spreading through some of the trees, sections where the bridges had collapsed, platforms where the lights had gone dark. It was subtle, but once you saw it, you couldn't unsee it—the realm was sick.

"What's causing it?" I asked.

"Many things. The balance has been wrong for a long time."

"Since my grandmother left?"

"Since before that. But her leaving accelerated it."

We flew in formation, the crew's bees moving with practiced synchronization. Nimor was barely visible on his mount, seeming to fade in and out of existence. Eltrien rode with careful grace, one hand occasionally glowing as he whispered something to his bee. Vashael was surrounded by her ever-present pollen cloud, making her bee sneeze occasionally. Sarnyx rode a bee with thorns actually growing from its fur, because of course she did. And Bryx was doing aerial tricks with Kevin that made my stomach turn just watching.

"Show off," Sarnyx called to him.

"It's not showing off if you're genuinely talented," Bryx called back, doing a loop that shouldn't have been possible on a giant insect.

"It's showing off if you're trying to impress the human," Vashael said, and even through her veil I could hear her smirk.

"I'm not trying to impress anyone. Kevin, tell them I'm not trying to impress anyone."

Kevin buzzed noncommittally.

"Traitor," Bryx muttered.

"How long have you all been together?" I asked Kaelren, needing distraction from the fact that we were very, very high up.

"Years," he said. "They each came to the crew for different reasons."

"What reasons?"

"Survival, mostly. The Crown wants them dead for various crimes."

"What crimes?"

"Existing incorrectly."

"That's a crime?"

"In Auradelle's kingdom, everything is a crime if you're not useful to him."

"And you? What's your crime?"

"Being born. Being promised something that was taken away. Refusing to accept it."

"The marks."

"Among other things."

We flew in silence for a while, the landscape below shifting from forest to something else. Here, the trees grew in spirals, creating natural clearings where villages clustered. I could see people—or things that looked like people from this height—working in fields that glowed with their own light. Harvest time in a realm where plants might harvest you back.

"There," Eltrien called, pointing ahead. "Vyn Hollow."

It rose from the forest like something out of a fever dream. Trees so massive they had their own weather systems, clouds actually forming around their middles. The structures built into and around them looked organic, like they'd been grown rather than constructed. Bioluminescent vines traced every surface, their glow shifting in slow ripples that moved from structure to structure like silent conversation.

"It's incredible," I breathed.

"It's dangerous," Kaelren corrected. "Vyn Hollow doesn't follow Crown law. They barely follow any law. The people there are outcasts, radicals, and worse."

"Worse than you?"

"Much worse."

"Then why are we going there?"

"Because outcasts and radicals are the only ones who might have answers about your marks. The legitimate sources would turn you over to Auradelle without blinking."

"Comforting."

"I told you—"

"You're not trying to comfort me, I know."

The bees began descending, and my stomach relocated somewhere around my throat. The landing platform was a mushroom the size of a basketball court, growing from the side of one of the enormous trees. Other bees were already there, their riders dismounting with the ease of people who did this every day.

"That was terrifying," I said.

"That was a trained mount on a clear day." His tone was flat. "If that terrified you, you're going to have a very short, very unpleasant time here."

"You could try being less of an asshole."

"I could. But coddling you won't keep you alive.

As we stood on the platform, I got my first real look at Vyn Hollow's inhabitants. They were wrong in ways that made my brain hurt trying to process them. A woman walked past with bark for skin and leaves growing from her scalp instead of hair, arguing with what looked like a man made entirely of morning mist except for his teeth, which were disturbingly solid and sharp. Children—or things child-sized—ran between the adults' legs, some with too many limbs, others with not enough, all of them moving with the casual ease of creatures who'd never known anything different.

The air smelled of rot and flowers and something chemical that made my nose burn. I saw what Kaelren meant about outcasts and radicals—these were people who'd been changed by magic or birth or choice, people who'd ended up here because they had nowhere else to go. A group huddled around a fire that burned without wood, passing around a pipe that released smoke that swirled in patterns of violet and green. Another cluster seemed to be trading goods that writhed in their containers, while a fight broke out near the platform's edge over what looked like a handful of teeth.

"Stay close," Kaelren said, his hand on my arm again, possessive and controlling. "They can smell the human on you, even with the marks. Some of them haven't had fresh meat in years."

"That's not funny."

"It's not a joke."

A figure approached from the shadows of the tree—tall, thin, with bark-like skin and eyes that glowed soft green. They wore robes that seemed to be made of living moss, and when they walked, flowers bloomed in their footsteps only to die seconds later.

"Kaelren," they said, their voice like wind through leaves. "You bring strangers to the Hollow."

"I bring someone who needs answers, Sage Willowmere."

The Sage's eyes turned to me, and I felt them looking not at me but through me, into me, at things I didn't know existed.

"The marked one," they breathed. "The one who shouldn't be." They moved closer, and I smelled earth and growing things and decay all at once. "May I?"

They reached out toward my collarbone where the marks were visible above my armor.

"Whoa, hey, personal space." I batted their hand away. "What happened to consent in this realm?"

The Sage tilted their head, curious rather than offended. "You object to being examined?"

"I object to being treated like a specimen. I'm a person, not a science experiment."

"You're both," they said simply. "And if I don't examine the marks, you'll be a dead person in within days."

"Everyone keeps saying that like it's supposed to make me cooperative."

"Elle." Kaelren's voice had that edge that meant he was running out of patience. "The Sage can help you. Let them."

"Or what?"

"Or you become something that isn't you anymore." For once, there was no cruelty in his tone. Just fact. "Your choice."

I looked down at the marks spreading across my collarbone, remembering the vision I'd had when they first appeared—every cell remembering something it had forgotten, being rewritten from the inside out.

"If this goes wrong—" I started.

"Then it goes wrong," the Sage interrupted. "But doing nothing guarantees the wrong outcome. Doing something at least gives you a chance."

I hated that they were right. "Fine. But you owe me an explanation after. A real one, not cryptic sage nonsense."

"I promise nothing but honesty." The Sage reached out again. "Which is often worse."

This time I let them touch me, but I didn't relax. Didn't trust it. Kept my eyes open and my guard up, even as their bark-rough fingers made contact with the golden lines on my skin.

The moment their skin touched my marks, the world exploded.

Not literally—though in this realm, that was always a possibility. But suddenly I could see everything. Every root beneath the ground, every leaf on every tree, every connection between every living thing. The realm was a web of light and life and power, and I was part of it, had always been part of it, would always be—

Time lost meaning. I could see centuries in a heartbeat—the first growth, the first bloom, the first death. The marks spread across my skin, golden vines reaching for my face, and I didn't care. Didn't want to care. Why would I need a human face when I could be forest? Why would I need thoughts when I could be pure growth?

Something was happening to the platform. I was vaguely aware of it— flowers blooming beneath me, roots cracking through ancient mushroom flesh. The crew was shouting. Or were they? Sound was strange now. Everything was strange except the connection, the perfect, terrible connection—

"ENOUGH."

Kaelren's hand clamped down on my wrist, his corruption flooding my marks with cold silver-black light, severing the connection like an axe through roots. The vision shattered. The Sage stumbled back, and I fell to my knees, gasping, shaking, my human lungs suddenly remembering they needed air.

"Fascinating," the Sage said, looking at their fingers, which were now traced with golden lines that matched my marks. "She's not just marked. She's becoming."

"Becoming what?" Kaelren demanded.

"Something new. Something that hasn't existed since the first growth." The Sage looked at me with something like pity. "You poor child. You have no idea what you're carrying."

"Then tell me," I managed, getting shakily to my feet.

"I cannot. The knowledge must come from within, or it will destroy you." They turned to Kaelren. "You know this. You've felt it through your— connection."

"We're not connected," Kaelren said quickly, too quickly.

The Sage laughed, a sound like trees falling. "Lie to yourself if you must, but don't lie to me. Your marks call to hers. Hers answer. Whether you admit it or not changes nothing."

"Can you help her or not?" Kaelren's voice was sharp, dangerous.

"I can teach her to not die immediately. Whether that's helping is debatable." The Sage turned back to me. "You have perhaps days before the marks consume you entirely. Unless you learn control."

"Days?" I felt cold despite the warm air. "What happens after days?"

"You become something else. Something that might save this realm or destroy it." They smiled, and it was terrible. "No pressure."

"Oh good, no pressure. Just the fate of an entire realm. That's totally manageable."

"Sarcasm," the Sage observed. "How wonderfully human. Try to hold onto that. You'll need something to anchor you when the power tries to take your mind."

"Again, not reassuring."

"Reassurance is for those with hope. You have something better."

"What?"

"Inevitability." They turned and began walking toward the tree. "Come. We have work to do, and not much time to do it."

I looked at Kaelren, who was watching me with an expression I couldn't read.

"What?" I asked.

"Nothing," he said, but I could tell he was lying. Something about what the Sage had said bothered him. The connection, maybe. Or the fact that I had days, not weeks or months.

"Look," I said, "about this connection thing—"

"There is no connection," he cut me off. "The Sage is wrong. Whatever you think you feel, it's just proximity. Nothing more."

"I didn't say I felt anything."

"Good. Because you don't. And neither do I."

He turned and followed the Sage, leaving me standing there feeling oddly rejected, which was stupid because I didn't want a connection with him anyway. He was angry and bitter and had literally threatened to kill me multiple times.

But still.

"He's lying," Peeble said, appearing on my shoulder. "About the connection. He feels it. It terrifies him."

"Why?"

"Because connections mean caring. And caring means pain when you lose someone. He's had enough of both."

I followed them into the tree, trying to ignore the weird awareness of Kaelren somewhere ahead of me. The Sage had said our marks were connected, but that didn't mean I had to feel it, right? Except I could feel something—a thread I could almost touch, a pulse that matched mine. I told myself it was just the aftereffects of having moss-person show me the entire history of plant life. Not a connection. Definitely not a connection.

Behind us, the crew dismounted their bees. Bryx was cooing over Kevin, telling him what a good bee he was. Vashael was already spreading her pollen, marking territory. Nimor had half-vanished into shadow. Eltrien was checking supplies with the methodical care of someone who knew everything could go wrong at any moment. Sarnyx was watching me with those blood-colored eyes, probably calculating how many pieces she could cut me into.

"Welcome to Vyn Hollow," she said as she passed me. "Try not to die on your first day. It sets a bad precedent."

"I'll do my best."

"That's what they all say." She paused, looking at me with something that might have been pity. "You know he's going to get you killed, right? Kaelren. He destroys everything he touches."

"Including himself?"

50

"Especially himself." She walked away before I could respond.

The inside of the tree was hollow, carved into spiraling chambers that went up beyond what I could see and down into darkness. Lights floated freely, little wisps of luminescence that followed people around like pets. The walls were covered in writing that shifted languages when I tried to read it.

"Don't look too closely," Eltrien advised, appearing at my side. "The writing here can drive you mad if you're not prepared for it."

"What does it say?"

"Everything. Nothing. The truth you most need to hear and the lie you most want to believe." He guided me away from the walls. "The Sage likes their games."

"Games?"

"Tests. Lessons. Tortures. In the Hollow, they're all the same thing."

"That's terrifying."

"Yes," he agreed simply. "But it's also effective. If you survive."

"And if I don't?"

"Then we'll burn your body with honors and Kaelren will blame himself for the rest of his probably-short life."

"He'd blame himself?"

Eltrien looked at me with those silver eyes, and I saw knowledge there, the weight of witnessing patterns repeat. "He blames himself for everything. It's his most consistent trait. Well, that and the brooding."

"He does brood a lot."

"It's an art form with him. Professional-level brooding. Sometimes I think he practices in the mirror."

Despite everything, I laughed. The sound echoed strangely in the hollow tree, bouncing off surfaces that shouldn't exist.

"Thank you," I said.

"For what?"

"For being kind. For treating me like a person instead of a problem."

"You're both," he said gently. "But person comes first. Kaelren forgets that sometimes. Don't let him forget it with you."

Before I could respond, the Sage's voice echoed through the hollow: "Come, marked one. Your education in not dying begins now."

I looked at Eltrien, who gave me an encouraging nod, then headed deeper into the tree, toward whatever fresh horror passed for education here.

Behind me, I felt Kaelren watching. Always watching, always calculating, always carrying the weight of failures that might not even be his.

But I didn't feel any connection. Definitely not. That would be ridiculous.

Even if our marks pulsed in perfect sync with each other's heartbeat.

6

Elle

"Again."

I pushed myself up from the moss-covered ground for what felt like the hundredth time, spitting out dirt and what I hoped wasn't blood. My entire body ached, the marks on my skin pulsed with an angry heat, and I was seriously reconsidering every life choice that had led me to this moment.

"I can't," I gasped.

"You can," the Sage said calmly, sitting cross-legged on a mushroom that glowed with soft purple light. "The marks wouldn't have chosen you if you couldn't."

"The marks made a mistake."

"The marks don't make mistakes. They make choices others don't understand."

We were in a training grove deep within the hollow tree, where the walls curved into a natural amphitheater. Bioluminescent fungi provided dim, uneven light that left pockets of darkness, making it hard to track movement. Which was probably the point.

"Try again," Sarnyx said from where she leaned against the wall, thorns extended from her arms like she was born with them. She'd been my opponent for the last hour, and she wasn't holding back.

"I don't even know what I'm trying to do," I protested.

"You're trying not to die," she said helpfully. "Very important skill here."

"I meant with the magic!"

"So did I."

She moved, faster than anyone covered in thorns should be able to move. I threw myself sideways, barely avoiding the thorned whip that grew from her hand. It cracked against the ground where I'd been, leaving gouges in the moss.

"Better," the Sage observed. "You're learning to read intent."

"I'm learning to run away."

"Same thing, initially."

Sarnyx came at me again, and this time I felt something. A pull in my chest, like someone had hooked a line behind my sternum and yanked. Without thinking, I slammed my hand against the ground.

The reaction was immediate and violent.

Roots exploded from the earth—not small ones, but thick, angry things the width of my arm. They shot toward Sarnyx with intent, wrapping around her legs before she could dodge. She cursed creatively as more roots responded to my unconscious call, creating a barrier between us.

"Finally!" Bryx cheered from where he sat watching, Peeble perched on his antennae like a tiny crown. "She did the thing!"

"I did the thing?" I stared at my hand, which was now traced with gilded light that matched my marks. "I did the thing!"

"You did the thing badly," Sarnyx corrected, slicing through my roots with her thorns. "But you did it."

"The Root responds to need," the Sage said, standing with fluid grace. "Your need to survive finally exceeded your fear of the power."

"I wasn't afraid of the power."

"You've been terrified of it since you arrived," Kaelren said from the shadows. I hadn't known he was watching. Of course he was watching. "Terrified of what you might be. What you might become."

"Thanks for the psychoanalysis, Dr. Brooding."

"It's not analysis if it's obvious."

He stepped into the light, and I tried not to notice how the fungi's glow played across his carved marks, making them look like living things.

"She needs combat training," he said to the Sage. "Magic is useless if she dies before she can use it."

"I'm standing right here."

"I'm aware." His silver eyes fixed on me with cold assessment. "You fight like someone who's never faced real violence. Like prey that's never been hunted."

"I've never even been hunting—"

"Irrelevant. You're soft. Weak. The realm will eat you alive, probably literally."

"And again, thanks for the pep talk."

"I'm not trying to encourage you. I'm trying to keep you breathing long enough to be useful." His voice was harsh, angry. "The marks chose wrong, but since they're stuck on you, you'd better learn to survive wearing them."

"Back in Arkansas, the worst danger was mosquito bites and the occasional tornado warning. Here, even the air wants to kill me."

"Then learn to kill it back," he said coldly. "Or die. Those are your options."

The Sage laughed, that sound like wind through dead leaves. "This should be educational. For everyone."

Before I could ask what that meant, Kaelren was moving. Not the supernatural speed the others had, but something worse—inevitable, like gravity deciding to take a personal interest in my destruction.

I managed half a step back before his hand was at my throat. Not choking, just present. A reminder of how easily he could end me.

"Dead," he said quietly.

"You didn't give me time to—"

His foot hooked behind mine, and suddenly I was on my back, looking up at him.

"Dead again," he said. "The realm won't give you time. Neither will I."

"This is stupid," I said, but I was already rolling away, some instinct screaming at me to move.

Good instinct. His hand hit the moss where my head had been, hard enough to leave an impression.

"Better," he said. "Fear is a teacher."

"You're enjoying this."

"I'm educating you. Enjoyment is irrelevant."

He came at me again, and this time I felt the Root respond. Not consciously—I was too busy trying not to die—but the marks on my skin flared, and suddenly there were vines between us. Thin ones, nothing like the roots from before, but enough to tangle his feet.

He destroyed them with a gesture, his carved marks flaring silver-black, but it had bought me seconds. I used them to scramble backward, my hand finding a fallen branch.

"Weapons are good," he said. "But only if you can keep them."

He moved, the branch was gone, and his hand was at my throat again. This time, though, something else happened. Our marks touched—his carved ones against my natural ones—and the world stuttered.

For a heartbeat, I saw through his eyes. Saw myself, dirt-covered and exhausted but still defiant. Saw the marks spreading across my skin like living art. Saw the moment he'd first felt them choose me instead of him, the rage that still burned—

We broke apart, both gasping. The grove had gone silent.

"What was that?" I breathed.

"Nothing," he snarled, backing away like I'd burned him. "A fluke."

"That wasn't nothing—"

"It was a mistake. The marks responding to proximity. It means nothing."

The Sage watched us with interest. "The connection is forming whether you want it or not."

"Then sever it," Kaelren said, and there was something close to desperation in his voice.

"I cannot. It is what it is."

"It's a curse," he spat. "Bad enough she stole the marks. Now I'm leashed to her incompetence?"

"The best bonds always are inconvenient," the Sage said mildly.

Kaelren looked at me, and for a moment his walls were down. I saw fear there. Not of me, but of what was happening between us. A connection neither of us had asked for, neither of us wanted.

Then the walls slammed back up, and he was cold again.

"Again," he said. "And this time, try to last more than three seconds."

"I lasted at least five that time."

"Four. And only because I was distracted."

"By our mystical proximity?"

"By your terrible footwork."

But I caught the lie in it. He was as shaken as I was.

We went again. And again. And again. Each time I lasted a little longer, learned a little more. The Root responded more readily, creating obstacles, diversions, sometimes actual weapons from the living wood around us. But it was wild, uncontrolled. I was as likely to trap myself as my opponent.

"You're thinking too much," Eltrien observed from where he was preparing some kind of healing salve. "The Root doesn't respond to thought. It responds to instinct."

"My instinct is to run away."

"Then use that. The Root excels at creative escapes."

Sarnyx laughed. "She needs to fight, not flee."

"She needs to survive," Kaelren corrected. "Fighting is optional. Living isn't."

"Pragmatic," Vashael said, her pollen cloud shimmering. "I approve."

"Nobody asked for your approval," Sarnyx muttered.

"Nobody ever does. I give it anyway. It's a service."

They continued bickering, but I wasn't listening. Something was happening with my marks. They were warm, almost hot, and spreading faster than before. I could feel them creeping down my arm, across my chest, like molten fire under my skin.

"Sage," I said, and something in my voice made everyone stop talking.

The Sage was beside me in an instant, their green eyes examining the spreading marks. "Interesting. It's accelerating."

"Is that bad?"

"That depends on your definition of bad."

"Death. Death is my definition of bad."

"Then yes, it might be bad." They touched my marks, and I saw their fingers come away with shimmering residue, like pollen. Their expression shifted to something like concern. "You're approaching the first threshold much faster than I anticipated."

"What threshold?"

"The point where you must choose: control the power or let it control you." The Sage's voice was grave. "Most marked ones have weeks to reach this stage. You have hours."

"Why? What's different about me?"

"Your grandmother suppressed your inheritance for your entire life. The marks were dormant, waiting, building pressure like water behind a dam." They traced the golden lines spreading across my skin. "When they finally manifested, all that accumulated power tried to emerge at once. And then you crossed realms, which forced them to activate to keep you alive. And then I touched them, which opened the floodgates further."

"So you're saying this is your fault?" I said, hearing the panic in my voice.

"I'm saying the marks were always going to consume you quickly. I simply accelerated the inevitable by a matter of days." The Sage's green eyes met mine. "Your body is trying to transform all at once rather than gradually. The threshold that should have taken months is happening in hours."

"Can you stop it?"

"No. I can only help you survive it."

"I choose control," I said, trying to sound more confident than I felt.

"Easy to say. Harder to do when the power is eating you from the inside out, when every cell is screaming to become something other than human." They looked at Kaelren, who had appeared at the edge of the training circle. "She needs to pass the threshold tonight. If she doesn't, the transformation will take her whether she's ready or not."

Kaelren kept his distance, careful not to let our marks touch again. "How long does she have?"

"Hours. Maybe less. The combat training accelerated it further—each time she used the Root, it claimed more of her."

"And if she fails?"

The Sage's expression was unreadable. "Then she becomes something else. Something the realm needs but that might not be you anymore. Pure Root incarnate, without the human consciousness to guide it."

"So I'd be alive but not... me?"

"You'd be a force of nature. Powerful. Necessary. But no longer Elle."

***

"You're still thinking like a human," the Sage said after my latest failure left a crater in the grove floor.

"I am human!"

"No. You were human. Now you're becoming something else."

"I don't want to become something else!" The words came out as a scream, and suddenly I was crying, really crying, for the first time since I'd fallen through that damned mirror. "I want to go home! I want my grandmother back! I want to wake up in my bed and have this all be some grief-induced nightmare! I didn't ask for any of this!"

The grove went silent. Even Sarnyx stopped sharpening her thorns to stare.

"I had a life," I continued, my voice breaking. "A normal, boring, human life. I drew pictures for romance novels and drank Dr Pepper and complained about my ex-fiance. Now I'm in some nightmare realm where everything wants to kill me, wearing magic tattoos that are apparently eating me from the inside out, and you're all acting like this is normal!"

"It is normal," Kaelren said coldly. "For us. You're the aberration."

"Thanks. That's really helpful."

"I'm not trying to help. I'm trying to make you understand that your wants are irrelevant. The marks chose you. That choice is final."

"How does it work then? The choosing?"

The Sage smiled sadly. "You surrender. You let the power reshape you. You hope that enough of who you were survives the transformation."

"That's not reassuring."

"It's not meant to be."

As the day wore on—or what passed for day in the hollow tree—I felt the threshold approaching. It was like standing at the edge of a cliff, knowing you were about to fall but not knowing if you'd fly or splatter.

The crew watched with varying degrees of concern. Bryx tried to lighten the mood with jokes that got progressively worse. Vashael offered advice that seemed designed to be confusing. Nimor observed silently, occasionally offering quiet corrections. Eltrien stood ready with healing, knowing he'd probably need it. Sarnyx was brutally honest about my chances, which were apparently "not good but not hopeless."

And Kaelren watched everything, keeping his distance, his anger palpable. He looked exhausted—something I hadn't noticed before, too busy being terrified or angry myself. Even standing at a distance, he was imposing— tall enough that most of the crew had to look up to meet his eyes, with the kind of build that came from actual combat rather than a gym. His dark hair was perpetually tousled, like he'd been running his hands through it, and the thorn-laced leather armor he wore looked like an extension of his corruption rather than protection from it.

"When it happens," he said abruptly, when the others were distracted, "don't fight it."

I looked at him, surprised. This was the first time he'd offered advice that wasn't wrapped in cruelty or contempt. "That seems like bad advice."

"Fighting makes it worse. Trust me." He gestured at his carved marks, and for a moment I saw past the anger to something else—regret, maybe. Or shame. "I fought. Look what it got me."

"Corruption? Pain? Slow death?"

"All of the above." His smile was bitter, and I realized this was the closest thing to kindness he'd offered since I arrived. Not comfort—he'd made it clear he didn't do comfort—but truth. Raw, honest truth that might actually keep me alive.

He was trying to save me from his fate. The thought hit me harder than it should have.

"Learn from my mistakes," he said, and there was something almost pleading in his voice, buried under layers of frost and fury.

"And if I can't?"

"Then you die horrifically instead of peacefully." The walls slammed back up, his expression going cold again. But I'd seen behind them, just for a moment. Seen someone who'd been where I was standing, who'd made the wrong choice, and who didn't want to watch someone else make it too.

Even if that someone was wearing marks he thought should be his.

Before I could respond—before I could acknowledge what he'd just given me—the marks flared. Not just warm now but burning, like someone had poured liquid lava under my skin. I gasped, doubling over, and suddenly everyone was moving.

"It's happening," the Sage said. "The first threshold."

"What do I do?" I gasped through the pain.

"Choose," they said simply. "Control or chaos. Master or servant. Human or other."

"Those are terrible options!"

"They're the only options."

The pain increased, and I felt myself starting to change. Not physically— not yet—but something fundamental was shifting. The human parts of me were being overwritten, replaced with something older, wilder, more in tune with the growing things.

"Get away from me," I gasped, terrified of what I might become.

"No," Kaelren said flatly. "If you lose control and kill everyone, I need to be close enough to stop you."

"How reassuring."

"It's practical. Someone needs to be ready to put you down if you become a threat."

Through the haze of pain, I felt a flash of anger. "You'd kill me?"

"Without hesitation," he said, and meant it. "The marks should have been mine. If you waste them by losing control, I'll end you myself."

The pain peaked, and suddenly I was somewhere else. Not physically—my body was still in the grove—but my consciousness was in the green. The space between spaces where all growing things connected. I could feel every root, every leaf, every flower in the realm. Could feel the rot eating at the edges, the corruption spreading, the slow death of everything.

And I could feel the Root itself. Ancient, patient, waiting.

Choose, it said without words.

"I don't know how," I said to the green.

Then learn.

The power flooded through me, and suddenly I understood. The marks weren't trying to control me. They were trying to connect me. To make me part of something larger, older, more necessary than individual consciousness.

But I could choose how that connection worked. I could be a conduit or a participant. A tool or a partner.

I chose partner.

The pain receded, replaced by something else. Awareness. Connection. Purpose.

I opened eyes I didn't remember closing and found myself standing in a grove that had been transformed. Where there had been moss, there were now impossible-looking flowers, growing in patterns that told stories in a language older than words. Where there had been fungi, there were now trees—saplings, but growing visibly, reaching toward light that shouldn't exist this deep in the hollow.

And where I stood, there was a garden. Small, wild, but undeniably mine.

"Interesting," the Sage said, and they sounded genuinely surprised. "You didn't choose control or chaos."

"I chose both," I said, and my voice had harmonics now, like wind through leaves.

"That's not possible."

"A lot of impossible things are happening lately."

I looked at my hands. The marks had spread to my fingertips, but they weren't just glowing anymore. Now they reflected the full spectrum of plant life—green of new growth, brown of fertile earth, red of autumn leaves, white of winter bark. They shifted and changed, never quite settling on one pattern.

"How do you feel?" Eltrien asked, healer's concern in his voice.

"Different. But still me. Mostly me, anyway." I flexed my fingers, watching the marks shift through their color changes. "Everything feels more alive. Like I can hear the plants breathing."

"The first threshold is the easiest," the Sage warned. "There will be others, each one taking more of your humanity."

"How many?"

"As many as it takes to become what you're meant to be."

"And what am I meant to be?"

"That remains to be seen."

Kaelren approached slowly, like I might explode. With the power humming through me, it wasn't an unreasonable concern.

"Your eyes," he said, his voice flat and emotionless.

"What about them?"

"They're changing. Gold with green, like sunset through leaves." He studied me with clinical detachment. "The transformation is accelerating."

"Thanks for sugar-coating it."

"Would you prefer pretty lies?"

"I'd prefer not being turned into a plant zombie."

"Then you should have stayed on Earth." His silver eyes were cold as winter. "But you're here now, wearing marks that should have been mine, so we'll make do with what we have."

Peeble landed on my shoulder, and I was surprised by how light they felt. Or maybe I was stronger now.

"Well," the beetle said, "you didn't explode. That's something."

"Was explosion a real possibility?"

"Oh yes. About thirty percent chance, actually. Though I've seen worse odds turn out fine. Well, mostly fine. There was that one time with the pixie who thought she could control lightning, but we don't talk about that."

The Sage clapped their hands, and the sound echoed wrong, like it bounced off surfaces that didn't exist. "She's passed the first threshold, but barely. The transformation will continue accelerating."

I looked at my accidental garden more closely. The flowers were moving, very slightly, tracking motion like tiny sentient things. Their appearance shifted when I wasn't looking directly at them, and I could have sworn one of them had teeth.

"That's disturbing," I said.

"That's the Root," Kaelren said, crouching to examine one of the flowers without touching it. "Everything it touches becomes more aware. More hungry. More dangerous." He studied the pattern of growth with the focus of someone analyzing a battlefield. "The way they're arranged—it's defensive. Instinctive territory marking."

"I didn't mean to—"

"You never mean to. That's the problem." He stood, brushing moss from his leathers. "Eltrien, check her vitals before she sleeps. Sarnyx, double the perimeter watch—the power spike will have drawn attention. Nimor, scout the approaches. Bryx, make sure Kevin and the other mounts are secure. We may need to move quickly."

The crew dispersed with practiced efficiency, and I realized this was the first time I'd heard him actually lead them. Not bark orders during combat, but plan. Strategize. Consider multiple threats at once.

"You think something's coming?" I asked.

"Something's always coming. The question is whether we're ready when it arrives." He looked at the Sage. "How long before the second threshold?"

"Days. Perhaps a week if she's careful."

"She won't be careful. She doesn't know how yet." He turned back to me, and his expression was harder to read than usual—not quite anger, more like calculation. "You need rest. Real rest, not collapse. Your body is rebuilding itself at the cellular level. That requires resources."

"I'm not hungry—"

"You will be. Bryx is bringing food that won't kill you. Eat it. All of it." He paused, then added, "The flowers you made? They're feeding off your excess power. As long as they're growing, you're stable. When they start dying, that's when we worry."

"Why?"

"Because it means you're not generating excess anymore. You're consuming everything you produce just to maintain the transformation." His silver eyes met mine. "That's when people start burning through their humanity to fuel the power."

64

It was the longest explanation he'd given me about anything, and the fact that he'd bothered felt significant.

"Thank you," I said.

He looked uncomfortable with the gratitude. "It's practical information. You're no use to anyone if you burn out before the second threshold."

"Right. Practical." But I saw Peeble's antennae twitch in a way that suggested the beetle didn't believe him either.

As evening approached—marked more by the dimming glow of the bioluminescent fungi than any actual sunset—the hollow settled into its own rhythm. I could hear the sounds of the community around us: arguments in languages I didn't recognize, laughter that sounded like breaking glass, children (or child-like things) playing games that seemed to involve a lot of screaming. The smell of cooking food drifted through the air, though I wasn't sure I wanted to know what was being cooked.

Bryx appeared with what he claimed was dinner—some kind of stew that glowed faintly and tasted like mushrooms and regret. "It's nutritious," he said when I made a face. "Probably won't kill you."

"Probably?"

"Ninety percent sure. Maybe eighty-five."

I ate it anyway because the alternative was starving, and my transformed body seemed to need more fuel than before. The marks on my skin pulsed gently as I ate, and I could feel them spreading incrementally, claiming more territory with each heartbeat.

"Hey," Bryx said suddenly, his compound eyes reflecting the fungal light in fascinating patterns. "Want to see something cool?"

"Does it involve potential death?"

"Only a little."

"Pass."

"Your loss. The honey wine here can dissolve metal."

"Why would anyone drink that?"

"For fun, mostly. Also, it makes you see colors that don't exist yet."

I looked around at my impossible garden, at the crew preparing for night watch, at Kaelren sharpening blades with methodical precision while

65

pointedly not looking in my direction. The marks on my skin continued their slow conquest, and somewhere in the distance, something howled in a register that human ears shouldn't be able to hear.

This was my life now. Strange foods that might kill me, people who definitely wanted to kill me, and marks that were slowly killing me while transforming me into something else. Tomorrow would absolutely be worse, and the day after that worse still.

But for now, in this moment between battles and transformations, sitting in a garden that shouldn't exist in a tree the size of a skyscraper, surrounded by dangerous outcasts who might eventually accept me or might eventually eat me—for now, I was surviving.

It wasn't much, but it was enough.

Even if I had no idea what I was becoming.

7

Elle

The smell of something burning dragged me from dreams of vines and violence.

"Shit, shit, shit—" Bryx's voice carried across camp, followed by the distinct sound of wings beating frantically.

I groaned, every muscle protesting as I sat up. My entire body ached from the journey here—days of riding giant bees and sleeping on the ground had left me feeling like someone had taken my bones out, put them back wrong, then decided to set them on fire for good measure. The marks at my collarbones pulsed with a dull ache, like the world's worst sunburn but under my skin.

The Sage had been right about passing the first threshold—it had bought me time. Instead of hours until I lost myself completely, I now had days, maybe a week before the second threshold hit. The transformation had slowed to a steady creep rather than a wildfire, though I could feel it eating away at my humanity with every heartbeat.

Outside my tent, the camp was already alive with morning activity. The air hummed with the sound of a thousand tiny wings—not just Bryx's bees, but the native insects of Wynmire that glowed faintly blue in the dawn light. Vashael tended to her mobile garden—plants growing in containers made from hollowed gourds and woven root baskets, their leaves releasing a scent like jasmine mixed with copper. Nimor flickered in and out of visibility near the perimeter, probably scouting or just enjoying making people nervous. Eltrien sat cross-legged near the fire, grinding something in a mortar that sparkled like crushed stars, organizing his healing supplies with the kind of methodical precision that suggested he'd seen too much chaos to leave anything to chance.

And Bryx was definitely burning breakfast.

I emerged to find him frantically trying to salvage what looked like fungus cakes, now more charcoal than food. Kevin, his favorite bee, hovered nearby making disapproving buzzing sounds.

"I just looked away for one second," Bryx protested to the bee.

"You were telling a story," Sarnyx corrected from where she sat sharpening her thorns. "A long story. With hand gestures."

"It was a good story!"

"Was it worth burnt breakfast?"

I made my way to the fire, trying not to limp. My ribs ached where I'd landed wrong during yesterday's "controlled falling" exercise, which was the Sage's fun way of saying "throw yourself at the ground and try to make plants catch you."

"There's porridge," Eltrien offered, gesturing to a pot that looked significantly less destroyed. "And some preserved fruit Vashael found."

"Thanks." I accepted a bowl gratefully, settling onto a log that someone had dragged near the fire. The porridge was bland but filling, with chunks of something sweet that might have been fruit or might have been crystallized tree sap. At this point, I didn't ask.

Kaelren stood at the edge of camp, his back to us, silver eyes scanning the forest. He hadn't acknowledged my presence, which was pretty standard. What wasn't standard was the way he kept flexing his left hand, the one where his carved marks were darkest.

He was in pain. I could tell by the tension in his shoulders, the careful way he held himself. But asking if he was okay would probably result in him glaring at me until I spontaneously combusted from embarrassment, so I focused on my breakfast instead.

Stop staring at him, I told myself. *He literally threatened to kill you three days ago. Multiple times. He's probably cataloging your weaknesses right now, figuring out the most efficient way to end you when you inevitably lose control.*

But damn it, even plotting my death, he was unfairly beautiful. The morning light caught in his dark hair, turned his pale skin to alabaster. His carved marks, visible through his shirt, created patterns that were horrifying and mesmerizing in equal measure.

Focus on not dying, not on how his jaw could cut glass.

"You're brooding into your porridge," Peeble observed, landing on my knee. "It's not that bad."

"I'm not brooding. I'm thinking."

"About our fearless leader's murderous tendencies or his cheekbones?"

I nearly choked. "What? Neither!"

"Liar."

"I'm thinking about training," I said firmly, though my face was definitely red. "The Sage said we'd work on shaping exercises today."

"After what happened with the trees yesterday? You nearly pulled three of them down on us."

"That was an accident."

"You said, and I quote, 'I wonder if I can make them dance.'"

"I didn't think they'd actually try!"

The Sage appeared then, materializing from wherever mysterious mentors go when they're not being cryptic. Today they looked more solid than usual, settling on the appearance of a middle-aged person with silver-streaked hair and eyes that held too much knowledge.

"Ready for your first real training?" they asked cheerfully.

"First? What do you call everything else that's happened?"

"Survival. This is education." They gestured to the cleared area near the camp. "Today we begin shaping your power properly."

I stood, brushing crumbs from my clothes. The vine belt had curled itself more comfortably around my waist while I ate.

"Still adjusting to the new clothes?" Vashael asked, noticing my fidgeting.

"My belt just rearranged itself," I said. "I know it's supposed to be learning me or whatever, but it's still weird."

"Give it another few days. They settle eventually."

They'd better. The first two days had been a nightmare of fabric that decided on its own when to tighten or loosen. I'd woken up the second morning practically mummified because the shirt thought I was cold. At least now the clothes were getting the hint about personal space.

Other things I'd gotten used to: bathing in freezing streams while keeping one eye out for the water beetles that Vashael swore were "mostly harmless." The soap concentrate she'd given me that first day worked miracles but smelled like crushed flowers and regret. Eltrien had taught me how to heat water using smooth stones from the fire, which had made everything infinitely more bearable.

And the bathroom situation—well. I'd learned which trees provided the most privacy and which plants were polite enough to look away. A low bar for civilization, but I'd stopped being precious about it after day two when something with too many legs had scared me mid-squat. Sarnyx had laughed for ten minutes straight.

Julian would have had a breakdown by now, I thought, watching the crew go about their morning routines with the casual efficiency of people who'd been living rough for years. He'd have demanded a hotel, proper plumbing, a shower with good water pressure. Would've been on the first metaphysical bus back to Earth.

The thought didn't sting as much as it used to.

"Everything here lives," Vashael said, apparently reading my expression. "The clothes, the trees, even the water sometimes. You're doing well, adjusting to it."

"Weird beats dead, right?"

"Exactly right."

As I walked to the training area, I caught Kaelren watching me. His expression was cold, calculating. Probably noting how the marks had spread slightly overnight, determining how many more days before he'd need to follow through on his promise to Josephine.

"Focus," the Sage said, drawing my attention back. "The Root responds to emotion, but it's controlled by will. Yesterday you shouted. Today, you'll whisper."

"How exactly does one whisper to an ancient magical force?"

"The same way you'd whisper to a lover—with intention and delicacy."

"Wouldn't know. My ex thought whispering was weird unless it was criticism about my life choices."

The Sage tilted their head. "Interesting baggage. We'll unpack that never. Now, start small. A single flower. Call it into being gently."

They gestured to the cleared training ground—a circle of packed earth surrounded by ancient stones that hummed with residual magic from countless exercises before mine. The crew had drifted to the edges, settling in to watch. Bryx perched on Kevin's back. Sarnyx leaned against a tree, already looking bored. Eltrien stood ready with his healing supplies, which was never a good sign. Even Kaelren had positioned himself within striking distance, arms crossed, face expressionless.

No pressure at all.

I moved to the center of the circle, feeling the weight of their attention. The ground here was different—softer, more receptive, like it had been waiting for someone to ask it to grow. I knelt, placing my palm on the earth. The marks at my collarbones warmed immediately, spreading heat down my arms. I could feel the Root beneath, vast and patient and eager. It wanted to explode upward, to transform everything into green chaos.

No, I thought. *Just one. Just a small one.*

The power pushed against my control like a dam about to burst.

"Breathe," the Sage instructed. "The Root follows breath. In for control, out for release."

I breathed. In, holding the power. Out, releasing just a thread of it.

A tiny shoot pushed through the soil. Then another. Then fifty.

"Too many," the Sage said mildly.

"I noticed." I tried to pull the power back, but the shoots kept growing, becoming stems, budding with flowers that shouldn't exist—blue roses, pale luminous daisies, something that shimmered with its own inner radiance.

"Control it." Kaelren's voice, sharp as a blade. "Or I will."

71

Right. Because if I lost control, ending me was his job. No pressure.

"I've got it," I said through gritted teeth, though I definitely didn't have it.

The flowers kept blooming, spreading in a circle around me. Some of them were starting to move, turning to track the sun like time-lapse footage on fast forward.

"You're fighting it," the Sage observed. "Stop fighting. Guide."

"That's not helpful!"

"Most truth isn't."

Instead of pulling or pushing, I tried to shape the power like water finding its course. The fifty flowers suddenly merged into one massive bloom the size of a dinner plate, petals shifting like oil on water.

"Better," the Sage said. "Now make it small again."

I focused on the flower, imagining it shrinking. The power resisted—it didn't like reversing growth. The flower shrank slowly until it was normal sized, then tiny as my thumbnail.

"Good. Now make it sing."

"I'm sorry, what?"

"Everything alive has a voice. Find it."

I reached for the flower with my mind, feeling for something like resonance. The flower chimed once, a clear, ringing note.

"Holy shit," I breathed.

"Focus," Kaelren said sharply, and I flinched before I could stop myself.

He'd moved closer without me noticing—close enough that I could feel the cold radiating from his corrupted marks, the way they seemed to pull at mine like opposing magnets. He was staring at the flower with an expression I couldn't read. Disgust, maybe. Or calculation. With him, it was always calculation.

"You're losing concentration," he said, but his voice had lost some of its edge.

"Hard to concentrate with you looming," I muttered.

"Get used to it. In actual combat, your enemies won't maintain a respectful distance."

He was right, which was annoying. But there was something else—the way he'd said *your enemies* instead of *enemies*. Like he'd almost included himself in that category, then thought better of it.

We spent the rest of the morning on precision exercises, and I became increasingly aware that Kaelren was watching every single one. Not from the edge of the training ground like the others, but close. Circling. Observing from different angles like he was cataloging my weaknesses—or maybe my strengths, I couldn't tell.

Each exercise pushed my control. The marks at my collarbones grew warmer, pulsing with increased intensity, but thankfully not spreading further. What *was* spreading was my awareness of him. The way he moved, silent as shadow. The tension in his shoulders that suggested pain he was ignoring. The moments when our marks pulsed in sync and his eyes would snap to mine before he looked away, jaw tight.

I tried to ignore it. Tried to focus on the Sage's instructions, on the flowers I was coaxing into existence, on literally anything except the fact that I could sense exactly where he was even when I wasn't looking at him.

That damned connection the Sage kept mentioning. Whether we wanted it or not.

"Stop thinking about him," Peeble whispered from my shoulder. "Your flowers are getting spiky."

I looked down. The beetle was right—the latest bloom had grown thorns.

"I wasn't thinking about him," I lied.

"Your subconscious disagrees."

Across the training ground, Kaelren's carved marks flared silver-black for just a moment, and I knew—*knew*—he'd felt whatever that was. Our eyes met. His expression was closed, cold, but something flickered behind it before his walls slammed back up.

"That's enough," the Sage announced at midday, their timing either impeccable or intentional. "You need rest."

"I'm fine."

"You're shaking."

I looked down at my hands. They were trembling, and there were thin green lines running through my fingernails like veins in leaves.

"That's new," I said, trying to sound casual about becoming part plant.

"Your body is adapting," Eltrien said, approaching with his healing supplies. "May I?"

I nodded, and he examined my hands with clinical efficiency.

"Three days since the first threshold and you're already this far along,' Eltrien murmured, examining the green lines. 'The transformation isn't just accelerating—it's compounding. Your blood is changing composition."

"Into what?"

"Something between human and plant. A bridge."

Kaelren made a disgusted sound and stalked away.

"What's his problem?" I asked.

"You're becoming what he can't," Sarnyx said bluntly. "The marks chose you. His were carved. You're evolution. He's just dying slowly."

"That's harsh."

"Truth often is."

I wanted to argue, but exhaustion was hitting hard. The precision exercises had drained me more than yesterday's power displays.

"Rest," the Sage said. "This afternoon, we'll work on communication."

"With plants?"

"With the Root itself."

I made my way back to my tent, pausing when I passed Kaelren. He was destroying training dummies with ruthless efficiency, corruption spreading from his strikes like disease.

"You're pushing too hard," I said without thinking.

He froze mid-strike. "Excuse me?"

"Your marks. The corruption's spreading faster when you push them."

"And you care because?"

"I don't. But Josephine would be pissed if you died before helping me figure this out."

"Josephine is dead. Her opinions are irrelevant."

"Wow. Cold even for you."

He turned to face me fully, silver eyes like winter. "Focus on your own

74

transformation. Mine is not your concern."

"Fine. Die of stubbornness."

"I intend to. After I fulfill my promise."

The threat was clear. I was just a task to complete before his own end.

"Good to know where we stand," I said, and walked away.

Inside my tent, I collapsed onto my bedroll, staring at my changing hands. The green veins were spreading, creating patterns that were beautiful if you didn't think about what they meant.

Julian would have called me reckless, I thought bitterly. *Said I was being 'unnecessarily dramatic' about a few scratches. He never understood that sometimes you had to bleed to grow stronger. Then again, he never understood much about growth at all—just control.*

"Your life is a disaster," I said to the tent ceiling.

"But an interesting disaster," Peeble replied, apparently having followed me.

"Is interesting worth dying for?"

"Better than dying of boredom with that imbecile you called a fiance."

They had a point. Even with the whole turning-into-a-plant thing and the assassin-bodyguard who'd kill me without hesitation, this was better than slowly disappearing into Julian's shadow.

"That's depressing."

"That's growth," Peeble said.

"Terrible pun."

"I'm a beetle. Terrible puns are my only joy."

Despite everything, I smiled. Then exhaustion pulled me under, and I dreamed of roots and roses and silver eyes that calculated the exact angle needed to end me efficiently.

8

Kaelren

She emerged from her tent the next morning looking like death warmed over, and I had to bite back several observations about her deteriorating condition.

Not your concern, I reminded myself. *She's a mission. Nothing more.*

I noticed the crew had settled into an easy rhythm. Bryx had taught Elle how to properly greet Kevin without getting stung—a delicate dance of humming and hand gestures that she'd fumbled through while the crew laughed. Even that simple moment of levity felt dangerous. She was integrating too well.

"We're going on patrol," I announced when she approached the fire for breakfast.

Elle looked up from the bowl Eltrien handed her, confusion clear on her face. "Patrol? The Sage said more training today."

"Training includes practical application. There are things moving in the forest—constructs. Bone and root fused together, drawn to concentrated Root power." I checked the knives at my belt. "Which means they're drawn to you."

"So I'm bait." Her voice went flat.

"You're the lure, yes. But you're also the weapon." I met her eyes. "You needed to know you could handle them in the field, not just in a controlled circle with the Sage watching. These things hunt at night. Better to face

76

them now, on our terms, than have them find camp while everyone's sleeping."

"You could have mentioned that before just announcing we're going on a death walk."

"Would you have agreed to come if I'd explained the full extent of the danger?"

She hesitated. "No. Probably not."

"Then discussing it beforehand would have been pointless. I would have brought you regardless—this needed to happen." I finished checking my weapons and looked at her directly. "We leave in ten minutes. Bring water, not breakfast. You'll want an empty stomach for this."

"Just the two of us?"

"The others have tasks. Perimeter checks, supply runs, scout rotations. Someone needs to stay with the Sage." I paused, considering whether to add more, then decided honesty served better than comfort. "And if this goes badly, better it's just me who has to deal with the consequences."

"This seems like a terrible idea."

"Most of mine are. But they keep us alive, so I keep having them." I gestured toward her tent. "Ten minutes. Don't make me come get you."

She muttered something under her breath that sounded like "no kidding" but stood to prepare.

Ten minutes later, we were walking through the deeper forest. Elle tried to look confident but jumped at every sound. Her marks glowed faintly with her nervousness.

"Stop broadcasting fear," I said. "Everything in a mile radius can sense it."

"How do I stop?"

"Remember you're more dangerous than most of them now."

"That's not reassuring."

"It's fact."

We walked in silence along a path that barely existed. The forest here was ancient, trees so old they'd developed their own ecosystems—moss gardens growing on bark, insects that only lived in specific branches, entire worlds contained in a single trunk.

Elle stared at the canopy with wonder that made her look younger, more vulnerable. Her mouth was slightly open, eyes tracking the way light filtered through leaves in colors that didn't exist on Earth. She'd stopped walking entirely, too absorbed in the beauty to remember she was supposed to be watching for threats.

Liability, I told myself. She's going to get herself killed staring at trees.

But I didn't push her forward. Didn't snap at her to focus. Just watched her take in the forest with the kind of unguarded awe I'd lost decades ago, if I'd ever had it at all. The marks on her skin were glowing faintly, responding to the life around us, and she didn't even notice. Didn't realize she was unconsciously reaching toward the trees, her power already trying to connect.

She was so clearly Jo's blood. That same wonder, that same instinct to commune rather than conquer. Jo had looked at the Thornwood like it was a miracle, even after everything it had taken from her.

Stop noticing such things, I commanded myself. She's a mission. A debt. Nothing more.

But then she smiled—just slightly, just for a moment—at something in the canopy, and I felt the connection between our marks pulse. Not painful this time. Just... present. Aware.

She was becoming more attuned to the Root with every passing hour, and I was dying from my failed attempts to force it. The irony would have been funny if it didn't make me want to destroy something.

"Movement," I said sharply, needing to break whatever moment this was. "Eleven o'clock."

Elle turned slowly, the wonder draining from her face as she spotted the bone-root construct. It moved like a spider, too many joints bending wrong, its form a mockery of both skeletal and plant life.

The marks on her skin flared bright with fear, and I felt the exact moment her survival instinct kicked in. Her posture shifted—less wonder, more coiled tension. She was learning.

Good, I thought. Fear will keep her alive longer than awe ever could.

"What the fuck is that?"

"Construct. I just told you."

"You didn't say they looked like nightmares had babies with trees!"

"Would that information have helped?"

"Maybe!"

The construct moved closer, drawn by her power but wary.

"What do I do?" Real fear in her voice now.

"Defend yourself."

"That's your advice?"

"You wanted practical training."

"I wanted to not die!"

"Then defend yourself effectively."

She glared at me, but the construct attacked. It moved faster than she expected, launching itself with bone claws extended.

Elle threw herself sideways, marks flaring. Thorns erupted from her arms—wild, desperate things. The construct twisted mid-leap to avoid them, landing behind her.

"Stop running!" I called. "You're not prey anymore."

"Easy for you to say!"

But she stopped retreating. When the construct lunged again, she met it. Her thorns caught its claws, holding them at bay.

"Now grow something inside it," I instructed.

"What?"

"You made a flower sing. Make this thing bloom."

Understanding flickered across her face. She pressed her palm against the construct's chest, marks pulsing.

Nothing happened for a heartbeat. Then the construct screamed.

Flowers erupted from inside it—violent, hungry things with their own thorns. They consumed it from within, using its body as fertilizer. Within seconds, a garden stood where the monster had been.

Elle staggered back, staring. "I killed it."

"You transformed it."

"That's just fancy words for killing."

"No. Look."

Insects were already investigating the flowers. Life returning to dead wood and old bone.

"You didn't destroy," I said, watching the insects investigate her gruesome garden. "You transformed it. Gave something twisted a chance to become something useful. That's rare."

She looked at me sharply, suspicion clear in her eyes. "I thought you believed I was an abomination."

"I believe you're dangerous. That's entirely different from being an abomination." I tilted my head, studying the flowers still blooming from bone and wood. "Abominations are mistakes. You're something the realm chose deliberately. I may not like what that means for me, but I can admit when something is well-crafted, even if it's inconvenient."

Before she could respond to that—and I could see she wanted to, probably with something cutting—more movement rippled through the undergrowth. Three more constructs emerged, and they'd clearly learned from their companion's spectacular death. They moved with caution now, coordinating their approach.

"Shit," Elle breathed.

"Really? We're fighting plant-bone nightmares and you're going with 'shit' as your battle cry?" I shook my head. "Standards remain regardless of circumstances, Elle. If you're going to swear at monsters, at least be creative about it."

"You're critiquing my language right now?"

"I'm a believer in maintaining civilization even when surrounded by things that want to eat us. Call it a character flaw." I watched the constructs circle, calculating angles and weaknesses. "Also, it annoys you, which makes this significantly more entertaining for me."

"You're unbelievable."

"I prefer 'consistent.' Now stop complaining and get ready—these ones look smarter than the first." I gestured with my blade. "Back to back. And try not to stab me with those thorns of yours. Friendly fire is embarrassing for everyone involved."

Elle pressed against me without hesitation. I ignored how her warmth felt through our clothes, how her marks hummed against my corruption.

"On three," I said.

"Three what?"

"One... two... three."

They attacked simultaneously. I let my corruption free—black rot spreading from my strikes, wasteful but necessary. Elle was learning, growing targeted vines instead of wild thorns, specific plants instead of random flowers.

But the third construct was smarter. It got past her defenses, claws raking her shoulder. Blood—red with gold threads—stained her tunic.

Rage, instant and absolute.

I moved without thought, corruption exploding in waves of decay. The construct didn't just die—it rotted to dust.

"Kaelren," Elle gasped.

I was still flooding the area with corruption. Trees withering, plants dying, air becoming toxic. I pulled back, but a circle of death surrounded us, everything within ten feet reduced to black rot.

"You're bleeding," I said, focusing on her shoulder.

"I'll live." She stared at the dead circle. "You killed everything."

"You were injured."

"So you committed botanical genocide?"

"It seemed efficient."

She laughed, slightly hysterical. "You're insane."

"Probably."

I reached for her shoulder, then stopped. "May I?"

"Since when do you ask?"

"Since now."

Because something in you shifted when you saw her blood, his corruption whispered. *Because she matters to you more than she should.*

She nodded. I examined the wound—three parallel cuts, deep but clean.

The golden threads in her blood were already knitting the wounds closed, flesh mending at a pace that would have taken a human days.

81

"You heal fast," I observed, watching the process with clinical interest. "Faster than yesterday, even. The transformation is accelerating the regeneration."

"Apparently being part plant has benefits." She tried to sound casual about it, but I caught the tremor in her voice. Fear of what she was becoming, probably. Or fear of how quickly it was happening.

"Don't rely on it. Fast healing makes people reckless—they start taking risks they shouldn't because they know they'll survive them." I pulled bandages from my pack, the motion automatic after years of field injuries. "Then one day they take a risk just slightly too large, and the healing isn't fast enough. I've seen it happen."

"Speaking from experience?"

"Yes. Multiple times, actually. I'm a slow learner when it comes to my own mortality." I gestured for her to hold still while I wrapped her shoulder. "The corruption speeds my healing too, in its own twisted way. It's kept me alive through things that should have killed me. But every time I rely on it, it claims more territory."

She was tense under my hands but didn't pull away. The bandage work required closeness—my fingers brushing her skin, her breath warm against my neck as I reached around to secure the wrapping. I focused on the task, ignoring how aware I was of her pulse, steady and strong beneath my fingertips.

"Why did you really bring me out here?" she asked quietly.

"Training—"

"Don't." Her voice was sharp. "The Sage would never approve this. They'd say I needed more controlled practice before facing constructs in the field. So why?"

I finished with the bandage, stepping back to put necessary distance between us. The truth sat heavy on my tongue, and I considered lying. Would have lied, usually. But something about her directness demanded the same in return.

"The constructs would have found our camp tonight. I saw the signs this morning—tracks converging on our location, probably drawn by the power spike from your threshold crossing." I met her eyes. "Better to face them here, in daylight, with preparation, than have them attack while everyone's sleeping. The Sage wouldn't have approved, which is why I didn't ask."

"You could have just said that from the beginning."

"Would you have believed me? Or would you have thought I was using it as an excuse to get you alone and test your abilities?"

She considered that. "Probably the second one."

"Then my initial approach was more efficient. Sometimes a small deception prevents a larger argument." I started walking back toward camp. "Though I'll admit the efficiency argument loses some merit when you end up injured anyway."

"Everything's about efficiency with you."

"Survival requires efficiency. Sentimentality is expensive." But even as I said it, I was remembering the rage that had flooded through me when she was wounded, the way I'd let corruption spread unchecked. That hadn't been efficient. That had been pure reaction, and I didn't know what to do with that information.

We stood there in the circle of death and growth—my corruption having killed everything, her power already reclaiming it. The contrast felt significant somehow. I wanted to move, to return to camp and the safety of routine, but something held me there.

"Kaelren?"

"What?"

"Thank you. For the save." She was looking at me with an expression I couldn't read. Not gratitude, exactly. Something more complicated. "I know you did it to protect Josephine's investment or whatever justification you're using, but... thank you anyway."

"You would have survived without my intervention. The healing would have kicked in."

"Maybe. But it would have hurt a lot more, and I might have panicked and done something stupid." She flexed her shoulder experimentally. "So. Thanks."

I nodded, not trusting myself to say more. The walk back to camp stretched in silence, but it wasn't the uncomfortable kind. Just... quiet. Contemplative.

When we arrived, the Sage was waiting at the camp's edge, arms crossed, disappointment radiating from them like heat.

"I said she needed rest."

"She needed more field experience. The constructs were coming regardless—better she face them prepared than surprised."

"She needed healing and controlled practice, not to be thrown at bone-monsters like bait."

"She needed to know she could survive when things went wrong. And now she does." I kept my voice level, meeting the Sage's eyes. "You can be angry about my methods, but the results speak for themselves. She's alive, she's learned, and the constructs won't be attacking camp tonight."

The Sage looked between us, taking in Elle's bandaged shoulder, the blood staining both our clothes, the exhaustion in her posture.

"What did you learn?" they asked Elle, voice careful.

"That I can kill things by making them bloom. Those constructs are horrifying. And that Kaelren's solution to everything is death."

"All valuable lessons," the Sage said dryly. "Tomorrow, controlled training only."

"Tomorrow might be complicated," Nimor said, his form solidifying from shadow at the edge of camp. His voice was quiet, but it carried the weight of bad news delivered too many times. "Crown scouts. Three miles out and closing."

The camp went still. Even the insects seemed to pause their humming.

"How many?" I asked, though I could already guess from Nimor's expression.

"Full patrol. Forty soldiers, maybe fifty. Standard search formation, moving methodically. They're not rushing—they know we can't have gone far." He flickered, checking over his shoulder as if they might appear at any moment. "They'll reach this location by mid-morning tomorrow if they maintain their current pace."

"They found us," Elle said, and I heard the resignation in her voice. The acceptance that this had always been inevitable.

"They were always going to find you. The marks are like a beacon to anyone who knows how to look." I started cataloging resources mentally— weapons, supplies, escape routes. "The only question was when, not if. Auradelle wants what you're carrying too badly to just let you disappear into Wynmire."

The crew exchanged glances, that silent communication that came from years of running together.

"We run," Eltrien said immediately, already thinking about how to pack his healing supplies quickly. "We've outmaneuvered patrols before. We can do it again."

"We fight," Sarnyx countered, her thorns extending as if the decision was already made. "I'm tired of running. Forty soldiers isn't impossible odds. Not with what she can do now." She jerked her chin at Elle.

"We prepare for both," the Sage interrupted, their voice cutting through the brewing argument with the authority of someone who'd survived more conflicts than any of us. "Tonight we plan every contingency. Tomorrow, when we see their actual formation and capabilities, we decide. Running blind gets you killed just as fast as fighting stupid."

The camp erupted into controlled chaos—Bryx checking the bees, Vashael gathering her plants, Nimor disappearing to set watches. Through it all, I watched Elle stand frozen, processing what this meant.

I caught her arm as she started toward her tent, pulling her aside where the others wouldn't overhear.

"Listen to me carefully," I said, keeping my voice low. "Whatever happens tomorrow—whether we run or fight or some combination of both—there's something you need to understand."

"What?" She looked up at me, fear evident but controlled.

"Don't let them take you alive."

She went very still. "What?"

"The Crown has methods of extracting power from marked individuals. Techniques refined over centuries, designed to pull every drop of magic out while keeping the host alive as long as possible." I held her gaze, making sure she understood. "You wouldn't survive it intact. The person they'd eventually release—if they released you at all—wouldn't be you anymore. Just an empty shell that remembers being Elle."

The color drained from her face. "That's... that's horrifying."

"That's reality. Which is why I'm telling you now, while you can still prepare for the possibility."

She swallowed hard, then asked the question I'd been expecting. "Would you do it?" Her eyes searched mine. "If it came down to it—if they were about to take me—would you kill me first?"

The honest answer sat between us, heavy and sharp.

"Yes."

"Without hesitation?" Her voice was barely above a whisper.

"Hesitation would be cruel. It would give you time to hope for a rescue that isn't coming, time to beg, time to believe there's another way." I kept my voice steady, clinical. "Quick is kinder. It's the last gift I could give you if it came to that."

She pulled her arm free from my grip, stepping back like I'd burned her. "Good to know exactly where we stand. You really are just waiting for permission to fulfill your promise to Jo, aren't you? This is just another acceptable outcome."

"Elle—"

"No. I get it. I'm a mission. A debt. An inconvenience wearing marks you think should be yours." Her voice shook, but whether from fear or anger I couldn't tell. "Thanks for the honesty, I guess. At least I know what to expect when things go wrong."

She walked away before I could correct her assumption, and I let her go. Better she think I was cold, calculating, waiting for an excuse. Better than her knowing the truth—that the thought of what the Crown would do to her made my corruption flare with a rage I couldn't afford. That I'd burn through the last of my life to prevent them from taking her, not because of Jo's debt, but because somewhere in the last few days, she'd stopped being just a mission.

I watched her disappear into her tent, shoulders rigid with hurt and anger.

Let her hate you, I told myself. *It's safer for both of you.*

Even if the cost of that safety was her thinking I'd kill her without a second thought.

Even if the truth was I'd already started counting all the ways I'd die to keep that from being necessary.

9

Elle

I couldn't sleep.

Every time I closed my eyes, I saw the construct blooming from the inside out. Saw the circle of death Kaelren had created. My shoulder throbbed where the construct's claws had raked me during our patrol earlier—three parallel cuts that had healed on the surface thanks to the shining threads in my blood, but still ached deep in the muscle. My ribs on the left side protested when I moved, bruised from when I'd slammed into a tree trying to dodge the second construct. Various smaller cuts decorated my arms from the thorns I'd manifested too wildly, not yet used to having weapons growing from my own skin.

The marks at my collarbones pulsed with each heartbeat. They'd grown slightly more vibrant during the fight, the golden vines at my collarbones seeming to glow from within, but they hadn't spread beyond their original boundaries. At this rate, I wondered how long before they would begin their inevitable creep across more of my skin.

Would that be so bad? The thought wasn't entirely mine. The Root speaking, maybe, or just my transformation.

I sat up, giving up on sleep. The camp was quiet except for whoever was on watch—probably Kaelren, because apparently the man never slept.

I needed air. The tent felt suffocating, the forest's whispers pressing in from all sides.

I emerged to find I was right—Kaelren sat by the dying fire, silver eyes scanning the darkness with the focused intensity of someone who'd spent years waiting for attacks that eventually came.

"Can't sleep?" he asked without looking at me, though I knew he'd tracked my movements from the moment I left my tent.

"The forest is too loud." I moved closer to the fire, drawn by its warmth and the one person who seemed immune to the overwhelming presence of all this living wood.

"It's completely quiet." He glanced at me then, one eyebrow raised. "I can barely hear anything beyond the fire."

"Not to me. Every root, every leaf—they're all talking at once. Communicating in ways I'm only just starting to understand." I rubbed my temples, where a dull ache had taken up residence. "It's like trying to sleep in the middle of a crowded room where everyone's talking directly into your ear simultaneously."

"Sounds like hell," he said flatly, and I appreciated that he didn't try to minimize it.

"Pretty much. Not everything can be fixed by just powering through it, you know." I sat on a log across from him, maintaining careful distance. The fire crackled between us, sending sparks dancing into the darkness.

"No. But complaining about it doesn't make it stop either." He stirred the fire with a stick. "You adapt or you break. Those are the options."

"Wow. Inspirational. You should write greeting cards." I watched the flames dance, remembering nights back home when the biggest concern was whether I'd remembered to lock the car. "Back home, I had this white noise fan. Ancient thing, sounded like a jet engine preparing for takeoff, drove my neighbors insane. But somehow it helped me sleep—just one constant sound to drown everything else out." I gestured at the forest around us. "Here, every single leaf has an opinion it wants to share, and they're all sharing them at once."

"Sounds peaceful," he said, and the dryness in his tone made it clear he understood exactly how not-peaceful it was.

"Oh, extremely. Very zen, having a thousand plants whispering commentary about everything. Even my bedroll has started trying to grow roots into me while I sleep, which is just fantastic for my already deteriorating mental state."

He actually looked at me then, attention fully focused. "Your bedroll is growing roots?"

"Small ones. Thin as hair, but definitely roots. I think it likes me. Or it's trying to absorb me slowly. Hard to tell the difference sometimes." I pulled my knees up, wrapping my arms around them. "Welcome to my life—where even the furniture is becoming sentient and possibly carnivorous."

"Burn it. Get a new one." He said it like the solution was obvious.

"The realm will just make the new one sentient, too. Everything here is alive. I'm starting to think that's the point—I'm supposed to get comfortable with being constantly surrounded by things that are aware of me."

Silence settled between us, heavier than before. In the distance, something howled—long and mournful and definitely not from any Earth species I'd ever heard.

"You saved me today," I said quietly, needing to acknowledge it even if he'd dismiss it. "With the construct. When it got past my defenses."

"You would have managed. The healing was already starting before I intervened."

"No, I wouldn't have." I met his eyes across the fire. "It was too fast, and I was too slow. I froze." I hated admitting weakness, but he deserved honesty. "You used your corruption to destroy it. I saw how much it spread after—that's accelerating your decline, isn't it?"

"Probably." He didn't sound particularly concerned about it. "But you being dead would have been inconvenient."

"Inconvenient. Right." I tried not to let that sting. "Well, thanks for preventing my inconvenient death."

"Don't mention it." His carved marks pulsed with dark light, and I felt a corresponding warmth in my own. That connection we kept pretending didn't exist, humming between us like a string pulled taut.

"Why aren't you asleep?" he asked, shifting the subject with all the subtlety of a battering ram.

"Besides the botanical chorus singing the song of their people directly into my consciousness? I keep thinking about tomorrow. About what's coming, about the Crown forces, about how many different ways this could go catastrophically wrong." I stared into the fire. "Hard to sleep when your brain won't stop cataloging potential disasters."

"Worrying doesn't change the outcome. Just makes you more tired when the disaster actually arrives."

"Says the man who never sleeps because he's always watching for threats that might materialize from the shadows." I gestured at his vigil. "How is what I'm doing different from what you're doing?"

"I'm doing something about it. You're just spinning in circles inside your own head." He leaned back, shadows playing across the sharp angles of his face. "There's a difference between preparation and panic."

"And what I'm doing is panic?"

He studied me for a moment. "What you're doing is human. Doesn't make it useful, but it's understandable."

Despite everything—the danger, the exhaustion, the fear—I almost smiled at the backhanded acceptance. "You know, back home my ex used to say—" I stopped, suddenly aware of what I was about to do. Why was I bringing up Julian? What was wrong with me?

"Your ex?" Something sharpened in his voice, an edge I couldn't quite identify. "The lawyer?"

"You remember that?"

"I remember most things. Especially the things people say when they think I'm not listening." He stirred the fire again, sending sparks flying. "You've mentioned him before. Multiple times."

"Have I?" I tried for casual and failed.

"You talk when you're nervous. I've noticed." He leaned back slightly. "Apparently you say a great deal when you're asleep, too."

"I do not—" I paused, remembering mornings where the crew had looked at me strangely. "Oh god. Fine. What else have I said in my sleep that I should be mortified about?"

"That he thought you were too much. Too intense, too dramatic, too invested in things that didn't matter. That you needed to be controlled, shaped into something more appropriate." His voice was matter-of-fact, but I caught something underneath. "That you spent two years trying to be smaller, quieter, less."

Great. Apparently, I'd been having therapy sessions unconsciously. "Can we please forget I said anything? I'd like to retain some dignity."

"Difficult, considering how much you talk. Both conscious and unconscious commentary." He met my eyes. "Your ex sounds like he was an idiot."

That startled me enough that I laughed. "Wow. Don't hold back."

"Why would I? It's true." He said it with the same casualness as commenting on the weather. "Anyone who tried to make you smaller was working against your nature. Doomed to failure from the start."

I didn't know what to say to that, so I stood, wrapping my arms around myself. The night was cool, but the marks kept me surprisingly warm, like I carried summer underneath my skin.

"The Crown patrol," I said, needing to shift to something tactical, something less personal. "Tomorrow. What are our real chances of getting out of this intact?"

"Slim." He didn't soften it, didn't dress it up. Just truth, stark and honest.

"That's it? Just 'slim'? No percentage, no strategic assessment, no contingency planning?"

"We're outnumbered, you're still learning control, and they have resources we don't. We might get lucky. Probably won't." He stood as well, and I was suddenly very aware of how tall he was, how the firelight cast shadows across the sharp angles of his face. "But we've survived worse odds before."

"Maybe a little encouragement wouldn't kill you. Just a small amount of false hope to get through the night."

"False hope gets people killed. I'd rather you go in scared and sharp than confident and careless." His voice was harsh, but I was starting to understand that was how he showed he cared—brutal honesty instead of

comfortable lies. "Fear keeps you alive. Hope just makes the disappointment hurt more."

"You're impossible."

"So I've been told. Frequently." Almost a smile, there and gone. "Usually
right before people try to kill me."

I started back toward my tent, exhaustion finally winning over anxiety.
But at the entrance, I paused, looking back at him silhouetted against the
firelight.

"Why did you save me today? Really? Not the tactical answer about me
being the marked one and strategically important. The real reason."

He was quiet for a long moment, and I thought he wouldn't answer. Then:
"Because watching you die would have been unpleasant. I've seen enough
people die badly—didn't feel like adding you to the list."

"Right. Of course." My chest tightened in a way that had nothing to do
with the marks. "How considerate of you."

"Elle—"

"No, it's fine. I get it. Good night, Kaelren."

"Get some sleep. Tomorrow's going to be brutal regardless, but it'll be
worse if you're dead on your feet."

His tone had that familiar edge of dismissal. I went back to my tent
without another word, because what else was there to say?

The marks at my collarbones warmed, spreading with intensity through
my chest but not actually expanding their territory, and I didn't fight it.
Whatever I was becoming, at least I wasn't facing it alone.

Even if my protector would kill me without hesitation if needed.

Morning came with Nimor's quiet report during breakfast. The camp was
shrouded in Wynmire's perpetual morning mist, which clung to everything
and tasted faintly of copper. Above us, the canopy filtered the dawn light

into moss and honey tones, and somewhere in the distance, I could hear the morning chorus of bell-birds—creatures that looked like sparrows but sounded like wind chimes.

"Crown patrol changed direction," Nimor said, materializing fully for once instead of his usual half-there state. "They're sweeping wider, but they'll still find us by midday if we stay."

"Then we move," Kaelren decided. "Everyone ready to leave within the hour. We head deeper into the Wyrmwood."

"That's the opposite direction from safety," Eltrien protested.

"Better than Crown territory."

Peeble landed on my shoulder with more force than usual, antennae drooping. "I don't suppose 'deeper into the Wyrmwood' means 'toward a nice safe hollow with excellent moss beds and no one trying to kill us'?"

"Probably the opposite of that," I muttered.

"Thought so. Just checking if optimism was warranted." The beetle's wings buzzed unhappily. "It never is."

As everyone prepared to leave, the Sage approached me with a vial of liquid moonlight. Peeble's antennae perked up with interest.

"Ooh, shiny. Is that for drinking or dramatic last-resort purposes?"

"Take this," the Sage said to me, ignoring Peeble entirely. "When the time comes, you'll know."

"What time? What is it?"

But they were already walking away, leaving me with yet another cryptic gift.

"I hate when they do that," Peeble grumbled. "Cryptic gifts are only mysterious the first three times. After that, it's just annoying."

"Elle!" Kaelren barked. "Stop staring at nothing. We leave in five minutes."

"I'm staring at a mysterious vial, not nothing!" I called back, but he'd already turned away.

"He's extra grumpy this morning," Peeble observed. "More than usual, I mean. Which is impressive given his baseline grumpiness."

Five minutes to pack what little I had. Five minutes before running into unknown danger. I tucked the vial away carefully, grabbed my few belongings, and tried not to think about how every step took me further from any hope of normal.

"You know normal was boring anyway," Peeble said, apparently reading my thoughts. "You complained about it constantly."

"I complained about my ex and my job. Not about, you know, basic safety and not being hunted by magical soldiers."

"Details. You're much more interesting now. Probably going to die more interestingly, too."

"That's not comforting."

"I'm a beetle. Comfort isn't in my skill set. Brutal honesty and excellent one-liners, that's what I bring to the table."

Not that normal had ever really been an option. The marks pulsed with something like agreement, and I let them. Whatever came next, at least it would be interesting.

Probably fatal, but definitely interesting.

"That's the spirit!" Peeble said cheerfully. "Embrace the inevitable doom with style."

"Ready?" Bryx asked, Kevin buzzing anxiously around his head.

"Do I have a choice?"

"There's always—"

"A choice, I know. Everyone keeps saying that."

"Because it's true," Vashael said, passing with her portable garden. "You could choose to give up. Let the transformation take you. Become the Root completely."

"Tempting, but I'm attached to having thoughts that are my own."

"Are they?" She tilted her head. "How can you tell which thoughts are yours and which are the Root's anymore?"

"She's got a point," Peeble whispered. "You've been talking to trees. That's not normal human behavior."

"Neither is having a talking beetle as a best friend, but here we are."

"Fair."

I didn't have an answer for Vashael. The truth was, I couldn't tell anymore.

The boundaries were blurring, and maybe that was the point.

"Mount up," Kaelren commanded. "We fly low, stay under cover."

I climbed onto the bee behind him, Peeble scrambling to adjust position on my shoulder. "I hate flying on these things. Too much wind. My antennae get all tangled."

"You can walk if you prefer."

"And miss all the action? Please. I have front-row seats to your doom. I'm not giving that up for comfort."

I tried to ignore the way my body automatically adjusted to Kaelren's, finding the familiar position. Through the space where our bond would be—if either of us acknowledged it—I felt his tension. He was expecting an attack.

"He's always expecting an attack," Peeble muttered. "That man thinks breakfast is an ambush waiting to happen."

"Hold on," Kaelren said, and the bee launched into the air.

Peeble dug tiny legs into my collar. "Why do I never hold on before he says that? You'd think I'd learn."

Below us, the forest fled by in a blur of emerald and bronze. I could feel every plant we passed over, their lives brushing against my consciousness like fingers through water.

"Stop projecting," Kaelren said over his shoulder. "You're leaving a trail they can follow."

"I don't know how to stop."

"Learn quickly."

"Your motivational speeches need work," I said.

"He doesn't do motivational speeches," Peeble supplied. "He does threats and tactical observations. It's his love language."

"I don't do—" Kaelren started.

The arrow came out of nowhere, catching our bee in the thorax. We spiraled down, Kaelren trying to control our descent while I held on for dear life.

"I KNEW THIS WOULD HAPPEN!" Peeble shrieked, clinging to my collar with all six legs. "I SPECIFICALLY SAID FLYING WAS A BAD IDEA!"

We crashed through the canopy, branches tearing at us, before hitting the ground hard. I rolled, thorns instinctively extending to protect me from the worst of the impact. Peeble went flying, tumbling through the air with an indignant buzz.

"Crown!" Nimor's voice, from somewhere above. "They were waiting!"

Soldiers in white emerged from concealment, weapons glowing with enforced reality. A trap. They'd herded us right into it.

"Elle, run!" Kaelren commanded, corruption already spreading from his hands as he intercepted the nearest soldiers.

"Don't run!" Peeble called from where they'd landed on a nearby fern. "Running is how people die! Stand your ground! Be scary!"

But running seemed pointless anyway. We were surrounded, and I was tired—tired of running, tired of being hunted, tired of being afraid of my own power.

The marks on my skin flared hot, and this time I didn't fight it. A soldier lunged at me, blade humming with that weird anti-magic resonance. My thorns met his steel, but instead of just blocking, I let them grow. They wrapped around his blade, up his arm, sprouting flowers that released spores. He stumbled back, coughing, eyes watering.

"YES!" Peeble cheered. "That's what I'm talking about! Spore attacks! I love spore attacks!"

"Non-lethal," I called to Kaelren, who was leaving a trail of decay through the Crown ranks. "I'm going with non-lethal!"

"Your funeral," he shot back, but I caught something like approval in his tone.

"It's not a funeral if she wins!" Peeble yelled. "It's a party! A spore party!"

Around me, chaos erupted in the best way. Sarnyx had gone full porcupine, thorns shooting in every direction. Bryx's bees weren't just swarming— they were synchronized, moving in patterns that confused and disoriented. Vashael's plants weren't trying to slow the soldiers down; they were actively pranking them. I watched one soldier's boots suddenly sprout roots that tickled, making him dance involuntarily.

97

"This is the best fight I've ever seen!" Peeble had somehow made it back to my shoulder. "No one's dying! Everyone's just very uncomfortable! It's perfect!"

"Surrender the marked one," a Crown captain called out, trying to maintain authority while pulling a vine from his helmet. "And the rest of you can live."

"That's a terrible offer," Peeble shouted. "Counter-offer time!"

"Counter-offer," I called back, kneeling to touch the earth. The power in my marks pulsed eagerly. "You leave now, and I don't ask every tree in this forest to drop branches on your heads simultaneously."

"Ooh, good threat," Peeble whispered. "Very specific. I like it."

"You don't have that kind of range," the captain scoffed.

I closed my eyes, feeling outward. Every root, every branch, every leaf for... oh. Oh wow.

"She totally has that kind of range," Peeble said gleefully. "This is about to get interesting."

"I can feel trees miles away," I said, opening my eyes. "There's an oak about thirty feet behind you that really doesn't like your captain. Something about you pissing on its roots last night?"

"GERALD!" Peeble exclaimed. "She's talking about Gerald! I love Gerald!"

"You can hear him, too?" I whispered.

"Everyone can hear Gerald. He's very loud. Mostly complains about people with no respect for nature."

The captain went pale. Several soldiers looked up nervously.

"That's impossible," he said, but his voice wavered.

"The oak's name is Gerald," I continued, because apparently I could know that now. "He's been here for three hundred years, and he's very protective of his forest. Want to know what he's thinking about doing to you?"

A branch cracked ominously overhead. Not because I'd done anything— Gerald was just dramatic.

"SEE?" Peeble shouted at the soldiers. "GERALD DOESN'T LIKE YOU! NONE OF THE TREES LIKE YOU! YOU SHOULD LEAVE!"

"Retreat," the captain ordered suddenly. "Fall back to the secondary position."

"Sir?" one of the soldiers questioned.

"I said retreat!"

They pulled back, dragging their spore-affected and vine-tangled comrades. Within minutes, they'd vanished into the forest, leaving us standing in a clearing covered in flowers, vines, and Kaelren's decay circles.

"WE WON!" Peeble did a victory dance on my shoulder. "We actually won! No one died! Well, probably no one died. Some of them looked pretty bad. But mostly no one died!"

"Did you really talk to a tree?" Bryx asked, Kevin buzzing excitedly around his head.

"I... maybe? I definitely felt something that thought of itself as Gerald."

"You definitely talked to Gerald," Peeble confirmed. "He's been talking to you for days, you're only just now listening properly."

"Trees having names isn't the problem," Kaelren said, his voice tight with something that might have been concern. "The problem is you shouldn't be able to communicate with them this clearly yet. Most Root-touched take years to develop that level of connection."

"Well, Gerald wasn't exactly subtle about introducing himself. He also wasn't subtle about his opinions on you—something about being 'an angry little death-walker who needs more sunlight.'"

Peeble buzzed with laughter. "Gerald's not wrong! You are very angry! And very death-oriented! More sunlight would probably help!"

Sarnyx barked out a laugh. "I like this tree."

"Everyone likes Gerald," Peeble said. "Except people who piss on his roots. He has strong opinions about that."

"We need to move," Kaelren said, trying to ignore the beetle. "They'll regroup and come back with reinforcements."

"Gerald says there's a grove about two miles north where the Crown never goes. Something about the mushrooms there giving them 'uncomfortable visions of their life choices.'"

"Those mushrooms are great," Peeble added. "Very therapeutic. Made me reconsider my life choices for three days straight."

Everyone stared at me. And Peeble.

"What? I'm just repeating what the tree said. Says? Is saying? Tree communication doesn't really follow normal temporal rules."

"You're talking to trees now," Eltrien said slowly. "That's... new."

"Everything about me is new. Yesterday I made a flower sing. Today I'm having philosophical discussions with oaks. Tomorrow I'll probably photosynthesize."

"Don't joke about that," Peeble said seriously. "Photosynthesis is actually really likely at this point."

"That's not funny," Kaelren said.

"It's a little funny."

"No, really, it's not," Peeble insisted. "I've seen it happen. It's weird. You turn slightly green in direct sunlight. Very disconcerting."

"Your transformation is accelerating beyond what we anticipated," Kaelren said, voice tense.

"Again, little bit funny if you think about—"

He grabbed my arm, and I felt his corruption pulse against my marks. It should have hurt, but instead it felt like... balance. Like two halves of something wrong trying to make something right.

"Ooh, that's new," Peeble observed. "The marks are doing a thing. A balancey thing. Is that supposed to happen?"

"This isn't a joke," Kaelren said, silver eyes boring into mine. "You're losing yourself faster than we expected. Days ago you could barely control a single flower. Now you're communicating with ancient trees across miles. That's not normal progression."

"Or finding myself," I countered, pulling free. "Did you see what I just did? I ended a fight without killing anyone. Well, Gerald might have killed someone if they hadn't run, but that's on Gerald."

"Gerald would have been justified," Peeble said loyally. "They pissed on his roots."

"You're anthropomorphizing plants."

"I'm communicating with them. There's a difference."

"Not much of one at this point," Peeble muttered.

"Is there?" Kaelren challenged.

Before I could answer, Nimor materialized fully. "We have a bigger problem. The Crown patrol we just faced? They were herding us."

"Herding us where?" Vashael asked.

"Toward a larger force. There are three full patrols converging on this position."

"How many?" Kaelren demanded.

"Over a hundred. Maybe more."

Silence fell over the group.

"Well, shit," Peeble said quietly.

"Gerald says there's another option," I said quietly. "But you're not going to like it."

"If Gerald suggests it, it's probably insane," Peeble said. "Gerald has terrible judgment. Remember when he suggested you eat that glowing mushroom?"

"That wasn't Gerald, that was you."

"Was it? Memory's fuzzy. Point stands."

"The tree has military advice now?" Kaelren's voice dripped sarcasm.

"Not Gerald. The forest itself." I could feel it, vast and patient and... amused? "There's a place. Old. Protected. The Crown literally can't enter it."

"Oh no," Peeble said. "Oh no, no, no. I know what you're sensing."

"The Bloom," the Sage said, appearing because of course they did. "You're sensing the Bloom."

"I KNEW IT!" Peeble's antennae drooped. "This is a terrible idea!"

"It's forbidden," Eltrien said immediately. "No one goes there and comes back unchanged."

"Look at me," I said, gesturing to my gold-veined marks. "That ship has sailed, hit an iceberg, and sunk to the bottom of the ocean."

"The Bloom would complete your transformation instantly," the Sage warned. "You'd become fully Root-bound."

"See? SEE?" Peeble waved his antennae frantically. "The Sage agrees with me! When I agree with the Sage, you know it's bad!"

"Or," I said, feeling the forest's ancient amusement, "it might teach me how to be both. Human and Root. A bridge instead of a replacement."

"That's never been done," Kaelren said.

"Lot of that going around lately."

"Because you keep doing impossible things!" Peeble practically wailed. "Stop doing impossible things! Do possible things! Safe, boring, possible things!"

He studied me for a long moment, and I could practically see him calculating odds, risks, probabilities.

"The Bloom it is," he decided.

"WHAT?" Peeble and Eltrien said simultaneously.

"Kaelren, that's—" Eltrien started.

"Our best option. Unless you'd prefer to fight a hundred Crown soldiers?"

"I'd prefer not to watch Elle dissolve into plant matter!"

"SAME!" Peeble added. "I'm very attached to Elle! In the literal sense—I live on her shoulder! If she becomes a tree, where do I live? On her branches? That's weird!"

"Hey," I protested. "If I dissolve into anything, it'll be very aesthetically pleasing plant matter. Maybe some nice flowers. Definitely better than whatever that decay thing Kaelren does."

"This isn't funny," Eltrien insisted.

"It's a little funny," Peeble said, though his voice had lost its usual cheer. "In a cosmic horror sort of way. Which is the worst kind of funny."

"We move now," Kaelren commanded. "Before the Crown forces converge."

As we prepared to leave, I touched the nearest tree—a young birch that practically vibrated with gossip.

"Tell Gerald thank you," I said.

The birch rustled, and I got the distinct impression of an old oak somewhere grumbling about 'youngsters' and 'their drama' but also something that might have been approval.

"Gerald says you're welcome and also he still thinks Kaelren needs therapy," Peeble translated. "And possibly a nap. Gerald's very concerned about everyone's stress levels."

"You're smiling," Vashael observed.

"Trees have personalities. Who knew?"

"Everyone who's been paying attention," she replied. "You're just finally speaking their language."

"I've been saying that for weeks!" Peeble complained. "No one listens to the beetle!"

We mounted the bees and took off, flying toward whatever the Bloom would make of me. Behind us, I could feel the Crown forces discovering our empty clearing, their frustration rippling through the forest network like angry static.

Peeble settled into their usual spot on my shoulder, quieter than usual. "You know this is probably going to change you even more, right? The Bloom. It's not gentle about transformations."

"I know," I said softly.

"And you're doing it anyway?"

"We don't really have a choice."

"There's always a choice. Just sometimes all the choices are terrible." They were silent for a moment. "For what it's worth, I think you'll still be you. Maybe different, but still you. You're stubborn that way."

"Thanks, Peeble."

"Don't mention it. Someone has to be optimistic, and it's clearly not going to be Mr. Death-walker up there." He gestured at Kaelren's back with one leg.

"The trees really don't like the Crown," I told Kaelren.

"The trees don't like anyone," he replied.

"They tolerate you. Although Gerald thinks you need therapy."

"Gerald can mind his own roots."

"Gerald's roots extend for about an acre, so technically everything in that acre is his business."

"Gerald sounds nosy," Peeble added. "But in a caring way. Like a nosy grandmother who's worried about you."

"Stop talking to trees and focus on not falling off."

But I could feel something in him through the space where our bond existed—not amusement exactly, but... interest. Like my tree-talking was another piece of a puzzle he was trying to solve.

The Root pulled at me as we flew, ancient and patient and deeply, cosmically amused by everything happening.

Come, it seemed to say. Let's see what you really are.

"Probably something weird," I muttered.

"Definitely something weird," Peeble corrected. "The question is what kind of weird."

"What?" Kaelren asked.

"Nothing. Just agreeing with the potentially sentient forest about my life choices."

"And discussing the various types of weird," Peeble added helpfully.

"That's not reassuring."

"Has anything about me ever been reassuring?"

"Or me?" Peeble chimed in. "I feel like I'm consistently unreassuring."

"No," Kaelren said, and for the first time, I thought I heard something that might have been the ghost of amusement in his voice. "Neither of you have ever been reassuring."

"Progress," Peeble whispered to me. "Weird, tree-talking, about-to-transform-completely progress, but progress nonetheless."

I couldn't have said it better myself.

10

Elle

Three days of flying on giant bees had taught me several things about Wynmire.

One: The realm was vast in ways that made no geographical sense. We'd flown what should have been hundreds of miles, yet the sun never seemed to move quite right, and sometimes I'd swear we passed the same mountain twice from different angles.

Two: My ass was going to be absolutely ripped by the time this was over. Hours upon hours of clenching every muscle in my lower body just to stay balanced on a bee's fuzzy back meant I was getting the world's most terrifying workout. I'd mentioned this to Sarnyx, who'd nearly fallen off her own bee laughing.

Three: Kaelren was watching me more than he probably thought he was.

I'd catch him sometimes—around the campfire at night, or during our brief rest stops when we'd land to let the bees forage. His silver eyes would track me as I talked with Eltrien about Wynmire's history, or when Bryx showed me how to properly secure my pack so it wouldn't shift mid-flight. The moment I'd look his way, he'd turn back to whatever he was doing, but not before I saw something in his expression I couldn't quite name.

"He's definitely softening," Peeble observed one evening as we made camp in a grove of trees that hummed with blue light. "Compared to the 'you'll die here' speech on day one, this is practically warm."

"That's a low bar," I grumbled back.

"Fair. But he did show you how to feel the forest network yesterday without making it sound like a lecture on your inevitable doom."

Also fair. Kaelren had been... not exactly friendly, but less aggressively distant. He still spoke in clipped sentences and maintained his careful physical distance, but there were cracks in the armor. Small ones. Like when he'd actually explained something about Wynmire's magic without being asked, or when I'd caught what might have been the ghost of amusement in his voice.

The Crown scouts were another story entirely. We'd spotted them twice — patrols sweeping the forest in organized grids, clearly searching for us. Each time, Nimor would scout ahead, we'd land and hide, and the group would set up wards that made us effectively invisible. Vashael's illusion magic combined with Eltrien's knowledge of Crown search patterns meant we stayed consistently one step ahead.

"They're getting more desperate," Eltrien had said after our second near-miss. "Expanding the search radius. Auradelle must be pushing hard."

"Good," Sarnyx had replied, thorns bristling. "Let them waste resources chasing shadows."

But I could feel the tension growing in the group. Every day we evaded capture was another day my marks spread, another day the corruption in Kaelren's carved lines deepened, another day closer to whatever the convergence actually meant.

I'd spent the flying hours learning what I could. Bryx taught me about the different bee breeds — apparently Kevin was a Northern Humming variety, prized for endurance. Eltrien shared stories about the time before the Bloom and Root split, when Wynmire was unified. Even Vashael, usually quiet, had explained how illusion magic worked differently here than in human folklore.

And sometimes, during those long flights, I'd catch Kaelren looking back at me over his shoulder, his expression unreadable but his marks pulsing with something that looked almost like concern.

Now, on the fourth day, the landscape began to change in ways that made my breath catch..

Below us, the forest grew denser, older. The trees here were titans, their trunks so vast they had weather systems. Mist clung to the middle canopy, and through gaps in the leaves, I could see bridges—actual bridges made of living wood connecting the massive trees. Smoke rose from what might have been chimneys.

"People live up there?" I asked.

"The Canopy Folk," Kaelren said over his shoulder, his tone clipped as always. "They haven't touched the ground in generations."

Before I could ask more, Nimor materialized on his bee beside us, more solid than usual—never a good sign.

"Crown patrol ahead. They've set up a blockade at the river crossing."

"How many?" Kaelren's voice sharpened.

"Twenty, maybe more. Armed with those reality-enforced weapons."

"Can we go around?" I asked.

"Not without adding days to our journey," Kaelren replied. "And we don't have days."

We descended carefully, landing in a grove of silver-barked trees that hummed with their own quiet energy. The moment my feet touched the ground, I could feel the forest's concern through my marks—not quite words, but impressions of danger, caution, old anger.

"We could try diplomacy," Eltrien suggested, though his tone suggested he knew how unlikely that was.

"They're not here to talk," Kaelren said flatly. "They're here to capture Elle."

"Then we fight?" Sarnyx asked, thorns already extending.

"We evade," Kaelren corrected. "There's an old smuggler's path through the root caves. It comes out past the crossing."

"Root caves?" I did not like the sound of that.

"Underground passages formed by the massive root systems," Vashael explained. "Dark, cramped, and occasionally inhabited by things that prefer not to be disturbed."

"Sounds delightful."

"Better than Crown custody," Peeble pointed out from my shoulder.

We moved on foot, leaving the bees who were too large for what came next. The entrance to the root caves was hidden beneath a curtain of phosphorescent moss, barely visible even when you knew where to look. The opening was just large enough for a person to squeeze through.

"I'll go first," Nimor said, his form becoming more shadow than substance. "I can scout ahead."

One by one, we entered the caves. The moment I crossed the threshold, the world changed. It was darker than dark—not just absence of light but presence of shadow. The air was thick, humid, tasting of earth and age and growing things. My marks provided a faint golden glow, just enough to see the person ahead of me.

The passages were formed by roots thicker than tree trunks, twisting and weaving through the earth. Some sections we could walk upright; others required crawling. The roots were warm to the touch, pulsing faintly with life.

"This is actually kind of amazing," I whispered, running my hand along a root that was probably older than human civilization.

"Quiet," Kaelren warned from behind me. "Sound carries strangely here."

As if to prove his point, I heard something in the distance—a sound like breathing, but too big to be human. We all froze.

"Keep moving," Nimor's voice drifted back, barely audible. "Slowly. It's sleeping."

We crept past whatever it was, and I tried very hard not to imagine what could make breathing sounds that deep. The passage opened into a small chamber where bioluminescent fungi provided dim blue light. We paused to rest, everyone checking equipment and catching breath.

"How did you know about this place?" I asked Kaelren quietly.

"I've had to evade Crown patrols before," he said, not meeting my eyes. "When you're labeled a failed prince, you learn the hidden paths quickly."

There was more to that story, but now wasn't the time to push.

We continued through the caves for what felt like hours but was probably less. Time moved strangely underground, each moment stretching like taffy. Finally, I saw light ahead—real sunlight, not fungal glow.

We emerged on the far side of the river, the Crown blockade visible in the distance but facing the wrong direction. We'd bypassed them completely.

"That was too easy," Sarnyx said what we were all thinking.

"They wanted us to go this way," Kaelren agreed, studying the forest ahead. "The question is why."

Before anyone could speculate, a figure stepped out from behind a massive tree. Not Crown, but not exactly friendly either. She was tall, willowy in that fae way, with bark-textured skin and eyes like amber. Her clothes seemed to be made of autumn leaves, constantly shifting between gold and brown. She was beautiful, even ethereal.

"Kaelren," she said, and there was history in that single word. "It's been a long time."

"Thessaly." His voice was carefully neutral. "I thought you were dead."

"The Crown thought so too. It was convenient to let them." Her eyes found me. "So this is the human causing all the fuss. She's smaller than expected."

"I'm getting really tired of people commenting on my size," I muttered.

Thessaly laughed, a sound like wind through leaves. "Fair enough. I'm here with an offer."

"We're not interested," Kaelren said immediately.

"You haven't heard it yet." She pulled out a scroll sealed with wax that seemed to move. "Safe passage through the Autumn Court's territory. Protection from Crown patrols. All we ask in return is one night's hospitality."

"The Autumn Court doesn't offer hospitality without price," Vashael said suspiciously.

"True. But the price isn't yours to pay." Thessaly looked directly at me. "The Court wants to meet the human who talks to trees. My mother is particularly interested."

"Your mother?" I asked.

"The Autumn Duchess. She governs this region of Wynmire." Thessaly's expression softened slightly. "She has... questions. About your marks. About what you're becoming." "She also has answers. About the convergence. About what's really coming."

I felt Kaelren tense beside me. "Absolutely not."

"Shouldn't that be Elle's choice?" Thessaly asked mildly.

Everyone looked at me. The marks at my collarbones pulsed with warmth, and through them, I could feel the forest's curiosity. The trees knew Thessaly, trusted her in their slow, ancient way.

"One night?" I asked.

"Sunset to sunrise. You'll be fed, rested, and protected. And my mother will tell you things the Crown doesn't want you to know."

"Elle," Kaelren warned.

But I was tired of running, tired of not understanding what was happening to me. "We accept."

Thessaly smiled, and autumn leaves swirled around us. "Then follow me. The Autumn Court awaits."

As we walked deeper into the forest, following paths that seemed to appear just for Thessaly, I noticed Kaelren's carved marks pulsing with agitation.

"You know her," I said quietly.

"I knew her. Before."

"Before what?"

"Before I became what I am. Before the Bloom rejected me. Before everything went wrong."

There was pain in his voice I hadn't heard before. Real, raw pain that his usual cold control couldn't quite hide.

"Was she...?"

"She was many things. None of them matter now."

But the way he watched Thessaly move through the forest, the way his marks flared when she looked back at us, suggested otherwise.

Great, I thought. *Magical ex-girlfriend drama. Because this situation wasn't complicated enough.*

"Jealous?" Peeble whispered near my ear.

"Shut up," I hissed back, but couldn't quite deny the twist in my stomach when Thessaly smiled at Kaelren with obvious familiarity.

The Autumn Court's entrance was marked by trees whose leaves were permanently caught in fall colors despite the season. The air was crisp here, smelling of apples and wood smoke and that particular scent of leaves turning.

"Welcome," Thessaly said, gesturing to an arched doorway that seemed to be carved from a single enormous tree, "to the Court of Eternal Autumn."

11

Kaelren

The Autumn Court hadn't changed.

It still existed in that space between waking and dream, where reality wore thin and seasons bled together. The great hall was carved from the heart of an ancient oak, its walls breathing with slow life. Fairy lights—actual fairies trapped in gleaming bubbles—provided illumination that shifted between honey and amber. The air tasted of harvest and endings.

And at its center, on a throne of woven branches and dying leaves, sat the Autumn Duchess.

Merithra looked exactly as she had 30 years ago, which meant she looked exactly as she had five hundred years ago. Ageless in that way of old fae, beautiful in that terrible way of predators. Her hair was every shade of autumn—gold, red, brown, burgundy—and her eyes held the patience of trees and the cruelty of winter's first frost.

"Kaelren," she said, and my name in her mouth was a weapon. "The failed prince graces our court again."

I didn't bow. I'd learned that lesson already. "Merithra."

"Your Grace," Thessaly corrected softly, but her mother waved dismissal. "He's earned the right to rudeness. Haven't you, carved one?"

Elle stepped forward before I could respond, and the entire court went still. The Duchess's attention fixed on her like a hawk spotting movement.

"You're the human," Merithra said. Not a question.

"I'm Elle," she corrected, chin raised in that defiance that was going to get her killed one day. "I have a name."

"Names have power here, child. Careful how freely you give yours."

"I'll keep that in mind, Your Grace." The title dripped sarcasm, but somehow Elle made it sound respectful enough to avoid offense.

Merithra laughed, delighted. "Oh, I like her. She has teeth." Her gaze shifted to me. "Different from your usual type."

"We're not—" I started.

"Together? No, of course not. The corruption in your marks would kill her if you tried. But you want to be." She stood, descending from her throne with predatory grace. "I can smell it on both of you. That desperate want that can never be satisfied."

Elle's marks flared at her collarbones, light pulsing. "You said you had information. Something about a convergence."

"Straight to business. How refreshingly human." Merithra circled Elle slowly, studying her like a specimen. "Your marks are Root-born but not Root-bound. Fascinating. You're becoming something unprecedented."

"Everyone keeps saying that. No one explains what it means."

"Because no one knows. You're writing new rules as you transform." The Duchess stopped in front of Elle. "But I know what's hunting you. And it's not just the Crown."

"What else?" I demanded.

Merithra's smile was sharp. "The Wild Hunt has been called."

The great hall erupted in whispers. Even Thessaly looked shocked.

"That's not possible," I said. "The Hunt only rides for—"

"For those who threaten the realm's fundamental nature. Yes." Merithra returned to her throne. "Someone has convinced the Hunters that your little human will destroy everything if she completes her transformation."

"Who?" Elle asked.

"Now that's the interesting question. The Crown wants to control you, not destroy you. So who benefits from your death?"

I thought of Eltrien's knowing looks, his careful words about patterns. But no—he'd helped us. Hadn't he?

"Tonight, you're under my protection," Merithra continued. "The Hunt cannot enter the Autumn Court without invitation. But tomorrow, when you leave..." She shrugged elegantly. "Well. The Hunt never fails."

"There must be a way to call them off," Vashael said from where she stood with the rest of our crew.

"Only one. Prove the threat has passed. Which means either the human dies, or she completes her transformation in a way that doesn't threaten the realm."

"How?" Elle's voice was steady, but I could see her hands trembling slightly. Peeble had gone very still on her shoulder—never a good sign.

"That, my dear, is what we're going to discuss over dinner."

"First, let me show you to your quarters," Thessaly said, gesturing for us to follow. "You'll want to... prepare."

The crew exchanged uneasy glances as we followed Thessaly through corridors that shouldn't connect. The Wild Hunt. Even Sarnyx looked shaken, her usual bravado dimmed. Vashael walked close to Elle, protective. Eltrien had gone very quiet—more quiet than usual—his expression unreadable.

"Try to rest," I told them as Thessaly began assigning rooms. "We'll strategize after dinner."

Elle caught my eye as she was shown to her door. The uncertainty there made something in my chest tighten painfully.

The rooms were each impossible in their own way. Mine had walls that aged and renewed in constant cycles, furniture that existed in multiple time periods simultaneously. I changed into the formal attire that had appeared—dark leather and silver thread that made my carved marks look intentional rather than the slow death they were.

I was adjusting the damned collar when there was a knock. I expected Nimor with some security concern.

I got Thessaly, wearing something that left very little to imagination and nothing to propriety.

"Hello, Kaelren," she purred, not waiting for invitation to enter. "I thought you might want... company before dinner."

"No."

She blinked, clearly not expecting the flat rejection. "No? You never said no before."

"Things change."

"Do they?" She moved closer, trailing a finger along my arm. "Or is it that someone else has caught your attention? The little redheaded human with her impossible marks?"

"Leave, Thessaly."

"She can't give you what I can. Her marks would kill you if you even kissed her properly."

"I said leave."

Something in my tone finally got through. She stepped back, studying me with those amber eyes. "You're different. Harder. Colder. She's done something to you."

"No," I corrected. "I did this to myself."

She left without another word, and I tried not to think about why rejecting her had been so easy. Tried not to think about green eyes and red hair and defiance that made me want impossible things.

I adjusted my collar again. Checked my marks in the shifting mirror— silver-black lines spreading like frost across my skin. Dying slowly, as always. The formal attire made them look intentional, decorative even. A lie wrapped in leather and silver thread.

The walk to Elle's quarters gave me time to rebuild my usual control. By the time I reached her door, I'd almost managed it.

Then she opened her door, and every carefully constructed wall shattered.

She was wearing starlight. Or spider silk. Or condensed moonbeams. The dress moved like water and light, revealing nothing and suggesting everything. Her marks looked like sunlight on her collarbones, seeming to pulse in rhythm with the fabric. Her red hair was pinned up, exposing the elegant line of her neck.

Peeble sat on her shoulder, looking remarkably dignified despite being a beetle. They'd somehow acquired a tiny bow tie that matched Elle's dress.

My body's reaction was immediate and mortifying. Heat flooded through me, my cock hardening so fast it was almost painful. I literally stopped breathing, frozen in her doorway like an idiot while every drop of blood in my body headed south.

"Well?" she asked, and there was uncertainty in her voice. "Is it too much? Thessaly said—"

"You look adequate," I managed, the words coming out strangled. I shifted my weight, trying to adjust without being obvious about it.

"Adequate?" Her eyebrow raised in that way that meant she was about to eviscerate me with sarcasm.

But then something shifted in her expression—recognition, maybe, or understanding. Her eyes flicked down briefly, then back up, and a faint flush colored her cheeks. She'd noticed. Of course she had.

Instead of the verbal destruction I'd been bracing for, she just pressed her lips together, fighting what looked suspiciously like a smile. "Court standards. Right."

"For court standards." I turned abruptly, offering my arm with stiff formality before she could say anything else. Before she could acknowledge what we both knew she'd seen. "We should go. The Duchess doesn't like to be kept waiting."

She took my arm, and the contact sent electricity through every carved line in my skin. I tensed, controlling the reaction ruthlessly—both the marks' flaring and the persistent evidence of my arousal that walking through the Court's corridors did absolutely nothing to diminish.

The feast was everything fae hospitality threatened to be—beautiful, dangerous, and laden with meaning. Food appeared that shouldn't exist: fruits that tasted of memories, wine that sparkled with actual starlight, meat from animals that might have been mythical.

Elle sat beside me, careful not to eat anything without checking with Peeble first. Smart. The Autumn Court's food could trap you in ways that had nothing to do with poison.

"This is weird," she muttered, poking at something that might have been bread if bread could be transparent.

"Don't eat that," I warned. "It shows your deepest desires to everyone present."

"Absolutely not," Peeble added from her shoulder. "Though I'm morbidly curious what the Court would make of your current desires."

Elle's face flushed. "Peeble."

"Just saying. The tension is very thick at this end of the table."

"Hard pass." She set it aside quickly. "So, you and Thessaly..."

"Were nothing."

"She seemed to think otherwise when she greeted you."

"Thessaly thinks many things. Most are wishful thinking."

Elle glanced across the table where Thessaly sat, beautiful in the candle-light. "She's very pretty."

"She's very dangerous."

"The two aren't mutually exclusive."

"In my experience, they're usually synonymous."

"Am I dangerous?" Elle asked, and there was something in her voice I couldn't identify.

"Increasingly so."

"Is that why you stay? Because I'm dangerous?"

Before I could answer—before I could figure out what I would answer—Merithra stood, commanding attention.

The great hall had filled while we'd been talking. Court members lined the long tables—fae in varying states of autumn, some with bark-textured skin, others with leaves for hair, all beautiful and dangerous in that way unique to the old courts. They'd been watching us, I realized. Watching Elle

117

specifically, with the kind of hunger that came from witnessing something unprecedented.

Our crew sat scattered along the table—Vashael to Elle's right, Eltrien further down looking increasingly uncomfortable, Sarnyx and Bryx together across from us. Nimor had taken a position near the shadows, as was his nature. Thessaly sat at her mother's right hand, amber eyes fixed on me with an expression I couldn't read.

The table itself was a work of impossible craft—living wood that grew and shifted, plates that seemed carved from solidified moonlight, goblets that held liquid starlight. Elle's dress caught the fairy-light, making her look like she belonged here, like she was part of the Court's impossible beauty rather than a human who'd stumbled through a portal.

"We have a tradition in the Autumn Court," Merithra announced, her voice carrying through the hall with effortless authority. The low conversations died instantly. "Stories for secrets. Entertainment for information." Her gaze found Elle, sharp and assessing. "Tell us a tale from your world, human, and I'll tell you what you need to know about the convergence."

Every eye turned to Elle—and to the beetle on her shoulder, who was regarded with the kind of wary respect usually reserved for unpredictable explosives.

She stood slowly, and I saw her hands tremble slightly before she clasped them together. The dress moved like water as she rose, her marks pulsing gently at her collarbones—the only sign of her nervousness beyond that brief tremor.

"What kind of story?" she asked, and her voice was steady despite the roomful of predators watching her.

"Something true. Something that matters. Something that explains who you are."

Elle was quiet for a moment, and I could feel the weight of the Court's attention pressing down on her. Could sense the danger in it—one wrong word, one perceived insult, and Merithra's protection might evaporate like morning frost.

Then Elle began, and something in her voice made even the ancient fae lean forward to listen.

"My grandmother had a garden. Not a magical one—just vegetables and flowers in Arkansas dirt. But she used to tell me that gardens were honest. They showed you exactly what you put into them. No lies, no pretense, just cause and effect."

The court had gone silent, listening.

"She died last year. Left me the house, the garden, everything. I went to settle the estate, to sell it all and move on with my neat, controlled life. But the garden was dead. Everything withered and brown." Elle's marks pulsed gently. "I sat in that dead garden and cried for the first time since finding my fiancé in bed with my best friend. Cried because the garden was honest—it showed exactly what happened when no one cared for something. When you assumed it would just keep growing without attention or love."

She looked directly at Merithra. "That's when the storm came. When the lightning struck. When I fell through to Wynmire. I think... I think maybe I was meant to. Because I finally understood that nothing grows without being tended. Not plants. Not love. Not even yourself."

The silence that followed was complete.

My entire body went rigid. My carved marks flared with sudden violence, corruption spreading across the table before I caught it.

I'd known about the ex-fiancé. She'd mentioned him in passing—an explanation for why she'd been at her grandmother's house, why she'd been vulnerable enough for the portal to take her. But she'd never told me this. Never said he'd been in bed with her best friend. Never explained the full scope of the betrayal that had broken her.

The rage that filled me was absolute and consuming. This wasn't just an ended relationship—it was a double betrayal. Two people she'd trusted most, destroying her in the same moment. Making her feel like she wasn't enough when the truth was they hadn't deserved her at all.

I wanted to find this man, this pathetic excuse for a partner. Wanted to show him what real betrayal felt like. What real pain could be. The corruption in my marks responded to the violence of my thoughts, spreading further before I caught it and forced it back.

My hand clenched on the table, wood beginning to transform under my touch.

Then Merithra began to clap, slow and deliberate. "A perfect story. Honest and raw and human." She smiled, and for once it seemed genuine. "So let me tell you about the convergence. What it really is, not the sanitized version the Crown would have you believe."

Elle sat back down slowly, still catching her breath from the vulnerability of her story.

"The convergence isn't Root and Bloom reuniting," Merithra continued. "It's the realm trying to reset itself. To return to a state before the split."

"What split?" Elle asked.

"Root and Bloom were one once. A single force of growth and preservation in perfect balance. But something broke them apart. Something that required them to become opposites instead of complements."

"What?" I demanded, still fighting the urge to destroy something in honor of Elle's piece of shit ex.

Merithra's eyes found mine. "You really don't know the full story? Or have you just accepted the sanitized version they teach in the Crown's histories?" She laughed, bitter and ancient. "Humans. Humans broke them apart. The first one to fall through, specifically. They made a choice that forced the split, and the realm has been trying to heal itself ever since."

I went still. I'd heard whispers, fragments of old stories that suggested humans were involved in the original schism. But the Crown had always dismissed them as myth, propaganda from the early wars. "That's not possible. The split happened before recorded history."

"Before official history," Merithra corrected. "The Crown has spent millennia burying the truth. Easier to blame natural forces than admit a human unmade the realm's fundamental nature."

Elle went very still. "Are you saying...?"

"I'm saying every human who falls through is an echo of that first breaking. And you, my dear, with your unprecedented marks and your impossible transformation—you might be the echo that finally shatters everything completely." Merithra leaned forward. "Or the one that finally heals it. The convergence will force you to choose."

"Choose what?"

"Whether to maintain the split or merge the forces back together. But here's what the Crown doesn't want you to know—both choices have been made before. Multiple times. And both have failed."

"That's impossible," I said. "The convergence is supposed to be a singular event."

"Is it?" Merithra's smile was sharp. "Or is that just what you've been told?"

The great hall went very still.

"How many times?" Elle's voice was barely a whisper.

I noticed Eltrien tense across the table, his hands stilling on his wine glass. He knew something—had known something all along. His eyes met mine briefly, a warning there I couldn't interpret.

"Who can say? The memories blur, fade, get overwritten. But sometimes they bleed through. In dreams. In moments of déjà vu. In the sense that you've done this before."

Elle's marks were glowing brighter now, pulsing with distress. I wanted to reach for her, to offer comfort, but my corruption would only hurt her.

"So I'm trapped?" she asked. "Doomed to make the same choice over and over?"

"Unless you make a different choice. One that's never been made before." Merithra stood. "But to do that, you'd have to become something that's never existed before. Something neither Root nor Bloom nor human."

"Something like what?"

"That, my dear, is what you'll have to discover for yourself."

I wanted to demand more answers. Wanted to force Merithra to explain exactly what Elle was supposed to become, how to stop the Wild Hunt, how to break a cycle that had apparently been repeating for who knew how long. But the Duchess had already turned away, the conversation clearly over by her decree.

The feast continued in form but not substance—people went through the motions of eating, drinking, conversing, but the earlier ease had evaporated.

Within the hour, court members began making excuses and departing. I watched Elle leave with Vashael and the others, the starlight dress making her look like she belonged to this impossible place even as I knew she must be drowning in revelations.

I retreated to my quarters, needing space to think. The room's constantly shifting timeline was actually soothing—it matched the chaos in my mind.

I was standing at my window, watching three seasons turn simultaneously, when Nimor materialized from the shadows.

"We have a problem," he said without preamble.

"Beyond the Wild Hunt coming to kill Elle at sunrise?"

"The Duchess's protection ends at her borders. The moment we step outside the Autumn Court, we're vulnerable. And the paths out are limited."

I turned to face him. "You've been scouting."

"Old habits." He solidified more fully, which meant he was genuinely concerned. "There's something else. Eltrien has been... strange. More than usual."

"Define strange."

"He keeps muttering about patterns and iterations. Drawing symbols I don't recognize. And tonight, when the Duchess mentioned deja vu and repetition, he looked terrified."

I thought of how Eltrien had tensed at dinner, that warning look he'd given me. "You think he knows something."

"I think he knows everything. The question is why he hasn't told us." As concerning as this was, we had more immediate issues to discuss.

"The Wild Hunt," I said, changing the subject. "What do we know about their weaknesses?"

"They don't have any. That's rather the point."

"Everything has weaknesses."

"Not things that exist outside normal reality." Nimor began to fade again. "But I'll keep scouting. Maybe there's something in the old stories."

He disappeared completely, leaving me alone with my thoughts and the turning seasons outside my window.

Tomorrow, we'd face something that had never been defeated.

Tomorrow, Elle would need me to be the strategist, the protector, the cold and calculating leader who could find victory in impossible odds.

But tonight, I stood in my impossible room and admitted a different truth: my carved marks were spreading faster since we'd arrived here. The corruption responded to emotion, and being near Elle—watching her in that dress, hearing her story, feeling her presence through the space where our bond existed—was accelerating my decline.

I was dying faster because of her.

And I didn't care.

The Wild Hunt could come. The convergence could demand its impossible choice. The realm could tear itself apart.

As long as Elle survived it, nothing else mattered.

That probably should have terrified me.

Instead, it felt like clarity.

12

Elle

The room they gave me in the Autumn Court was impossible.

Not impossible like "hard to believe," but literally impossible. The walls were made of falling leaves that never landed. The bed was carved from platinum driftwood. Outside my window, autumn held its eternal moment—leaves frozen mid-fall, suspended in time.

"This is giving me a headache," I told Peeble, who was investigating a vase that kept flickering in and out of focus.

"The Autumn Court likes its paradoxes," they replied. "Makes them feel sophisticated."

A knock at the door interrupted my attempt to figure out if the bathroom was physically accessible or just a very convincing illusion. Thessaly entered without waiting for permission, carrying a tray of something that smelled amazing and probably shouldn't be trusted.

"Thought you might want something to help you sleep," she said, setting a crystal decanter on the table that materialized just for that purpose. "Dream wine. It's safe—guest-right protected."

"Thanks." I eyed the wine suspiciously. It seemed to contain actual dreams, swirling like smoke in liquid. "I'm not really in a drinking mood."

Thessaly sat uninvited on the edge of the impossible bed. "Kaelren seems very protective of you."

There it was. The real reason for the visit.

"He's protective of the mission," I corrected.

"Is that what you think?" She laughed, musical and somehow sad. "Oh, you really don't know him at all."

"And you do?"

"I knew him before. When he was still trying to be what everyone expected. Still believing he could earn the Bloom's acceptance through sheer will." She picked at the moonlit bedding. "Did he tell you why it rejected him?"

"No."

"He fell in love."

I tried to hide my reaction, but she saw it anyway.

"Not with me," she clarified quickly. "With the idea of power. Of being more than what he was born to be. The Bloom saw that hunger and recognized it as corruption. Root-touched, they called it. Too much destruction in his heart."

"But his marks are carved, not natural."

"Yes. He tried to force what wouldn't come naturally. And now they're killing him slowly." She looked at me directly. "Your marks, though— they're nothing like I've ever seen. Natural but not. Root but not. You're rewriting the rules."

"So everyone keeps telling me."

"It frightens them. Kaelren especially."

"Why?"

"Because he can't protect you from yourself. And that's all he knows how to do—protect things. Even when they don't want protection."

Before I could respond, another knock interrupted. This time it was Vashael.

"The Duchess requests your presence," she said to me, then noticed Thessaly. "Both of you."

I exchanged a glance with Thessaly. A summons this late couldn't be good news.

We followed Vashael through corridors that seemed to breathe, the walls contracting and expanding with the Court's slow pulse. Peeble had gone very still on my shoulder—their version of high alert. The air grew colder as we descended, tasting of frost and copper.

"Where are we going?" I asked.

"The memory garden," Thessaly answered. "My mother does her best thinking there."

We emerged into a courtyard that made my impossible bedroom look normal by comparison. Plants grew here, but not from soil—they grew from moments, from emotions given physical form.

"This is deeply unsettling," Peeble observed in my mind. "I don't like gardens that remember things."

A rose bloomed from what felt like first love, its petals the exact color of longing. A gnarled tree twisted upward from what could only be last words, its bark carved with names. Vines climbed the walls from broken promises, thorned and reaching.

"Tell me," the Duchess said without preamble, "what do you know about the nature of time?"

"Um. It's linear? Usually?"

"Usually. But not always. Not here." She gestured to the garden. "The convergence bends time. Makes it flexible. Past, present, future—they bleed together at the edges. You will start feeling like you've done things before. Moments will feel familiar even when they shouldn't."

"That makes my head hurt."

"It should. Mortal minds aren't meant to perceive time as it truly is—a garden where everything grows simultaneously." She plucked a flower whose petals were translucent as morning frost. "But you're becoming less mortal with each passing day."

"What does this have to do with the convergence?"

"Everything. The convergence isn't just a meeting of Root and Bloom. It's a temporal nexus. A point where all possibilities exist at once. Where you could make any choice, including ones that haven't been thought of yet."

"But you said the choices have all been made before."

"The obvious ones, yes. Root or Bloom. Both or neither. But what if there's a fifth option? A sixth? What if the choice itself is the wrong question?"

My marks pulsed with warmth, responding to something in her words.

"You know something," I said. "Something specific."

"I know that when the convergence comes—still weeks away, if the signs are right—you'll stand before the Bloom in the Heartspire. I know you'll be asked to choose. And I know that everyone who matters to you will suffer the consequences of that choice."

"But why now?" I asked. "Why is the convergence happening at all?"

Merithra's expression grew grave. "The realm has been tilting toward imbalance for decades. Root growing stronger while Bloom weakens— or perhaps the reverse, depending on who you ask. The scholars have been tracking it, sensing the convergence approach like a storm on the horizon." Her eyes found mine. "But your arrival accelerated it. You're not just a symptom of the imbalance—you're a catalyst. Your transformation is forcing the realm toward a reckoning it might have avoided for another century."

"So it's my fault?"

"Fault implies choice. You didn't choose to fall through. You didn't choose these marks." She gestured at my collarbones where the gold light pulsed. "But your presence here, your impossible nature—it's like dropping a stone into already turbulent water. The ripples become waves."

"So when the convergence happens, I have to choose something. And that choice affects...?"

"Everyone who matters to you," Merithra finished. Her eyes held ancient knowledge and something that might have been pity. "Especially him. The failed prince who carved his own destruction into his skin for power. Your choice will either save him or damn him completely."

"Everyone?" I whispered.

Her eyes found mine, ancient and knowing. "Especially him. The failed prince who carved his own destruction into his skin for power. Your choice will either save him or damn him completely."

"No pressure then."

"Pressure is what creates diamonds. Or crushes coal to dust." She handed me the flower. "Keep this. When the moment comes—and you'll know the moment—crush it. It might give you just enough time to think of something impossible."

"Why are you helping me?"

"Because I'm curious. In all the iterations I half-remember, no one has ever been quite like you. Marked but not chosen. Human but transforming. Connected to the failed prince by a bond that shouldn't exist." She smiled. "You're an anomaly. And anomalies are the only things that can break patterns."

We were interrupted by commotion from inside—shouting, running feet, the sound of weapons being drawn.

"What—" I started.

"The Wild Hunt," Merithra said calmly. "They're testing my boundaries. They can't enter, but they can make their presence known."

My blood went cold. The flower in my hand suddenly felt very fragile.

"We should get inside," Thessaly said, her usual composure cracking. "Now."

We didn't run—running would show fear—but we moved quickly through the memory garden, past the emotional plants that seemed to shrink away from whatever was coming. Peeble pressed tight against my neck, their small body trembling.

"This is bad," they whispered. "This is very, very bad."

Inside the great hall was in controlled chaos. Through the massive windows, we could see them—riders on horses made of shadow and pale light, circling the Court's borders. Their hounds were worse—massive things with too many teeth and eyes that glowed like dying stars, bodies that seemed to phase in and out of existence with each stride.

"Well, this is going great," Peeble muttered from my shoulder. "Really stellar evening. Five stars, would not recommend."

And at their head, the Hunter himself. I couldn't look at him directly—my eyes kept sliding off like he existed in a dimension slightly to the left of reality. But I got impressions: antlers that were also crown that were also thorns, a face that was beautiful and terrible and ancient beyond measure.

"Elle Hawthorne of Earth," his voice echoed through the hall without him speaking. "You are called to answer for crimes against the realm's nature."

"Oh good, a formal accusation," Peeble whispered. "That's always a positive sign."

"She's under my protection," Merithra called back, authority ringing in every word.

"Until sunrise. Then the Hunt claims its right."

"What crimes?" I shouted, surprising everyone including myself. "What am I supposed to have done?"

The Hunter turned toward me, and looking at him felt like falling into the space between stars. "You exist outside the pattern. You break what should be whole. You are becoming something that should not be."

"According to who?"

"According to the laws written before the first seed was planted."

"Well, maybe those laws need updating!"

"Oh brilliant," Peeble hissed. "Yes, definitely sass the ancient death god. What could possibly go wrong?"

Silence. Complete, total silence.

Then the Hunter laughed, a sound like wind through graveyards. "Perhaps they do. We shall see at sunrise."

They vanished—not gradually but all at once, leaving only the echo of howling and the scent of endings.

"That was either very brave or very stupid," Thessaly said.

"I'm going with stupid," Peeble added. "Definitely stupid."

"Both," Kaelren said, appearing at my side. His marks were glowing with agitation. "It was both."

"The Hunt hasn't been challenged in a thousand years," Merithra said thoughtfully. "This should be interesting."

"Interesting?" I spun to face her. "They want to kill me at sunrise and you find it interesting?"

"Everything about you is interesting, dear. Including whether you'll survive to see another sunset." She studied me with those ancient eyes. "But sunrise is hours away. Tonight, rest. Tomorrow, we'll face what comes."

As the court dispersed, servants—or what passed for servants in a place where reality was negotiable—showed us back to our quarters. I found myself walking beside Kaelren through corridors that shifted with each step.

"You were quiet during dinner," I said.

"I was listening."

"To what?"

"Everything. The way Merithra's words had multiple meanings. The way Eltrien kept trying not to react. The way you..." He paused. "The way you talked about your past."

"Oh." I hadn't realized he'd been paying such close attention to my grandmother story. "It wasn't that interesting."

"Your fiancé." The words came out sharp, edged with something dark. "He hurt you."

It wasn't a question.

"It's in the past."

"Is it?" He stopped walking, turned to face me. His carved marks were pulsing with barely controlled violence. "Because you still flinch when someone mentions betrayal. You still expect people to find you 'too much.' You still—"

"Stop." I held up a hand. "Just stop. You don't get to psychoanalyze me. Not when you won't even admit you have feelings beyond 'mission parameters.'"

We stared at each other in the shifting corridor, tension crackling between us like lightning about to strike. His silver eyes were dark, his jaw tight, and those carved marks were pulsing with barely restrained emotion.

"You think I don't have feelings?" His voice was low, dangerous. He took a step closer. "That's the problem, Elle. I have too many of them."

My breath caught.

He took another step, close enough now that I could feel the heat radiating from his marks, could see the corruption spreading through them in real-time like silver-black lightning. Close enough that if I reached out—

"You should go inside," he said, his voice strained. "Get some rest before tomorrow."

"Kaelren—"

His hand lifted, trembling slightly, and for a heartbeat I thought he'd touch my face, tuck the loose strand of hair behind my ear. His fingers hovered near my cheek, so close I could feel the warmth of his skin.

Then he pulled back, jaw clenching. "If things were different—" He stopped himself, shaking his head. "Go, Elle. Before I do something we'll both regret."

"Like what?"

His eyes met mine, and the heat in them made my stomach flip. "Like finding out if wanting something impossible makes it any less dangerous."

The words hung between us, heavy with implication.

"I should check on the others," he said finally, already backing away. "Make sure everyone's quarters are secure."

"Right. Of course. Security." The words came out more bitter than I intended.

He hesitated for just a moment, his eyes finding mine one last time. "Tomorrow, when the Hunt comes—stay close. Whatever happens, stay close."

Then he was gone, and I was left standing in the shifting corridor alone, my cheek still tingling from the almost-touch, from the heat of his hand that had gotten so close.

I shook my head and walked back into my room, and changed out of the starlight dress and into something more comfortable—soft pants and a tunic that the Autumn Court had provided, made from fabric that felt like clouds. I was just settling into the impossible bed when there was another knock at my door.

"Seriously?" I muttered. "What now?"

"Maybe it's Kaelren coming back to brood attractively in your doorway," Peeble suggested from the nightstand where they'd been investigating a candle that burned with frozen fire.

I opened the door.

Thessaly stood there, wearing something that could generously be called a nightgown if nightgowns were made of shadow and suggestion.

"Oh, for fuck's sake," I said before I could stop myself.

"Can't sleep either?" she asked, not waiting for an invitation to enter.

"I could be sleeping if people would stop knocking on my door." I closed it harder than necessary. "This is your second visit tonight. What could you possibly want now?"

"Charming as ever," Peeble observed. "This is definitely going to end well."

Thessaly moved around my room with casual familiarity, settling on the window seat. "He turned me away, you know."

"What?"

"Kaelren. I went to his room. Offered to help him... relax before tomorrow." She smiled ruefully. "He literally closed the door in my face."

"Oh." I didn't know what to say to that. Part of me wanted to feel victorious, but mostly I just felt exhausted.

"Awkward," Peeble whispered.

"He's never turned me away before," she continued. "Even after the Bloom rejected him. Even when he was at his lowest. But now..." She looked at me directly. "Now there's you."

"There's nothing between us." The words felt like a lie even as I said them.

"Really getting a workout tonight, that particular denial," Peeble muttered.

"No? Then why did his marks nearly destroy the dining table when you mentioned your ex-fiancé? Why does he watch you like you might disappear if he blinks? Why did he just reject the comfort of someone familiar for the possibility of someone impossible?"

"Because he's focused on the mission."

Thessaly laughed, soft and knowing. "If that's what you need to tell yourself. But tomorrow, when the Hunt comes, when everything goes to hell—and it will—remember that he chose you. That means something, even if neither of you is ready to admit what."

She stood to leave, pausing at the door. "For what it's worth, I hope you both survive long enough to figure it out."

Then she was gone, taking her shadows and suggestions with her.

"Well," Peeble said into the silence. "That was almost sincere at the end there. Character growth."

"Shut up, Peeble."

"You know I'm right though. About all of it."

I climbed into the impossible bed, pulling the covers up. Tomorrow the Wild Hunt would come. Tomorrow everything would change. But tonight, I could still feel the ghost of Kaelren's hand hovering near my cheek, close enough to feel the heat but not close enough to touch.

"He almost did it," I whispered into the darkness.

"I know," Peeble replied, gentler now. "That's what makes it worse."

Outside, autumn held its eternal moment, and somewhere in this impossible Court, Kaelren was probably standing guard, probably overthinking, probably hating himself for pulling away when all he wanted was to reach out.

At least some things stayed consistent.

13

Elle

Dawn came like a blade through silk—sudden, sharp, and irreversible.

I'd barely slept. Every time I closed my eyes, I felt the ghost of Kaelren's hand hovering near my face, heard his voice saying *before I do something we'll both regret.* What did that mean? What would he regret?

"Stop overthinking," Peeble muttered from my shoulder. "You'll give yourself a headache."

Too late for that.

The Autumn Court saw us off with all the ceremony of escorting condemned prisoners to execution. Merithra stood at the border, looking almost sorry—which, coming from her, was unsettling.

"Try not to die immediately," she said. "It would be anticlimactic."

"I'll do my best."

"The plan hasn't changed," Kaelren said as we gathered at the border, his voice all business, his back rigid, deliberately not looking at me. "We continue to the Heartspire to see the Bloom. It's our best option for—"

"For completing my transformation in a controlled way," I finished. "I remember the plan."

He'd been like that since we'd gathered at dawn—all clipped orders and cold efficiency, the man from last night completely buried under layers of control.

Fine. If he wanted to pretend nothing happened, I could pretend too.

Except I couldn't stop noticing the way dawn light caught in his silver eyes, or how his marks seemed to pulse in sync with mine when we got too close, or how his jaw clenched every time someone said my name.

"The Heartspire is still several days' travel," Vashael added. "If we can avoid the Hunt that long."

"We won't," Kaelren said flatly. "Merithra's protection ends at her borders. The moment we cross, they'll come."

"Ready?" Vashael asked, appearing at my side.

"Absolutely not."

"Good. Honesty is refreshing." She glanced toward Kaelren. "Whatever happened between you two last night, work it out fast. Tension like that gets people killed."

"Nothing happened."

"Right. And I'm the Queen of the Summer Court." She moved away before I could respond.

The Autumn Court's borders shimmered as we crossed them, Merithra's protection falling away like a discarded cloak. The moment my foot touched unclaimed ground, I felt them. The Wild Hunt. Not just their presence but their hunger, pressing against my consciousness like fingers probing for weakness.

"Move," Kaelren commanded, his voice clipped and cold. Still not looking at me. "They're already coming."

Our eyes met for half a second—just long enough for me to see the storm behind his carefully controlled expression—then he looked away first, jaw tight.

Right. We were doing this, then. Pretending.

We'd barely made it fifty yards into the forest when the first horn sounded—not heard but felt, vibrating through bones and blood. The trees around us shuddered, leaves falling like tears.

"Bees won't help us," Bryx said, Kevin buzzing anxiously around his head. "The Hunt drives them mad."

"Then we run," Sarnyx said, thorns already extending.

"Running just delays the inevitable," Eltrien murmured, and there was something in his voice—resignation? Recognition? "The Hunt never fails."

Another horn, closer. Through the canopy, I caught glimpses of them—riders that flickered between solid and transparent, neither fully there nor fully gone. Their mounts were worse, horses made of mist and darkness that moved through trees like they weren't there.

"This way," Nimor called, materializing from shadow. "There's a ravine—"

The hounds found us first.

They came from everywhere and nowhere, massive things with too many teeth and eyes that glowed like dying stars, bodies that seemed to phase in and out of existence with each stride. When they howled, reality itself rippled, trees bending away from the sound.

"You know what would be great right now?" Peeble muttered. "Literally anything else. Sarnyx's cooking. A corruption infection. Listening to Kaelren explain tactical formations for six hours."

"Form up!" Kaelren commanded, and the crew instinctively fell into defensive positions. "Back to back, don't let them separate us!"

"Don't look at them directly!" Vashael warned, but one of the hounds had already locked eyes with Bryx.

He froze mid-step, compound eyes going wide with terror. "No, no, no—" His voice rose to a panicked buzz. "Kevin, I'm sorry, I should have—"

"Bryx!" Sarnyx grabbed him, shaking him hard. "It's not real! Whatever you're seeing, it's not real!"

But it was real to him. That was the hounds' power—they didn't just show you fear, they made you live it.

Another hound circled toward me, and I made the mistake of meeting its void-like gaze.

Suddenly I wasn't in the forest anymore. I was back in Grandmother's house, watching her take her last breath, but this time I was frozen, unable to reach her bedside. Unable to say goodbye. Unable to tell her I understood now, understood what she'd tried to protect me from. The portal opened behind me, lightning crackling, and I was falling through—but Grandmother's hand reached out, accusing: You left me. You left everyone.

"Elle!" Kaelren's voice cut through the vision like a blade. His hand caught my arm, hauling me upright with bruising force. "Fight it. You're stronger than fear."

The hound snarled, frustrated its hold had broken. It lunged.

Kaelren's corruption met it mid-leap. Black tendrils of decay spread from his marks, wrapping around the hound like chains. The creature's howl turned to something almost like pain as its ethereal form began to solidify, to rot, to become something that could be hurt.

"Now!" he shouted.

Sarnyx's thorns struck true, piercing through what was now partially solid flesh. The hound dispersed into mist, but we could all hear its whimper echoing from somewhere else, somewhere between.

"They can be fought," Vashael said, her pollen already creating golden clouds of illusion around us. "But not for long."

She was right. For every hound we drove off, two more materialized from the shadows. They were testing us, wearing us down, driving us toward—

"It's a trap," Eltrien said suddenly. "They're herding us."

"Where?" I demanded.

"Does it matter?" Nimor materialized beside me, more solid than I'd ever seen him. "We can't fight them all."

One hound lunged at Bryx, who had finally broken free of the fear-vision but was still disoriented. It left three parallel scratches across his chest that bled light instead of blood—not physical wounds, but something worse.

"Those are essence wounds," Eltrien said, pulling Bryx back. "They're tearing at what makes him him."

"Oh good," Peeble said. "Because regular deadly wounds would be too boring."

The riders appeared then, surrounding us in a perfect circle. They'd stopped herding us—we were exactly where they wanted us. The Hunter himself dismounted, and looking at him was like trying to focus on a migraine—painful and impossible. He was beautiful and terrible, ancient and newly born, everything and nothing all at once.

"Elle of Earth," his voice came from everywhere and nowhere. "You run from judgment."

"I run from bullshit," I shot back, my marks flaring brightly at my collarbones. The Root responded to my anger, roots beginning to push up through the forest floor around my feet. "What crime am I guilty of besides existing?"

"Existing as an *abomination*," he replied simply. "You are becoming something outside the pattern. Something that breaks the wheel."

"Good. The wheel sucks."

"Oh brilliant," Peeble hissed. "Yes, definitely sass the ancient death god. What could possibly go wrong?"

He laughed, and birds fell dead from the trees around us, their small bodies hitting the ground with soft thumps. "Such defiance. It will make the hunt sweeter."

He raised his hand, and the hounds tensed to spring—

Nimor didn't wait. He charged.

Not at the Hunter—that would be suicide—but at the nearest hound, his shadow-form wrapping around the creature like chains of darkness. The hound howled, thrashing, snapping at something it couldn't quite catch, and the Hunt's attention divided.

"Move!" Kaelren commanded, already dragging me backward.

"Nimor!" I screamed, but he was already fighting three hounds at once, his form flickering wildly as they tore at his essence with teeth and claws that shouldn't exist.

Two more hounds peeled off from the circle to join the attack on him. Then another. He was outnumbered, outmatched, and he knew it—but he kept fighting anyway, kept drawing their attention, kept buying us seconds.

"He's buying us time!" Vashael shouted, golden pollen already creating illusion-clouds around us. "Don't waste it!"

The Hunter's attention snapped back to me, and his spear—which hadn't existed until it did—materialized in his hand. "The shadow-walker cannot save you. Only delay—"

Nimor screamed—not in pain but in defiance—and exploded into pure shadow, engulfing half the hounds in darkness so complete it seemed to eat light itself.

"GO!" Kaelren commanded, his hand like iron on my arm, hauling me into motion. "NOW!"

We fled.

Behind us, I could hear the battle—Nimor's howls of rage, the hounds' frustrated snarls, the Hunter's cold commands. But Nimor had done it. He'd given us an opening, a chance.

The forest became a blur of motion. Kaelren led us along paths that appeared just long enough to use them, through hollows that existed in spaces between spaces. My marks burned with heat and desperation, and I felt the Root responding—opening ways that shouldn't exist, bending trees aside, creating passages through barriers that should have been impassable.

"Keep moving!" Vashael shouted from behind me. "Some of them broke off—they're gaining!"

I could feel them—three, maybe four hounds that had abandoned the fight with Nimor to pursue us. Their presence was like ice down my spine, their hunger pressing against my consciousness.

We burst through a wall of thorns that parted at my approach—the Root recognizing me, responding to my need—and stumbled into a glade I didn't remember creating.

The moment we crossed the boundary, everything changed.

The sounds of pursuit cut off like someone had thrown a switch. The oppressive weight of the Hunt's presence vanished. Ancient wards hummed in the trees around us, so old they were more feeling than sight, thrumming with power that made my marks resonate in sympathy.

"Safe," Vashael gasped, doubling over to catch her breath. "For now."

But we weren't all there.

For a long moment, there was just our ragged breathing and the gentle hum of the wards. Then—

A shadow crawled across the ground at the glade's edge, reforming into something almost human. Nimor collapsed just inside the boundary, more gap than person, his form flickering between states like a candle in wind.

"Did we... make it?" he whispered, eyes dim and fading.

"You idiot," Kaelren's voice broke—actually broke. He was across the glade in three strides, dropping to his knees beside his friend, hands hovering like he was afraid to touch and make it worse. "You absolute idiot."

Vashael was right behind him, her usual sultry composure completely shattered. She fell to her knees beside Nimor, and I realized with a shock that there were tears cutting tracks through the gold dust on her cheeks. "Nim, you fool." Her voice was raw, stripped of all pretense. "We had a plan. You weren't supposed to—"

"Had to," Nimor managed, his form flickering like a dying light. "She's... important. The pattern... needs breaking." He looked at me, and I saw knowledge in those fading golden eyes. "You feel it, don't you? That sense that you've... done this before. All of you."

"What are you talking about?" I asked.

"The wheel," he whispered. "Turning and turning... but this time... different."

Peeble pressed closer to my neck, trembling. "He shouldn't know about that," they whispered. "How does he know?"

Before anyone could answer, Nimor's form scattered like smoke in a strong wind, then pulled back together weaker than before, barely holding shape.

"He's dispersing," Eltrien said urgently, kneeling beside him. His marks glowed as he reached out with healing magic. "His essence is too damaged to hold form."

"Fix it," Kaelren commanded, and it wasn't a request.

"I can't." Eltrien's voice cracked with frustration. "He exists between states now. Neither living nor dead, neither here nor there." His healing threads passed through Nimor like he wasn't there at all. "He saved us, but the cost..."

"The cost is acceptable," Nimor whispered, barely audible. "Always knew... wasn't meant to finish the story. Just... help it along."

"Stop talking like you're dying," I said, my voice fierce as I dropped to my knees beside them. "We'll figure this out. There has to be a way to—"

"Not dying," he said, and somehow he managed a smile. It was heart-breaking. "Just... becoming something else. Something useful." His form flickered again, more transparent than before. "The Hunt will follow. Can't enter here, but... they'll wait. Forever if necessary."

"Then we make sure it's not necessary," I said, though I had no idea how.

"This is bad," Peeble said from my shoulder, their voice unusually serious. "This is really, really bad."

As Eltrien worked desperately to stabilize what was left of Nimor's essence, I stood and walked to the edge of the glade. I could feel them out there—the Hunt, patient as stone, inevitable as sunrise. They'd wait at the borders until we emerged, and then...

But something else was happening. My marks were responding to this place, warming against my skin, resonating with the ancient wards humming in the trees. This glade was old—older than the Hunt, older than the Autumn Court, maybe older than the split between Root and Bloom itself.

"What is this place?" I asked aloud.

The air shimmered near one of the massive oaks at the glade's edge. Not like heat distortion, but like reality remembering something it had forgotten. A figure stepped out of the shimmer—or perhaps they'd been there all along and were only now choosing to be seen.

The Sage.

"Wait—" Bryx spun around, his compound eyes going wide. "Where did you come from? How did you—we would have seen you!"

"Would you?" The Sage tilted their head, amused. Their form was more solid here than it had been at the Autumn Court, as if this ancient place gave them substance. "I've been following since the Autumn Court. Did you think the Duchess would let you leave without... insurance?"

"You could have helped during the chase!" Sarnyx snarled, thorns extending toward them even as she stayed protectively near Nimor's flickering form.

"The Hunt cannot harm me, true." The Sage moved toward Nimor with careful, deliberate steps, their feet barely disturbing the grass. "But interference would have broken older laws. Laws that even I do not break lightly." They looked down at Nimor with something like sadness. "This is neutral ground. One of the few places left where the old laws still hold. The Hunt cannot enter, but neither can you leave without facing them."

"So we're trapped," Vashael said bitterly.

"You're protected. There's a difference." The Sage knelt beside Nimor, studying his dispersing form. "He knew the cost. He's known for—" They stopped, shaking their head. "Time is difficult here. Difficult to explain."

"Can you help him?" I demanded.

"I can keep him from dispersing completely." They placed their hands on either side of where Nimor's head flickered in and out of existence. "But what he becomes... that depends on choices yet unmade. By all of you."

As the Sage began working with Eltrien, combining their ancient knowledge with his healing magic, I felt Kaelren's presence behind me—dark, furious, barely controlled. His corruption was spreading visibly now, black veins crawling up his jaw like angry cracks in porcelain.

"This is your fault," he said quietly, voice rough with barely suppressed emotion.

I turned to face him. "I didn't ask him to—"

"You didn't have to." His silver eyes were molten with rage and pain. "You exist, and people die protecting you. That's what you are. A catalyst for destruction."

The words hit like physical blows, and I felt Peeble tense against my neck. But I could see beneath Kaelren's anger—the terror, the grief, the guilt of a leader watching his people fall.

"I'm sorry," I said simply, because what else was there to say?

"Sorry doesn't fix this." His hands clenched into fists at his sides, corruption spreading across his knuckles. "Sorry doesn't bring him back."

"No. But maybe something else can." I looked at my marks, feeling the power coiled beneath my skin, the Root responding to my distress. "The Root opened those paths for us. Created this opening in the barrier. Maybe it can—"

"Don't." His hand shot out, catching my wrist before I could reach for the power. His touch burned—not painfully, but with the heat of his corruption meeting my transformation. "Every time you use it, you change more. Eventually, there won't be enough human left to save."

"Maybe that's a price worth paying. If it can help Nimor—"

"Not to me," he said, and the rawness in his voice made my chest tighten. Then he seemed to realize what he'd admitted, what he'd revealed. He released my wrist like it burned him. "We wait. We plan. We find another way."

"There might not be another way," I said softly.

"Then we make one." He turned away, jaw clenched. "We always do."

But as the sun began to set and the Hunt's presence pressed against the glade's borders like a physical weight—patient, inevitable, eternal—I wondered if there really was another way.

Or if Nimor's sacrifice had only delayed the inevitable.

14

Kaelren

Night had fallen hours ago, but something was different.

I noticed it first in the way the firelight seemed to pulse—not with the wind, but with something else. A rhythm from outside our reality. Then the temperature dropped, not cold exactly, but *thin*. Like the air itself was holding its breath.

"Does anyone else feel that?" Vashael asked, her hand going to her throwing knives.

Elle stood, turning in a slow circle. "The wards. They're... singing?"

She was right. The ancient protections woven into the glade had begun to hum, a frequency that bypassed the ears and resonated in the chest. In the bones. In the marks we all carried.

Then the first silver thread appeared in the sky.

"Oh shit," Bryx whispered. "Is that—"

"The Star Veil," I finished, my voice rough with disbelief. "I never thought I'd see it."

More threads materialized, rippling across the darkness like the universe was showing its seams. Within minutes, the entire sky was latticed with silver light, weaving patterns that hurt to look at directly—not because they were bright, but because they were true. Reality laid bare.

Elle moved to my side, her face tilted up in wonder. "When was the last time this happened?"

"Five hundred and seventy years ago," Eltrien said softly. "In the Breaking Fields, right before the Fracture War began. It's said the Veil appears when the world stands at a threshold. When decisions made in one moment will cascade through centuries."

"So no pressure then," Peeble muttered.

The silver threads reflected in Elle's eyes, making them look like captured galaxies. Her marks had calmed since the chase, glowing soft amber—but I could see they'd spread, delicate vines now creeping up the sides of her neck.

"It's beautiful," she breathed.

"It's dangerous," I corrected, settling beside her. Close enough that our bond hummed with the proximity, with the weakened boundaries between us. "The Veil doesn't just weaken barriers between waking and sleeping, between real and possible. It erases them. Everything becomes permeable. Vulnerable."

"Including us?" she asked.

I met her eyes. "Especially us."

"Between you and being an ass?" she suggested.

Despite everything—Nimor barely holding form, the Hunt waiting beyond our sanctuary—I almost smiled.

"That boundary doesn't exist," I said.

"Clearly."

Through the bond—because yes, it was a bond, I could admit that much—I felt her amusement like warmth against my ribs. What I refused to name was what kind of bond. Magical necessity, I told myself. The result of our marks existing in tandem, nothing more. Certainly not the other thing. The thing that made my chest ache when she smiled. The thing that made me want to kill men I'd never met for hurting her.

Not that.

The others were scattered around the fire. Bryx unusually subdued, one hand resting on Kevin who'd shrunk back to pocket-size and hadn't stopped anxious buzzing since the chase—even small, his distress was palpable. Sarnyx sharpening thorns with mechanical precision. Vashael organizing supplies we might never get to use. Eltrien and the Sage still working on Nimor, who flickered in and out of visibility like a bad transmission.

"I've seen this before," Eltrien said suddenly, looking up at the Star Veil. "Or... I will see it. Or I'm seeing it now in multiple ways." He shook his head. "The Veil makes time strange."

"Everything here makes time strange," Elle muttered.

Peeble landed on her shoulder, looking up at the lights. "Pretty though. In a 'reality might collapse' kind of way."

"Comforting," Elle said.

"I live to serve."

The fire crackled, sending sparks up toward the silver threads. Where they met, tiny explosions of color bloomed—memories given form. I saw glimpses of other times, other places. Elle in my arms, both of us covered in blood. Elle with silver hair, ancient and terrible. Elle dead at my feet while I screamed at uncaring stars.

"Did you see—" she started.

"Echoes," I said quickly. "The Veil shows what might be. Don't trust it."

"Alright, enough of this doom and gloom!" Bryx said suddenly, his usual cheer forced but welcome. Kevin buzzed anxiously from his perch on Bryx's shoulder—even at pocket-size, the bee's distress was palpable. "We need a story. Something fun, something dramatic, something with at least one questionable life choice. Anyone? Please? Before I start spiraling about how Nimor might be dying and we're trapped and—"

"I'll go," Vashael said, surprising everyone despite Bryx's prompting. She rarely shared anything personal. "How about I tell our lovely Elle how I ended up in this rowdy group of misfits."

She settled into storyteller posture, the firelight making her gold-dusted skin shimmer. "I was a courtesan in the Petal Courts. Trained from childhood in the arts of pleasure and poison. I had a lover—a noble who thought he owned me."

The fire dimmed as she spoke, responding to her voice.

"He was beautiful the way weapons are beautiful—all sharp edges and deadly purpose. He said he loved me, but what he loved was possession. The idea that something as dangerous as me could be contained."

Elle shifted beside me, and I wondered if she was thinking of her ex-fiancé. The one who'd betrayed her. The one I'd kill if I ever met him.

"One night," Vashael continued, "he brought another to our bed. Said I should be honored to share him. Said I should be grateful." Her smile was sharp as her throwing knives. "I poisoned them both. Slowly. Made him watch her die first, so he'd know how betrayal felt. Then I watched him follow, and I felt... nothing. No satisfaction. No regret. Just empty."

"That's horrible," Elle said softly.

"That's survival," Vashael corrected. "The Petal Courts don't forgive that kind of defiance, even when it's justified. They would have executed me—made an example of the courtesan who dared strike back. But I'd heard stories about a disgraced prince who'd disappeared into the Thornwood. One who understood what it meant to be cast out for refusing to be what others demanded."

She glanced at me, and I kept my expression neutral.

"I knew Kaelren from court functions. Knew he was the kind of monster who had rules. Who protected his people." Her smile turned softer, almost fond. "So I ran. Tracked him through half the realm until he finally stopped trying to lose me and let me join his crew of outcasts."

"And now you're stuck with us," Bryx added cheerfully.

"And now I'm stuck with you," she agreed. Then her amber eyes fixed on Elle. "We all have our befores. Our reasons for being here, outcasts in the deep woods. What's yours, little human? What broke you enough that falling into another world seemed like escape?"

Elle was quiet for a moment. Then: "I wasn't broken. I was... bent. Bent trying to fit into spaces too small for me. My ex, Julian—he needed me smaller. Quieter. Less. And for two years, I tried. Tried to be the supporting character in his story instead of the lead in mine."

My marks flared with possessive rage. This Julian had tried to diminish her. Tried to contain something meant to be wild.

"Then I caught him with my best friend," Elle continued. "In our bed. And you know what he said? 'You're too much, Elle. She's easier.'" She laughed, bitter. "Easier. Like I was some kind of challenge to overcome instead of a person to love."

"I would kill him," I said, the words escaping before I could stop them. Everyone turned to look at me.

"Slowly," I clarified, not backing down. "I would kill him very slowly."

Elle stared at me, something shifting in her expression. "That's... weirdly sweet. In a psychotic way."

"I don't do sweet."

"No," she agreed. "You do vengeful protection. It's different but... not unwelcome."

The moment stretched between us, the Star Veil making everything feel more intense, more real. Through the connection we both pretended wasn't there—that pull I refused to call a bond—I felt her pulse quicken, felt her lean slightly toward me—

"I should check on Nimor," I said abruptly, standing.

"Right," she said, and I caught disappointment in her voice. "Of course."

I retreated to where Nimor lay—or existed, or whatever state he was in. But I could still feel Elle's presence, her warmth, her want mixing with mine until I couldn't tell where I ended and she began.

Later, exhaustion finally claimed us. One by one, the crew settled into sleep. Elle curled near the fire, using her pack as a pillow, her face soft in the flickering light. I took first watch, settling against a tree where I could see both the glade's borders and her sleeping form.

The Star Veil continued its dance overhead, glittering threads weaving tighter, reality thinning with each passing hour. The boundary between waking and dreaming grew gossamer-thin. Permeable.

I should have expected what happened next.

There was no transition. No sensation of falling asleep. One moment I was awake, watching the fire's embers pulse in rhythm with my marks. The next, I was standing in sunlight that felt like a memory given form.

Elle's dream.

The garden materialized around me in layers—first the skeleton of hedge and pathway, then color filling in like stained glass catching light, each hue sharp and deliberate. Her grandmother's garden, I realized, but wrong in ways that made my chest ache. Half the roses were skeletal, thorns black as obsidian. The other half bloomed with flowers from fever dreams—petals that opened and closed like breathing, stems that bled light when broken, leaves that sang in harmonics only dreams could hear.

Elle stood at the garden's heart, and she was devastating.

Her marks didn't just cover her skin—they *were* her skin, glowing vines that pulsed with each heartbeat, spreading across every visible inch in patterns that hurt to look at directly. They wrapped around her throat like a lover's hands, cascaded down her arms in spiraling fractals, disappeared beneath the white dress that seemed woven from mist and regret. Her eyes were pure light, no iris, no pupil—just radiance that saw through me, past me, into me.

"You're not supposed to be here," she said, but she was smiling. That smile was wrong too—too knowing, too hungry, too much like the smile I'd imagined in a hundred moments I refused to acknowledge.

"The Veil." My voice came out rougher than intended. "It's making boundaries weak."

"Or maybe you just can't stay away." She tilted her head, and her hair moved like it was underwater, defying physics the way everything here defied reason. "Maybe you've been trying so hard not to think about me that the Veil dragged you straight into my dreams."

She moved toward me, and reality rippled with each step. Flowers bloomed where her feet touched earth, then withered, then bloomed again in an endless cycle of creation and decay. I wanted to run. Should run. In dreams, our marks couldn't hurt each other. In dreams, we could—

"Don't," I said, but my voice lacked conviction. My marks were already reaching toward hers, corruption spreading across my hands like ink in water.

"Why?" She was close now, close enough that I could smell roses and rain and something underneath that was purely her—that scent I'd been trying not to notice for weeks. Close enough that I could see myself reflected in those light-filled eyes, see how broken I looked, how desperate. "We both want this. I can feel it through the bond. Every time you look at me. Every time you *don't* look at me because looking would mean admitting—"

"The bond isn't real," I said, the lie tasting like ash. "It's just magical proximity."

"Liar." She reached up, her fingers stopping just shy of my face. This close, I could see her marks moving, vines shifting and growing, flowers opening and closing like breathing. "You feel it too. Have felt it since that first day when I defied you in the tent. When I looked at you like I wasn't afraid. When you looked at me like you wanted to destroy me and save me in the same breath."

"Elle—"

"I'm so tired of almosts," she whispered, and there was such raw need in her voice it felt like a physical blow. "Aren't you? Tired of stopping ourselves. Tired of pretending. Tired of all the reasons we can't when we both know we *want*."

Her fingers made contact with my cheek, and the world exploded.

Not with pain but with *rightness*. Like two halves of something ancient and broken finally remembering how to fit together. The sensation crashed through me—her marks meeting mine, dream-logic allowing what reality forbade. I felt her gasp echo in my own chest, felt her surprise and relief and desperate hunger as if they were my own emotions.

I pulled her against me, and she made a sound that was part gasp, part laugh, part sob. Her body fit against mine like it had been designed for this exact purpose, every curve and hollow aligning perfectly.

"This is a dream," I said, my voice barely recognizable. "Only a dream."

"Then let me dream," she whispered against my throat, and pulled my head down to hers.

The kiss detonated between us.

Desperate, hungry, tinged with the knowledge that this couldn't be real, that reality would rip us apart the moment we woke. Her hands tangled in my hair, pulling hard enough to hurt, and I welcomed the pain. Mine spread across her back, then lower, pulling her impossibly closer. Through the dream-bond—vivid and overwhelming in ways our waking connection never was—I felt everything she felt. The want that had been building since the day we met. The frustration of every interrupted moment. The need that scared her as much as it scared me. And underneath it all, something deeper. Something that felt dangerously close to—

No. I couldn't think that. Not even here.

"I hate you," she gasped against my mouth, then bit my lower lip hard enough to draw blood.

"I hate you too," I agreed, then kissed her again, deeper, trying to memorize the taste of her, the feel of her, knowing this was all we'd ever have.

The garden around us responded to our emotions like a living thing. Flowers bloomed and died in rapid succession, their petals falling like snow. Seasons changed with each heartbeat—spring's soft green to summer's lush abundance to autumn's golden decay to winter's stark beauty and back again in an endless, dizzying cycle. The hedge maze grew wild, thorns lengthening, roses opening mouths filled with teeth. The fountain at the garden's center ran backward, water defying gravity, reaching toward the sky.

We were destroying her grandmother's memory with our desperate need, warping this sacred space into something feral and hungry, and neither of us cared.

"We could stay here," she said between kisses, her voice breaking. "In the dream. Never wake up. Just this, forever."

"We'd die." I pulled back just enough to see her face, to watch how the light behind her eyes pulsed with each rapid breath.

"Maybe it would be worth it." She traced the carved marks on my face with trembling fingers. "Better than waking up. Better than pretending. Better than watching you walk away from me again and again because we're too dangerous together."

I pulled back farther, holding her face in my hands. Her skin was fever-hot beneath my palms, or maybe I was the one burning. "No. You're meant for more than dying in a dream. You're meant for—"

"What?" she demanded, and there was fury mixed with her want now. "What am I meant for, Kaelren? To survive? To become whatever the marks want me to become? To watch you destroy yourself while I can't touch you, can't help you, can't—"

"To *live*," I said, and the word came out like a wound. "To have more than this. More than me."

"With you, though," she said, and there was something broken in her voice that matched the broken thing in my chest. "I'd be dying with you. And maybe that's enough. Maybe that's everything."

"Elle—"

The dream shattered like glass.

One moment I was holding her, the next I was slamming back into my body with enough force to make me gasp. My marks screamed with frustrated want, burning like brands across my skin. Across the fire, Elle jolted awake, her eyes snapping open with a sound that might have been a sob or a scream.

We stared at each other while the Star Veil danced overhead, both knowing exactly what had happened, both knowing we couldn't acknowledge it. Her chest heaved with rapid breaths. Her marks glowed amber-bright, pulsing in the same rhythm as mine. I could still taste her on my lips, still feel the ghost of her body against mine.

"I should—" she started, her voice wrecked.

"Yes," I agreed, not trusting myself to say more.

She stood on shaking legs and walked to the other side of the glade, as far from me as she could get while staying within the wards. She didn't look back, but through the bond—the one we both pretended didn't exist—I felt her want warring with her fear, felt her trying not to remember the way I'd kissed her like I was drowning and she was air.

I remained where I was, trying to forget the taste of her mouth, the feel of her body against mine, the way she'd said my name like a prayer and a curse combined. Trying and failing. The memory was branded into me, deeper than any mark I'd ever carved into my own flesh.

The Star Veil began to fade with approaching dawn, silver threads dissolving into ordinary darkness. But the memory of that dream-kiss burned like corruption in my veins, like Bloom-marks spreading, like something that would consume me from the inside out if I let it.

We'd crossed a line we couldn't uncross.

And we both knew it would destroy us.

The only question was whether we'd be able to stop ourselves from crossing it again.

15

Elle

Two days after the dream-kiss we didn't talk about, we finally left the glade.

The Wild Hunt had withdrawn—not gone, but waiting at a distance like wolves who knew their prey would eventually leave the sheep pen. Nimor could move again, though he still flickered between solid and shadow, sometimes mid-sentence.

We traveled on foot through the Thornwood, keeping to hidden trails the Sage knew. The bees had scattered after the chase—Bryx said they'd find their own way home, that Kevin would track him down when things were safer. For now, we walked in tense silence, everyone hyper-aware of the Hunt's horns echoing in the distance, never quite close enough to engage but never far enough to forget.

"There's a settlement ahead," the Sage finally said on the second evening. "Thornhaven Hollow. Neutral ground, markets, relative safety. A place to resupply and plan."

What they didn't mention was that Thornhaven had a tavern.

The Nectar Nook squatted between two massive trees like something that had grown there by accident—all curves and organic architecture, windows that glowed amber with promises of questionable decisions. The sign above the door featured a beetle in what could generously be called a corset, holding a tankard and winking.

"Oh no," I said flatly. "Absolutely not."

"Too late!" Bryx exclaimed, already through the door. "I need alcohol and poor choices!"

I followed reluctantly, Kaelren a silent presence at my back.

The interior was exactly what the sign threatened—a riot of color and light, bioluminescent lanterns hanging like jewels, tables carved from twisted roots. The space was packed with patrons of every variety: Root-marked fae playing cards in shadowy corners, Bloom-touched merchants haggling over drinks, what looked like a group of forest sprites doing shots that glowed an alarming shade of green. Music thrummed through the walls themselves, making the floor pulse with bass that I felt in my chest.

The servers were Florakith—seven-foot-tall beings with skin like flower petals, wings that sparkled with pollen, and outfits that were more suggestion than clothing. One glided past our group, leaving a trail of sweet scent that made my head spin.

"Is this a brothel?" I asked.

"It's whatever you pay for," Peeble said from my shoulder, already examining a menu made of pressed mushroom. "But mostly it's just aggressively flirtatious."

A Florakith host appeared, all smiles and calculated charm. "Table for...?" Their eyes swept over our ragtag crew with obvious interest.

"Eight," Kaelren said curtly.

"And would you prefer intimate or... exposed?" The host's smile suggested they already knew which would make us more uncomfortable.

"Back corner," Sarnyx said before anyone else could answer. "Away from the windows."

The host led us through the crowded tavern, past tables where deals were being made and romances were being negotiated, to a large round table tucked into the far corner. It was partially hidden by a support beam grown from living wood, offering some privacy while still giving us clear sightlines to both exits.

Kaelren immediately claimed the seat with the best view of the room, back to the wall. I slid in beside him—safer than sitting across where we'd have to look at each other—and the rest of the crew arranged themselves around the table.

Kaelren hadn't said a word since we entered. He sat like a storm cloud, arms crossed, jaw tight. Every time a server looked his way, his marks flared with irritation.

"Relax," Vashael purred from across the table, clearly enjoying his discomfort. "They're just friendly."

"They're predatory."

"Pot, meet kettle," I muttered.

He shot me a look that could have frozen fire, but before he could respond, our server arrived. She was devastating—lavender skin that shifted to pink at the edges, eyes like midnight, and a smile that promised trouble.

"Well hello there, sweetlings," she drawled, leaning one hip against the table in a way that made her filmy skirt shift dangerously. "First time at the Nook?"

"Unfortunately," Kaelren said flatly.

She laughed, a sound like wind chimes. "Oh, I like the grumpy ones. They're fun to crack." She leaned closer to him than necessary, giving him a view that would have made most men forget their own names. "Let me know if you need anything. Anything at all."

"We'll start with water," he said, voice like ice.

"I'll have whatever's strongest," I said, partly because I needed it, partly because his obvious discomfort was amusing.

"Ooh, adventurous," the server said, straightening to look me up and down with obvious appreciation. "I have just the thing for you, sweetling. It'll make you forget all your troubles."

"Perfect. Bring three."

The server sashayed away, and Kaelren's glare could have powered a small city.

"What?" I asked innocently.

"Three?"

"I'm thirsty."

"You're reckless."

"You're annoying."

"Children," Sarnyx interrupted, sharpening one of her thorns on the edge of the table. "Can we have one evening without you two eye-fucking or fighting?"

"We're not—" Kaelren and I said in unison, then glared at each other for the synchronization.

Thank goodness the drinks chose that minute to arrive. They were mesmerizing, something that glowed purple and tasted like bad decisions. I was halfway through my second an hour later, warm and buzzing, when I excused myself to find the bathroom.

The Nectar Nook's facilities were predictably bizarre—a carved alcove with a door made of woven vines and a mirror that showed me looking slightly more attractive than I actually was. Flattering enchantments, probably. When I emerged, he was waiting.

"Did the garden grow you just for me?" the man said, blocking my path back to the table. He was handsome in that obvious way—all sharp cheekbones and artful stubble, shirt open enough to show geometric tattoos that pulsed with their own light.

"That's a terrible line," I said, trying to step around him.

He moved with me, still blocking. "Is it working?"

"Absolutely not."

"Then let me try another." He leaned closer, and I caught the scent of honeywine and something darker, more predatory. "You look like someone who appreciates danger."

"I look like someone trying to get back to her table."

He laughed, hand landing on my arm. His touch was warm, confident, possessive in a way that made my skin prickle. "I'm Fenric. And you're the human everyone's talking about." His fingers traced up my arm, getting bolder.

"People say a lot of things they don't understand." I tried to pull away, but his grip tightened slightly.

"They also say you're with the failed prince." His eyes flicked toward our corner table, where I could just make out Kaelren's dark silhouette. "But he seems... distracted."

I followed his gaze to see one of the Florakith servers practically draped over Kaelren's chair, laughing at something Bryx had said. Kaelren looked like he wanted to commit murder, but he wasn't moving away. My chest tightened with something ugly and irrational.

"We're not together," I said, the words tasting bitter.

"Perfect." Fenric's hand slid from my arm to my waist, pulling me slightly off balance. "Dance with me. Just one song."

"I should get back—"

"They won't even notice you're gone." His other hand found my hip, and suddenly we were moving toward the dance floor whether I'd agreed or not. "Come on. You look like you need to forget about brooding princes for a while."

The alcohol and his insistent pulling made it easier to give in than fight. The dance floor was crowded, bodies pressing close in the dim light. The rhythm was hypnotic, compelling, pulsing up through the floor and into my bones.

Fenric could dance, I'd give him that. He moved like water, confident and smooth, pulling me into the rhythm until I forgot to be self-conscious. His hands started at my waist but grew bolder with each song—sliding lower, pulling me closer, fingers spreading possessively across my lower back.

"You're beautiful," he murmured in my ear, close enough that his lips brushed my skin. "Especially the marks. They make you look wild."

"Wild?"

"Untamed. Free." His hand slid even lower, just above the curve of my ass. "Like someone who doesn't follow rules. Someone who takes what she wants."

I should have stopped him. Should have pushed away. But the alcohol made everything soft-edged, and some petty part of me wanted Kaelren to notice, to care that someone else was touching me.

"Smooth talker," I managed.

"When properly motivated." He spun me, then caught me against his chest, both hands on my hips now, holding me flush against him. His fingers traced the edge of where my marks disappeared beneath my clothes. "And you're very motivating. I bet those marks go everywhere, don't they?"

"That's—"

His hand slid up my side, thumb brushing the underside of my breast through the fabric. "I'd love to find out. There're rooms upstairs. Private. Comfortable."

"I don't think—"

"Don't think." His lips were at my ear now, his hand growing more insistent. "Just feel. Just—"

Fenric suddenly wasn't there anymore.

One moment he was pressed against me, the next he was flying backward, slamming into the wall hard enough to crack the living wood. Kaelren materialized from the crowd like violence given form, carved marks blazing black, corruption spreading from his hands in visible waves.

"Kaelren!" I stumbled forward, but he was already moving.

He had Fenric pinned with one hand around his throat, the other—oh gods, the other held a knife. Not one of his throwing blades, but something crueler. A Root-touched dagger that made the air around it taste like rot.

"Touch her again," Kaelren snarled, and his voice was barely recognizable, "and I'll feed you to the Root piece by piece. Starting with the parts that touched her."

"Kaelren, stop!" I tried to grab his arm, but he shook me off without looking away from Fenric.

"He had his hands on you." Each word came out like broken glass. "His filthy fucking hands on what's—"

"Dancing! We were just dancing!"

"That wasn't dancing." Kaelren pressed the blade against Fenric's palm— the hand that had been on my hip, on my back, touching me. "That was claiming. Marking. Hunting what isn't his to take."

Fenric made a choked sound, eyes wide with genuine fear now. "I didn't— I didn't know—"

"You knew." The blade pressed harder, drawing a bead of blood. "You saw her sitting with me. Saw her marks responding to mine. And you thought you could just take her anyway."

"Kaelren, please—" I tried again.

"Did he touch you here?" The knife traced up Fenric's arm, leaving a thin red line. "Here?" Another line across his chest. "Where else? Tell me where else his hands went, Elle, and I'll carve those parts off him."

The entire tavern had gone silent, everyone watching. Even the music had stopped.

"Let him go," I said, and this time I put command in my voice. The kind I'd been learning to use with the marks, with the power growing inside me.

Kaelren's eyes finally found mine, and what I saw there made my breath catch. Rage, yes, violence barely contained. But underneath it—possessive hunger that matched what I'd felt in the dream. Raw need that bordered on feral. His marks were spreading up his neck, black veins pulsing with corruption that made the air shimmer.

"Please," I said more softly. "Not like this."

Something in my voice cut through his fury. The knife trembled in his hand.

"He touched you," Kaelren said, and his voice cracked. "He put his hands on you like he had the right. Like you were his to take."

"But I'm not his," I said quietly. "And he didn't take anything I didn't allow."

That was the wrong thing to say. Kaelren's expression shuttered into something cold and terrible. The knife moved with brutal precision, slamming through Fenric's hand and into the wall behind him, pinning him there like an insect in a collection.

Fenric screamed.

"Kaelren!" I lunged forward, but Vashael caught me, holding me back.

"Let him finish," she murmured in my ear. "This has been building since the glade. Better he takes it out on someone who deserves it."

"Next time," Kaelren said, his voice deadly calm now, "when you see a woman whose marks are responding to someone else's, when you see power calling to power, you walk away. You don't touch. You don't pursue. You don't presume. Understand?"

Fenric nodded frantically, tears streaming down his face.

Kaelren yanked the knife free with a wet sound that made several patrons flinch. Fenric collapsed, clutching his bleeding hand.

Then Kaelren turned to me, and the look in his eyes was pure possession. "We're leaving."

"We're not—"

In one fluid motion, he bent and threw me over his shoulder like I weighed nothing.

"Kaelren!" I beat at his back, but he was already moving, carrying me through the stunned crowd toward the door.

The crew watched with expressions ranging from shock to entertainment. Bryx whooped. Vashael looked deeply satisfied. Even Sarnyx cracked a rare smile.

"Have fun, kids!" Bryx called. "Try not to kill each other! Or do—actually that would be very entertaining!"

"Put me down!" I demanded, but Kaelren ignored me, shouldering through the door and into the cool night air.

He carried me into the narrow alley between the massive trees, where the bioluminescent lights from the tavern barely reached. Only when we were shrouded in darkness did he set me down—not gently, but not roughly either. Just with enough force that I stumbled back against the rough bark of a tree.

"What the hell is wrong with you?" I shoved at his chest, but he didn't budge.

"He was touching you." Each word came out like gravel, like violence barely contained.

"So?" I shoved again, harder. "People touch when they dance!"

"Not like that." He stepped closer, and I could see his marks blazing even in the dim light, black veins crawling up his neck, across his jaw. "Not with hands that wanted to own. To claim. To take what isn't theirs."

"I can decide who touches me!"

"Can you?" He was closer now, so close I could feel the heat radiating off him, could smell corruption and pine and something wild underneath. "Because from where I was sitting, watching his hands slide down your

161

body, watching him pull you against him, watching him whisper things that made you smile—it looked like you were deciding to let him have you."

"And what if I was?" I challenged, anger and alcohol making me reckless. "What if I wanted someone who actually wants me back instead of—"

"Instead of what?" His hands slammed into the tree on either side of my head, caging me in. "Instead of me? The one who can barely breathe when you're near? The one who dreams about tasting you every fucking night? The one who wanted to rip that man's throat out with my bare hands for daring to touch what's mine?"

"I'm not yours!"

"Aren't you?" He leaned in, his face inches from mine, and I could see the wildness in his eyes, the barely-leashed violence. "Then why does your pulse spike every time I get close? Why do your marks respond to mine even when you're trying to ignore me? Why did you kiss me in that shared dream like I was everything you needed?"

"That was just—"

"Don't." His voice dropped to something dangerous, something raw. "Don't lie to me. Not about this. I watched you dance with him. Watched him touch you. Watched you let him, and do you know what I felt?"

"What?" The word came out breathless.

"Murderous." He shifted closer, his body almost flush against mine now. "Possessive. Feral. I wanted to kill him. Wanted to make it hurt. Wanted to carve my name into every inch of skin he touched so everyone would know—"

"Know what?"

"That you belong with me." His forehead dropped against mine, his exhales ragged. "That you've been meant for me since the moment you looked at me with fire instead of fear. Since you challenged me. Since you—"

"Stop." But I wasn't pushing him away. My hands had somehow ended up fisted in his shirt, holding him close instead of shoving him back.

"I can't." His hands left the tree, sliding down to grip my waist, fingers digging in hard enough to bruise. "I've tried. Gods, I've tried. But watching him touch you, seeing his hands where mine should be—"

"Your hands?" I challenged, even as my body betrayed me, arching slightly into his grip.

"Yes." One hand slid up my side, achingly slow, burning everywhere it touched. "My hands. My mouth. My—" He made a frustrated sound. "You have no idea what you do to me. How badly I want to—"

"What?" My marks were flaring hot at my collarbones now. "What do you want to do, Kaelren?"

His hand came up to cup my face, thumb brushing across my lower lip. "Everything. Things that would terrify you. Things I shouldn't even think about doing to someone like you."

"Someone like me?"

"Someone good." His pupils had swallowed his irises completely. "Someone who deserves better than a monster who wants to mark every inch of her skin, who wants to make sure no one else ever touches her, who wants to—"

I grabbed his face and kissed him.

For a heartbeat, he froze, shocked. Then he made a sound—something between a growl and a groan—and kissed me back with a hunger that stole my breath. His fingers tangled in my hair, gripping tight, angling my head so he could deepen the kiss. The other arm wrapped around my waist, hauling me against him, and I could feel every hard line of his body, the way his marks pulsed against mine, the corruption spreading between us like wildfire.

This wasn't like the dream. This was real. Raw. Desperate.

He kissed me like he'd been starved and I was a feast. Like he'd been suffocating and I was oxygen. His teeth caught my lower lip, and I gasped, which he took as an invitation to kiss me deeper, harder, until I couldn't tell where I ended and he began.

My back pressed harder against the tree, bark biting through my clothes, but I didn't care. His touch was everywhere—my waist, my hips, sliding up my ribs, one hand venturing to cup my breast through the fabric and I gasped into his mouth.

"This is insane," I managed when he moved to kiss down my jaw, my neck, finding the place where my marks pulsed hottest.

"Yes." His teeth scraped against my throat, and I made a sound I'd never made before. "We should stop."

"We should," I agreed, but my fingers were in his hair now, holding him against my throat as he kissed and bit and marked me with his mouth.

"Someone could see."

"Let them." His hand slid down to grip my thigh, hitching it up around his hip, and suddenly we were pressed together in a way that made coherent thought impossible. "Let everyone see. Let them know you're—"

"Don't say it," I warned, but there was no heat in it.

"Mine." He said it anyway, against my skin, and I felt the word like a brand. "You're mine, Elle. Say it."

"I—"

His hand slid higher on my thigh, fingers digging in possessively. "Say it."

"This doesn't mean—"

"Say. It." His mouth found that spot behind my ear that made me shake.

"Yours," I finally gasped. "I'm yours. But you're—"

"Yours." He pulled back just enough to look at me, and what I saw in his eyes made something in my chest crack open. "I've been yours from the start. From before I understood what that meant. From before I could admit it to myself."

"HEY!" Bryx's voice carried from somewhere close by, loud and urgent. "HUNT'S BEEN SPOTTED! WE NEED TO MOVE NOW!"

Kaelren pulled back with a snarl that was pure frustration. We stared at each other, both gasping for air, both disheveled, both marked with swollen lips and blown pupils.

"This isn't over," he said, voice wrecked.

"I know," I replied, still trying to remember how to breathe normally.

He stepped back reluctantly, and the loss of his warmth felt like a physical ache. His hand caught mine, threading our fingers together in a gesture that felt more intimate than everything that had just happened.

"We need to run," he said.

"I know."

But neither of us moved for another heartbeat, just standing there in the darkness, holding hands like the world wasn't ending around us.

Then Bryx's panicked shout came again, and reality crashed back.

We ran back to find the crew already moving, weapons drawn, supplies gathered. The Wild Hunt's horns were closer now, close enough to make my teeth ache. Fenric was nowhere to be seen, but the Florakith servers watched from the doorway with knowing smiles.

As we fled into the night, Kaelren's hand never left mine.

We were spiraling toward something inevitable.

And whether it would save us or consume us entirely, neither of us could say.

16

Kaelren

The Wild Hunt's horns tore through the night, each note a promise of violence.

We ran through the twisted paths beyond Thornhaven Hollow, the gaudy lights of the Nectar Nook already swallowed by darkness behind us. My kiss with Elle still burned on my lips—that desperate collision against the alley wall, the way she'd gasped my name, the possessive claim we'd both made. Now we fled with the Hunt bearing down on us like inevitability given form.

"Move!" I barked, pushing the crew harder.

Elle ran beside me, matching my pace despite the uneven ground. Through our bond, I felt her exhaustion from the tavern confrontation, the emotional toll of our confession, and underneath it all, a simmering frustration that even that moment had been stolen from us.

"Oh good," Peeble buzzed sarcastically from Elle's shoulder, somehow maintaining perfect balance despite our breakneck speed. "Running for our lives in the dark. My favorite Tuesday night activity."

The horns sounded closer. Too close.

"They're pushing us toward the old market square." Sarnyx observed, her blade already drawn as she ran.

A killing ground. Open space, nowhere to hide, perfect for the Hunt's mounted charge.

"Then we don't go there," Elle said, and without warning, she veered left into the thick undergrowth.

The crew followed without hesitation—we were learning to trust her instincts. The Root whispered to her in ways none of us fully understood, and right now, those whispers were keeping us alive.

But the Hunt adapted. They always did.

The shadows ahead of us erupted.

Shadow riders materialized from nothing. Their mounts were creatures of smoke and stolen starlight, shifting forms that hurt to look at directly. The hounds came with them, all teeth and hunger, circling us with predatory patience.

We'd run straight into their trap anyway.

"Back to back!" I commanded, and the crew formed a defensive circle instinctively.

Elle pressed against my side, and the contact sent power crackling through both of us. After what had happened in that alley—the claiming, the confession, the way we'd finally stopped pretending—every touch felt charged with possibility and danger.

"So much for one night of peace," Elle muttered.

"Peace was never an option," I replied, corruption already spreading from my marks like veins of darkness.

"Shocking," Peeble chimed in, their metallic voice dripping with sarcasm. "The brooding murder prince doesn't believe in peace. Someone alert the press."

The Hunt's leader spoke, and its voice resonated through the air itself, ancient and absolute.

"The Convergence approaches. The human carries what was never meant for mortal hands. Surrender her now, and the rest may flee. Resist, and we take her by force. Either way, she comes with us. She will not be allowed to choose again."

"Over my dead body," Elle shot back, her marks blazing in response.

The Hunt attacked.

Three riders broke formation, all targeting Elle. They could sense what she carried—Root magic that no human should possess, power that called to them like a beacon.

Sarnyx had her blade out before I could even shout commands, the steel singing as she carved through a hound that materialized from the shadows. Vashael's fingers danced, releasing pollen that bloomed into golden clouds, creating illusions that sent Hunt riders crashing into trees as they chased phantoms through the darkness. Even Nimor, still unstable from the Star Veil's effects, managed to phase partially into mist, making himself a harder target as he darted between the twisted trunks.

But it was Elle who truly answered their violence.

She stood at the center of our formation, and the Root sang through her. Not the hesitant power she'd been learning to control, but something ancient and terrible and beautiful. The forest floor erupted with growth— vines and roots bursting from the earth, already there and just now choosing to manifest. They formed barriers of thorn and bark that even the Hunt's supernatural mounts couldn't penetrate, protecting our flanks as we fought.

"Holy shit," Peeble buzzed from somewhere above, dodging a shadow-hound's leap with nimble aerial maneuvers. "When did you learn to do that? Because last week you could barely make a flower bloom without passing out!"

She didn't answer because three more riders were already closing in, weaving between the twisted trees that lined the path.

I intercepted the lead rider with violence that would have horrified me once.

My corruption slammed into the rider mid-charge. Rot spread across its body in seconds—skin blackening, armor flaking away like ash. Its scream cut off as the decay reached its throat. The mount underneath dissolved into wisps of shadow that scattered on the wind.

Elle's power erupted beside me again. The forest floor responded to her will, roots bursting from the earth to strike and protect. She caught a Hunt hound mid-leap, vines wrapping around it and squeezing until it dissolved into shadow and regret.

Bryx had transformed into something massive and terrifying—a beetle the size of a small house, wreathed in bioluminescent fury. He barreled through three riders at once, his chittering war cry echoing through the twisted woods. Kevin, full-sized now and buzzing with rage, dove at the Hunt's flanks with his stinger extended.

Nimor flickered in and out of visibility, using his unstable form as an advantage. He couldn't maintain solidity long enough to strike effectively, but he could distract, confuse, make the Hunt chase shadows through the darkness.The Sage stayed close to Nimor, their steady presence somehow keeping him more solid, more present.

Vashael's pollen clouds created dozens of illusory copies of our crew. The Hunt wheeled in confusion, striking at phantoms while the real us repositioned among the trees.

Eltrien moved through the chaos like he knew where every rider would be before they arrived, his mycelial markings pulsing as he guided crew members away from danger with uncanny precision.

But there were too many. For every rider we destroyed, two more materialized from the shadows.

"We need cover!" Sarnyx shouted, her blade carving through another hound.

"Working on it!" Elle replied, and I felt her pulling deeper into the Root's power than ever before.

What happened next shouldn't have been possible.

Elle didn't just grow new trees—she made trees that had somehow always been there. Ancient oaks with thick trunks and deep roots appeared around us. The open market square we'd been herded toward transformed into a dense grove in seconds.

"That's new," I observed.

"I'm improvising!" she shot back, sweat streaming down her face.

Through our bond, I felt the cost—she was burning through energy too fast. The Root's power wasn't meant to bend reality like this.

A rider got past our defenses, its blade aimed at Elle's heart. I moved without thinking, my hand shooting out to catch the blade bare-handed. It should have severed my fingers.

Instead, my corruption destroyed it. Not just broke it—erased it. The blade flickered like a dying candle, then vanished completely.

The rider stared at its empty hand, and in that moment of confusion, Elle struck. Vines erupted from its chest—not piercing through but growing from inside it. The rider screamed as it transformed, becoming a twisted tree of shadow and pale light.

Elle stumbled, and I caught her arm. The moment we touched, power exploded between us—my corruption and her Root-force not fighting but working together. Where our magic combined, reality started bending.

The remaining Hunt riders hesitated. These beings that never showed fear—they paused.

"Don't let go," Elle gasped, gripping my hand tighter.

We moved together without speaking. Our joined power spread outward in waves. Hunt riders caught in it didn't just die—they changed. Some became shadow-trees. Others dissolved into flowers. One hound transformed into a fountain that sang in voices that made my ears ache.

Around us, the forest path looked distorted now. Trees flickered between green and bare. The ground shifted from moss to stone and back. The air tasted strange.

But more riders kept coming.

Elle and I ended up back to back in the center of the fight.

We moved in sync. Her Root-power and my corruption flowed out in opposite directions. Where they met, something new formed—something that defied nature.

Through our bond, I felt Elle's mind expanding to hold power that should have killed her. She was channeling forces older than time itself. And she was doing it with the same stubborn defiance she'd shown when she first fell into Wynmire, covered in dirt and pissed off.

She was incredible. And she was mine.

The possessive thought should have bothered me. Instead, it kept me grounded, kept my corruption from consuming everything.

"Keep going," Elle said through gritted teeth, and I felt her hand find mine, our fingers lacing together.

Again, when our palms touched, the bond erupted. Power flowed both ways—my darkness giving her light something to push against. We became one weapon, impossible and deadly.

The remaining riders pulled back. These beings that had never known fear—they retreated, melting back into the shadows, leaving destruction behind.

The forest path was destroyed. Trees were split and transformed, the ground torn up. What had been a simple trail now looked like a battlefield where reality itself had fought. The transformed Hunt riders stood frozen—shadow trees, strange flowers, singing fountains.

Elle and I still stood back-to-back, hands clasped, power fading but not gone. Through the bond, I felt her exhaustion, her horror at what we'd done.

"We did that," she whispered.

"Yes."

She turned to face me, eyes wide with fear and lingering power. "Kaelren, what we just did... that wasn't natural."

"No," I agreed. "We changed them into something unnatural."

"But it saved us."

"Did it?" I looked at the transformed riders, the impossible trees. "We didn't save anyone. We just remade them into something else. Something that shouldn't exist."

She pulled her hand from mine, and the loss felt like part of me had been ripped away. "Is that what we are? Something that shouldn't exist?"

Before I could answer, Vashael approached, golden skin splattered with blood. "We need to move. Now. The Hunt doesn't retreat—they regroup. Next time will be worse."

Nimor flickered into view, barely holding his shape. "There's a safe house. Three miles north. Old Root-cult monastery. The Hunt won't follow us there."

"Why not?" Elle asked.

"Because," Eltrien said quietly, stepping forward with the Sage beside him, "it's where you died in iteration fifteen. Even the Hunt respects cursed ground like that."

Everyone stared at him.

"What?" He blinked, genuinely confused. "Did I say that out loud? I meant... it's warded. Very strongly warded."

I grabbed his throat, lifting him off the ground. "What aren't you telling us?"

"Everything," he wheezed, completely calm. "But right now, Elle needs somewhere safe to process what just happened. Look at her."

I looked. Elle's marks were pulsing erratically. Reality around her was unstable—flowers grew from her footprints, died, then grew again. Her hair floated like she was underwater. Her eyes kept changing colors.

"She's hitting the second threshold," Eltrien continued despite my grip on his throat. "Your combined powers accelerated it. The first threshold was choosing to accept the power. This one... this is where she becomes something more than human. If we don't get her somewhere with proper Root-resonance to anchor her through the transition, she might not survive it."

"Don't say it," I snarled, dropping him.

"I warned you all there would be more thresholds," the Sage interrupted. "Each one takes more of her humanity. This one's happening faster because of what you two just did together."

Elle laughed, sharp and bitter. "Great. So I'm not just destabilizing—I'm transforming again?"

"The second threshold is always the hardest," the Sage said, stepping forward with unusual gravity. "This second transformation is surrender. You must let go of what you were to become what you're meant to be."

"That's not ominous at all," Elle muttered.

"Only if we don't move," Vashael said urgently. "Kael, she needs—"

"I know what she needs." I moved closer to Elle but kept my hands at my sides. Through the bond, I could feel her unraveling, her existence becoming uncertain. Every instinct screamed at me to grab her, to anchor her like I had during the battle. But I could also feel how unstable she was—one wrong touch might shatter her completely.

It was killing me, standing this close without touching her. My marks burned with the need to connect, to claim, to protect. But I wouldn't risk breaking her.

"Elle, look at me," I commanded.

She did, and I saw multiple versions of her reflected in her eyes—like looking at her through broken glass where each piece showed something different.

"I don't know what's happening," I admitted. "But we'll figure it out. Together. Right now, just focus on me. On my voice. Stay with me."

"Which me?" she asked, and her voice echoed strangely. "I can feel different versions. Different choices. Like I'm being pulled in multiple directions at once."

"Choose this one," I said. "Choose the Elle standing in this destroyed forest, covered in dirt and flowers, who just helped me fight the Wild Hunt. Choose her."

She focused on me, and gradually, the other versions faded. Reality solidified around her again, though flowers still bloomed where she stood.

"You're becoming something I never could," I admitted. "Human enough to choose. Powerful enough for it to matter."

"That terrifies you," she observed.

"Yes."

"Good." She swayed, exhaustion hitting her. "Because it terrifies me too."

I caught her as she stumbled, and the contact sent shockwaves through both of us. But I didn't let go.

"The safe house," I ordered the others. "Now."

"Safe house?" Peeble landed on Elle's shoulder, wings twitching. "You mean that creepy monastery that looks like it eats people? Great. Love that for us."

As we fled the destroyed forest, leaving impossible trees and strange flowers behind, I played what the Hunt's leader said one more time:

"She will choose. And this time, her choice will break everything differently."

I didn't know what that meant.

But I was starting to suspect we were about to find out.

17

Elle

The monastery clung to the hillside like a wound that refused to heal—all twisted spires and warped buttresses that defied every natural law. This wasn't architecture. This was what happened when desperation carved shelter from tortured wood and neither the tree nor the blade survived intact.

"Root-cult buildings aren't built," the Sage explained as we approached, their voice carrying an unusual reverence. "They're grown. Coaxed. Pleaded with. The ancient cultists would spend years in communion with a single tree, convincing it to reshape itself into shelter. This one..." They paused, studying the structure with critical eyes. "This one was grown during the Fracture War, when there wasn't time for patience. You can see where they forced it."

They were right. The walls curved where they should corner, bulging like scar tissue. Windows sat at stomach-turning angles, their frames twisted as if the wood had been screaming when it solidified. And the door—gods, the door was definitely breathing, expanding and contracting in a slow, wet rhythm that made my skin crawl.

"Charming," I muttered, still feeling disconnected from my own body after whatever had happened in the forest. "Very 'abandoned horror chapel' aesthetic."

"It's safe," Nimor insisted, though his form flickered worse than ever—

sometimes solid, sometimes just an outline of where a person should be. The fight had cost him. Cost all of us. "The Root-cults used places like this for meditation and communion with the deepest powers. The resonance should help stabilize you. Hopefully stabilize us both."

"Should?"

"Will." Kaelren's voice cut through the doubt with absolute certainty. No question, no comfort—just cold fact delivered like a blade. His hand still gripped my arm like I was something he'd claimed and had no intention of releasing. "It will help."

Peeble buzzed near my ear, wings producing an anxious hum I'd learned meant genuine worry. "Famous last words. 'The creepy breathing building will definitely help and not turn you into fertilizer.'"

Kaelren hadn't let go of my arm since catching me at the battle site. His touch was the only thing keeping me anchored, keeping me from dissolving into all those other versions of myself. Through our bond, I felt his determination like iron. He would not let me fade. It wasn't a choice—it was a certainty he'd decided and would enforce with violence if necessary.

"The Fracture War," Eltrien said quietly, running his fingers along the warped doorframe with something like grief. "This monastery was a healing house. The Root-cultists took in soldiers from both sides—Bloom-touched and Root-marked alike. They tried to prove that the two powers could coexist, could heal together." His mycelial markings pulsed softly. "Three hundred cultists died when the Crown discovered what they were doing. Burned them alive inside their own sanctuary."

"Wait," I said, the term catching in my mind. "What does Bloom-touched mean? I know what Root-marked is—" I gestured at the golden veins spreading under my skin, "—obviously. But I don't understand the other thing you're talking about."

Kaelren's jaw tightened, and through our bond I felt something dark and bitter rise to the surface. "The Bloom lives in the Heartspire. Guarded by the Crown. Controlled by the Crown."

"Controlled?"

"Originally, the Bloom was created as a semblance of balance," he continued, his voice flat with old anger. "A counterweight to the Root's wild power. But the Crown learned that if they could bind with it, they could control elements of the Root itself. Use it. Shape it. Corrupt it." His carved marks pulsed darker. "That binding shifted the balance of everything. Created the rot you've seen spreading through Wynmire. The Crown's precious control is killing the realm piece by piece."

"Delightful history," Bryx muttered, though for once his mandibles weren't clicking with amusement—just nervous energy that set my teeth on edge. Even he looked shaken, still steaming from his combat transformation.

"The wood remembers," Vashael added, pressing her palm against the breathing door. "That's why it looks like this. Every twist, every wrong angle—that's pain given form. The trees were trying to protect the people inside when the fire came. They failed, but they never stopped trying. That's why places like this are safe. The wood knows betrayal. It won't allow it again."

The door opened without us touching it, exhaling warm air that smelled of earth and old grief.

Inside, the monastery was worse. Better. Both.

The walls were definitely breathing—I could see them expand and contract, see veins of pale sap pulsing beneath translucent bark. But it was oddly soothing, like being inside something alive and benign. Something that had survived unimaginable trauma and chosen kindness anyway.

Phosphorescent moss carpeted the walls in constellations of light, shifting between jade and bronze. The floor was soft beneath our feet—not carpet but living wood that had chosen to be gentle, that cushioned each step like it understood how badly we hurt.

In the center of the main chamber, a massive tree grew up through the floor and out through the ceiling. Its trunk was thick as a house, bark silver-white and covered in carved names. Hundreds of them. Thousands.

"The Witness Tree," the Sage said softly, approaching it with unusual reverence. "Every person who died here during the burning—the cultists carved their names before the end. So someone would remember. So their choice to heal rather than harm would mean something."

I moved closer, drawn by something I couldn't name. The carvings were beautiful—not just names but tiny scenes. A cultist holding the hand of a dying soldier. Two enemies sharing bread. A child being born during the siege. Moments of grace in the middle of horror.

"Meira of the Copper Grove," I read aloud, tracing one carving. "Healed fourteen before the smoke took her."

"Zoltin Rootwalker," Kaelren added, his voice rougher than usual. "Gave his life force to keep the flames back for three more minutes. Saved twenty children."

Through our bond, I felt his grief—not for strangers dead three centuries ago, but for the proof that good people could try everything and still fail. That sacrifice didn't guarantee salvation. That sometimes, the world just burned anyway.

In the heavy weight of the silence, the others dispersed to explore, but there was none of the usual banter. Even Bryx was quiet as he collapsed in a corner, still steaming from his transformation, Kevin curled protectively on his chest.

Eltrien took Nimor aside, guiding him to sit against the Witness Tree. His mycelial markings glowed brighter as he placed both hands on Nimor's chest, threads of light spreading from his fingers into Nimor's unstable form.

"This is going to hurt," Eltrien warned.

"Everything hurts," Nimor replied, his voice echoing strangely. "Do it."

The light intensified, and Nimor screamed—a sound that rippled through multiple dimensions at once. But when it faded, he was solid. Fully solid. More present than I'd seen him since the Star Veil.

"Thank you," Nimor gasped, tears streaming down his now-visible face. "Gods, thank you. I thought I was going to disappear completely."

"You almost did," Eltrien said quietly. "The Hunt's touch destabilizes everything it marks. I've bought you time, but you need to be careful. No more phasing for at least five days, or you might not come back."

Watching them, I realized how little I actually knew about my companions.

Nimor, who'd been slowly disappearing and said nothing. Eltrien, whose mycelial marks pulsed with power I didn't understand and who sometimes spoke in riddles that felt like warnings. Bryx, whose humor hid genuine fear. Sarnyx, who guarded us all with a loyalty she'd never explain. Vashael, who'd murdered her way to freedom and now fought to protect ours.

They weren't just placeholders in my story. They were people with their own traumas, their own reasons for being here in this breathing building full of ghosts.

"We should tell stories," Bryx said suddenly, still lying on his back. Kevin buzzed indignantly on his chest, clearly annoyed at being used as a pillow. "Something to remind us we're still alive. Otherwise, Kevin here is going to keep judging my life choices with his tiny bee eyes."

"That's surprisingly thoughtful," Sarnyx said.

"I contain multitudes," Bryx replied. "Shallow, panic-driven multitudes, but multitudes nonetheless."

I hadn't expected Kaelren to stay. Honestly, I'd half-expected him to disappear into the shadows or find some broody corner to lurk in while glowering at potential threats. Instead, he stayed close, his presence a steady warmth at my side, his hand occasionally brushing mine like he needed to confirm I was still solid.

The others shared their stories—Nimor talked about the shadow-weavers who'd raised him before the Crown wiped them out. Even Sarnyx spoke, though her tale was brief.

"I'll tell you how I met the brooding prince here," Sarnyx said, settling against the wall with her usual predatory grace. "I was on a scouting mission for my village. Tracking a Crown transport that was supposed to deliver supplies to us—food, medicine, things we desperately needed. The shipment was a week late, and we were starting to starve."

She smiled, sharp and dangerous. "Then I found someone robbing it. This arrogant bastard in a cloak, loading goods onto his own transport like he owned them. Those were *our* supplies. My people's supplies. So I attacked him."

"You gave me a black eye," Kaelren said dryly.

"Almost took your head off," Sarnyx corrected. "Would have, too, if you weren't so damn fast. We fought for twenty minutes before he finally pinned me. I was waiting for the killing blow—figured I'd die trying to save my village. Instead, he explained who he was. A rebel. Someone fighting against the Crown that had been stealing from us for years."

"She's been my second ever since," Kaelren finished. "Best decision I ever made, even if she did nearly cave in my skull."

"Your turn," Bryx said, looking at me after the laughter died down. "Tell us about your grandmother. The one who started all this."

I hadn't planned to. I sat there trying to control my breathing, willing the tears to not break through at the thought of how much I missed her. But surrounded by their stories, by their trust, the words came anyway.

"She used to garden in the moonlight," I began. "My grandmother. She'd wait until after midnight, when the neighbors were asleep, and she'd go out in her nightgown with this old trowel and just... talk to the plants. Like they were people."

"Did they talk back?" Bryx asked, genuinely curious for once.

"I thought she was losing it," I admitted. "Grief does that, right? Makes you a little unhinged. But now..." I gestured at my glowing marks. "Now I wonder if she heard them the same way I do. If she knew what I'd become."

"She knew," the Sage said softly. "Josephine knew exactly what you'd inherit. Why do you think she ran away from this world?"

"And yet you're here anyway," Kaelren observed. "Destiny, or just bad luck?"

"Maybe both," Peeble chimed in from my shoulder. "Though if we're ranking bad luck, Elle's really cornered the market. Falls into murder realm, immediately gets marked for cosmic doom, finds the one guy in Wynmire who's emotionally constipated—"

"I'm not emotionally constipated," Kaelren said flatly.

"You're seventy percent repression and thirty percent murder instinct wrapped in a very attractive package of doom."

"That's not—" He paused. "Actually, that's depressingly accurate."

Everyone laughed, even Sarnyx, and the sound echoed warmly off the breathing walls.

"Your turn, murder prince," Bryx said, gesturing at Kaelren. "Tell us something we don't know. Something that doesn't involve you being terrifying."

"I'm always terrifying."

"Try anyway."

Kaelren was quiet for a long moment, his hand still wrapped around mine. Through our bond, I felt him weighing what to share, testing the words before speaking them.

"I had a brother," he finally said, his voice colder than before—distance as armor. "Before the marks. Before everything went to hell."

The room went silent. Even Peeble stopped buzzing.

"Older or younger?" I asked gently.

"Younger. By two years." Kaelren's jaw tightened, but his voice remained flat, emotionless. "Therin. He was everything I wasn't. Warm. Easy to love. The kind of person who made things better just by existing in the same room."

"What happened to him?" Nimor asked, though his tone suggested he already knew the answer wouldn't be good.

"The marks happened," Kaelren said simply. "When I tried to take the power, when I carved these into my skin, the corruption didn't just affect me. It spread. Therin tried to stop me, grabbed my arm right as I completed the final mark." His free hand moved to his carved marks, tracing them without expression. "The corruption jumped to him. Instantly. Ate through him in seconds—not slowly like it's doing to me, but fast. Violent. He screamed once. Then he was gone."

Through the bond I felt the chasm of grief beneath the words, but his face revealed nothing.

"That's why you're so desperate to fix this," Eltrien said quietly. "Not just for yourself. For him."

"I made him a promise," Kaelren replied. "That I'd make the marks work. That his death wouldn't be meaningless. Every day I fail is another day I've broken that promise. Another day he stays dead for nothing."

I squeezed his hand, not knowing what else to offer.

"Well this took a dark turn," Peeble said after a moment, their voice uncharacteristically subdued. "Anyone want to hear about the time I accidentally started a war between two hives by insulting both queens' honey-making techniques?"

There was a collective groan from the group, but that didn't deter the overly eccentric beetle.

Peeble launched into an elaborate tale involving diplomatic honey, very offended queen bees, and what they called "the Great Pollination Incident." It was completely ridiculous, probably half-fabricated, and exactly what we needed.

The stories continued flowing—lighter now, safer. Bryx described the dryad who'd chased him through half a dozen territories in increasingly creative attempts at seduction. Sarnyx told about a hunt that had ended with her prey outsmarting her so thoroughly she'd recruited them instead. Even Nimor shared about his first attempt at shadow-walking, which had resulted in him getting stuck halfway between states for a week.

I felt myself relaxing, the tension from the battle finally starting to unwind. The Root-resonance of the monastery thrummed through me, steady and soothing. My marks had settled to a gentle amber glow, no longer threatening to tear me apart.

"Elle's falling asleep," Vashael observed with a smile.

I tried to protest, but a yawn ambushed me. "No, I'm fine. Keep going."

"You're barely upright." Kaelren's voice wasn't gentle. "You need actual rest."

"But…"

"Sleep, child. You've earned it," the Sage assured me.

My eyes were already closing. Through the pleasant haze of exhaustion, I felt Kaelren shift beside me. Then strong arms slid under my knees and back, lifting me as easily as if I weighed nothing.

"I can walk," I mumbled against his chest, though I made no move to prove it.

"You can barely stand," he replied with slight amusement in his voice.

"Stop arguing."

He carried me through the monastery, his footsteps soft on the living floor. I felt him navigate turns, felt the air change as we entered a different chamber. Warmer here. Quieter.

Then I was being lowered onto something impossibly soft—moss, I thought distantly, or maybe the wood had simply chosen to be gentle. A blanket settled over me, smelling faintly of pine and that particular scent that was just Kaelren.

"Stay," I whispered, not quite awake enough to be embarrassed.

"I wasn't planning on leaving," he said, and I felt him settle beside me, close enough that I could feel his warmth.

The last thing I registered before sleep claimed me completely was his hand finding mine in the darkness, our fingers interlacing, the bond between us humming softly.

Safe. For now, I was safe.

I stood in a garden stitched together from pure magic.

But calling it a garden was like calling the ocean a puddle. This was Wynmire distilled to its purest essence—every impossible wonder, every breathtaking beauty, every magical absurdity concentrated into a dreamscape that made my chest ache with how magnificent it was.

The trees weren't just trees—they were living sculptures of light and shadow, their trunks spiraling upward in impossible helices. Their leaves weren't green but every color imaginable, shifting and shimmering like oil on water. Some branches grew downward, their roots reaching for the sky. Others simply floated, untethered by anything as mundane as physics.

Streams that resembled flowing honey mixed with morning dew cut through pathways of petrified flowers, their movement thrumming like roots seeking water. Fish made of pure luminescence swam upstream, leaving trails of phosphorescence in their wake. And above—gods, above— the sky was a kaleidoscope of every sunset and sunrise that had ever existed, layered over each other in impossible beauty.

"We really need to stop meeting like this," Kaelren's voice came from behind me, and I could hear the dark amusement in it. "People will talk."

I turned, and he was... different. The weight of his failures momentarily lifted. His carved marks glowed with silver-blue light instead of their usual corruption-black, and his eyes—his eyes were actually warm.

"Let them talk," I shot back, grinning. "Besides, this is my dream. I can do whatever I want."

"Our dream," he corrected, stepping closer. He was dressed in something that looked like raven feathers woven seamlessly together, practical but somehow elegant. "You pulled me here. Just like you pulled the monastery's resonance to stabilize yourself. You're getting stronger."

"Did I?" I looked down and realized I was wearing a dress made of living flowers—petals that bloomed and shifted with each breath, vines that wrapped around my waist like a belt. "Huh. Subconscious fashion choices."

"It suits you." His eyes traveled over me with an intensity that made my skin warm. "Very 'forest deity who could destroy you but might kiss you instead.'"

"That's specific."

"I'm a man of specific tastes."

Before I could respond, something bright blue zoomed past my head, leaving a trail of glittering dust. I turned to see a dragonfly the size of a cat hovering nearby, its wings creating miniature rainbows with each beat.

"Okay, that's adorable," I said.

"Wait until you see the rest." Kaelren held out his hand. "Come on. If we're going to be trapped in a magical fever dream, we might as well enjoy it."

I took his hand, and the moment our fingers touched, the world shifted.

We were standing on the edge of a clearing filled with mushrooms—not the normal kind, but massive toadstools the size of houses, glowing with bioluminescent patterns that pulsed like heartbeats. Some were as tall as trees, their caps broad enough to use as platforms. Others clustered in groups, creating natural steps and ramps between levels.

"No," I said, immediately understanding what he was suggesting. "Absolutely not."

"Absolutely yes." He was already grinning, that rare expression that transformed his entire face. "When's the next time you'll get to jump on magical mushrooms in a dream?"

"This is ridiculous."

"This is perfect." He tugged my hand, pulling me toward the nearest mushroom. "Trust me."

Before I could protest further, he stepped onto the mushroom's cap. It compressed slightly under his weight, then launched him upward with a springing sound that was somehow both musical and hilarious. He flipped in the air—showing off—and landed on a higher mushroom, which sent him bouncing to another.

"Your turn!" he called down, grinning.

I couldn't help it—I smiled too. Then I ran and jumped.

The mushroom caught me with a bounce that sent me soaring. My stomach dropped in that wonderful way of freefall, and then I was flying, the wind rushing through my hair as I arced through the air. I landed on another mushroom with a giggle that surprised me.

"This is insane!" I shouted, bouncing to the next one.

"This is Wynmire!" Kaelren bounced past me, graceful as a cat. "Everything's insane!"

We bounced from mushroom to mushroom, the bioluminescence leaving trails of light in the air. Each landing sent up puffs of glowing spores that tasted like lavender and sweet wine. I found myself doing flips, trying increasingly ridiculous aerial maneuvers just to make Kaelren laugh—and gods, when he laughed, really laughed, it was like the sun breaking through clouds.

"Catch me!" I called, launching myself from a particularly tall mushroom toward him.

He did, arms wrapping around me as we both landed on a mushroom together. The momentum sent us bouncing higher, tangled together, laughing so hard we could barely breathe. When we finally landed on solid ground, we were both glowing with spore-dust and grinning like idiots.

"That was—" I started.

"Amazing," he finished, still holding me. "You're amazing."

The clearing around us shifted, reality bleeding into something new.

Now we stood at the edge of a vast meadow that stretched to a horizon made of dreams. The grass wasn't green—it was every color of the rainbow, each blade a different hue that shifted when the wind touched it. And the creatures...

"Oh my gods," I breathed.

The meadow was alive with impossible animals. Deer made of porcelain and pearl pranced past, their antlers branching into trees that bloomed with tiny stars. Rabbits with butterfly wings hopped between flowers that were larger than they were. A fox with four tails watched us with knowing eyes.

Overhead, sprites danced in spirals—tiny beings of pure light that left trails of laughter in the air. They wove between each other in patterns that made my throat tight with wonder, their joy so palpable I could taste it.

"It's like every fairytale I ever read as a kid," I said, unable to look away. "Every magical creature, all in one place."

"This is the Wynmire I grew up knowing," Kaelren said softly, and there was something raw in his voice. "Before all the rot and corruption. This is everything I hoped I could show you." He turned to me, and his expression was more open than I'd ever seen it. "I don't know how much longer we have in this dream, but I have one more place I would like you to see before this is over."

A unicorn approached us—not the white horse kind, but something stranger and more wonderful. It had the body of a stag, scales instead of fur that reflected light like opals, and a spiral horn that seemed to be made of frozen lightning. It lowered its head to me in a gesture that felt like a blessing, and when I touched its nose, I felt the entire realm pulse through my fingertips.

My breath caught in my throat. This wasn't just a dream—this was

Kaelren showing me what he was fighting for. What he'd lost. What he wanted to protect.

"Thank you," I whispered, not sure if I was thanking the unicorn or him.

The unicorn dissolved into mist that spiraled upward, joining the dancing sprites.

Kaelren took my hand again. "Come on."

The meadow faded, and we were walking through a forest of giant ferns and flowering vines. The air here was thick with perfume and possibility, warm and humid in a way that made my skin tingle. I could hear water rushing nearby, growing louder with each step.

We emerged into a hidden grotto, and I stopped breathing.

A waterfall poured down from heights I couldn't see, but it wasn't made of water. Light fell instead—actual light that flowed and splashed, ranging from ghost-pale where it was thin to deep bronze where it thickened. When it struck the pool below, the collision produced music: clear ringing tones that traveled through the ground and into my bones. The pool's surface remained smooth as glass everywhere except where the falls disturbed it, and when I looked into that mirror-stillness, I didn't see my reflection. I saw other things: moments that hadn't happened yet, scenes from different choices, glimpses of paths not taken.

Around the edges of the pool, impossible plants took root in the moss-covered stone. Flowers opened petals made of actual flame—red and orange and blue—that gave off warmth but left nothing scorched when I brushed against them. Vines climbed the rocks, heavy with fruit that wasn't quite solid: translucent spheres that chimed when they knocked together, each one holding what looked like captured giggles frozen mid-sound. Lily pads broad as dining tables drifted across the surface, and perched on them were tiny people no bigger than my thumb. They had dragonfly wings that blurred with movement and faces that were fully formed—sharp little grins and knowing eyes that tracked my every move with obvious amusement.

"It's perfect," I breathed.

"It's ours," Kaelren said. "For tonight, at least."

Then, without warning, he pulled his shirt over his head and tossed it

186

aside.

I forgot how to breathe.

I'd felt his body before—through combat, through the bond, through stolen moments of closeness. But seeing him like this, in the dream-light of this impossible place, was something else entirely.

His torso was a canvas of controlled violence. Lean muscle carved sharp lines across his chest and abdomen, the kind of build that came from years of fighting. His carved marks continued down from his face and neck, spreading across his shoulders and chest in intricate patterns that seemed to pulse with their own light here in the dream. They should have been ugly—self-inflicted scars born of desperation. Instead, they were mesmerizing, like watching lightning frozen in skin.

But it wasn't just the marks or the muscle that made my mouth go dry. It was the scars. So many scars. Some thin and precise—knife wounds. Others jagged and brutal—claws, perhaps, or worse. A few looked like burns, twisted tissue that had healed wrong. Each one was a story of survival, of a man who'd been broken and refused to stay that way.

"You're staring," he said, and there was dark satisfaction in his voice.

"You knew I would," I managed.

"I hoped you would." He moved to the edge of the pool, the light catching on his skin. "Are you coming, or are you going to keep pretending you don't want to?"

It wasn't a request. It was a challenge.

My flower dress dissolved at a thought, and I was grateful for dream-logic that let me skip the awkward process of undressing. His eyes tracked over me with the same hunger I'd felt looking at him, but he didn't move closer—just waited at the water's edge like a predator giving prey one last chance to run.

I didn't run.

I walked to the pool's edge, and without giving myself time to second-guess, I dove in.

The water—if it could be called water—was perfect. Warm but not hot, with a texture like satin against my skin. It seemed to hum with the same magic that filled everything in this dreamscape, making every nerve ending sing with sensation.

I surfaced to find Kaelren already in the water beside me, droplets of liquid sliding down his chest and catching in the hollows of his collarbones. His hair was slicked back, making the sharp angles of his face even more pronounced.

"Show off," I said.

"You dove in first," he pointed out, moving closer. "What does that make you?"

"Impulsive?"

"Brave." His hand found my waist under the water, pulling me closer. "Or reckless. I haven't decided which I prefer."

We swam together, and it was easy—playful even. He showed me how the mystical water responded to movement, creating patterns and ripples that sang different notes depending on how you disturbed them. I splashed him, and he retaliated by pulling me under briefly, both of us emerging laughing.

This was Kaelren without the weight of failure, without the corruption eating him alive. This was who he might have been if the world hadn't broken him.

"There's something behind the waterfall," he said after a while, nodding toward the cascade of light. "Want to see?"

I did.

We swam toward it, the current creating resistance that made us work for it. But then we were through, behind the curtain of radiance, in a hidden alcove where the sound of the waterfall created a cocoon of privacy.

The alcove was lined with moss that glowed softly, providing gentle light. The air was thick with mist that tasted like magic and promises. And the way Kaelren was looking at me—like I was something he wanted to devour and worship in equal measure—made every nerve in my body light up with anticipation.

"Elle," he said, and my name in his mouth sounded like a prayer and a threat.

"Kaelren," I replied, moving closer.

He caught me before I could close the distance, one hand fisting in my wet hair, tilting my head back. "I need you to understand something."

"What?"

"This might be a dream, but what I want to do to you?" His voice dropped lower, intimate and dark. "That's real. And when we wake up, when we're back in the waking world, I'm going to make every moment of this a reality. Do you understand?"

I could barely breathe. "Yes."

"Good." He released me, stepping back. "Now, I'm going to show you exactly what I've been thinking about since the first time you challenged me in that forest."

Wisteria vines erupted from the moss-covered walls—vibrant purple blossoms releasing a heady scent that made my head spin. They moved with purpose, wrapping gently but firmly around my wrists, my ankles, lifting me out of the water and slightly off the ground until I was suspended in the alcove, spread bare before him.

"Kaelren—"

"No," he said, his voice hard. "Words are done. From now on, the only things I want to hear are the sounds you make when you lose control and scream my name. Understood?"

I nodded, my heart pounding so hard I could feel it in my throat.

"Good girl."

He moved to sit on a moss-covered ledge, deliberately putting distance between us. His eyes roamed over me with possessive hunger, taking in every detail like he was memorizing the moment.

"Do you know what I thought the first time I saw you?" he asked, his voice conversational but edged with darkness. "I thought you were going to die. That you were too soft, too human, too unprepared for this world. I thought I'd have to watch you break."

More vines emerged, these ones thin and delicate, beginning to trace patterns across my skin. They moved like living things—curious, exploratory, maddeningly gentle.

"But you didn't break," he continued. "You fought. You adapted. You

189

challenged me at every turn. And gods, Elle, do you have any idea how much that made me want you?"

A vine circled my breast, squeezing gently, and I couldn't stop the gasp that escaped.

"That's it," he said, his voice rough with approval. "I want to hear every sound you make. Every gasp, every moan, every desperate plea when you need more."

The vines continued their exploration. Some traced patterns across my stomach, my thighs, leaving trails of tingling sensation. Others were more direct—one wrapping around my other breast, squeezing in rhythm with the first. The sensation was maddening, too gentle and too much all at once.

"When we do this for real," Kaelren said, and I watched his hand move to stroke himself slowly, "I'm going to take my time. I'm going to taste every inch of you, learn what makes you tremble, what makes you beg."

Venus fly traps bloomed into existence, smaller than their mundane counterparts but no less fascinating. They attached themselves to my nipples with gentle pressure that made me cry out—not quite pain, but intense sensation that bordered on overwhelming.

"Fuck," I gasped, and he smiled—dark and satisfied.

"You like that?" He stroked himself faster, his eyes never leaving me. "You like being at my mercy, spread out for me to watch?"

"Yes," I admitted, past the point of pride.

"Yes, what?"

"Yes, I like it. I like—" I broke off as a vine slid between my thighs, not entering but teasing, sliding through the wetness that had nothing to do with the pool. "Oh gods—"

"Not gods," he corrected. "Me. I'm the one doing this to you. Making you shake, making you wet, making you desperate."

He was right. The vine between my legs continued its maddening exploration, sliding through my folds with deliberate slowness. Another joined it, this one focusing entirely on my clit with small, pulsing movements that made me whimper.

"That's better," Kaelren said, his breathing heavier now. "Keep making those sounds. I want to know exactly how close you are."

I was already close—embarrassingly so. The combination of sensations, of being watched, of his dark promises about what he'd do when this was real, was pushing me toward the edge faster than I'd thought possible.

A thicker vine pressed against my entrance, not demanding but offering. When I tried to shift my hips, tried to take it inside, it pulled back teasingly.

"Please," I begged, pride completely abandoned.

"Please what?" His hand moved faster on himself, and I could see how close he was too—muscles tense, jaw clenched. "Tell me exactly what you want."

"I want you inside me. I want—"

The vine thrust in, and I screamed.

"That's my good girl," Kaelren groaned. "Taking it so well. Looking so perfect spread out, desperate and dripping for me."

The vine began to move—slow, deep strokes that made me shake in my bonds. The one on my clit intensified its rhythm, and the venus fly traps pulsed in time with the thrusts. It was too much, too intense, too perfect.

"When I fuck you for real," Kaelren growled, his control fraying, "I'm going to make you come just like this. Tied up, at my mercy, begging me for more. And I'll give it to you, Elle. I'll give you everything until you can't remember anything but my name."

"Kaelren—" I was right on the edge, every nerve singing.

"Come for me," he commanded. "Now."

I shattered.

The orgasm ripped through me in waves, made more intense by the vines that didn't stop, that carried me through the pleasure until I was sobbing with the intensity of it. Through the haze, I heard Kaelren groan my name, watched him come with his eyes locked on me, claiming me even from a distance.

The vines lowered me gently, releasing their hold but remaining close like a living blanket. Kaelren moved to me immediately, gathering me against his chest, both of us breathing hard.

"When we do this for real," I said against his skin, "I want everything.

No holding back."

"You'll have it," he promised, his voice rough. "All of me. Every dark, corrupted, possessive part. And you're going to love it."

"I already do," I said with absolute certainty.

We stayed tangled together as our breathing slowed, as the alcove filled with softer light.

But then the alcove began to shake.

"What's happening?" I asked as cracks appeared in the moss, as the waterfall's light started to flicker.

"You're waking up," Kaelren said, regret heavy in his voice. "The dream's ending."

"No, wait, I'm not ready—"

"Elle." He cupped my face, forcing me to meet his eyes. "Remember this. Remember that we're possible. That we can be more than destiny's puppets."

"Kaelren—"

The world shattered like glass.

I jolted awake with a gasp, my heart pounding, my body still singing with phantom sensations. I was back in the monastery, lying on soft moss, covered with a blanket that smelled like pine.

And Kaelren was beside me, his hand still clasped in mine, his eyes snapping open at the same moment mine did.

We stared at each other in the dim phosphorescent light, both breathing hard, both knowing without words that we'd shared the same dream.

"That wasn't—" I started.

"Just a dream," he finished, his voice rough. "No. That was something else."

Through our bond, I felt the echo of everything we'd done, everything we'd felt. Real or not, it had changed something between us.

Something we couldn't take back.

And as I looked into his eyes, saw the same hunger and possessive intensity reflected there, I realized I didn't want to take it back.

Whatever came next—convergence, corruption, the weight of seventeen failed iterations—we would face it together.

But first, we had to survive long enough to make that dream a reality.

18

Elle

The dream had changed everything, and the two days since had been an exercise in pretending it hadn't.

We'd left the monastery at dawn—too early, moving with the kind of desperate efficiency that came from needing to outrun both the Hunt and our own thoughts. The crew noticed, of course. How could they not? Kaelren and I orbited each other like binary stars, pulled together by gravity we couldn't control but held apart by the very real danger of what might happen if we touched.

Every accidental brush of hands sent flowers blooming. Every shared glance made reality ripple at the edges. The bond between us thrummed with tension that was equal parts desire and terror—one wrong move and we'd either tear the realm apart or finally, finally give in to what we both wanted.

"You're doing the thing again," Peeble observed from my shoulder as we navigated another narrow forest path.

"What thing?"

"The 'staring at him while pretending you're not staring' thing. Very subtle. Extremely convincing. Nobody suspects a thing."

"I'm not—"

"He's doing it too, by the way. Currently examining the back of your head like it contains the secrets of the universe. Which, given your general situation, it might."

I didn't look back to confirm. I didn't need to—I could feel his attention like heat between my shoulder blades, could sense through our bond that he was remembering exactly what I was remembering. The waterfall. The vines. The promises we'd made.

"This is torture," I muttered.

"Welcome to sexual tension," Peeble said cheerfully. "Population: you two idiots who can't touch without potentially destroying reality. Sad trombone noise."

The worst part was that everything reminded me of the dream. The way sunlight filtered through the canopy became the light-waterfall. The sound of wind through leaves turned into his voice saying my name like a prayer and a threat. Even the flowers growing along the path seemed to mock me with their innocent beauty.

Sarnyx noticed, because of course she did. On the second morning, she'd pulled me aside with an expression that managed to be both knowing and exasperated.

"Whatever happened in that monastery," she'd said, "get it under control. We can't afford distractions right now."

"Nothing happened," I'd lied.

She'd given me a look that said she wasn't buying it. "The flowers growing everywhere you walk say otherwise. As does the way he watches you like a man dying of thirst looking at water he can't drink."

I'd had no response to that.

The others handled our tension differently. Bryx made increasingly inappropriate jokes that nobody laughed at. Vashael and Nimor exchanged glances that suggested they were taking bets on when we'd finally crack. Even the Sage seemed amused, though they at least had the grace not to comment directly.

Only Eltrien remained characteristically cryptic. "The convergence approaches," he'd said that morning, his mycelial markings pulsing in that unsettling rhythm. "And you two are preparing for it whether you know it or not. What happens in dreams has a way of becoming real in this realm. Be careful what you promise."

Now, as the sun began its descent toward the horizon, we finally emerged from the dense forest paths into something that made me stop breathing.

The Thornwood Throne wasn't what I'd expected.

After days of running, fighting, and nearly dissolving into pure possibility, I'd built up this image in my head of a dark fortress, all thorns and shadows and brooding rebellion. Instead, as we emerged from the forest paths, I found myself staring at something that looked like it had been dreamed rather than built.

The base spread through a massive hollow where trees had been coaxed into living architecture. Colossal blossoms—each the size of a small house—had been hollowed out and transformed into dwellings, their petals glowing with soft incandescent light that shifted from rose to bronze to violet as the sun set. Vines thick as bridge cables wove between the structures, creating walkways that pulsed with their own gentle light. Pollen lanterns floated freely through the air, casting dancing shadows that seemed to move independently of their light sources.

And it was alive with celebration.

"What is this?" I breathed, taking in the whirl of activity around us.

"The Harvest Moon Festival," Nimor said, his form solid and stable since Eltrien's intervention. "I'd forgotten it was tonight."

"Of course it is," Peeble muttered. "Because arriving at rebel headquarters during a massive public festival is exactly the kind of tactical brilliance I've come to expect from this operation."

"The Hunt won't breach our defenses here," Kaelren said, though his carved marks pulsed with tension that had nothing to do with external threats. "Not tonight. Even they respect certain boundaries."

His eyes met mine across the space between us, and I felt the echo of the dream—the waterfall, the promises, the way he'd looked at me like I was something he wanted to devour and worship in equal measure.

Two days of walking. Two days of wanting. Two days of knowing exactly what we'd do to each other if we could just touch without consequences.

The festival spread before us like a test, like a dare, like an inevitability we'd been careening toward since the moment we'd woken tangled together on monastery moss.

"Well," Peeble said with obvious glee, "this is definitely going to end badly. Shall we?"

But I barely heard them. The scene before me was overwhelming in its strange beauty. Insect drummers created rhythms that seemed to bypass my ears and go straight to my bones. Florakith acrobats twisted through the air on silk ribbons, their wings catching the light like stained glass. Tables groaned under the weight of feasts—glowing fruits I'd never seen, sweets that looked like they were enchanted, bread that released luminous steam.

It was magical. It was impossible. And it made my chest ache with a homesickness so sharp I had to catch my breath.

"Elle?" Kaelren's voice, closer than expected.

"It reminds me of the county fair," I said, not looking at him. "Grandma Jo used to take me every summer. The lights, the music, the chaos of it all. Except there the biggest attraction was a butter sculpture of a cow, not..." I gestured at a performer who appeared to be juggling balls of living light.

Through our bond, I felt his conflict—wanting to comfort but not knowing how, not without touching, not without risking another reality-warping moment.

"We should find quarters," he said instead, falling back on practicality. "Rest while we can."

But the moment we entered the festival proper, the crew began to scatter like seeds on the wind.

Bryx immediately got pulled into some kind of game involving thrown daggers and moving targets, his laughter bright and genuine. Vashael drifted toward where Nimor stood watching the acrobats, and I saw her hand brush his—deliberate, testing. His form solidified further at the touch, and something passed between them that made me look away.

Sarnyx remained with us, but she was on high alert, watching the crowd like a bomb was about to detonate.

"I need to check our supplies," she said abruptly. "Don't do anything stupid."

Then she was gone, leaving Kaelren and me standing awkwardly at the edge of the celebration.

"You should enjoy it," he said, his voice carefully neutral. "We don't get many nights like this."

"What about you?"

"I need to report to the other cell leaders. Explain..." He gestured vaguely at me, at the flowers that had started growing around my feet without my conscious input. "This."

"Right. The anomaly needs explaining."

"Elle—"

"Go," I said, sharper than intended. "Do your rebel leader thing. I'll try not to accidentally transform reality while you're gone."

He hesitated, and through our bond, I felt words he wanted to say but couldn't. Then he was gone, his corruption leaving cold spots in the warm festival air.

"Well," Peeble announced, landing on my shoulder with a metallic chime. "That was sufficiently awkward. Should we find something to eat, or would you prefer to stand here growing increasingly elaborate depression flowers?"

I looked down. The flowers around my feet had turned blue—not midnight like the cosmos, but a deep, melancholic blue that hurt to look at.

"Food," I decided. "And maybe something to drink that will make me forget I'm apparently stuck in a cosmic shit show."

"That's the spirit!" Peeble said cheerfully. "Nothing says coping like festival wine and denial!"

We wandered deeper into the celebration, and I tried to lose myself in the wonder of it all. A vendor offered me something that looked like candied daffodils and tasted like summer rain. Children ran past trailing ribbons that painted colors in the air. Music shifted and swirled, sometimes sounding like home, sometimes like nothing that I'd heard before.

But everywhere I went, I felt the stares. Some curious, some fearful, some calculating. I was the anomaly, the thing that shouldn't be, the human wearing marks meant for their realm.

"She's the one," I heard someone whisper. "The one who turned Hunt riders into trees."

"Look at her marks—they're spreading."

I glanced down at my arms. They were right. The marks had crept past my collarbone, delicate tracings now visible on my forearms when the light hit right. But there were dark veins too, shadows of corruption that matched Kaelren's. They appeared when I woke up from the dream. Kaelren assumed it was a symptom of the deepening connection of our bond.

I paused at a stall selling bottled memories—actual memories trapped in perriwinkle-like gems that played when you held them to the light. The vendor, a creature made entirely of shifting sand, offered me one for free.

"For the prophet," they whispered, pressing it into my palm before I could refuse.

The memory bloomed in my mind—warm and comforting, like a hug from the person you love most.

A Florakith mother teaching her daughter to dance for the first time. The child's wings weren't fully formed yet, just translucent nubs that trembled with excitement. They stood in a garden that had existed a hundred years ago, maybe more, surrounded by flowers that no longer grew in Wynmire. The mother's laughter was like wind chimes, and when the little one stumbled over her own feet, she caught her gently, spinning her in the air until the stumble became part of the dance itself.

"See?" the mother's voice echoed across time. "There are no mistakes in dancing, my bloom. Only new steps we haven't learned yet."

The child giggled—a sound so pure it made my chest ache—and tried again. This time her wings caught the rhythm, and for a moment, just a moment, she floated. The joy in her face was so fierce, so bright, that it hurt to witness.

Then the memory shifted. The same daughter, grown now, teaching her own child the same dance in the same garden—except the flowers were different, the realm older, the steps slightly changed. She spoke the same words her mother had spoken: "There are no mistakes in dancing, my bloom."

It was a tradition, I realized. Passed down through generations, evolving but never lost. A small moment of beauty and continuity in a realm that seemed built on chaos and change.

The memory faded, leaving me gasping—not with horror this time, but with something deeper. Loss, maybe. Longing for traditions I'd never had, for roots that went deeper than one generation, for the kind of love that survived through teaching and time.

"Beautiful, isn't it?" The sand vendor's voice rippled like water over stone. "That family line stretches back four hundred years. The current daughter still teaches that dance every Harvest Moon."

I looked down at the crystal in my palm, its surface still warm. "Why give this to me?"

"Because you're building something new," they said simply. "And sometimes, when building the new, it helps to remember what's worth keeping from the old."

Despite everything, I smiled. It felt good, real.

That's when I saw the dancers. The vendor nodded his head in their direction and shooed me away.

They moved in the center of the festival, bodies telling stories without words. Some had wings, some had too many limbs, some seemed to be made of plants themselves. But they all moved together, creating patterns mesmerizing.

"You should join," a voice said beside me. A local, her bark-skin glowing with health, her leaf-hair rustling with the music. "The dance chooses its partners, and tonight, it's calling for you."

"I don't know the steps."

"The dance knows them for you." She smiled, and it was kind despite the sharp thorns that served as her teeth. "Besides, the one with stormy eyes has been watching you all night. Perhaps the dance will call him too."

I didn't have to ask who she meant. Even without looking, I could feel Kaelren's presence at the edge of the festival, his attention like a weight between my shoulder blades.

"Maybe later," I said.

But later had a way of becoming now in this realm.

The music shifted, and suddenly dancers were reaching for me, pulling me into their spiral. I tried to resist, but their joy was infectious, their movement hypnotic. Before I knew it, I was spinning with them, my feet finding steps I didn't know, my body moving to rhythms that were both beautiful and sensual all in one.

The world became a blur of light and sound and motion. I forgot about death and doom. Forgot about choosing between love and realm. Forgot everything except the dance and the way it made me feel—alive, present, real.

That's when I felt him.

Kaelren stood at the edge of the dance, his darkness a sharp contrast to the swirling lights. Our eyes met across the spinning bodies, and something electric passed between us.

Come, the dance seemed to whisper. *Both of you. Show us what impossible looks like.*

"This is definitely going to end badly," Peeble observed from somewhere above. "Which means it'll be entertaining. Carry on!"

The dancers parted, creating a path between us. The music slowed, deepened, became something that thrummed in my bones.

Kaelren took a step forward. Then another.

And I knew, with the certainty of someone who'd been warned by oracles, that this dance would change everything.

Or destroy everything.

With us, there never seemed to be a middle ground.

19

Kaelren

The council chamber hadn't been made for comfort. Carved from the heart of the Thornwood Throne itself, it was a reminder that rebellion grew from pain. The walls wept sap that never dried, and the table was scarred from years of desperate planning and bitter arguments.

Tonight's meeting needed to be different. We had perhaps two weeks before the convergence, and Auradelle was moving.

"She's stabilizing," Fenwick said, surprising me by not starting with criticism. The scarred rebel leader had lost half his face to Auradelle's forces, and the remaining half perpetually scowled. "The anomaly, I mean. Her power grows, but it's... controlled."

"Controlled is generous," Sarnyx added from across the room. "She turned reality into a garden in Vyn Hollow."

"To save us," I reminded them. "Without her intervention, the Hunt would have taken us all."

Maris, the elderly strategist whose blind eyes somehow still managed to convey disapproval, leaned forward. "The question isn't what she's done, but what she'll do. The convergence approaches. We need strategy, not sentiment."

I stood, letting them see the corruption that had spread again during the walk here—black veins now visible up my neck, creeping toward my jaw.

"Strategy then," I said, my voice rough. "Auradelle masses forces at the Heartspire. Our scouts report three battalions of Crown guard, plus whatever abominations his pet mages have created. The outer walls are reinforced with wards. The inner sanctum..." I paused, remembering. "The inner sanctum is where he'll try to force Elle to choose."

"How do we breach it?" Fenwick asked, all business now.

"We don't breach. We infiltrate." I pulled out recent maps of the Heartspire we had thanks to a Crown guard who fled to join the rebellion after growing a conscience. "There are tunnels beneath the Heartspire, Root-carved passages that predate Auradelle's rule. They were sealed when he took power, but—"

"But seals can be broken by someone the Root recognizes," Maris added, her blind eyes somehow knowing exactly where to focus. "Or someone chosen by it."

"Elle," the Sage said from the doorway. They'd been observing quietly waiting to impart their wisdom to the group. "You're planning to use her as a key."

"I'm planning to give her options," I corrected. "When the convergence comes, she'll need every advantage we can provide."

"What about the second wall?" Fenwick asked, spreading his own intelligence on the table. "Forty feet high, jagged spikes that burn Root-touched on contact. Your corruption especially would light up like a beacon."

"That's where you come in," I said, looking at each of them. "We divide our forces. A direct assault on the main gates—loud, obvious, drawing their attention. Meanwhile, a smaller team uses the tunnels."

"Suicide for the assault team," Fenwick observed.

"Not if we time it right. Not if we coordinate with the convergence itself. The realm will be... unstable. Reality will be malleable. Elle's not the only one who can take advantage of that."

"You're gambling everything on cosmic timing and underground passages that may not even be accessible," Maris said quietly.

"Yes."

"And if we fail?"

"Then we die fighting for something that matters."

Silence fell like a stone.

"There's more," Sarnyx said, leaning forward. "Tell them about the connection. About what happens when you and Elle..."

"When we touch, reality bends," I said bluntly. "Our bond amplifies both our powers. It's dangerous, unpredictable, and probably our best weapon against Auradelle."

"It's also killing you both," Sarnyx said sharply. "Look at yourself, Kaelren. Have you forgotten who the true ruler of this realm is?"

The temperature in the room dropped twenty degrees. Frost spread from where I stood, and several council members stepped back.

"That person died in the Heartspire," I said softly. "When the Bloom rejected me. When Auradelle arranged my parents' 'accident.' When I was exiled for the crime of not being enough."

"Yet here you are," Maris observed quietly, "carving marks into your skin, forcing a connection that was always meant to come through her."

Through the bond, I felt Elle's emotions shift—joy from the dance mixing with something deeper. She could sense the tension in the room through me.

"I need to go," I said abruptly.

"The meeting isn't—"

"The meeting is what it needs to be. You have your orders. Prepare the assault teams. Scout the tunnel entrances. In two weeks, we move on the Heartspire." I headed for the door, corruption leaving frost in my wake. "And if anyone has a problem with that, find another rebellion to lead."

I left them to their arguments and fears, drawn by the pull of the bond toward the festival. Toward her.

I found her at the edge of the dancers, flowers blooming around her feet in colors that matched her emotions—deep purple frustration, silver uncertainty, and underneath it all, a thread of gold that pulsed when she saw me. The music drawing us together on the dancefloor without even realizing it.

She took one look at me and frowned. "How bad was it?" she asked without preamble.

"Productive. We have a plan."

"Which is?"

"Something I'll tell you about tomorrow. Tonight..." I held out my hand. "Dance with me?"

She looked at my outstretched hand like it might bite. "Is that wise?"

"Probably not. But wisdom hasn't gotten us very far, has it?"

"Point." She took my hand, and the familiar electricity sparked between us. "Try not to unmake reality while we're dancing?"

"I make no promises."

20

Elle

The dance was everything and nothing like I expected.

Kaelren moved with a grace that shouldn't have been possible for someone carrying so much darkness. His hand in mine was steady, warm despite the corruption that traced silver-black veins up his neck. The other dancers gave us space, creating a pocket of intimacy in the chaos of celebration.

"You're a good dancer," I said, surprised.

"You sound shocked."

"I just figured brooding rebel leaders were too busy plotting revenge to learn party tricks."

He spun me, and the world blurred into streams of light. "It's called the Spiral of Seasons. Each movement represents a different time of year in the realm."

"What season is this?" I asked as he pulled me closer, our bodies moving in perfect synchronization.

"Winter into spring. Death into rebirth. Ending into beginning."

"Subtle."

His lips quirked in what might have been a smile. "The realm isn't known for its subtlety."

The music shifted, became something lighter, and suddenly we were laughing as he lifted me, spun me through air. For a moment, we weren't the anomaly and the corrupted prince. We were just two people dancing badly and enjoying it.

"Your flower crown is crooked," he said when he set me down.

"I have a flower crown?" I reached up and felt petals that hadn't been there before. "When did—"

"You've been growing them all evening. Every time you laugh." He adjusted it gently, fingers barely grazing my hair. "The children have been following you, collecting the fallen petals."

I turned and saw them—a small group of young beings, some with wings, some with bark for skin, all clutching handfuls of petals like treasure.

"Oh," I said softly.

"You're already changing things here," Kaelren said. "The Hollow hasn't seen flowers like these in decades."

The music ended, and I expected him to pull away. Instead, he kept my hand in his.

"Let me show you something," he said.

"Now?"

"Now."

He led me away from the dancing, through the winding paths of the Thorn-wood Throne. Peeble followed, occasionally making sarcastic comments about "romantic midnight tours" that we both ignored.

"This is the Healer's Grove," he said, guiding me through an archway of living wood. Inside, glowing moss covered everything, and the air smelled of mint and medicine. "Eltrien grows his remedies here."

A few healers looked up from their work, nodding respectfully to Kaelren. One, a young woman with leaves for hair, approached me shyly.

"You're the one who saved Nimor," she said. "Who turned the Hunt riders into trees."

"That was more accident than intention," I admitted.

"The best magic usually is," she replied with a smile, pressing a small vial into my hand. "Essence of moonbell. For when the marks burn."

Before I could thank her, Kaelren was guiding me onward.

"The Archives," he said, showing me a hollow tree so massive its interior held multiple levels of books and scrolls. "Every piece of knowledge we've saved from Auradelle's purges."

An elderly scholar looked up from his work. "Ah, the prophet arrives at last."

"I'm not a prophet," I said automatically.

"Aren't you?" He winked. "Time will tell. It always does."

We continued through the Thornwood Throne—the training grounds where rebels sparred with weapons made of steel, the nurseries where seedling-children grew in pods of soft light, the kitchens where the feast was being prepared by beings who cooked with magic as much as heat.

Everywhere we went, the inhabitants watched us with expressions ranging from hope to curiosity to fear. But they all nodded to Kaelren with genuine respect, and many smiled at me with something that looked like welcome.

"They're not afraid of you," I observed as we climbed a spiraling staircase carved from a single massive vine.

"They're terrified of me," he corrected. "But they trust me anyway. Fear and faith aren't mutually exclusive."

"That's depressing."

"That's leadership."

We emerged onto a balcony I hadn't noticed from below—a platform woven from branches that extended out over the entire Hollow. The view was breathtaking. The festival continued below, dots of light and color swirling in patterns that looked almost like writing from this height. The moon hung enormous overhead, tinting everything silver.

"This is my favorite place," Kaelren said quietly. "When the responsibility gets too heavy, I come here."

"It's beautiful."

"It's dying."

I turned to look at him. "What?"

He moved to the edge, hands gripping the railing. "This wasn't always a hollow. When I first came here after my exile, it was corrupted. The realm's sickness had spread so deep that nothing could grow. The rebels who'd made it their base were dying, one by one."

"But now it's thriving."

"At a cost." He turned to face me, and in the moonlight, I could see the exhaustion he'd been hiding. "I made a bargain, Elle. The corruption wanted to spread—it always wants to spread. So I gave it a path."

I gasped, realization hitting me as I took in his pulsing black marks on his skin. "Through you."

"Through me, yes. But more than that. I became a filter. Every dawn, I bleed shadows into the earth, feeding the barriers that protect this place. Every dusk, I pull them back into myself. The Hollow thrives because I'm... processing its poison."

My heart clenched. "That's killing you."

"Everything's killing me. The marks I carved, the corruption I channel, the bargain I made—it's all just a matter of time."

"How long?"

"Two weeks, maybe three. Long enough to see you through the convergence."

"And after?"

"There is no after for me, Elle. There never was."

"Bullshit." The word came out sharp, angry. "You don't get to sacrifice yourself for everyone else and call it noble."

"It's not noble. It's necessary."

"It's both, and that's what makes it infuriating." I moved closer, and flowers bloomed at my feet—not the sad blue ones from earlier, but fierce red things with thorns. "You think you're the only one who can carry darkness? The only one who can filter poison?"

"You have your own burden—"

"Then let me share yours." I reached out, not quite touching him. "Our bond already connects us. When we touch, our powers amplify. What if we could use that? What if we could share the load?"

"It would corrupt you."

"I'm already corrupted. Look." I held up my arms, showing him where his darkness had started threading through my golden marks. "It's already happening. The only question is whether we do it intentionally or let it happen chaotically."

He stared at the marks, and through our bond, I felt his conflict—hope warring with fear, desire fighting against protection.

"After the convergence," he said finally. "If we survive. If we somehow break whatever cycle we're trapped in... then we'll try."

"Promise?"

"I promise."

The words hung between us, heavy with possibility. Below, the festival continued, but up here, it felt like we were the only two people in existence.

"I should take you to your quarters," he said softly. "You need rest."

"Probably," I agreed, though rest was the last thing on my mind.

He led me back through the Thornwood Throne, this time taking quieter paths. The rooms he'd arranged for me were in one of the giant flower houses, the petals glowing soft amber in the darkness. Inside was simple but beautiful—a bed that looked like it had been grown rather than built, windows that were actually gaps between petals, and a small table with a vase of those impossible black and gold roses.

"From earlier," he explained. "When we... they grew where we danced. The children collected them."

"They're beautiful."

"They're impossible. Darkness and light shouldn't blend like that."

"And yet they do."

We stood in the doorway, neither moving to separate. The bond hummed between us, warm and electric and patient.

"Thank you," I said. "For showing me your home. For trusting me with the truth about the barriers."

"Thank you for not trying to fix everything immediately."

"Oh, I'm absolutely going to fix it. Just... after the convergence."

He laughed, soft and real. "Of course you are."

"Someone has to save you from your own nobility."

"And you've appointed yourself?"

"I'm uniquely qualified. Anomaly, remember?"

He reached up, brushing a strand of hair from my face. "How could I forget?"

The touch was electric, sending sparks across my marks. His corruption pulsed in response, and for a moment, the very air between us felt alive with possibility.

"Elle," he said, my name a question and a warning and a prayer.

But then he leaned down and kissed me—soft, careful, barely there. It lasted only a moment before he pulled back, but that moment was enough to make flowers bloom everywhere—on the walls, the ceiling, carpeting every surface with blossoms.

"Goodnight, Elle," he said, stepping back before we could do something truly dangerous.

"Goodnight, Kaelren."

He turned to go, then paused. "The meeting tomorrow—we'll discuss the plan. What happens when we move on the Heartspire."

"I'll be there."

"I know."

Then he was gone, leaving me alone with a room full of impossible flowers and a kiss that tasted like promises we might not live to keep.

"Well," Peeble said, landing on the table. "That was disgustingly romantic."

"Shut up," I said, but I was smiling.

"You know this ends badly, right? These things always end badly."

"Maybe," I said, touching my lips where I could still feel the ghost of his kiss. "But maybe that's the point. Maybe the ending isn't what matters."

"Philosophy from the anomaly. We're all doomed."

I laughed, and more flowers bloomed—hopeful things that glowed in the darkness.

Tomorrow would bring plans and strategies and the weight of impossible choices. But tonight, I'd danced with a corrupted prince, toured a miraculous hollow, and been kissed like I was worth dying for.

For now, that was enough.

Even if it wouldn't be for long.

21

Elle

The morning of our second day at the Thornwood Throne dawned with that same impossible beauty—petals shifting from deep burgundy to violet in the early light, pollen lanterns drifting lazily through the air like sentient fireflies. I'd barely slept, too aware of Kaelren's presence in the adjacent chamber, separated only by a wall of living wood.

"You look like hell," Peeble announced, landing on my shoulder with their usual grace—which is to say, like a small drunk person falling off a barstool.

"Good morning to you, too, asshole."

"I'm just saying, the dark circles under your eyes are approaching corpse territory. You look like you haven't slept since we got here—which, judging by the amount of sighing and pacing I heard through the wall last night, is accurate."

I threw a pillow at them. They dodged with insulting ease.

"Come on," they said, once they'd finished laughing at my expense. "I found something yesterday you're going to want to see. Trust me, it'll distract you from all that unresolved sexual tension radiating through the walls. Kevin and I could barely sleep with all the pining."

"I'm not pining."

"Sure. And I'm not devastatingly gorgeous for an insect. We're both liars, let's move on."

I dressed quickly, pulling on the clothes someone had left for me—soft fabrics that felt like wearing clouds, in shades of green and gold that somehow matched my marks exactly. The Thornwood rebels had been nothing but kind since we'd arrived, but there was still an edge of uncertainty in how they looked at me. The human. The prophet. The walking apocalypse.

No pressure or anything.

Kaelren was already awake when I emerged, because of course he was. Did the man ever sleep? He stood on the balcony of our shared common area, looking out over the Hollow with that statue-still quality he had when he thought no one was watching.

"Going somewhere?" His voice was carefully neutral.

"Peeble wants to show me something. They won't tell me what it is but insist I'll love it."

"That's code for 'I've found something potentially dangerous but entertaining,'" Kaelren said, the barest hint of amusement warming his tone.

"Probably." I hesitated, then added, "Want to come?"

His marks pulsed once, that quick tell I'd learned meant he was surprised. "If you'd like company."

"I would." The words came out softer than I'd intended, carrying weight we both felt through the bond.

He turned to face me fully, those silver-shot eyes catching the morning light. "Then I'm yours."

My breath stuttered. The way he said it—like a vow, like a promise, like something that meant more than just accompanying me on a walk.

"Great! Perfect!" Peeble chirped from my shoulder, sounding far too pleased. "Let's go, team emotionally-stunted-but-sexually-tense! Adventure awaits! We're going to need Kevin for this one," Peeble announced, already making the complicated whistle-buzz combination that summoned his favorite bee.

Kevin arrived moments later, his fuzzy body catching the morning light as he landed on the balcony with surprising grace for something the size of a horse.

"Where exactly are we going?" Kaelren asked, eyeing the bee with his usual wariness.

"You'll see!" Peeble sang out. "It's a bit of a flight, but trust me, totally worth it. Kevin, be a gentleman and don't let them fall to their deaths. It would really ruin the mood I'm going for."

Kevin buzzed something that might have been agreement or might have been sass—with Kevin, it was hard to tell.

"After you," Kaelren said, gesturing to Kevin's back.

I climbed on, and the bee's fur was just as soft as I remembered—like velvet made of sunshine. A moment later, Kaelren settled behind me, his arms coming around my waist to hold on.

"This feels familiar," I said, remembering our first flight together.

"Last time you squeaked when we took off," he murmured against my ear.

"I did not squeak."

"You absolutely did."

Kevin's wings began their thrumming beat, and we lifted into the air. The Thornwood Throne fell away beneath us as we flew over sections I hadn't seen—meditation groves where monks tended to plants that hummed with their own songs, armories carved into living trees, libraries with books growing directly from branches.

"How far out are we going?" Kaelren called to Peeble, who was flying alongside us, looking far too pleased with themself.

"Just to the outer gardens! The really old section that nobody maintains anymore! For absolutely no suspicious reasons!"

"That's not reassuring," I said.

"Good! Reassurance is overrated!"

We flew for what felt like an hour, the Thornwood Throne's main structures becoming distant behind us. The forest here was wilder, older, with trees that looked like they predated the Bloom itself.

Kevin began their descent, landing in a small clearing I never would have found on foot. The moment my feet touched the ground, I felt it—that same heavy sweetness in the air, but stronger now.

"Welcome," Peeble announced with a dramatic flourish of his antennae, "to the Pleasure Grove!"

Of course that's what it had to be called, because nothing else would fit. The garden spread before us like something out of a very specific kind of fantasy. Flowers in shades of pink and gold released visible pollen that drifted through the air like glitter made of want. Vines thick as my thigh wound through the space, their leaves shimmering with some internal light. Mushrooms grew in clusters, their caps glowing soft blue-green, and—

"Are those blueberry bushes?" I asked, distracted despite everything else.

"Oh wow, they are!" Peeble said. "Weird, right? Must have been cultivated by someone who crossed to Earth. You know, like your grandma. Who definitely came through here. Frequently. With companions. For reasons I'm sure were very innocent and botanical in nature."

My face burned. "Peeble."

"What? I'm just saying, Grandma Jo had excellent taste in gardens. Very... stimulating variety of plants. Educational. Medicinal, even."

"I'm going to let Kevin eat you."

"Kevin would never. We're in love."

Kaelren had gone very still beside me, and I could feel his awareness through the bond—the same recognition that was dawning on me. The sweet heaviness in the air wasn't just pleasant; it was doing things. Specific things. Very specific things to very specific parts of my body.

"This is an aphrodisiac garden," Kaelren said flatly.

"Is it?" Peeble's voice was the picture of innocence. "Gosh, how'd we end up here? What an unfortunate accident. Anyway, I'm going to go now. Very quickly. To somewhere extremely far away. You two have fun! Don't do anything I wouldn't do! Which, considering I'm a beetle, leaves you a LOT of options! Bye!"

They launched into the air before I could grab them, leaving us standing at the garden's edge.

Alone.

In a garden full of plants specifically designed to make people want to fuck.

"We should go," Kaelren said, but he didn't move.

Neither did I.

Because here's the thing—I could feel it affecting me, the pollen or the flowers or whatever magical bullshit was in the air. Heat was pooling low in my belly, my skin hypersensitive, every nerve ending suddenly aware of Kaelren's proximity. But I'd wanted him before we walked into this garden. I'd wanted him since that damn waterfall, since before that if I was honest. The plants weren't creating desire. They were just removing my ability to pretend I didn't feel it.

"What if I don't want to go?" I heard myself say.

His marks flared, black veins pulsing against his skin. "Elle."

"We've been dancing around this for weeks. Since the monastery. Since that kiss that bent reality." I turned to face him fully. "I'm tired of pretending. I'm tired of being careful. I'm tired of wanting you and not having you."

"The plants—"

"Aren't making me lie." I stepped closer, close enough to feel the heat radiating off him. "They're just making me brave enough to tell the truth."

His control was cracking; I could see it in the way his hands clenched, in how his breathing had gone shallow. "If we do this—"

"Then we do this." Another step. "Don't you remember what you said to me?"

"I think about it constantly." The admission was rough, dragged from somewhere deep. "Every moment. Every breath. You're in my head, in my blood, in every thought since I saw you laid bare before me behind the waterfall."

"Then stop thinking," I said, reaching up to trace the marks along his jaw, "and just feel."

He caught my wrist, but not to push me away. His thumb pressed against my pulse, feeling it race. "Elle. Are you certain? Is this what you want, or is it the garden..."

"It's me." I met his eyes, let him see the truth there. "It's been me since the first moment you saw me."

Something in him shattered. I felt it through the bond—the last wall of his restraint crumbling like crystal under pressure.

His mouth found mine with bruising intensity, one hand tangling in my hair while the other pulled me against him. This wasn't like any kiss previously. This was need made physical, weeks of tension released all at once.

I gasped against his mouth and he swallowed the sound, walking me backward until my back hit one of the massive bloom-houses that dotted the garden. The petals were soft against my shoulders, glowing faintly at the contact.

"Weeks," he growled against my throat, his lips tracing the marks at my collarbones. "Weeks of watching you, wanting you, trying to maintain some semblance of control."

"I don't want your control." My hands found the laces of his tunic, fumbling with them. "I want you."

He pulled back just enough to look at me, and the raw want in his expression made my knees weak. "Once we do this, there's no going back. You understand that?"

"Good," I breathed. "I don't want to go back."

The kiss this time was different—slower, deeper, a claiming. His hands mapped my body through my clothes like he was memorizing topography, and everywhere he touched left trails of heat.

"Wait," I said against his mouth, and he froze instantly.

"Too much?"

"Not enough." I pulled back with a grin, reaching for one of the vines nearby. Its leaves were glistening with morning dew, sparkling in the light. I plucked one, brought it to my nose. The scent was pure peppermint, sweet and sharp. "These are flavored."

His eyebrows rose. "Flavored."

"Peppermint. There are others—look." I pointed to different vines. "Chocolate. Bubblegum. Some kind of berry." I traced the peppermint leaf over his lips, watched his pupils blow wide at the cooling sensation it left. "Guess I found my own personal candy cane."

217

"You're going to be the death of me," he said, but his voice was rough with want.

"Hopefully not before we get to the good part." I kissed him again, tasting peppermint on his lips, and felt his control slip another notch.

His hands found the hem of my tunic, hesitated. "May I?"

The formality of it, in this moment, undid something in my chest. "Yes. Please, yes."

He pulled the fabric over my head in one smooth motion, and for a moment just looked at me. The marks at my collarbones had spread again, golden lines tracing patterns down my chest.

"Gods, you're beautiful," he said, reverent. His fingers traced the marks, making me shiver.

He kissed me again, and this time there was no hesitation. His hands learned the curve of my waist, the dip of my spine, and I did the same—mapping the planes of his chest, the ridges of his muscles, the places where his marks pulsed under my touch.

"The vines," I murmured against his mouth. "They're moving."

He glanced to the side, then smiled—an expression I'd rarely seen, and it transformed his face. "Pleasure vines. They respond to desire."

Even as he said it, the vines were weaving themselves into a structure behind us—supportive, responsive, creating something like a nest.

"That's convenient."

"That's intentional. This garden was designed for exactly this." His hands were working at the laces of my pants now. "The rebels who founded the Thornwood knew that pleasure was as much a part of life as duty. That joy could be revolutionary."

"Revolutionary fucking. I like it."

He laughed—actually laughed—and the sound went straight through me. "You're impossible."

"You like it."

"I do." He kissed me again, slower now, thorough. "Root and Bloom, I do."

My clothes disappeared in stages, his following, until we were skin to skin in the golden light. The vines had created a bower around us, supporting but not confining, adjusting to our movements like living furniture.

"Elle," he said, his voice dropping to that register that made everything inside me clench. "I need you to understand something."

"What?"

"I've lived hundreds of years, and I have never—" He pressed his forehead to mine, breathing hard. "I have never felt like this. Never wanted someone the way I want you. It's not the bond, it's not the prophecy, it's not anything except you."

I pulled back to look at him, saw the vulnerability there, the fear under the want. "Then have me. I'm yours."

The vines adjusted as he lay me down, creating a nest that was impossibly comfortable. The mushrooms growing nearby began to glow brighter, responding to our arousal, casting everything in soft blue-green light.

"Wait," I said, remembering. "The mushrooms—Peeble said something about them once. During one of their more educational rants."

"What about them?"

I reached for one of the glowing caps, carefully broke off a small piece. It left luminescent residue on my fingers. "Body paint."

His eyes darkened. "Show me."

I traced glowing patterns across his chest, following the natural lines of his marks, watching how the light made them stand out even more. He shuddered under my touch, his hands clenching in the moss beneath us.

"Your turn," he said, taking a piece of mushroom for himself.

His hands were careful, almost reverent, as he painted patterns on my skin—constellations, spirals, runes in languages I didn't know. Every stroke left tingling warmth in its wake.

"You know what the best part is?" I asked, breathless.

"What?"

"You get to lick it off."

His control snapped.

His mouth traced the glowing trails he'd painted, and the mushroom was sweet on my skin—earthy and bright, with an effervescent quality that

219

made every nerve ending sing. He took his time, learning what made me gasp, what made me arch into his touch.

"My turn," I said, flipping us over when I couldn't take it anymore, pushing him back into this makeshift bed.

I painted him with deliberate care—patterns down his chest, following the ridges of muscle. God, he was beautiful. Not in a soft way, but like something carved from marble. His abdomen was a study in controlled power, each muscle defined, the kind of physique that came from centuries of training and fighting. He looked like an Adonis—if Adonis had been forged in darkness and marked with corruption.

"You're staring," he said, voice rough.

"You're worth staring at." My hands traced lower, following the trail of marks that disappeared beneath the vines. "Has anyone ever told you that you're obscenely gorgeous?"

"Not in those words."

"Then everyone you've met has been a coward." I leaned down, pressing kisses to follow where I'd painted. The mushroom glow made his skin look almost ethereal. "I'm going to take my time with you."

"Elle—"

"Shh. My turn to explore."

When my hand finally wrapped around his cock, his sharp intake of breath was gratifying. He was substantial—impressively so—and the look on my face must have shown my thoughts because he actually smiled.

"Is that concern or appreciation?" he asked.

"Definitely appreciation." I stroked slowly, watching his eyes darken. "With maybe a touch of 'this is going to be interesting.'"

"I'll be careful—"

"I don't want careful right now." I reached for one of the chocolate-flavored leaves, showing it to him. "Do you know what a lollipop is?"

"A... what?"

"Earth candy. You lick it." I traced the leaf along his length, coating him with the chocolate essence. "Let me educate you."

The moment I took him in my mouth, chocolate and salt and him, he made a sound that wasn't quite my name. His hands found my hair, not pushing, just holding on like I was the only thing keeping him anchored to reality.

"Root and Bloom," he gasped. "What are you—"

I pulled back just enough to answer. "Showing you what a lollipop is. Educational."

"This is not—" His words cut off as I took him deeper, the chocolate leaf creating a sweetness that made the act even more decadent.

The peppermint leaves came next, alternating sensations—cooling, warming, the slight effervescence of the mushroom glow still on my lips. I could feel him trying to maintain control, trying not to thrust, trying to be careful even now.

"Let go," I told him, my hand working where my mouth couldn't reach. "I want all of you."

His control shattered beautifully. Through the bond, I felt his pleasure building, felt the moment he stopped fighting it, and when he came with my name on his lips, I stayed with him through it—taking everything he gave, feeling powerful and desired and absolutely perfect.

When I finally pulled away, his chest was heaving, marks pulsing erratically across his skin. He looked thoroughly undone. His eyes bulged when I ran my tongue along my lips, swallowing the last of him.

"That," he said when he could speak again, "was not educational."

"No?"

"That was devastation." He pulled me up to kiss me, tasting chocolate and himself on my lips. "You're dangerous."

"You like it."

"I'm obsessed with it." His hands were already exploring again, returning the favor. "Your turn."

He pulled me up, kissing me deeply, tasting chocolate and peppermint and want. When I pulled back, he was already hard again—impossibly quick recovery that made me raise an eyebrow.

"Fae stamina?" I asked.

"Among other benefits." His marks pulsed with renewed hunger. "If you're interested."

"Very interested."

The vines responded to our desire, weaving themselves into supportive straps that positioned me above him. They created loops that I could grip with my hands, while other vines wrapped gently around my thighs and hips—not restraining, but supporting my weight like a sex swing.

"Oh," I breathed, understanding the mechanics. "That's—"

"Perfect leverage," Kaelren finished, his hands settling on my hips as he lay back into the nest of moss and vines beneath him. "You control the rhythm. The vines will hold you."

I straddled him, the swing-like support taking most of my weight while still letting me move. From this angle, I could see all of him—the sculpted planes of his chest still gleaming with traces of mushroom paint, his marks pulsing in rhythm with his heartbeat, the way he looked at me like I was something sacred and profane all at once.

"Like this?" I asked, positioning myself above him, feeling the head of him pressing against my entrance.

"Exactly like that." His voice was strained, hands flexing on my hips. "Take your time. Set the pace."

I sank down slowly, inch by inch, watching his face as I took him. The vines adjusted with me, supporting my weight so I could control the depth, the angle. When I was fully seated, we both groaned at the sensation— deeper than before, the angle hitting something inside me that made stars burst behind my eyelids.

"Fuck," I gasped.

"Move," he urged. "Please, Elle, move."

I gripped the vine-straps with both hands and lifted myself up, then sank back down. The support made it effortless—I could bounce, could control the rhythm completely while the vines held my weight. And the eye contact—god, the eye contact was intense. Every expression on his face, every flutter of his lashes, every clench of his jaw as I moved on him.

"You're perfect," he said, watching me ride him. "Absolutely perfect."

I experimented with the angle, shifting my hips, finding what felt best.

The vines adjusted with every movement, tightening or loosening their support to give me exactly what I needed. When I found the right angle—the one that made me cry out—his hands tightened on my hips.

"There," he said, helping guide me. "Right there."

I built the tempo gradually, using the vine-straps for leverage, bouncing faster as pleasure coiled tighter in my belly. He thrust up to meet me when I came down, the dual motion driving him impossibly deeper.

"Touch yourself," he commanded, and the edge in his voice sent shivers through me.

One hand left the vine-strap to slide between us, finding where we were joined. The added sensation made me clench around him, and he groaned my name like a prayer.

"That's it," he encouraged, his eyes dark with lust as he watched me pleasure myself while riding him. "Take what you need. Use me."

The combination—the perfect angle, my fingers on myself, the way he filled me completely, the swing support letting me move faster and harder than I could have on my own—it was overwhelming. I could feel the orgasm building, could feel him getting close through the bond.

"I'm going to—" I gasped.

"Yes. Come for me. Let me feel it."

When I shattered, the vines held me through it—supporting my weight as my body convulsed with pleasure, keeping me positioned perfectly so he could thrust up into me as I clenched around him.

The aphrodisiac plants intensified everything. Every touch was electric, every kiss was consuming, and the bond between us amplified sensation until I couldn't tell where I ended and he began. I felt his pleasure bleeding through, his wonder at this—at us—at how good it was.

"The leaves," I gasped, reaching for more. "Try them."

He understood immediately, creating trails with different flavors—chocolate warming his skin, bubblegum creating tiny bursts of sensation, peppermint cooling and soothing. We painted each other, tasted each other, learned what made the other come apart.

The vines responded to our shared desire, creating new configurations—

spinning, adjusting, finding angles that made us both gasp. They held me suspended, allowed movement I'd never imagined possible, rotating me slowly as he moved within me. The sensation was dizzying, overwhelming, perfect.

My hands found his pointed ears—sensitive, I'd learned—and when I traced them he made a sound somewhere between a groan and my name.

"There," I said, doing it again. "You like that."

"You're going to unravel me completely."

"Good."

The pleasure built in waves, each one higher than the last. The mushrooms glowed brighter, responding to our mounting arousal, painting us both in ethereal light. Flowers bloomed where my hands gripped the vines—unconscious magic responding to overwhelming sensation—and his corruption marks pulsed in counter-rhythm, creating patterns of light and shadow across our skin.

The vines shifted us through different positions—playful, exploratory, finding what made us cry out. Every configuration brought new sensation, new connection, new ways to come apart together.

When my climax hit, it was like being struck by lightning—every nerve ending electrified at once, current racing through my body in waves that left me trembling and gasping his name. Through the bond, I felt his release follow, felt the way it broke something open in him, something he'd kept carefully locked away.

The vines lowered us gently to the soft moss. We were thoroughly sated—covered in glowing mushroom paint, flavored leaf residue, flower petals, and the evidence of our pleasure. My hair was full of blooms I'd unconsciously created, and his marks had left temporary shadows on my skin—dark where he'd gripped me, darker where he'd kissed me.

"That was," I started, then laughed because words seemed insufficient.

"Revolutionary," he finished, smiling against my shoulder.

"Definitely revolutionary."

We lay there for long moments, breathing together, heartbeats gradually slowing to something approaching normal. The garden had dimmed slightly now that the intensity of our desire had passed, returning to its baseline glow.

"Grandma Jo definitely had sex here," I said eventually. "Multiple times, probably."

He laughed, the sound vibrating through where we were still pressed together. "Almost certainly."

"That's... actually kind of sweet. In a weird way."

"Your family has excellent taste in pleasure gardens."

"Apparently, we also have excellent taste in impossible fae lords."

"Impossible?"

"Impossibly stubborn. Impossibly dramatic. Impossibly hot."

"The last one redeems the first two."

"Barely."

"I'm going to make you regret that."

"Promise?"

He kissed me, thorough and deep, and I felt the promise in it—that this wasn't just once, wasn't just the garden, wasn't just hormones and aphrodisiac pollen.

"We should probably clean up," I said eventually. "Before someone comes looking for us."

"There's a spring nearby. The garden is designed for... aftercare."

"Of course it is."

The spring was clear and surprisingly warm, fed by some underground source that kept it perfect. We washed the evidence from our skin— mushroom glow, leaf residue, the physical traces of what we'd done. But nothing could wash away the marks Kaelren's corruption had left on my skin, or the flowers still blooming in my hair, or the way we couldn't stop touching each other—small contacts, reassurance that this was real.

"As whatever you want us to be." His hands stilled on my shoulders, turning me to face him. "I'm yours, Elle. However you'll have me."

"Even knowing your time is limited?"

His jaw tightened. "Especially then." He turned me back around, continued working the laces with careful precision. "I told you before—

225

my corruption is accelerating. I have enough time to see you through the convergence. To make sure you survive what's coming. After that…" He didn't finish.

He didn't need to.

My chest constricted, an ache that had nothing to do with the marks at my collarbones. Of course. Of course I'd finally find someone who looked at me like I mattered, who made me feel something real, and he came with an expiration date stamped across his soul.

My mother died when I was two. Too young to remember her, but old enough to spend my whole life feeling the absence.

My father checked out after that—physically present but emotionally gone, lost in grief that had no room for a daughter who looked too much like the woman he'd lost.

Julian chose someone else. Chose her over me, over the life we'd planned, over promises that turned out to mean nothing.

Grandma Jo left me, though that one wasn't her choice. Cancer didn't care about timing or fairness or the fact that she was the only person who'd ever made me feel like I belonged somewhere.

And now Kaelren. Not leaving by choice either, but leaving all the same. The universe apparently had a sick sense of humor about giving me people just long enough to need them before ripping them away.

"Elle?" His voice was concerned. "Your marks are flaring."

I realized my hands had clenched into fists, flowers blooming aggressively from my knuckles—thorned things with petals like knives.

"I'm fine."

"You're lying."

"I'm—" My voice cracked. "I just got you. I finally have something that feels real, that feels like mine, and you're already telling me I'm going to lose you."

He turned me to face him, his hands cupping my face with a gentleness that made my throat tight. "You're not losing me. Not while I'm still here. Not while I can still choose to be yours."

"But after—"

"After doesn't matter." His thumbs brushed away tears I hadn't realized were falling. "Listen to me. I have lived more years than you can imagine, and I have never—" He pressed his forehead to mine. "I have never felt this. Never wanted someone to survive more than I wanted my own survival. Whatever time we have, it's more than I thought I'd ever get."

"That's not fair."

"None of this is fair." He kissed me, soft and fierce all at once. "But I'm done pretending I don't want every moment I can steal with you. Even if it's not enough. Even if it ends badly. I'm choosing this. I'm choosing you."

I kissed him back, tasting salt and chocolate and the bittersweet knowledge that our time was borrowed. Part of me wanted to pull away, to protect myself from the inevitable grief. But I'd spent my whole life trying to protect myself from loss, and it had never worked. People left anyway.

At least this time, I'd know what I had before it was gone.

"Okay," I whispered against his mouth. "Okay. We'll take what we can get."

"That's all anyone gets, really. The rest is just an illusion of control."

"You're terrible at reassurance."

"I've been told." He smiled, and it was real despite everything. "But I'm excellent at making the most of borrowed time."

"Prove it."

So he did.

We returned to the main Thornwood compound looking thoroughly debauched despite our best efforts. My hair, even wet, still had flowers blooming in it—softer ones now, pink and gold instead of thorned. Kaelren's marks were more prominent than usual, pulsing contentedly. And neither of us could stop the occasional touch—his hand at my lower back, my fingers brushing his arm.

The physical contact felt like a promise. Or maybe a prayer. *Please let this last. Please let him survive. Please, for once, let me keep something good.*

Peeble was waiting on the balcony of our chambers, sitting next to Kevin the bee and looking extremely pleased with themselves.

"Have a nice trip?" they asked innocently.

"You're the worst," I said without heat.

"I'm the best. You'll realize that when you name your first child after me. Little Peeble Junior, or maybe Peeblina if it's a girl—"

"Never happening."

"We'll see. I'm very good at long-term manipulation." They paused, then added more seriously, "You two look happy. For once. It's gross, but also kind of nice."

"Thanks, Peeble," Kaelren said, surprising us both.

"Don't mention it. Seriously, don't. I have a reputation to maintain as a sarcastic asshole." They launched into the air, Kevin following. "I'm going to give you lovebirds some privacy. Try to keep the magical reality-warping orgasms to a minimum—some of us are trying to maintain a stable lifestyle here."

They disappeared before I could throw something at them.

"I like him," Kaelren said.

"Everyone does. It's infuriating."

He pulled me close, and I let myself lean into him, breathing in his scent— pine and storms and the garden still clinging to our clothes. I pressed my ear to his chest, listening to his heartbeat. Counting the beats like borrowed coins.

"Tomorrow there's a council meeting," he said quietly. "Strategy planning. It's going to be brutal."

"Politics always is."

"They'll want to use you. As a weapon, as leverage, as bait." His arms tightened around me. "I won't let them. But I need you to be prepared for how they'll see you."

"As a tool?"

"As our only chance." He pulled back to look at me. "The convergence is coming fast. We have maybe two weeks. Auradelle is moving, and we're running out of time to prepare."

Two weeks. Maybe less. Two weeks of Kaelren's heartbeat. Two weeks of this feeling, this belonging. Two weeks before I'd be alone again.

No. I shoved the thought away. I'd promised myself I wouldn't waste our time grieving what we'd lose. I'd grieve later, when it mattered. Right now, he was here. Solid and real and mine.

"Then we'd better make these two weeks count," I said.

"Every moment." He kissed me, soft and sure. "Starting with actually sleeping. You need rest."

"Bossy."

"Practical."

"Broody and practical. Such a catch."

"And yet you're still here."

"Lucky me," I said, and tried to mean it.

He led me inside, and for the first time since arriving in Wynmire, I fell asleep in his arms—ignoring the countdown running in my head, ignoring the certainty that I was setting myself up for another loss, choosing instead to hold onto the warmth of now.

Outside, the Thornwood Throne glowed with bioluminescent life. To-morrow there would be council meetings and strategy sessions. The convergence was coming, corruption spreading through both of us, time running out with every heartbeat.

But tonight, we had each other.

And I was going to pretend that was enough.

Even though I knew better.

Even though I'd learned this lesson before.

Even though loving people who leave had never once protected me from the pain of losing them.

22

Elle

We'd spent three days at the Thornwood Throne—three days of strategy meetings I was barely included in, of watching Kaelren disappear into war councils while the corruption spread another inch up his jaw, of feeling the weight of the convergence approaching like storm clouds on the horizon.

Three days of stolen moments between the planning sessions. His hand finding mine under the council table. Flowers blooming unconsciously in my hair whenever he looked at me. The ache of wanting more time when time was the one thing we didn't have.

We left Thornwood at dawn. By mid-morning, we were deep in the forest, following paths that seemed to shift when I wasn't looking.

Everything felt different now. Charged. Like the realm itself knew what had happened between us in the Pleasure Grove—knew that we'd stopped pretending, stopped holding back, stopped acting like we had forever when we both knew the countdown had already begun.

Kaelren had been quiet during those three days of planning, but I'd felt him through our bond—the constant drain of maintaining the Thornwood's barriers, the weight of decisions that would send people to their deaths, the way his corruption pulsed whenever he looked at me. And underneath it all, something new: a fierce protectiveness that made my chest ache, knowing it came with an expiration date.

The note he'd slipped under my door last night had been typically brief:

We leave at dawn. The convergence won't wait.

But when I'd opened the door to leave, he'd been standing there in the hallway—waiting, like he couldn't bear to let the night end without seeing me one more time. He'd kissed me against the doorframe, thorough and desperate, and I'd felt through the bond what he couldn't say: I'm running out of time to memorize this.

Now, hours into our journey, the landscape had shifted from the living architecture of the Thornwood into something wilder, more primal. The trees here were ancient, their trunks so massive that the entire crew could have linked hands and still not encircled them. Their roots dove deep into earth that hummed with old magic, the kind that predated kingdoms and courts and carved marks. Mist clung to everything, turning the world soft at the edges.

"My feet hurt," Bryx complained for the third time in an hour, always so dramatic. "Why couldn't we take the bee highways? Kevin misses me."

"The bee highways are watched," Sarnyx replied without looking back. She'd been leading our group with the kind of rigid precision that suggested she was holding herself together through pure will. "The Hunt has eyes everywhere now."

"Paranoid much?" Bryx muttered, but quietly. We'd all noticed how Sarnyx had been since the planning sessions—wound tighter than a spring, her hand never straying far from her weapon.

Vashael and Nimor walked together, their shoulders occasionally brushing in a way that would have been casual if not for how Nimor's form solidified each time they touched. Something had shifted between them during our time at the Thornwood, something tender and unspoken that made my chest ache with recognition.

I understood that now—the desperate need to hold onto connection when the world was ending. The way touch became prayer.

"We'll rest here," Kaelren announced suddenly, his voice cutting through my wandering thoughts.

The clearing looked like someone had designed it specifically for rest. Morning glory vines formed natural canopies overhead, their deep purple blooms releasing a faint glow. Thick moss cushioned every step. The air was heavy with sweetness—honey, rain-soaked soil, and unfamiliar blossoms.

But it was the lake that drew my attention, pulled to it like a magnet draws iron.

It stretched before us like captured sky, its surface so still it could have been glass. The water was impossibly clear, showing stones at the bottom that glowed faintly with their own light—some blue, some green, some with a pearl-like radiance. The edges were lined with cattails that chimed softly in a breeze I couldn't feel, their sound like distant bells.

Something about it made my marks tingle, a sensation somewhere between warning and recognition. The marks on my arms seemed to pulse in rhythm with something beneath the water's surface.

"Mirror Lake," Nimor said, materializing beside me in that unsettling way he had. His shadow form was more solid today, but I could still see through him if I looked at the right angle. "They say it shows truth to those brave enough to look."

"Or foolish enough," Vashael added, but her attention was on Nimor, not the water. Her pollen-touched skin seemed to glow in response to his proximity, little sparkles dancing across her cheeks.

"Why do mystical lakes always have to show truth?" Peeble complained, landing on my shoulder with their familiar weight. "Why can't they show something helpful, like tomorrow's weather or where you dropped that thing you were looking for?"

The crew dispersed to set up camp—Bryx immediately challenging anyone who'd listen to a game of dice, his carved wooden set appearing from somewhere in his many pockets. Sarnyx began checking the perimeter with her usual paranoia, placing small ward stones at strategic points. Eltrien wandered toward a cluster of strange mushrooms, pulling out vials and muttering about "fascinating spore patterns."

But I couldn't look away from the lake. It pulled at something deep in my chest, a yearning I couldn't name.

"Don't go near it," Kaelren said, suddenly at my shoulder. His hand found mine instinctively, fingers threading through mine with the ease of new habit. Through our bond, I felt his unease.

"Why?" I asked, though part of me already knew the answer would be cryptic and unhelpful.

"The Mirror Lake isn't just water. It's a threshold. Sometimes things come through. Sometimes things get pulled in."

I took a step toward it, fascinated, but his hand tightened around mine—gentle but firm.

"Elle. I'm serious. Stay away from it."

The intensity in his voice made me look at him, really look. The corruption had spread another fraction up his jaw since morning, and his eyes held genuine fear—not for himself, but for me.

"Okay," I said, squeezing his hand back. "You're right. Sorry. It's just... it's beautiful."

"Beautiful things are often the most dangerous in this realm," he said, then added more quietly, his thumb brushing across my knuckles, "Present company excluded."

Despite everything, I smiled. "Did you just make a joke?"

"I've been known to try. The results are usually unfortunate."

"That's because your delivery needs work." I stood on my toes to kiss him quickly, tasting concern and something softer beneath it. "But I appreciate the effort."

He pulled me closer for just a moment, pressing his forehead to mine. Through the bond, I felt what he couldn't say: I can't lose you. Not when I just found you. Not like this.

"I'll be careful," I promised.

"You're terrible at careful."

"Then it's lucky I have you to keep me from doing anything stupid."

Something flickered across his face—grief, maybe, or guilt. Because we both knew his time to keep me safe was running out, measured in days now, not weeks.

For the next hour, I helped the others set up camp properly. Refilled everyone's canteens from a small stream that fed into the lake—but from a safe distance, always with Kaelren watching. The water from the stream was cold and tasted of minerals and something green, like drinking the essence of the forest itself.

"At least eat something," Vashael insisted, pressing dried fruit and something that might have been jerky into my hands. "You barely touched breakfast."

The food tasted like nothing, my appetite gone since we'd left the Thornwood, but I forced it down anyway. Everyone was trying so hard to act normal, like this was just another day on the run, not the prelude to something terrible.

"I need to..." I gestured vaguely toward the tree line, the universal signal for bathroom needs.

"Take Peeble," Kaelren said immediately.

"I don't need a bathroom buddy," I protested. "I'm twenty-nine years old."

"Take Peeble," he repeated, and there was no room for argument in his tone.

"Oh joy, I get to be the pee guardian," Peeble complained but landed on my shoulder anyway. "The glamorous life of a cosmic beetle."

I walked into the trees, found a suitable spot, and took care of business while Peeble politely faced the other direction, humming something off-key and vaguely rhythmic.

"Are you making that up or is that an actual song?" I asked as I finished.

"Does it matter? I'm a beetle with excellent taste."

On the way back to camp, I took a slightly different path—not intention-ally, but the trees seemed to have shifted while I wasn't looking. Or maybe I was just disoriented. The forest did that sometimes, rearranged itself when you weren't paying attention.

That's when I saw it again—the lake, but from a different angle. This side was hidden from the camp by a thick stand of willows whose branches trailed in the water like fingers. The surface here was even more still, even more perfect.

And in the reflection, I saw her.

"Jo?" The name escaped before I could stop it.

My grandmother stood in the water's reflection, young and beautiful, wearing a crown of roses that bloomed and died and bloomed again. She was pressing her hand against the surface from below, her mouth moving urgently, and this time I could almost hear her—

"Elle, don't—" Peeble started, but I was already moving.

The closer I got, the clearer she became. Not just clear—actively luminous, as if lit from below by something that had never known the sun. The surface tension looked wrong too, more like mercury than water, holding its shape with an unnatural perfection.

My reflection stared back at me, but it was wrong in ways that made my skin crawl. My marks glowed brighter in the reflection than they did on my actual skin, pulsing with a rhythm that didn't match my heartbeat. My eyes held knowledge I didn't possess, older and sadder than they should be. And there was something about my expression—a resignation that didn't belong on my face.

Then the surface rippled, though no wind touched it. The ripples moved in perfect concentric circles, originating from nowhere and everywhere at once.

The reflection changed.

Not me anymore—or not just me. I saw the Hunt behind my reflected self, tall figures in armor curated from my worst nightmare, their edges blurring where they met regular air. They stood motionless, patient, waiting with the terrible patience of predators who knew their prey had nowhere to run. Their mounts stamped feet that might have been hooves or claws or something worse.

But that wasn't what made my breath catch, what made my heart stutter in my chest.

It was what appeared next.

Grandma Jo's garden materialized in the water, as real as if I was looking through a window into Earth. Every detail was perfect—the heritage tomatoes hanging heavy on their vines, so ripe they seemed about to burst. The roses climbing their careful trellises, each bloom exactly as I remembered. The herb spiral with its mysterious plants that had never quite seemed to belong. Even the greenhouse was there, its glass panels catching late afternoon sunlight in a way that made them gleam like burnished metal.

And there—there by the greenhouse door—stood a figure I knew too well.

"Julian?" The name escaped before I could stop it, scraped raw from my throat.

My ex-fiancé stood in Jo's garden, but not as a memory. This was current Julian, wearing the blue button-down I'd bought him for his birthday last year. There was a fresh cut on his cheek—had he been in an accident? He looked lost, confused, searching as he called out.

"Elle? Elle, where are you? Your dad's worried sick. We all are. The police said you just vanished, but I know you wouldn't just leave. Please, just come home. We can work this out. I know I messed up with Melissa, but—"

It was impossible. There was no connection between Earth and this realm. But the water showed him turning, searching, and I could see the engagement ring he still wore on a chain around his neck—the one I'd thrown at him when I'd found him with Melissa in our bed, in our apartment, on what was supposed to be our anniversary.

"That's not real," Peeble said urgently, their voice sharper than usual. "Elle, you know that's not real. The lake shows what you want to see, what you fear to see. It's a trap."

"I don't want to see Julian," I said, but my voice came out wrong, uncertain.

"Don't you? Some part of you that wishes you could go back? Pretend none of this happened?" Peeble's words stung, but they were trying to break through whatever hold the lake had on me.

Before I could answer—before I could even process the truth in their words—the image shifted again.

Now it was Jo herself, but young Jo from the locket, standing in the water-garden. She wore a dress that seemed to be made of flower petals and morning dew, still wearing the crown of roses. Her eyes were the same warm brown I remembered, but there was power in them that made my marks burn.

She pressed her hand against the surface from below, and I could see her lips moving, forming words I couldn't hear but somehow understood.

"Come home," she seemed to say. *"Come back where you belong. This isn't your fight. This isn't your world."*

"My grandma died weeks ago," I said, but my hand was already reaching for the water, moving without my conscious control.

"Elle, don't—"

My fingers touched the surface.

The contact triggered an avalanche of sensation. Not pain—something stranger. Like every memory and feeling I'd ever had was trying to surface at the exact same moment. I saw myself at seven, planting seeds with Jo, her weathered hands guiding mine as we tucked tomato seedlings into the earth. At fifteen, screaming at my dad that he didn't understand me, that I was meant for something more than his suburban dreams. At twenty-six, saying yes to Julian's proposal in that restaurant where he'd hidden the ring in the tiramisu, feeling like I was settling even as the word left my mouth. At twenty-eight, about a year ago, watching him with Melissa, seeing them tangled together in sheets I'd picked out, and feeling more relief than heartbreak.

The water gripped my wrist, but it felt nothing like water. Warm and dense, it moved with purpose—pulling with a strength no liquid should possess. Steady as a tide, patient as stone. I tried to pull free, but I was already in past my forearm. Through the surface, I could sense the other side. Warmth. Real warmth, not the strange temperatures of Wynmire. The warmth of grass in sunlight and houses with central heating. The warmth of the world I'd lost.

I could smell it through the water—freshly cut grass and barbecue smoke from the neighbors. Could hear distantly familiar sounds—cars passing on the street, a dog barking, someone's music playing too loud. All the mundane symphony of the life I'd left behind.

"Elle, no! Hold on!" Peeble's voice was pure panic now. "He's coming—I can see him running—just hold on!"

But the lake was stronger, older, hungrier. It pulled me through the surface up to my shoulders, and now I could see both worlds—the realm above, Earth below, and me suspended between like I'd always been.

Through the bond, I felt Kaelren's awareness snap to attention—felt the exact moment he realized something was wrong. Felt his terror spike like lightning through my chest.

"Find me," I managed to say to Peeble, to the air, to whoever might hear. The words felt important, necessary, like a key being fitted to a lock. "Tell him—in this lifetime or any other. Tell him to find me."

The water surged, and suddenly I was through, pulled into depths that couldn't exist in a lake so shallow. But through the water, through the crushing weight of it, I saw him—Kaelren, running full speed from the camp, his mouth open in what must have been a scream of my name though I couldn't hear it underwater. His corruption spread like wings of darkness behind him, beautiful and terrible, as he dove for the lake without hesitation.

The last clear thing I saw before the darkness took me was his hand reaching through the water toward mine, fingertips almost touching, the thread of our bond stretching between us like it could defy physics itself.

Almost.

But almost had never been enough.

Through the muffling water, I heard Peeble's voice, not sarcastic for once, laden with a grief that suggested this wasn't the first time they'd witnessed this:

"Not again. Please, not again."

Then there was nothing but water and memory and the sensation of drowning.

The water was every temperature at once—burning, freezing, body-warm, nonexistent. I couldn't tell if I was breathing it or if it was breathing me. Images flashed behind my eyes like a film reel running too fast:

Jo young and beautiful, choosing love over duty. Jo old and dying, pressing a locket into my hand. My mother as a child, golden marks spreading up her small arms before Jo took her away. My mother dying when I was young, the marks having turned to cancer on Earth. Kaelren as a child, hope bright in his eyes. Kaelren screaming, corruption spreading from that first wound. Myself in a crown of living wood, power radiating from me like heat from a star. Myself dead, nothing but a failure.

When I finally surfaced I was somewhere else entirely.

The Hunt was waiting on the other side.

They stood in a perfect semicircle, tall and terrible and patient. Their armor caught light, reflecting it back in sharp flashes that made my eyes water.

"Prophet," one of them said, and their voice majestic and horrifying all at once. "You're exactly on time."

I tried to speak, to make some sarcastic comment that would make this feel less like a nightmare, but lake water poured from my mouth instead— silver water that evaporated before it hit the ground, leaving only the ghost of moisture.

"The convergence approaches," another Hunt rider said. "The wheel turns."

"I just want to go home," I managed, though the words came out waterlogged and wrong.

"Home," the first rider mused, tilting their helmed head. "Such a simple word for such a complex concept. Is home the Earth you left? The Thornwood where you danced? Or perhaps..." They gestured, and I felt the weight of their attention like pressure in my skull. "Perhaps home is wherever he is."

Through the bond, thin as spider silk now but still there, I felt Kaelren's rage like a distant wildfire. He was coming. Of course he was coming. He would tear apart the world to reach me.

"I'm sorry," I thought through the bond, not knowing if he could hear me. *"I'm sorry we don't get more time."*

"Take her," the lead rider commanded. "Auradelle awaits."

Hands lifted me onto a mount that smelled of old leather. Restraints that might have been rope or might have been living vines wrapped around my wrists, burning with a cold that went deeper than skin.

As we rode—flew? —I caught glimpses of what we passed. The realm was dying, sick, corrupted. Not just in patches but systematically, spreading out from the Heartspire like infection from a wound. Trees stood as blackened skeletons. Rivers ran backwards, their water thick and dark as old blood. The very air seemed to rot, leaving tears in reality that showed nothing but void.

And somewhere behind us, following the pull of our bond, Kaelren was coming—bringing his own corruption, his obsession, his determination.

The Hunt rode on, and I closed my eyes, trying not to see how each hoofbeat left another piece of the realm a little more broken.

Trying not to think about how we'd had three days together, and I'd wasted at least half of them in strategy meetings.

Trying not to count the hours we'd lost that we could never get back.

23

Kaelren

The bond didn't break—it stretched and tore and muted until I could barely feel her. One moment Elle was there, angry and bright in my consciousness, a flame I'd grown dependent on without realizing. The next, almost nothing. A whisper where there had been a shout. A cold ember where there had been fire.

The loss hit me like a physical blow, doubling me over at the lake's edge where I'd just watched her disappear beneath impossible water.

"ELLE!"

The roar tore from my throat, inhuman, primal. The golden vines that had appeared on my arms in the Pleasure Grove—the ones I hadn't told her about, hadn't let her see when she'd traced patterns on my skin with glowing mushroom paint—turned black instantly, spreading up my forearms like poison through veins. I'd kept my sleeves down these past three days, unwilling to show her that being with her had marked me permanently. Where they touched my carved marks, the silver-blue light died, replaced by something that ate light rather than created it.

I dove back into the Mirror Lake without thinking, but the water rejected me—burned like acid against my corrupted marks. Each stroke felt like swimming through molten glass. But she wasn't there. The lake had taken her somewhere else, somewhere beyond my reach.

I surfaced gasping, scanning the water that had become hatefully serene.

"Get away from the water!" Vashael commanded, but I was already moving, running in the direction my corrupted instincts said she'd been taken.

Trees split where I passed, their trunks cracking not from physical force but from the wrongness radiating from my skin. Roots erupted from the earth, reaching for enemies that weren't there, responding to the violence in my blood.

The others followed, trying to keep up, but I was beyond caring about them. Beyond caring about anything except the growing emptiness where Elle should be.

"Kaelren, stop," Peeble's voice came, frantic. "You're going the wrong way. They took her east, but you can't just—"

"Then tell me where she is!" I snarled at the tiny creature now perched on my shoulder, having grown to the size of a cat during the chaos.

"I'm trying, but you're not listening! You're just destroying everything!"

I stopped, finally noticing the devastation behind me. A trail of dead vegetation, trees withered to husks, the ground itself cracked and wrong. The corruption wasn't just in my marks anymore—it was leaking out, poisoning everything I touched.

"Where?" The word came out as a growl.

"East. Toward the Heartspire. But Kaelren, you can't just charge in—"

I started moving, but Sarnyx stepped into my path.

"We need a plan," she said, thorns extended but trembling slightly. She'd seen what I'd done to the forest. "Charging in will just get her killed."

"Move."

"No."

The rage that had been building since Elle's capture finally found a target. I had Sarnyx by the throat before she could react, lifting her off the ground. Her thorns pierced my arm, but I didn't feel them. All I felt was rage—pure, corrupted, absolute.

"You should have stopped me from sending her off with just Peeble," I snarled, my grip tightening. Black veins spread from where I touched her, and she gasped in pain. "You knew the lake was dangerous. You should have gone with her. You should have—"

"Kaelren!" Vashael's voice cut through the red haze. "Put her down. This isn't helping."

"She lost her!" I squeezed tighter, watching Sarnyx's face turn purple. The black veins from my touch were spreading up her neck now.

Vashael's blade pressed against my ribs. "Put. Her. Down. Or I'll put you down."

"Try it," I said, and my marks pulsed with such violent light that she staggered back.

Nimor tried to grab me from behind, manifesting from shadow, but the moment he touched me, he screamed. The corruption burned him, sent him reeling back with black marks spreading across his hands.

"Someone stop him!" Bryx shouted. "He's going to kill her!"

Then Peeble landed on my hand—the one crushing Sarnyx's throat.

"She wouldn't want this," the creature said, and suddenly I wasn't hearing Peeble's voice but something of Elle channeled through our dying bond. *"Kaelren, please. Don't become the monster they think you are. Not for me."*

My grip loosened. Not much, but enough.

"She's scared," Peeble continued. "She's in pain. The Hunt has her, and they're taking her to Auradelle. She needs you functional, not feral. She needs you to be smart, not just strong."

I dropped Sarnyx, who collapsed gasping. The black veins I'd left on her throat were already fading, but the memory of them wouldn't.

"I'm sorry," I said, but the words felt hollow. I wasn't sorry. I wanted to destroy everything between me and Elle. I wanted to paint the realm in blood until she was back where she belonged—with me.

"That's the corruption talking," Peeble said. "Look at yourself."

I looked down. The golden vines that had been beautiful just days ago—when Elle had smiled up at me from that nest of moss and flowers, when she'd told me she wanted me despite knowing our time was limited—were now black as midnight, spreading past my elbows, up my biceps. Where they met my carved marks, they twisted together into patterns that hurt to look at. My skin between the marks was pale, almost gray, like something dead.

"We need to get to Silverpine Hollow," Vashael said, helping Sarnyx to her feet. "There are rebels there. People who can help. Resources."

"How long?" My voice was rough, barely controlled.

"Three days if we push hard."

"The convergence—" I stopped, calculating. The days we'd spent at Thornwood Throne, plus three more days of travel to Silverpine would just give us over a week until the convergence. "We have time. Barely."

"Before what?" Eltrien asked, his mycelial markings pulsing with that disturbing rhythm.

"Before the convergence," I said. "Before whatever Auradelle plans comes to pass. Before this realm either survives or is destroyed completely."

His marks pulsed, steady and knowing. "Then we'd better move," he said quietly.

We ran through the day and most of the night. I couldn't stop, wouldn't stop. Every moment we delayed was another moment Elle suffered. Through our bond, faint as gossamer, I felt flashes—cold that burned, marks turning gray at the edges, someone's voice saying something about the Bloom. Pain. Fear. But also defiance, that stubborn refusal to break that was so essentially Elle.

"*I'm coming*," I sent through the bond, not knowing if she could hear me. "*Hold on. I'm coming for you.*"

And impossibly, faintly, I felt her response—not words, but the memory of her voice from our last night together: "*Find me. In this lifetime or any other. Find me.*"

By the time we reached Silverpine Hollow on the third day, I was more corruption than man.

The settlement was built into living pines, massive trees that had been coaxed to grow shelters within their trunks. It should have been beautiful. But the moment I entered, the trees recoiled. Leaves withered. Bark cracked. The living wood recognized what I was becoming and feared it.

"Who is that?" someone whispered.

"That's not a who anymore," another replied. "That's a what."

Thrak, the rebel leader of Silverpine, was a scarred veteran missing his left eye. He may not have been tall as me, but he was built for war nonetheless. He took one look at me and reached for his weapon.

"He's with us," Vashael said quickly. "This is our leader, Kaelren. He's... sick."

"That's not sick," Thrak said. "That's corrupted. That's dangerous."

"Yes," I agreed, meeting his gaze with eyes that had gone silver-white. "I am. And I'll be worse if you don't help me get her back."

"Her?"

"The marked one. The human. Elle."

Something shifted in Thrak's expression. "The prophecy girl? She's been taken?"

"By the Hunt. To Auradelle. Three days ago."

"Shit." He lowered his weapon slightly. "That changes things. Come on, we need to talk. Away from the trees you're killing."

We were taken to the center of the settlement, where an ancient pine served as a meeting hall. The moment I entered, frost spread across the floor from my footsteps. The torches flickered, dimming. Several rebels backed away, fear plain on their faces.

Thrak gestured to the others already assembled. "My inner circle. Vera—" A woman with bark-textured skin and calculating eyes nodded. "Former Crown guard, turned when she saw what Auradelle was building. Knows the Heartspire inside and out." He indicated a massive being whose body seemed carved from living stone. "Gorak. Demolitions. If it needs breaking, he breaks it." Finally, a slight figure wreathed in shadow. "Lysandra. Seer. She's the one who told us you were coming."

"These are the people I trust with my life," Thrak said, meeting my corrupted gaze steadily. "You can trust them with yours."

"Tell us everything," he continued. "From the beginning."

So I did. Or Vashael did, mostly, because every time I tried to speak, the corruption made my voice into something that terrified everyone. She told them about Elle's arrival, her marks, the growing bond between us, the Hunt's attack at Mirror Lake.

"We have nine days until the convergence," I managed to rasp out. "Auradelle will try to force her to merge Root and Bloom."

"And if she refuses?" Thrak asked.

"Then the convergence fails," I said. "The imbalance between Root and Bloom becomes permanent. The realm tears itself apart." I met his gaze. "Elle is human. She's the only one who can bridge both forces. Without her, there's no convergence. Just collapse."

"And you know this how?"

"The bond," I said. "I feel what she feels. I see glimpses of what Auradelle plans. He needs her alive, needs her willing, or his ritual fails and takes everything with it."

Thrak studied me with his one good eye. "So we're not just rescuing the girl. We're preventing the end of the realm."

"I don't care about the realm," I said flatly. "I care about her. But yes—saving her saves everything else." I stood, and the corruption spread another inch, visible through my shirt now—black veins creating a web across my chest. "Help me get her back, or get out of my way."

Thrak studied me for a long moment. "My grandfather helped build the Heartspire," he said finally. "Before Auradelle took power. Before the walls became a prison. He told me about tunnels beneath the fortress. Root-carved passages that predate the Crown's occupation."

We'd discussed this at Thornwood, during the strategy sessions I'd barely been able to focus on because all I'd wanted was to find Elle, pull her away from the council table, and steal more time with her while we still had it.

Hope, painful and sharp, flared in my chest. "The sealed passages. Can we break through?"

"Seals can be broken. Especially by someone the Root recognizes." He looked meaningfully at my marks. "Or someone corrupted enough to force their way through."

"Then we use the tunnels."

"It's not that simple," Vera spoke up. "The Heartspire has two walls—the outer is ceremonial, easy enough if you're not spotted. But the inner wall..." She pulled out an old map, hand-drawn on leather. "Forty feet high, topped with massive spikes that burn Root-touched on contact. Your corruption especially would light up like a beacon."

"I don't care about burns."

"You should. These wards don't just burn—they mark. Every Crown soldier in the Heartspire would know exactly where you are."

The corruption pulsed, and I had to grip the table to keep from destroying it. The ancient wood began to rot under my touch, centuries of growth withering in seconds.

"Stop destroying my furniture," Thrak growled, but there was no real heat in it. He'd seen what I'd done to the trees outside—an entire grove withered because I'd leaned against one trunk while trying to feel Elle through our dying bond.

Through the muffled bond, so faint I might have imagined it, I felt Elle's defiance like a distant flame. She was fighting. She was surviving. She was waiting for me.

"Mine," I sent through the connection, pushing so hard that dark blood ran from my nose. *"Always."*

And impossibly, faintly, I felt her response—not words, but a feeling. Recognition. Love. Fear for me, even now. And underneath it all: *"Hurry."*

"How long to prepare?" I asked.

"Give us four days," Thrak said. "We can gather forces, plan the assault properly—"

"Four days?" I stood so fast the chair disintegrated. "We have nine days until convergence. I'm not wasting half of our time planning when she's suffering right now."

"That's suicide."

"That's necessary." The corruption surged, and several people stepped back as the temperature dropped twenty degrees. "I leave in three days, with or without help. That gives us six days to reach her and get out before the convergence."

Thrak and Vashael exchanged looks.

"Three days to prepare, five days to travel, and one night of rest before all hell breaks loose" Vashael said slowly. "That's... tight. But possible."

"It has to be," I said. "Because I'm done waiting. I'm done being careful. I'm done watching the people I—" I stopped, the words catching. "I'm done losing what matters."

Peeble landed on my shoulder again.

"She knows you're coming," the creature said quietly. "She can feel you through the bond. It's the only thing keeping her from breaking."

"Then we'd better not disappoint her," Thrak said, already pulling out more maps. "Three days to prepare. You're going to need every advantage we can give you. Because breaking into the Heartspire before convergence? That's not a rescue mission. That's a declaration of war."

"Good," I said, and my smile made several rebels step back. "I've been wanting to burn something down."

The corruption spread another inch, and somewhere in the distance, I felt Elle shiver.

Nine days until convergence.

"Hold on," I whispered into our dying bond. *"I'm coming. And I'm bringing Hell with me."*

And through the fading connection, I felt her response—not words, but a memory. The taste of peppermint and chocolate. The feeling of her hands in my hair. The sound of her laugh when I'd tried to tell a joke and failed spectacularly.

The memory of three days at Thornwood when we'd had everything, before the world had stolen it away.

I was getting those days back.

Even if I had to destroy the entire realm to do it.

24

Elle

I came to with my face pressed against something that might have been leather and definitely smelled like death warmed over and left in the sun for a week. My head pounded in rhythm with hoofbeats—or what should have been hoofbeats but sounded more like breaking glass on stone, like ceramics shattering in slow motion. Every part of me hurt in new and creative ways, from my hair follicles to my toenails, with special attention paid to my spine, which felt like someone had replaced it with a string of hot coals.

"She wakes," a voice said above me, cultured and cold as winter moonlight, with an accent that wasn't quite British, wasn't quite anything from Earth.

I tried to sit up and immediately regretted every life choice that had led to this moment. My wrists were bound by restraints that felt alive, aware, and deeply offended by my existence. Root-forged restraints, my scattered mind supplied helpfully, as if naming the thing hurting me would somehow make it hurt less.

"I'm going to be sick," I managed, and I wasn't lying. My stomach was doing gymnastics that would have won Olympic gold.

"If you vomit on my mount, I'll drag you behind it instead." The threat was delivered so casually it took a moment to register. Like someone mentioning they'd forgotten to buy milk.

I forced my eyes open. The light was strange—dim and gray, making

249

everything look faded. The air felt heavy in my lungs, harder to breathe than it should be.

The rider looming over me was tall and armored in dark metal etched with silver. Frost clung to the edges of their armor despite no cold in the air. Their helmet had no openings except for the eyes, which burned with a dull red glow.

"Where are you taking me?" My voice came out rough, like I'd been gargling gravel.

"Where you were always meant to go."

Helpful. Super specific. I loved cryptic non-answers when I was bound and being kidnapped by supernatural beings. Really added to the ambiance of the whole situation.

I turned my head—slowly, carefully, trying not to trigger another wave of nausea—to take in our surroundings. What I saw made my stomach drop through the floor and possibly through several sub-basements of reality.

The landscape was dying.

Not dead—dying. Present tense. Active tense. Very much currently in the process of dying. I watched grass blacken and curl in real-time, like watching those time-lapse videos of fruit rotting, but at normal speed. Trees withered to husks as we passed, their leaves falling as ash that disappeared before it touched the ground. The very air tasted of decay, sweet and cloying and wrong, like flowers left too long in a funeral home.

This wasn't natural corruption like Kaelren's—his darkness had a purpose, a logic to it. This was systematic destruction, deliberate and thorough and absolutely certain. The kind of death that didn't allow for resurrection.

"The realm," I whispered, horror making my voice small. "You're killing it."

"We're cleansing it," another rider said, pulling alongside us. This one's voice was feminine, but I couldn't make out their form clearly—they kept blurring at the edges, shifting slightly whenever I tried to focus. "The rot was already here, spreading from the Heartspire outward. We merely... accelerate the process."

"That makes no sense—"

"Doesn't it?" The first rider adjusted their grip on me as one of their horrific mounts navigated a fallen tree. "The Crown Prince has been spreading corruption for years, trying to force a bond with power that won't have him. You've been warping reality just by existing. The realm recognizes the threat you both pose."

"So you're what—antibodies?" The scientific metaphor felt absurd in this context, but my brain was grasping for familiar concepts.

"We are servants of the cycle," they said, and I could hear the capital letters in their voice. "We ensure the wheel turns as it must. That patterns hold. That stories end as they're meant to end."

I just blinked at them like I knew whatever the fuck that meant.

Through the bond—muffled but still there, like hearing music from another room—I felt Kaelren's rage like a distant wildfire. He was coming. Of course he was coming. The idiot was probably destroying everything in his path to reach me, leaving a trail of corruption a mile wide, which was exactly what these things wanted.

"You're using me as bait."

"You're using yourself as bait," the rider corrected with what might have been amusement. "Every choice you've made has led here. Every moment of defiance, every refusal to accept your role—it all ends the same way. The lake, the capture, the convergence. Sixteen times before, and now the seventeenth begins."

"Are you on drugs? Do you even hear yourself?"

"You'll see soon enough."

I was too exhausted to even try and unravel whatever nonsense riddle they were spitting my way.

The Heartspire rose before us like a cancer made of diamonds and light, and my first thought was that someone had fucked up spectacularly in the architecture department. It should have been beautiful—a palace of living glass that caught and refracted sunlight into rainbow cascades that danced across every surface. Instead, it hurt to look at, its perfection somehow wrong, like a smile with too many teeth or a laugh that goes on too long. Every angle was precise but felt off, like someone had built it according to

251

mathematics that didn't quite match reality.

The rot was worse here, so much worse. The gardens that should have been paradise were nightmares of decay, flowers blooming and dying in accelerated cycles—bud to bloom to empty husk in seconds. Trees growing and withering in moments, their entire lifecycle compressed into seconds. The fountains ran with something that wasn't quite water—too thick, too dark, with an oily sheen that made my stomach turn.

The very air felt sick, heavy with the scent of corrupted magic that made my marks burn like someone had traced them with acid.

"The Crown Prince's work," the rider said, noting my horror with what might have been satisfaction. "He's been trying to force the realm to accept him for years. This is the result—a kingdom dying from the inside out because its would-be ruler carved false marks into his skin. Because he couldn't accept rejection. Because he had to have what wasn't his."

"Kaelren didn't cause this." The defense came automatically, even though I wasn't entirely sure it was true.

"No? Look closer."

And I did, though I wished I hadn't. The patterns in the rot, the way it spread in veins and fractals—it matched the corruption I'd seen in Kaelren's marks. But reversed, somehow. Like a photo negative. Like an echo bouncing back wrong. Like—

"A rejection," I breathed, understanding hitting like cold water. "The realm is rejecting him."

"The realm is rejecting both of you. But Auradelle believes he can change that. Fix you. Use you. Shape you into what the realm needs rather than what you are."

We passed through gates that opened without touch, into a courtyard where fountains ran aqua-blue water. Guards in thorned armor watched us pass, their faces hidden behind mirrors that reflected nothing—not us, not the world, just empty silver that suggested voids where people should be.

The throne room was worse than the gardens, worse than my worst expectations. Beautiful and terrible in equal measure, every surface reflecting and refracting light until reality became a kaleidoscope of possibility.

Standing there was like being inside a prism, broken into component parts and scattered. My reflection appeared on every surface, but each one was different—some younger, some older, some corrupted like Kaelren, some glowing with power I didn't possess. Yet.

And there, at its heart, stood Auradelle.

He looked exactly as I remembered from our first encounter—that sharp, cold beauty that made you want to look away and stare at the same time. His platinum hair caught the fractured light, and his winter honey eyes held that same frozen core I'd noticed before. But something was different now. He seemed more tired, more desperate, though he hid it well behind that practiced royal composure.

His robes had changed—they seemed to shift between white and gold, more elaborate than when I'd first met him. Like he was trying harder to project power, to convince himself as much as anyone else that he was in control.

And his smile—his smile was the worst thing about him. Warm and welcoming and absolutely sincere, like he was genuinely delighted to see me. Like we were old friends reuniting after too long apart.

"Miss Hawthorne," he said, and my name in his mouth sounded like a prayer and a curse all at once. "Welcome back. I've been waiting for this moment since you slipped through my fingers."

The Hunt released me, and I stumbled, catching myself before I could fall because I'd be damned if I was going to collapse at this asshole's feet. The restraints on my wrists dissolved, but I could still feel their echo, burning under my skin like phantom pain.

"Usually people just send a nice invitation." I managed, proud that my voice didn't shake. "Not supernatural bounty hunters. But then again, you've never been one for normal social conventions."

His laugh was genuine, delighted, which somehow made it worse. "Still that wonderful defiance. Even better than when we first met. That fire—you're so much like her."

"Like who?"

"Your grandmother, of course. Josephine." He stepped closer, and I saw his gaze catch on my throat. "And wearing Jo's locket. How wonderfully sentimental."

Everything in me went cold, then hot, then cold again. "You know about Jo?"

"Know about her?" His smile widened, showing teeth that were just slightly too white, too perfect. "My dear child, I knew her personally. Before she fled to Earth. Before she abandoned the realm that needed her."

He reached out as if to touch the locket, and I jerked back hard enough to stumble. My back hit one of the mirrors, and I hit my head hard enough to see stars.

"Stay away from me."

"You're lying," I said, but my voice shook. "My grandmother would never—she wouldn't have—"

"Wouldn't have what? Fallen in love with a prince? Borne his child?" Auradelle tilted his head. "She was human once too, before the marks changed her. Before she became something more."

My stomach twisted. My mother had been a bastard princess. Auradelle was my uncle. The man who'd captured me, who was trying to use me for some twisted ritual, was family.

"No," I whispered. "That doesn't make any sense. Why would she run? Why would she hide my mother on Earth?"

"Because she saw what she'd become," he said simply. "And she feared the Bloom would take her daughter from her as a sacrifice."

"You see, the convergence is in nine days. The celestial alignment accelerated when you went through the lake—the realm recognized your presence and responded. Nine days to convince you to save this realm. Nine days to undo the damage your grandmother's choice caused."

"And if I refuse?"

"Then the convergence collapses. The imbalance between Root and Bloom becomes permanent. The realm tears itself apart over decades instead of finding harmony." He leaned forward. "And your Kaelren dies with it. The corruption is eating him alive, you know. Faster now, since you've been taken. By the time he reaches you—and he will try to reach you—there might be nothing left but a monster wearing his face."

"Don't talk about him like you know him."

"But I do know him, Princess. I trained him, once." Auradelle's voice went soft with something almost like regret. "After Jo left, my father forced me to face the Bloom. To prove I was worthy despite my bastard half-sister's existence. The Bloom rejected me. Violently. Left me with these." He gestured to his corruption marks. "For years afterward, I searched for another candidate. Someone the Bloom might accept where I had failed."

He smiled, cold and bitter. "A seer told me about a boy. Said he was the key to everything. So I trained Kaelren from childhood. Made him a prince. Taught him to control Root magic, to understand the balance, to be everything I couldn't be. And when he was finally ready, when I presented him to the Bloom..." He paused. "It rejected him too. Nearly killed him. The corruption you see consuming him now? That's where it started. That's the wound that never healed. He carved those marks desperately trying to make the prophecy come true. Little did I know he was the key, the key that unlocked the door to you."

My heart broke for Kaelren. Knowing all he had sacrificed. Knowing he thought he was never enough, with all the weight of the realm on his shoulders.

Auradelle gestured, and guards stepped forward—not threateningly, but present. Making it clear I wasn't a guest but wasn't quite a prisoner either.

"I've prepared quarters for you," he continued, back to that horrible sincere warmth. "Comfortable ones. You'll find I'm not the villain young Kaelren has painted me as. I'm simply a man trying to save a dying realm with the tools available. A regent holding a throne for a ruler who ran away, waiting for someone worthy to claim it properly."

"By kidnapping me?"

"By showing you the truth." His eyes glittered with something cold and hungry, the kind of certainty that had burned witches and started wars. "Your grandmother was a coward who ran rather than face her destiny. Your mother was weak, dying pathetically on Earth rather than returning where she belonged. But you..." His smile turned predatory. "You know deep down, beneath all that defiance, you know what you are. Property of this realm. Mine to shape. Mine to use."

"I belong on Earth."

"No, my dear. You belong to the realm. And in nine days, willing or not, you'll understand why." He gave me one last evil smile as he stalked out the door leaving me standing in the room full of mirrors.

Through the bond, I felt Kaelren's presence—distant but furious, corruption spreading with every mile he traveled toward me. "*I'm coming,*" his feelings seemed to say. "*Hold on. Burn the world. Save you. Hold on.*"

I pressed my hand to the locket, feeling its unusual warmth against my palm. It pulsed in time with my heartbeat, or maybe my heartbeat was matching it. Jo had secrets—that much was becoming clear. Auradelle had plans that involved using me in ways that promised pain. Kaelren had corruption eating him alive, consuming him from the inside out to reach me.

And I had nine days to figure out how to save them all.

Or how to destroy everything trying.

25

Elle

I woke up slowly, my mind foggy and reluctant to focus. The last thing I remembered were the guards escorting me to my quarters Auradelle promised would be "comfortable." I opened my eyes to find he hadn't lied. The room was luxurious to the point of insult: a four-poster bed with purple silk sheets that probably cost more than most people saw in a year, an ornate wardrobe already filled with gowns in my exact size, floor-to-ceiling windows showing a spectacular view of the dying realm below.

But luxury didn't hide the cage. Root-forged restraints circled my wrists, the living wood humming with wrongness that made my markings writhe and retreat beneath my skin. The chain connecting them to the wall was long enough to let me move around the room but not reach the door or windows. When I tested them—and of course I tested them immediately—they burned cold, spreading frost up my arms.

"Fuck," I muttered, yanking against them harder. The chain rang out a mocking chime, and my markings flickered like a flame being smothered.

Through the bond—that connection with Kaelren that had become as natural as breathing—I felt almost nothing. Like trying to hear someone shouting through miles of vast nothingness. Occasionally a spike of rage so pure it made my chest ache, but even that was muted, distant. The restraints weren't just holding me; they were drowning our connection.

"*Still there, angry boy?*" I thought as hard as I could, pushing against the

257

magical dampening.

Nothing. Not even an echo.

The door opened without warning. A serving girl who couldn't have been more than twenty entered, carrying a tray that smelled amazing despite my circumstances. A bruise darkened her jaw, carefully hidden by powder but not carefully enough.

"Lord Auradelle requests your presence for the evening meal," she squeaked, not meeting my eyes.

"Did they hurt you?" I asked, softer than I'd intended.

She shook her head quickly—too quickly. "Please, miss. It's better if you don't resist. For all of us."

The implication was clear: my defiance had consequences for more than just me. The Crown was too smart to torture me directly when they could hurt others instead.

"Fine," I said, hating myself a little. "Lead the way."

She gestured to clothes laid out on the bed—a gown in deep green with gold threading that would complement my markings perfectly. "You're expected to change first."

"Expected to—how exactly am I supposed to change with these?" I raised my shackled wrists, the chain between them clanking mockingly.

The girl's face went pale. "I'll... I'll help you, miss."

"This is humiliating," I muttered, but let her assist me. Her hands shook the entire time, and she kept apologizing under her breath like this was somehow her fault.

We'd barely gotten the dress fastened when the door slammed open, making us both jump.

"Taking your sweet time, anomaly?" A Bloomguard filled the doorway—massive, with marks that crawled up his neck like diseased vines. "The Crown Prince doesn't like to be kept waiting."

"Maybe he should have thought of that before putting me in chains," I shot back.

His backhand caught me across the cheek before I saw it coming, hard enough to make my ears ring. The serving girl let out a small sob.

"You speak when spoken to, Earth-trash." He grabbed my arm, fingers digging in hard enough to bruise. "And you move when we tell you to move."

He dragged me out of the room, the serving girl trailing behind us. More guards fell into step as we walked, and their commentary was a steady stream of cruelty.

"Look at her boys, dressed in silk like she's Court-born."

"The anomaly playing at nobility."

"The Crown Prince is too generous. After what her kind has done to the realm, she should be crawling through the rot-tunnels."

"Maybe after the binding. If her mind survives it."

"Back off, gentlemen. The Crown Prince gets first rights," the guard guiding my arm said, his tone making my skin crawl. "But after the ritual, after you're properly broken in? The garrison's been promised time with what's left."

"If there's anything left," a woman with marks spreading like disease across her face, corrected. "The last one who went through the binding ritual came out wrong. Still screaming, three days later, before the Crown Prince finally let her die."

"This one's different, though. Natural marks. Might last longer."

"Might scream prettier too."

I bit my tongue hard enough to taste blood, refusing to give them the satisfaction of a response. But inside, fear was spreading cold through my chest.

The dining hall was smaller than expected, intimate rather than grand. A table set for two dominated the space, carved from what looked like a single piece of coal-colored wood that reflected the green flames of the candles like water. The chairs were high-backed, throne-like, making me feel even smaller than I was.

Auradelle waited at the far end, rising as I entered—as if we were at a dinner party instead of a kidnapping. He wore robes that shifted between purple and black depending on how the light hit them.

"Elle," he said, gesturing to the chair across from him. "You look lovely, dear niece. That color suits you."

"Fuck you," I said pleasantly, but I sat anyway since standing seemed pointless with the weight of the chains.

Servants appeared from shadows I hadn't noticed, placing plates before us with practiced silence. The food was beautiful and wrong—fruit that glowed faintly from within, meat that might have been venison if venison bled silver, bread still warm but somehow giving off cold steam. My stomach clenched with hunger I hadn't realized I felt, but I didn't trust any of it.

"Such language," he said, lifting his wine glass—the liquid inside thick and dark with an oily sheen on top. He took a deliberate sip but didn't touch the food. "Your grandmother at least pretended to have manners."

"Yeah, well, Arkansas didn't exactly come with a finishing school," I said. "You get what you get."

He actually smiled at that, and it was almost worse than his threats. "I can see why he's so taken with you. That fire, that defiance—you're so much like her."

"Like who? Jo?"

"In spirit, if not in temperament." He set down his glass, the liquid clinging to the sides wrong. "Did you know he's left a trail of dead forests from Mirror Lake across the realm? Entire groves withered to ash just from his presence. The corruption is spreading faster without you to balance it."

The words hit like ice water, but I kept my expression neutral. "He's stronger than you think."

"Is he?" He produced a scrying mirror from nowhere, its surface rippling to show Kaelren in what looked like a rebel hideout. His corruption had spread past his jawline, black veins mapping his face like cracks in porcelain. He was destroying training equipment with methodical violence, and each piece didn't just break—it rotted, corrupted by his touch.

My throat tightened. "Stop. Just stop."

Auradelle dismissed the mirror with a wave. "If you don't accept what you are by the Convergence, he dies. You die. The realm dies. Everyone dies."

"Except you," I said bitterly. "Let me guess—you get to watch it all happen because you've found some loophole."

His eyes went sharp, predatory. "Ah. So you did hear about that at the Autumn Court. Yes, they told you about the wheel, didn't they? About how a human split Root and Bloom, how the realm has been trying to reset itself. But they didn't tell you everything, did they?"

"What do you mean?"

He leaned back, and a servant immediately appeared to refill his wine. "They told you a human broke the realm. What they didn't tell you—what they couldn't have known—is which human."

My blood went cold. "What?"

"It was you, Elle. You were that first human who fell through. You made the choice that split Root and Bloom apart. And you've been paying for it ever since." His smile was sad now, almost pitying. "Sixteen times you've lived this same life. Sixteen times you've come through that portal, developed those marks, met Kaelren, been dragged into this impossible choice. Sixteen times you've failed."

"That's not possible," I whispered, but my hands were shaking. "I would remember—"

"Would you? The wheel erases memories when it turns. Resets the board. But patterns remain. Connections persist." He gestured between us. "Do you think that bond with Kaelren is coincidence? You're drawn to each other because you've been drawn to each other sixteen times before. You were always going to meet. Always going to fall for him. Always going to be trapped in this same dance."

"You're lying."

"Am I? Then explain why you've adapted to Wynmire so naturally. Why it was so easy to fall for him. The way you knew how to use your marks without training, as if muscle memory reached across iterations." He leaned forward. "I discovered this recently, you see. Found records that survived the resets—fragmentary, scattered, but enough to piece together the truth. Sometimes you and Kaelren are lovers. Sometimes enemies. Sometimes allies who never quite cross that line. But every single time, you fail. Every single time, one of you chooses Root and the other chooses Bloom, or you both refuse to choose, or you choose the same one and create imbalance.

Every single time, the realm collapses and iteration seventeen becomes iteration eighteen, eighteen becomes nineteen, on and on forever."

I was going to be sick. The room spun. "No," I managed. "My grandmother—she figured it out. She found a different way—"

"Did she?" His laugh was bitter. "Your grandmother ran to Earth and hid your mother there, thinking that would break the cycle. That if you never came to Wynmire, the wheel couldn't turn. But it didn't work, did it? Because here you are anyway. The wheel pulled you back. It always does."

Through the bond, I felt Kaelren's rage spike—he was closer now, fighting his way through whatever stood between us. But underneath that rage, I felt something else. A terrible, familiar ache. Like recognition. Like remembering something you'd forgotten but your body never did.

"He knows," I breathed. "Doesn't he? He knows about the iterations."

"Fragments. Pieces. Enough to drive him half-mad with déjà vu." Auradelle stood, the untouched feast between us vanishing as if it had never existed. "That's why his corruption spreads so fast this time—he's carrying the weight of sixteen failures, even if he can't consciously remember them. Every time he looks at you, some part of him remembers watching you die, or watching you choose Bloom and dissolve, or watching you walk away, or a thousand other endings, none of them happy."

"Then what's the point?" My voice broke. "If we're trapped in this cycle, if we always fail, why are you even bothering with this ritual?"

"Because I learned something from all those iterations. Something your grandmother never figured out." He moved closer, and I saw genuine desperation in his eyes beneath the cold calculation. "Every time before, you've had to choose between Root and Bloom. Between him and the realm. Between love and duty. But what if you didn't have to choose? What if there was a way to merge them properly, to become both, to finally break the pattern?"

"The binding ritual."

"The binding ritual," he confirmed. "It's never been tried before—not in any iteration I could find records of. Your grandmother was too afraid, Kaelren was too corrupted, previous versions of you were too... limited. But you? You're different this time. Stronger. More adaptable. You've already started merging Root and Bloom in small ways. I've seen the reports from your time in Wynmire, how you used both powers simultaneously."

"So you're going to force me into this ritual and hope it works."

"Hope?" He laughed, cold and sharp. "I'm going to *make* it work. I've spent fifty years studying every iteration, every failure, every version of you that came before. I know exactly where each one broke, exactly how to push harder this time." His voice dropped, losing any pretense of warmth. "Eight days, Elle. Eight days to learn what you are, what you've been, and what you could become. Eight days for me to break you down and reshape you into something that can finally serve its purpose."

He pushed back his chair and stood, taking one last sip of wine like he was savoring a victory already won. He started for the door, then paused, glancing back with a smile that made my skin crawl.

"Oh, and don't worry about Kaelren. He'll come for you—he always does. It's quite romantic, really, in a cosmically doomed sort of way. Sixteen times he's torn through my forces, corruption spreading with every step, thinking *this time* he'll save you." His smile widened. "This time, I'll be ready. This time, I'm going to let him reach you—just in time to watch you dissolve into the ritual. His corruption will peak at the exact moment you're most vulnerable, and you'll have no choice but to merge or die. Perfect synchronization."

"And if we can't?" My voice was barely a whisper.

His expression went cold, any pretense of sympathy evaporating. "Then you fail again, the realm dies, and we reset. But you'll carry the weight of seventeen lifetimes of failure into iteration eighteen. And I?" He touched his corruption marks almost lovingly. "I'll remember *everything*. Every scream, every failure, every version of you I've broken trying to fix this. I'm tired of being gentle. I'm tired of giving you choices."

He moved to the door, his robes shifting like living shadows. "So no, Elle. I'm not hoping. I'm ensuring. Whether you survive it with your mind intact is entirely up to how quickly you learn to obey."

Then he was gone, leaving me alone with impossible truths.

I sat there for a long moment, trying to process it all. Sixteen previous iterations. Sixteen versions of this same story, all ending badly. Sixteen times I'd met Kaelren, loved him or hated him or something in between, and watched everything fall apart.

Through the bond—muffled but still there—I felt his rage. Distant, like hearing someone shout from miles away, but unmistakable. He was planning. Gathering forces, probably, rallying rebels for an assault that Auradelle was already prepared for.

"I remember you," I thought into the silence, testing the words. *"I don't remember remembering you, but some part of me knows. Some part of me has always known."*

There was no response, but for just a moment, I felt something back—recognition and rage and desperate love all twisted together.

The door opened. The same terrified serving girl stood there, not meeting my eyes. She gestured for me to follow, keeping her distance from my restraints. The walk back was silent. She kept glancing at the chains on my wrists but never reached to help.

Back in my room, the restraints still burned cold against my skin. My markings writhed beneath them, trying to pull away from the Root-forged metal. Through the bond, I felt Kaelren's fury building, even from however many miles separated us.

I stood at the window, looking out at the dying realm. Twisted forests stretched to the horizon. Rivers flowed backward, defying gravity. Reality itself was coming undone at the edges, and I tried not to think about sixteen other versions of myself who had stood at windows just like this one, facing the same impossible choice.

"Hold on," I thought into our bond. *"I'm going to figure this out. This time has to be different. This time, we're going to change the ending."*

There was no response. Just that distant rage, burning steady somewhere far from here.

Eight days. Seventeen iterations. One chance to finally break the wheel.

I pressed my hand against the cold glass and tried to believe it was possible.

26

Elle

The serving girl woke me by dropping the breakfast tray.

The crash of porcelain shattering against stone jerked me from whatever passed for sleep, and I bolted upright to find her on her hands and knees, frantically trying to gather the pieces before anyone noticed.

"Shit, I'm sorry," I said, moving to help before the chain on my wrist snapped taut, yanking me back. "Are you hurt?"

"Don't—please don't tell anyone," she whispered, not looking at me. Her hands were shaking so badly she could barely hold the broken pieces. "They'll think I did it on purpose. They'll think I was trying to..."

The door slammed open.

A Bloomguard filled the doorway, his expression already twisted with suspicion. "What's going on here?"

"I dropped it," the girl said immediately, her voice high and thin with panic. "It was an accident, I swear—"

"Clumsy bitch." He grabbed her by the hair, yanking her to her feet. She didn't even cry out, just went rigid and silent like she'd learned this was the best way to survive it.

"Let her go," I said. "It was my fault. I startled her."

He looked at me then, and his smile was cruel. "Oh? The Crown Prince's special guest thinks she can give orders now?"

"I said let her go."

"Or what?" He twisted his grip, and the girl's face went white. "You'll burn me with your pretty marks? Oh wait," He gestured to my restraints with his free hand. "You can't. Because you're just a chained-up anomaly playing at being important."

Something in me snapped.

I lunged forward as far as the chain would let me, felt my marks flare hot despite the restraints trying to smother them, and spat directly in his face.

The guard froze. The girl froze. Even I froze, a little shocked at what I'd just done.

Then he dropped the girl and moved toward me, and his expression promised pain.

"You're going to regret that, Earth-trash."

"Add it to the list," I said, lifting my chin even as my heart hammered against my ribs.

His hand caught me across the face hard enough to split my lip. I tasted blood and saw stars, but I didn't give him the satisfaction of crying out. The second blow caught me in the stomach, driving the air from my lungs.

"Stop," the serving girl sobbed from the floor. "Please stop, she didn't mean—"

"Oh, I think she meant it." Another blow, this one to my ribs. Something cracked. "I think the anomaly needs to learn some manners."

He raised his hand again, and I braced for the impact.

"That's enough."

Auradelle's voice cut through the room like a blade made of ice.

The guard went still, hand frozen mid-swing. "My lord, I was just—"

"Just what? Damaging my most valuable asset a week before the convergence?" Auradelle moved into the room with that predatory grace of his, and the guard actually stepped back. "Do explain how beating her unconscious helps my plans."

"She—she disrespected—"

"She's human. She doesn't understand respect yet." His eyes found mine, cold and assessing. "Though she's learning."

He gestured, and the guard's corruption marks flared painfully enough that the man gasped. "Get out. Send someone to clean this mess. And if you touch her again without my express permission, I'll show you what real pain feels like."

The guard fled.

Auradelle watched him go, then turned his attention to the serving girl still on the floor. "You. Out."

She scrambled to her feet and ran, leaving the broken dishes scattered across the stone.

Then it was just the two of us.

"Don't expect a fucking 'thank you' from me," I glared at him.

"That was foolish," Auradelle said, moving closer. I tried to back away, but the chain kept me in place. "He could have killed you."

"Would have saved you the trouble," I managed through my split lip.

"No. It wouldn't have." He produced a cloth from nowhere—because of course he did—and reached toward my face. I flinched, but he just dabbed at my bleeding lip with surprising gentleness. "You're no use to me dead. Broken, perhaps. Frightened, certainly. But not dead."

"How reassuring."

"You defended her." His eyes searched mine, curious. "The servant. Why?"

"Because she was scared and he was hurting her. I don't need a better reason than that."

"Even when defending her got you hurt instead?"

"Especially then."

Something flickered across his face—surprise? Respect? It was gone too quickly to identify. He stepped back, and the bloody cloth vanished as mysteriously as it had appeared.

"Your grandmother would have done the same thing," he said quietly. "She could never stand by and watch suffering, even when standing up meant suffering herself. It's what made her perfect for the Root. And what made her too weak to survive this world."

"She survived fine. She lived a whole life on Earth."

"She ran away and died young, her power eating her from the inside because she refused to use it properly." His voice hardened. "That's not survival. That's slow suicide."

He manifested a chair from the floor—roots growing and twisting with sounds like breaking bones—and sat with elegant precision. "But we're not here to discuss Josephine's failures. We're here to discuss yours."

I stayed standing, even though my ribs screamed in protest. "I don't have any failures yet. This is my first iteration, remember?"

"Is it?" His smile was cold. "Or is this just the first one you remember?"

"You look tired," he observed as he tossed me a robe on the bed, his eyes taking in what I'm sure was a spectacular case of bed head and bags under my eyes. "The Heartspire takes getting used to. Most people never do. They usually go mad within the first three days."

"Most people aren't held here against their will with magical restraints suppressing their power," I shot back, finally getting the robe tied despite the split lip making it hard to talk. My ribs ached with every breath.

"Aren't they?" He tilted his head, and I noticed that his marks moved when he did—the golden corruption under his skin following the motion like it was always a half-second behind. "Every person in Wynmire is held by something. Duty, fear, love, prophecy. You're just more honest about your chains."

"Philosophical bullshit before breakfast? You really are a villain."

He smiled, and I hated that it almost looked genuine, like he actually found me amusing rather than just a tool to be used. "Your grandmother said something similar when I first met her. Though she was more polite about it. She called me 'exhaustingly metaphorical.'"

"Yeah, well, she didn't have the benefit of knowing what a complete bastard you'd become."

"Become?" He leaned forward, and the chair grew with him, adjusting to his movement. "I haven't changed, child. I've always been exactly this. The only difference is that now I have the power to reshape the world according to my vision instead of merely dreaming about it."

"And what vision is that? Turn everything into this?" I gestured at the writhing walls, trying not to flinch when one of the face-shapes turned to track my movement. "Make the whole world into your personal nightmare palace?"

"No, my vision is to make the whole world alive. Connected. No more separation between the Root and the Bloom, between growth and decay, between the mortal and the eternal." His corrupted marks pulsed with golden light, and I felt them reaching for mine again. "Your world—Earth—it's dying. You know this. You've seen it. The gardens failing, the green things retreating, the slow strangling of everything natural and wild."

I wanted to argue, but he wasn't entirely wrong. Grandma Jo's garden had been an oasis in an increasingly concrete world. Every year, fewer butterflies. Every season, less magic.

"So what?" I said instead. "You're going to save Earth by corrupting Wynmire? That's brilliant logic."

"I'm going to save both by making them one." He stood, and the chair dissolved back into the floor with a wet sound. "The barrier between worlds is already weakening. Your presence here proves that. But it's been a slow decay, a gradual dissolution that will end with both worlds simply... fading."

He moved closer, and I pressed back against the headboard despite myself, the chain rattling mockingly. My cracked rib protested.

"Unless," he continued, "someone takes control of the process. Guides it. Shapes it into something new instead of letting it collapse into nothing."

"Unless you take control, you mean."

"Who else? The old courts, playing their political games while the rot spreads? The rebels, so focused on opposing me they can't see the bigger picture? Or perhaps your precious Kaelren, too consumed by his own corruption to think beyond his next act of violence?"

"Don't talk about him," I snapped before I could stop myself.

"Protective of him still? Even knowing what I made him to be?" Auradelle reached into his coat and pulled out something that made my blood freeze and my markings burn simultaneously.

A locket. Not mine—I could still feel Grandma Jo's, warm against my throat, hidden under my shift. But identical to it in every way that mattered.

"Recognize this?" he asked softly.

"That's... how?"

"Your grandmother's wasn't the only one made. There were three, originally. Tokens of the first compact, when the barriers between worlds were established. One for Earth, one for Wynmire, and one..." He opened it with a click that echoed too loudly in the breathing room, revealing not a picture but a small, perfect seed that pulsed with inner light. "One for the bridge between them."

My markings responded to the seed's presence, flaring so hot I gasped and doubled over. I could feel them spreading—from my collarbone up toward my throat, down toward my heart—and everywhere they touched felt like being rewritten at a cellular level.

"Stop," I gasped, my hands clawing at my chest. "Whatever you're doing—"

"I'm not doing anything." He closed the locket but didn't put it away. "This is what you were meant to be. What your grandmother refused to become."

He began to pace, and where he stepped, small flowers sprouted and immediately withered. "She could have been the bridge. Could have held both worlds in balance. Instead, she chose love. Chose your grandfather. Chose to let the compact fragment and decay rather than accept her responsibility."

"Good for her," I managed through gritted teeth.

"Is it? Look at the result. You, bearing marks that are killing you without proper control. Kaelren, carved into a weapon that's consuming itself. Two halves of what should have been whole, both destroying yourselves because she was too selfish to accept her role."

"Or maybe," I said, forcing myself to stand straighter despite the pain in my ribs and the burning in my marks, meeting his eyes with defiance I didn't entirely feel, "she was smart enough to know that some roles aren't worth accepting. That some prophecies are better broken than fulfilled. That maybe people should get to choose their own destinies instead of having them carved into their skin."

He studied me for a long moment, and I saw disappointment in his face. Real, genuine disappointment.

"You really don't understand yet, do you? This isn't about prophecy or destiny. This is about survival. Mathematics. Inevitability." He moved to the wall, pressing his hand against it, and I could see through the semi-translucent surface to the world outside—Wynmire dying, Earth fading, both worlds bleeding into each other through widening cracks.

"The Root chose you because you're strong enough to bear what's coming. Strong enough to channel the power needed to fuse the worlds properly. Not destructively, not chaotically, but with purpose. With design."

"And if I refuse?"

"Then both worlds die slowly instead of being reborn quickly." He turned back to me. "I tried to force this with Kaelren. Trained him from childhood to be the perfect vessel, presented him to the Bloom knowing it would accept him. But it rejected him. Violently. Publicly. So he carved those marks into himself, trying to force what wouldn't come naturally. But forced marks corrupt. They consume instead of creating. The experiment failed."

"He's not a failure," I said, heat in my voice.

"No? Then why is his corruption spreading faster every day? Why does he look at you like you're salvation and damnation combined? Why can't he stay away from you even though proximity to your marks accelerates his decay?" He moved closer, and I could smell old books and funeral flowers and something medicinal. "He knows what he is—a mistake I'm going to correct through you."

"By doing what? Forcing me through some ritual?"

"No." His smile was terrible in its certainty. "By letting your natural marks do what they were designed to do. By feeding them the right catalyst at the right moment. By making you bloom, Elle Hawthorne, in ways your grandmother never could."

He gestured, and guards entered—Bloomguards, but different from the ones I'd seen before. These looked like they'd been changed by prolonged exposure to the Heartspire itself. Their armor had fused with their skin in places, crystal and flesh merging into something that made my stomach turn. Their faces were almost normal until you looked closely and realized their eyes reflected light wrong, their mouths opened at odd angles, their hands had too many joints.

"Take her to the ritual chamber," he commanded, his voice carrying harmonics that made my teeth ache. "It's time to begin."

They grabbed me with hands that felt like stone and bone combined, their touch leaving marks that burned cold. I fought, kicked and bit and tried to summon any power I could through the restraints. One of them I caught where the knee should be, and something cracked, but the guard didn't even slow down.

My split lip opened again, blood running down my chin. The cracked rib screamed with every movement.

"Oh," Auradelle said as they carried me past him, his voice conversational, "I should mention—your friends will arrive just in time for the Convergence. Silverpine Hollow to here, pushing hard with whatever forces they can muster. They're making better time than I expected, considering the obstacles I've placed in their path."

I stopped struggling, my whole body going still. "What?"

"Did you think I didn't want them to come? This only works with both halves present. You to be the vessel, Kaelren to be the final catalyst. His corrupted marks calling to your pure ones. The failed experiment and the successful one, joining to create something unprecedented."

"You're using me as bait."

"I'm using you as what you are—the key to everything. Your friends' arrival is just... convenient timing." His golden marks pulsed brighter. "This gives us time for several preparatory sessions. I want you properly conditioned for what's to come. Your marks need to spread further, your connection to the Root needs to deepen, your resistance needs to... soften."

"Fuck you."

"Such spirit. Your grandmother had that too, until the very end." He smiled, and it was almost sad. "I wonder if you'll break the same way she did, or if you'll find new ways to shatter."

As the guards dragged me away, their bony hands leaving frost burns on my arms, he called after me, "Don't worry about the pain, child. By the time Kaelren arrives, you'll barely remember what it felt like to be merely human."

The door slammed shut behind us, and I was carried deeper into the Heartspire's living corridors, toward whatever nightmare he'd prepared for me.

The guards' grip tightened as we descended into darkness, and I felt my marks pulse in response—not with pain this time, but with something that felt almost like anticipation.

The Heartspire recognized what I was becoming.

And it was hungry for it.

27

Elle

The ritual chamber wasn't what I expected.

After being dragged through the Heartspire's corridors by those corrupted guards, I'd braced for something dramatic—-a throne room with an ancient altar, maybe some ominous sacrificial setup. Instead, they brought me to a circular room deep underground. The walls glowed a sickly green with pulsing light. The floor was wood, but it was warm under my bare feet and gave slightly when I stepped on it, like standing on skin.

At some point during the journey down here, they'd stripped me to a simple shift. Between that, the aching throb in my ribs, and the burn of my split lip, I felt exposed and raw.

The guards, those things with armor fused to their skin and too many joints in their fingers, didn't speak as they positioned me in the center of the room. A platform rose from the floor, grown from the same wood. It looked like a cross between an operating table and an altar, and my stomach turned looking at it.

"On your back," one said, its voice grinding like stone on bone.

"Fuck you," I managed through my swollen lip, tasting copper.

But there were four of them and one of me, and my restraints were still suppressing any power I might have used. My cracked rib screamed as they forced me down, not roughly, but with steady, relentless pressure.

The moment my back touched the platform, the wood moved. Tendrils grew up and wrapped around my ankles, my thighs, my waist. Not tight enough to crush, but firm enough that I couldn't budge. More wrapped around my arms, pinning them at my sides. A final one grew across my forehead, locking my head in place.

The frost burns on my arms from the guards' earlier grip throbbed with cold pain where the wood touched them.

"Comfortable?" one guard asked. I could have sworn the thing was smiling.

I tried to spit blood at him, but it fell short thanks to the restraints.

They roared with laughter as they left me there. Alone. Waiting.

Time moves differently when you can't move, can't see anything but the pulsing ceiling, can't do anything but think. I tried counting my breaths, but the Heartspire's rhythm kept interfering, making me lose track. I tried focusing on the bond with Kaelren, but the restraints turned every attempt into static and pain.

So I thought about escape. About the serving girl with the bruise on her jaw who'd helped me dress. About Auradelle's exhausted eyes and what fifty years of wearing a crown that burned must feel like. About seventeen iterations of this same story, playing out over and over. What was different this time? What variable had changed?

Me, obviously. But I was just another Elle in a long line of Elles, wasn't I? Unless...

The door opened—or rather, a section of wall split apart—and Auradelle entered. He'd changed from his morning robes into something that looked almost like a surgeon's garb. Behind him floated a tray of implements that made my stomach turn just looking at them.

"I apologize for the wait," he said, approaching slowly, studying me like I was something pinned to a board. "I had to ensure the calculations were correct. Your markings are spreading faster than anticipated, which changes some variables."

"Let me go."

"Eventually." He pulled on gloves that looked like they were woven from petal-threads, each finger lighting up with a different color as he flexed them. "But first, we need to understand exactly what we're working with."

He moved to stand beside the platform, looking down at me with those tired, ancient eyes. For a moment, I saw something flicker there—curiosity? Hunger? But it was gone before I could be sure.

"The first test," he announced, as if speaking to an audience that wasn't there, "is to see how your natural marks respond to direct Bloom exposure."

"Test?" I yanked against the wood holding my arms, ignoring the scream from my cracked rib. "I'm not your fucking experiment."

"No," he agreed, his voice flat and clinical. "You're far more valuable than that."

He didn't gesture, didn't speak a word. More roots simply emerged from the floor, wrapping around my already-bound ankles, my waist, my wrists. They tightened this time, making the earlier bonds feel gentle by comparison. The restraints on my wrists hummed in harmony with them, creating a resonance that made my teeth ache and my skull feel like it was cracking open.

"Your grandmother," Auradelle said, "managed to resist the Bloom's call for three days when we tested her. But she had mental preparation, years of knowing what she was. You..."

He pressed his hand against my collarbone, right where my markings originated, and the world went white.

It wasn't pain. It was worse than pain. It was like every nerve in my body suddenly remembered every sensation it had ever felt, all at once. The summer heat of home. The cold of Mirror Lake. The burn of Kaelren's corrupted touch. The gentle warmth of my grandmother's hugs. All of it, compressed into a single moment that stretched into eternity.

My markings responded violently, spreading across my skin like they were trying to escape my body. This wasn't the gentle creep I'd grown used to—this was aggressive, ravenous, trying to claim every inch of me at once. Golden vines raced down my arms, across my chest, up my neck. I could feel them trying to reach my face, my eyes, trying to burrow into my brain.

I screamed. The sound tore out of my throat raw and animal.

"Fascinating," Auradelle murmured, taking notes in a journal that materialized from nowhere. His voice was completely detached, like he was observing something mildly interesting rather than listening to me scream. "The acceleration is even faster than predicted. Your body wants this, Elle. It's been waiting your whole life for this moment."

"Stop," I gasped, but the word came out wrong, harmonizing with itself like I was speaking in multiple voices. "Please—"

"Not yet. We need to see your threshold."

He increased the pressure, and the sensation intensified until I couldn't tell where I ended and the pain began. I wasn't just feeling my memories now. I was being forced into other people's minds. My grandmother as a young woman, standing in this very room, screaming just like I was. My mother, whom I barely remembered, dying when I was just a toddler. Kaelren, carving marks into his own skin with desperate precision, blood running down his arms. Even Auradelle himself, younger, hopeful, before decades of holding a realm together had turned him into this monster.

"Please," I sobbed, hating myself for begging, unable to stop. "Please stop—"

"There we are," he said, like I'd passed some kind of test. He removed his hand, and the sensations stopped so abruptly I would have collapsed if the roots weren't holding me. I gasped for air, tasting blood and bile. "Two minutes, thirty-seven seconds. Your grandmother lasted forty-three seconds on her first exposure."

"Fuck you," I spat through the blood in my mouth. My split lip had opened wider. "Fuck you—"

"This isn't torture, child. This is calibration." He walked to a table I hadn't noticed before, covered in implements that looked medical and mystical in equal measure. His tone was so matter-of-fact it was worse than if he'd been cruel. "We need to understand exactly what you're capable of before the Convergence. How much power you can channel. How much transformation you can endure before you break."

"Why?" My voice was hoarse from screaming, and I could feel my markings still spreading, though slower now. They pulsed with heat under my skin. "Why not just throw me at the Bloom and see what happens?"

"Because I've spent fifty years preparing for this moment, and I don't intend to waste it on chance." He selected something that looked like a tuning fork made of petrified wood. "Your bloodline is the key to saving both worlds. But keys can be turned different ways. I need to ensure you turn the right way. My way."

He struck the tuning fork against the table, and it rang with an impossible sounding note—too pure, too complex, like an entire orchestra compressed into a single tone. My markings responded immediately, resonating with the sound, and I felt something deep in my bones shift and crack.

"What are you doing to me?"

"Attuning you. The Bloom operates on specific frequencies, specific patterns. Your natural marks are close, but not quite right. Like an instrument that needs tuning." He struck the fork again, and this time the note was different, darker. The sound made my teeth vibrate and my vision blur. "This will help them align properly when the time comes."

The session continued for what felt like hours. Different tools, different tests, each one pushing my markings in new directions, each one making me scream until my throat was raw. He never paused, never showed mercy, never acknowledged my pain except to make clinical observations in that damned journal.

By the time he finally called for the guards to take me back to my quarters, I could barely stay conscious. My marks had spread to cover most of my torso, creeping down my thighs. Every breath felt like swallowing fire, every movement sent lightning through my nerves. My cracked rib was agony with each shallow breath.

"Tomorrow," Auradelle said as they peeled me off the platform—the wood releasing me reluctantly, leaving red welts and deep bruises where it had held me. "We'll test your capacity for holding Root-energy while channeling Bloom-force. It should be... illuminating."

I tried to respond, but all that came out was a broken sound that might have been a sob. My vision was going dark at the edges, and I could taste blood from where I'd bitten through my tongue.

"Careful with her," Auradelle instructed the guards as they hauled me upright. My legs wouldn't hold me—they buckled immediately. "I need her functional for tomorrow's session. Damaged is acceptable. Dead is not."

The journey back to my quarters was a blur of pain and half-consciousness. I was vaguely aware of the guards' cruel laughter, of passing through a maze of corridors, of my markings flickering under my skin like dying embers. When they finally dumped me on my bed, I couldn't move, couldn't think, could barely breathe around the pain in my ribs.

The serving girl—the same one from before—appeared with a basin of water and clean cloths. She worked in silence, gently cleaning the sweat and blood from my skin. Her touch was careful around my markings, which were still spreading, still burning, still trying to consume me.

"It gets easier," she whispered, so quiet I almost missed it.

"What?"

"The tests. The pain. After a while, you learn to... go somewhere else. In your mind." She wrung out the cloth, and I saw her own marks—faint, wrong, creeping up her arms like disease. "I was tested too. Before. When he thought I might be the one."

"You have marks?"

"Failed ones. Forced ones. He tried to make me into what you naturally are." She pulled her sleeves down, hiding them. "It didn't work. But I survived. You will too."

"How do you know?"

"Because you have something I didn't." She glanced at my restraints, which were still humming, still suppressing my connection to Kaelren. "Someone waiting for you. Someone coming for you. Hold onto that."

She left before I could respond, taking the basin with her. I lay there on the silk sheets, my body feeling like it had been taken apart and reassembled wrong.

"Kaelren," I thought desperately into the muffled bond. "Please. I don't know how much more of this I can take."

There was no response. There never was, with these restraints.

But that night, as exhaustion finally pulled me toward sleep, something changed.

28

Elle

The dream didn't start like a dream. It started like being yanked from the bottom of the ocean by an invisible hand—sudden, disorienting, gasping into awareness.

I found myself in another fantastical garden, but different from before.

Roses grew downward from clouds that drifted at waist height, their petals glowing with sunset hues. Trees sprouted from pools of bright, flowing water, their branches reaching down instead of up, heavy with fruit with surfaces like oil slicks—rainbow patterns constantly moving. The grass beneath my bare feet felt like silk and hummed with a melody I almost recognized—something my grandmother used to hum while tending her tomatoes.

I walked deeper into this impossible place, drawn by the sound of water. A stream flowed in spirals through the air, fish made of golden light swimming against gravity. Where droplets looked like candy, flowers bloomed in midair, their roots dangling like jewelry.

There was a swing hanging from nothing—just two ropes extending up into empty sky that somehow held my weight when I sat. My cheeks heated when I thought about the Pleasure Garden, and the last time I was in a swing. As I swayed back and forth, butterflies with wings of stained glass gathered around me, each one carrying a different memory reflected in its wings. My first day of school. My mother's laugh. The taste of birthday cake. Kaelren's eyes when he'd first really seen me.

I reached out to touch one—the memory of my grandmother's hands teaching mine to braid—when I heard footsteps approaching from behind.

"Elle?"

I turned, nearly falling off the swing, and there he was. Kaelren, but not quite as I'd last seen him. His corruption was present but controlled here, creating patterns across his skin that looked like calligraphy written in ash. His eyes—those impossible silver eyes—were looking at me like I was something he'd lost and found again.

"How—" I started, but he was already moving.

He hit me like a wave, crushing me against him with desperate force that drove the air from my lungs. His hands were everywhere—my face, my hair, my back—like he was trying to confirm I was real through touch alone.

"Elle. Elle. *Elle.*" He kept saying my name like a prayer, his face buried in my neck, his whole body shaking. "I felt you dying. Through the bond, I felt you *screaming*, and I couldn't reach you. I couldn't—"

"I'm here," I gasped, clinging to him just as desperately. "I'm here, I'm okay—"

"You're not okay." He pulled back just enough to look at me, and the anguish in his face made my chest ache. His hands came up to frame my face, tilted it toward what passed for light in this place. "I can see the marks. The welts. Your lip—" His thumb ghosted over my split lip, and his eyes went black. "What did he do to you?"

"Kaelren—"

"What. Did. He. Do."

"Tests," I said, and my voice broke despite my best efforts. "He's trying to tune me. Make my marks align with the Bloom properly. It's—" I couldn't finish. Couldn't find words for what Auradelle had done to me.

The space around us responded to his fury—the stars beneath our feet went dark, the roots above writhed and screamed, and something that might have been thunder, if thunder could exist here, rolled through everything. The temperature dropped so fast I could see my breath.

"I'm going to tear him apart," Kaelren said, and his voice was barely human. "Cell by cell. I'm going to make him experience every moment of pain he's inflicted on you magnified a thousand times, and when he begs for death I'm going to keep him alive just to continue—"

I kissed him.

Hard and desperate and probably stupid given my split lip, but I needed to ground him, ground us both. He made a sound low in his throat—half growl, half sob—and kissed me back like I was oxygen and he'd been drowning. His hands slid into my hair, angling my head, and I tasted copper and salt and desperation.

When we finally broke apart, we were both shaking.

"Where is this?" I asked, my forehead pressed against his. "How are you here?"

"I don't know." His hands were still in my hair, his thumbs tracing small circles against my skull like he couldn't bear to stop touching me. "I've been pushing against the bond for days, trying to find you through the suppression. And then suddenly, I felt you. Like a light in the dark. Your mind created this, I think."

"So this is a dream?"

"No." His eyes searched mine, silver and desperate and more alive than anything else in this impossible place. "Or maybe. I don't know. But it feels real. You feel real. The bond between us—it's clearer here than it's ever been, like all the interference has been stripped away." He pulled me closer, if that was even possible. "I can feel everything you're feeling right now. The fear. The pain. The exhaustion."

"Then you know I don't have much time." I forced myself to say it. "He's breaking me down, Kaelren. Systematically. Tomorrow he's going to try something worse—"

"We're coming." His voice was steel. "Tonight. We leave Silverpine tonight. The rebels have found tunnels under the Heartspire, old Root-pathways that—"

"No." I grabbed his face, making him look at me. "Not yet. Auradelle's expecting you. He told me you'd arrive 'just in time for the Convergence.' He *wants* you to come. It's a trap."

"I don't care if it's a trap—"

"I care." My voice cracked. "I care because if you walk into whatever he's planned, he'll use you against me. He'll hurt you to make me cooperate, or he'll hurt me to make you cooperate, and either way we both end up exactly where he wants us."

"Then what do we do?" His hands tightened in my hair. "You want me to just leave you there while he tortures you? I can't—Elle, I physically cannot do that. The corruption is eating me alive without you. Every hour we're apart, it gets worse. I've destroyed three groves just by walking through them. I'm becoming the monster everyone always said I was."

"You're not a monster."

"I will be if he hurts you again." It wasn't a threat. It was a promise. "I will burn down both worlds if that's what it takes to get you back."

I believed him. That was the terrifying part—I believed him completely.

"How much time do we have?" I asked. "Before you get here?"

"Five days if we push hard. Maybe six if the tunnels are worse than Sarnyx thinks." His forehead pressed against mine. "But Elle, I don't think you have that long. I can feel your marks through the bond right now, and they're spreading faster than—"

"I know." I cut him off before he could finish that thought. "I can feel it too. But if you come early, he wins. We need—we need a plan. A real one. Not just charging in and hoping for the best."

"Then help me make one." His hands slid down to my shoulders, my arms, like he was mapping every inch of me he could reach. "Tell me everything. The layout, the guards, the restraints, everything. We'll find a way through this that doesn't end with both of us as his puppets."

So I told him. Everything I could remember through the haze of pain and fear. And he held me while I talked, his hands never stopping their gentle movement, grounding me in this impossible space where we could finally touch without suppressions or barriers or the weight of two dying worlds between us.

"I'm going to get you out," he said when I finished, and the certainty in his voice almost made me believe it. "I promise you, Elle. I'm going to get you out, and then I'm going to make him pay for every second of pain he's caused you."

"Just don't die doing it," I said. "Because I've gotten really attached to you, and I'd hate to have to burn everything myself to bring you back."

He laughed—short and sharp and almost surprised, like he'd forgotten how. Then he kissed me again, softer this time, like he was trying to memorize the taste of me.

"Hold on a little longer," he whispered against my lips. "Just a little longer. I'm coming."

"I know," I said. "I can feel it."

And I could, I could feel his determination, his rage, his absolute refusal to let Auradelle win. It wrapped around me like armor, and for the first time since the guards had dragged me to that ritual chamber, I felt something other than fear.

I felt hope.

Kaelren

She was trying to protect me. Even here, even after everything Auradelle had done to her, she was trying to protect me.

The realization hit me like a physical blow, and the garden around us responded shuddering, almost seeming to collapse in on itself. My corruption spread further across my dream-form, turning my hands nearly black.

"Elle," I said, and her name tasted like prayer and damnation combined. "How much time do we have?"

"Seven days until convergence," she said immediately. "Auradelle was very specific about that. He wants me 'properly conditioned' before it happens."

Seven days. Five of those would be spent traveling from Silverpine Hollow to the Heartspire, pushing hard through hostile territory. That left us one day here to plan, and one night to rest in the tunnels beneath the fortress before the convergence. One night between me and her, with an entire realm in between.

"Tell me what happened," I said, pulling her closer, needing her solid against me despite knowing she was so impossibly far away. "I need to understand what I'm walking into."

She hesitated, and I felt her exhaustion through the bond—bone-deep, soul-deep, the kind that came from being systematically broken down. But she nodded.

"He tortured me," she said bluntly. "Called it calibration, testing, tuning. Strapped me to this living wood platform and pushed Bloom-energy through my marks until I screamed. Made me experience every sensation I've ever felt all at once. Hours of it, while he took notes like I was a fucking science experiment."

The garden around us darkened. My corruption flared.

"But that's not the worst part," she continued, her voice steady despite the tremor I could feel through our bond. "The worst part is what he told me. About why he's doing this. About the iterations."

"Iterations?"

"Sixteen of them." She looked up at me, and her eyes held knowledge that shouldn't be there—ancient, terrible knowledge. "Sixteen times this story has played out. Sixteen times I've come to Wynmire. Sixteen times you've tried to save me. Sixteen times we've failed, and the cycle resets. Now we are at the end of the seventeenth wondering if we will make the same mistakes again."

The words hit me like physical blows. "What are you talking about?"

"Auradelle told me." Her hands fisted in my shirt. "About other timelines. I've died sixteen different ways, Kaelren. I saw you become a monster trying to save me, over and over. I saw us fail every single time."

"That's not possible—"

"Isn't it?" She pulled back enough to look at me fully. "Think about it. Think about the things that don't make sense. The way Eltrien talks about patterns and wheels. The way he always seems to know what's coming next. The way he mentioned me dying in iteration fifteen before and then tried to cover it."

My mind was racing, corruption spreading faster as pieces clicked into place with sickening clarity.

"On the way to the monastery," I said slowly. "I thought he was being cryptic, being Eltrien, but—"

"He knows." Elle's voice was certain. "He's been carrying this knowledge the whole time. Watching us repeat the same mistakes, following the same pattern, failing the same way. And he never told us."

The garden around us was dying rapidly now, my rage destroying everything my corruption touched. "How long has he known?"

"I don't know. But Auradelle talked about being able to remember across iterations now that he's done the research. I wonder if Eltrien is the same. Like he's been watching this play out over and over, and he's just been waiting to see if this time would be different."

"Different how?"

"Me." She touched my face, forcing me to focus on her instead of the fury building in my chest. "I'm different this time. The pattern is 'woman arrives, falls for you, has to choose between saving you or saving the realms, chooses wrong, everyone dies, reset.' But this time, I know about the pattern. I know what Auradelle's planning. I know there have been sixteen other Elles who stood where I'm standing, and they all failed."

"So what does that mean?"

"It means we can break it." Her voice held desperate determination. "If we know the pattern, we can change it. We can choose differently. We can—"

"We can't do anything if you don't survive the next session," I interrupted, my hands tightening on her shoulders. "Elle, you're asking me to leave you in hell for another day while that bastard breaks you down further, and now you're telling me this has all happened before? That there are sixteen dead versions of you because we keep failing?"

"Yes." Her voice didn't waver. "But charging in blind is exactly what you've done in every other iteration. You storm the Heartspire, corrupted beyond recognition, so focused on saving me that you walk right into his trap. And it never works. It never has."

"How do you know that?"

"Because he told me." She swallowed hard. "He wanted me to know. Wanted me to understand that resistance is futile, that the pattern always wins, that I'm just another Elle in a long line of Elles. He thought it would break me. Make me accept my role."

"Did it?"

"No." Her smile was fierce and defiant. "It pissed me off. Because if there have been sixteen iterations where I failed, that means I get to be the seventeenth one who doesn't. The one who breaks the fucking wheel instead of being crushed by it."

I stared at her—this impossible woman who'd crashed into my world and refused to accept any ending that wasn't her own. Even now, even tortured and trapped and told she was doomed to fail, she was fighting.

"I've seen it."

That halted all my thoughts. "What have you seen, Elle?"

"Other versions of us. When he tortured me and tested me against the Bloom it brought visions of some of the cycles before."

"Show me," I said suddenly. "Let me see these other iterations."

She hesitated, fear spiking through the bond. Not fear of showing me, but fear of reliving it.

"I need to understand," I said more gently. "If we're going to break the pattern, I need to know everything."

She nodded. The garden shifted, reality bending, and suddenly I was experiencing her memory.

The ritual chamber. The platform. The wood binding her while she was still injured from the guard's beating. Her cracked rib screaming. The frost burns from the guards' hands.

Then Auradelle, clinical and detached, pressing his hand to her collarbone and *pushing*.

I felt it all through her senses, and then started getting glimpses of other timelines.

Me, storming the Heartspire so corrupted I looked more shadow than man. Cutting through guards, destroying everything in my path. Reaching Elle just as Auradelle completed his ritual. Watching her dissolve into the Bloom while I screamed and the corruption consumed me.

Another version: Elle making a different choice, sacrificing herself to save me. The realms collapsing anyway. Both of us dying as reality tore itself apart.

Another: Me arriving too late. Elle already gone. My corruption eating the Heartspire itself in rage before it consumed me too.

Sixteen failures, each slightly different but all ending the same way. A wheel turning endlessly, grinding us both to dust.

When the memories finally released me, I realized I'd destroyed the entire garden. We stood in an empty void now, nothing left but Elle and me and the all-consuming rage threatening to tear me apart.

"Kaelren." Her voice was distant. "Come back to me. Stay present."

I was shaking, my whole dream-form vibrating with fury so intense it was rewriting what little reality remained around us. Not just fury at Auradelle, though that burned hot and bright. Fury at Eltrien. At the healer who'd been guiding us, advising us, watching us, all while knowing we were repeating a pattern that had failed sixteen times before.

"He knew," I snarled, and my voice made the void itself shudder. "Eltrien knew about the iterations. About the failures. About all of it. And he never told us. Never warned us. Just watched us stumble toward the same ending like we were pieces in a game he'd already lost sixteen times."

"I know. Maybe that's the only way he's stayed sane through sixteen iterations of watching everyone he cares about die."

"I don't care about his sanity." The words came out cold and vicious. "I care that he's been playing puppet master while pretending to help. I care that he's known the exact shape of the trap we're walking into and he's been letting us walk anyway."

"What if he thinks we need to walk into it?" She grabbed my face, forcing me to focus on her. "What if the only way to break the pattern is to understand it first? To see how it fails so we can change it?"

"That's too fucking convenient—"

"Or it's the truth." Her eyes searched mine. "Kaelren, I know you're angry. I'm angry too. But think—if Eltrien could just tell us how to win, wouldn't he have done it by now? Maybe the pattern doesn't work that way. Maybe we have to figure it out ourselves, or the wheel just keeps turning."

I wanted to argue. Wanted to reject the idea that Eltrien's deception might serve a purpose. But she was right—if there was an easy answer, sixteen iterations wouldn't have failed.

"I'm going to have words with him when this is over," I said darkly. "Extensive words. Possibly involving my hands around his throat."

"Get in line." She managed a weak smile. "But first, we have to survive. And that means you can't come charging in like every other Kaelren in every other iteration."

"Then what do I do?" The question tore out of me. "How do I break a pattern that's been repeating for—what, centuries? How long has this been going on?"

"I don't know. But I know what doesn't work—you, corrupted and desperate, storming in exactly when Auradelle expects you. That's the pattern. That's what fails every time."

"So I wait." The words tasted like ash. "I wait while he tortures you again. While he pushes your marks further. While he breaks you down piece by piece."

"One more day," she said, her voice cracking slightly. "Give me one more day to find his weakness. To understand what he's really planning. To figure out how to sabotage it from the inside."

One more day. Which meant waiting while she was tortured again, while I was too far away to help.

"You're asking me to let him torture you," I said, the words like broken glass in my throat. "I'll feel it through the bond—muffled, but there—and I won't be able to reach you."

"I know." Her hands tightened on my shirt. "But in every other iteration, you arrive early and walk right into his trap—exactly when he expects you to do. That's the pattern, Kaelren."

"And if I wait?"

"You strike at dawn on Convergence day when he's preparing for the ritual."

She was right. I hated that she was right, but she was. The tactical part of my mind could see it—arriving early meant fighting through his full defenses. Arriving the night before meant catching him mid-preparation.

But it also meant leaving her there longer to be tortured.

"I can survive if it means you don't walk into a trap," she said, reading my hesitation. "I can hold on if it means breaking this never-ending cycle."

"You're asking me to trust that this time will be different when sixteen other versions have failed."

"No." She pulled me closer, her forehead pressed against mine. "I'm asking you to trust me. Not the pattern, not the prophecy, not some cosmic fucking wheel—me. Elle. The woman you've gotten really attached to and would burn both worlds for."

Despite everything, the rage, the fear, I almost smiled. "That's not what you said before."

"I'm paraphrasing. The point stands." Her hands slid up to frame my face. "I'm not the same Elle from the other iterations. I know about them now. I know what fails. And I'm too stubborn and too pissed off to let Auradelle win just because sixteen other versions of me couldn't figure it out."

I studied her face—exhausted, marked, but absolutely fierce. She was right. This Elle wasn't like the others. And I did. Trust her. Completely.

Even though it meant five days of travel with her pain echoing through the bond. Even though it meant feeling every moment of tomorrow's torture session and the next day's, unable to reach her, unable to help. Even though every instinct I had screamed at me to leave now, to close that distance as fast as physically possible.

"Just don't lose yourself before you get there," she whispered.

"I won't." I kissed her forehead. "You're my anchor."

"And we're both alive," she added.

"That too."

The space around us was starting to destabilize—her physical body pulling her back, exhaustion and pain too deep to maintain this connection much longer.

"Wait," I said. "I'll make sure our assault is different from the other timelines." I pulled her close for one last desperate kiss. "No charging in blind. No walking into obvious traps. No repeating the same mistakes."

"Good." She kissed me back fiercely. "Because I'm tired of dying in other timelines. This one needs to stick."

"It will." I made it a vow, a promise, a threat to reality itself. "This iteration breaks the wheel. Or I'll tear through time itself to make sure it does."

She was fading faster now, her form becoming translucent.

"Stay alive," I commanded. "Whatever happens tomorrow, whatever he does to you—stay alive."

"You too. Don't let the corruption—"

But the connection shattered before she could finish.

One moment she was in my arms, solid and real. The next, I came back to myself standing in the middle of the rebel camp, my corruption having carved a perfect circle of destruction around me. Trees were dead within twenty feet. Grass turned to ash. Even the stones looked scorched.

The others stood well back, watching me with the usual mix of fear and wariness. But my eyes found Eltrien immediately.

He stood at the edge of the group, mycelial marks pulsing with that infuriating calm, watching me with eyes that held too much knowledge.

"You knew," I said, and my voice came out more growl than speech. "About the iterations. About the sixteen failures. You've known the whole fucking time."

Silence fell over the camp like a shroud.

"Sixteen what?" Thrak asked, confused.

"Timelines," I said, not taking my eyes off Eltrien. "Sixteen times this story has played out. Sixteen times Elle and I have tried to stop Auradelle. Sixteen times we've failed and the cycle resets. And our dear healer has been carrying that knowledge like a dirty little secret."

Eltrien's marks pulsed faster, but his expression remained calm. "Yes." Just that. Yes. No denial, no explanation, just flat admission.

"You want to elaborate on that?" Vashael demanded, her voice sharp. "You want to explain why you've been guiding us through a pattern you knew was doomed to fail?"

"Because every other time I tried to change it actively, we failed faster." Eltrien's voice was steady, but I could see cracks forming in his composure. "Sixteen iterations, and I've tried everything. Warning you early—you don't believe me. Telling you the prophecy—you try to fight it and fail worse. Hiding information—you make the same mistakes. No matter what I do, the wheel keeps turning."

"Except this time?" I took a step toward him, and he actually stepped back. Smart of him. My corruption slithering across my body like serpents ready to strike.

"This time is different," he insisted. "Can't you feel it? The way reality responds to you both? The impossible flowers, the creatures following you, the way the Convergence itself is behaving? This time, Elle knows about the pattern. That's never happened before. And that might—*might*—be enough to break it."

"Might," I repeated, ice in my voice.

"I don't have certainties!" For the first time, Eltrien sounded desperate. "I have sixteen timelines of failure and one that's finally, *finally* diverging from the pattern. Do you want me to risk that by interfering more than I already have? Do you want me to become the thing that makes us fail again?"

"I want you to stop playing games with our lives!" The words came out as a roar, backed by corruption that made everyone except Eltrien step further back. "I want you to tell us the truth so we can make informed decisions instead of stumbling through someone else's cosmic fucking joke!"

"The truth?" Eltrien laughed, and it was a terrible sound. "The truth is that we're trapped in a story that's been told sixteen times. The truth is that no matter what Elle chooses—save you, save the realms, sacrifice herself—we all die. The truth is that I've watched everyone I care about die sixteen times, and the only thing keeping me sane is the tiny, desperate hope that this time might be different."

His marks exploded with light, bright enough to make people shield their eyes. And in that light, I saw them—fragments of other timelines, ghosting through reality like afterimages. Other versions of this moment. Other versions of me, confronting other versions of Eltrien, having this same argument sixteen different ways.

I watched as the rest of the crew looked on with horror. Their eyes shifting between the two of us.

"So yes," Eltrien continued, his voice echoing across iterations, "I've been keeping secrets. I've been playing games. I've been desperately trying to nudge this timeline in a direction that doesn't end with all of you dead and me alone in the ashes, waiting for the cycle to reset so I can watch it all happen again."

The Sage stepped forward, and there was no look of concern on their face. Almost as if they knew this was coming. Great, another fucking person keeping us in the dark. "If Elle has remembered other iterations, then that means the second transformation is complete. All that is left is the final communion with the Bloom."

Bryx, who had been unusually quiet said, "Gods, did everyone know but us? The people who are constantly dying? I for one, would like a heads-up next time if I'm about to be hacked into a million pieces. Oh my gods, what about Kevin! Poor Kevin!"

The Sage shook their head. "My child, you know not what you speak. As we have said, there are things that cannot be shared if we do not want to further alter the timeline. And this is where I must leave you. If I continue further, we risk resetting everything, again."

We all stood there in the scorched circle, processing what they'd both just admitted.

"How do we know you're not just making us fail in a new way?" Sarnyx asked quietly.

"You don't," Eltrien said simply. "You have to trust me. Which, given that I've been lying by omission for the entire time you've known me, is a big ask. I understand that."

"You're damn right it is," Vashael spat.

Peeble landed on my shoulder then, their mental voice cutting through the tension. "He's telling the truth. About the iterations. About trying to change it. I can feel the echoes too—all the times I've died, all the times Elle died, all the times we got this far and failed."

"How long have you known?" I demanded.

"Since Elle's marks started really spreading. The memories started coming back—fragments from other timelines bleeding through." Peeble's tone was somber. "He's not lying about trying to change it, Kaelren. He's just been doing it quietly. Hoping we'd find our own way to break the pattern."

I looked at Eltrien—still furious at his admission.

"When do we move?" Thrak asked into the silence, always practical.

"Day after tomorrow at dawn," I said, forcing my voice back toward something human. "That gives us one more full day to plan, gather supplies, and prepare. We have to know everything we can about those tunnels."

"That's cutting it dangerously close," Vashael pointed out. "If anything delays us on the road—"

"Then we push harder." My corruption flared.

"Why wait at all?" Sarnyx asked. "Why not leave now?"

"Because leaving now means arriving when he expects us. That's the pattern." I looked at each of them. "Elle saw the other timelines. Saw how they failed. Every iteration, I charge in early, corrupted and desperate, exactly when Auradelle is ready for me. This time, we arrive right before. We catch him mid-preparation. We break the pattern."

"And if it doesn't work?" Sarnyx asked. "If we just fail in a new way?"

I smiled, and several people stepped back. "Then we try again in iteration eighteen. But I don't plan on giving the universe that chance."

"Alright, everybody, get moving. You heard the man." Thrak said, already moving into command mode. "Check weapons. Review the tunnels. Gather supplies for five days of hard travel. Make ready."

The others dispersed, some to prepare, some just to process what they'd learned. Within minutes, only Eltrien and I remained in the circle of death.

"I'm still angry at you," I said.

"I know."

"When this is over, we're having a very long conversation about trust and honesty and not playing with people's lives."

"I look forward to it." He actually smiled slightly. "It'll mean we survived."

"It'll mean Elle survived," I corrected.

Eltrien's expression softened. "You're doing the right thing. The strategic thing. The thing that gives you both the best chance."

"I know." I looked up at the stars. "Doesn't make it any easier."

He started to walk away, then paused. "For what it's worth, I think she can do it. This Elle—your Elle—she's different in ways I can't quite articulate. Stronger. More stubborn. More willing to break the rules."

"She's perfect," I said simply.

"Yes." Eltrien looked back at me, and his expression was sad and knowing. "Let's make sure she stays that way. Alive and whole and perfect. This timeline. Not the next one."

He left me alone in my circle of death, standing under stars that were just beginning to appear. Somewhere beyond those stars, hundreds of miles away, Elle was waking in pain. Facing another day of torture. Another day of holding on.

"Hold on," I sent through the muffled bond, knowing she probably couldn't hear but saying it anyway. *"I'm coming."*

Different. This iteration would be different.

It had to be.

Because I couldn't survive watching her die again.

29

Elle

The days blurred together after that first dream with Kaelren.

Day after day, Auradelle tested me. Tuned me. Each session was different—resonance chambers where he hunted for my "core frequency," calibration rituals, tests whose purposes I stopped trying to understand. I just endured.

Between sessions, there was Mora.

The servant girl who'd been assigned to care for me had become something more than a keeper—perhaps not quite a friend, but the closest thing I had to one in this nightmare. She was young, maybe twenty, with mouse-brown hair perpetually escaping its severe bun and gray eyes that had seen far too much for someone her age. Forgettable prettiness that helped servants survive in dangerous courts, but there was a steadiness to her, a quiet strength that reminded me of nurses who worked in war zones— someone who'd seen too much but kept going anyway.

She brought food I could barely eat, helped me bathe when my hands shook too badly to manage alone, and cleaned the welts and burns that appeared after each "tuning." She never said much during the torture sessions' immediate aftermath, letting me have silence when words would have shattered what little composure I had left. But in the quiet moments, she filled the windowless hours with stories about her grandmother, about the time before the rot when the realm was whole.

She'd even taught me curse words in the old tongue. My favorite translated roughly to, "your face looks like a rotted asshole," which seemed particularly appropriate given the circumstances.

"How long?" I asked her one morning—or afternoon, time had lost all meaning in my time at the Heartspire. My voice was raw, rasping from yesterday's screaming.

"Four more days until the convergence," Mora said quietly, helping me sit up. Her hands were gentle as she assessed the new welts across my shoulders. "Lord Auradelle says you're exceeding his expectations."

I wasn't sure if that was good or bad.

Four days. The number settled in my chest like a stone. Somewhere beyond these walls, Kaelren was fighting his own battle against corruption, pushing through hostile territory to reach me. We'd managed to connect in the dream space once since that first night—brief, desperate, filled with more strategy than tenderness. But in the nights since I'd felt nothing. Just emptiness where our bond should be.

"Different robe today," Mora said, holding up white silk with silver threading. Not the crimson from yesterday's resonance testing, not the gold from the day before's frequency calibration. White. The color of endings, or beginnings. I couldn't tell which anymore.

"What's different about today's session?" I asked as she helped me stand. My legs trembled, still weak from yesterday's ordeal.

"I don't know exactly." She began fastening the robe, her fingers working quickly. "But the testing chambers have been sealed since dawn. Even the servants aren't allowed near them." Her gray eyes met mine, and I saw real fear there. "The girl before you—the one who lasted longest—she made it through two days of testing before she broke."

"What happened to her?"

Mora's hands stilled completely. "No one knows. She's alive, but not what she used to be. Lord Auradelle keeps her in the deep chambers. Sometimes at night, you can hear her singing. It doesn't sound fae anymore."

Ice ran through my veins, but I forced my voice steady. "Cheerful. And you? How long have you been here?"

She resumed working on the robe, but I caught the way her fingers trembled slightly. "Since I was seven. My village started to show signs of the rot. My parents thought sending me to serve at the Heartspire would save me." A bitter smile crossed her face. "They were half right. I'm alive."

"But not saved."

"No one who enters the Heartspire is ever truly saved." She finished with the robe and stepped back, studying me with an expression I couldn't read. "We just learn to survive."

I'd asked her once, in a moment of curiosity between torture sessions, about the twisted marks on her forearms—forced into her skin rather than growing naturally, patterns that hurt to look at. She'd told me Lord Auradelle tested her when she was eleven, hoping her Root-touched blood might manifest marks strong enough to hold his power. They'd been hollow. Empty. When it failed, he kept her as a servant, saying she might be useful for understanding the real marked one when they finally arrived.

"You understand what he's doing to me, don't you?" I'd asked her then.

She'd met my eyes and said simply: "I understand that you're terrified. That you miss him—your Kaelren. That you're trying to be brave but inside you're screaming." Her voice had softened. "I understand because I felt all of that too. The difference is, you have someone coming for you. Someone who loves you enough to tear the world apart to get you back."

Now, as she stepped back from adjusting my robe, that same knowing look was in her eyes.

"Be strong today," Mora whispered. "Remember who you are. You're Elle. The woman who told Lord Auradelle to his face that his crown looked like a diseased mushroom."

I almost laughed despite everything. I had said that, two days ago, delirious with pain and exhausted past the point of self-preservation.

"You're stronger than they know," she continued. "Stronger than you know."

Before I could respond, the door opened. Four guards entered, their faces hidden behind ceremonial masks that looked like twisted vines.

"Time to go," one said, voice muffled and strange. "Prince Auradelle can't be kept waiting."

They didn't grab me roughly like the first day. They'd learned I would come willingly to spare Mora from being dragged into the testing chambers "for comparison purposes," as Auradelle had so delicately phrased the threat. I stood, the white robe swirling around me, and followed them out.

The route was different from yesterday. We went deeper into the Heartspire, down stairs that seemed to grow from the walls themselves, through corridors where the air grew hotter and thicker with magic that made my marks burn. The temperature rose with each step until sweat beaded on my skin beneath the silk robe. Finally, we arrived at a chamber I hadn't seen before.

It was larger than yesterday's testing room, circular, with a vaulted ceiling that disappeared into shadow. The walls were covered in mirrors with surfaces that showed different versions of reality—me with marks covering every inch of skin, me as pure corruption, me as something between human and tree. But what made my stomach drop were the figures already in the chamber.

Seven robed figures stood in a circle, swaying in unison to a rhythm I couldn't hear but could feel in my bones. Their faces were hidden behind dark masks that left what they were to the imagination. They hummed—a low, discordant sound that made my marks pulse with painful heat.

At the center of the circle stood not Auradelle, but someone else.

The mage was tall and thin, draped in robes the color of old blood. But it was their face that made me freeze—half of it was ruined, melted and twisted into a grotesque parody of features. Burn scars ran from their left temple down their neck, disappearing beneath the robe. The unmarred right side was beautiful in a cruel way, all sharp angles and cold eyes the color of winter ice.

"Ah," the mage said, and their voice was like something from a horror movie. "The prince's little toy. How delightful." The guards pushed me to the middle of the room and the robed figures circled me slowly as I caught the scent of burned roses. "Do you know who I am, vessel?"

"Should I?"

The mage barked a humorless laugh. "Your corruption-touched pet didn't mention me? How disappointing. I am Malachar, formerly of the Winter Court, before your Kaelren decided I was too 'cruel' in my interrogation methods." They traced one finger down their scarred cheek. "He gave me this. Corruption-fire, burning so hot it melted through my protective wards like they were cobwebs. It took days before the healers could stop the spread."

Ice flooded my veins. "You were torturing someone."

"I was extracting information vital to the realm's security," Malachar corrected, still circling. "But Kaelren has always been... sentimental about such things. Weakness, really. A weakness you seem to share." They stopped directly in front of me. "But Prince Auradelle has given me a gift—the chance to break something he loves. To make you scream the way I screamed. To burn you from the inside out with your own power until you beg for death."

"Charming. You must be delightful at parties."

Malachar's unmarred eye twitched. "Strap her down."

The guards forced me into a chair at the circle's center. This time the restraints were thick vines that grew from the chair itself, wrapping around my wrists, ankles, waist, and throat with enough pressure to make breathing difficult. They were covered in thorns that pressed into my skin without breaking it—yet.

The seven dancers moved closer, their humming growing louder, more discordant. I could feel it now—their power building, feeding into whatever Malachar was about to do.

"Today we test your resonance," Malachar said, producing a crystal blade from their robes. It pulsed with sickly light. "Every marked one resonates at a specific frequency. Finding it is usually a delicate process, requiring patience and precision." Their smile was vicious. "But the prince has given me permission to be... less delicate. After all, we have so little time, and I have so much pain to repay."

"This seems personal for you."

"Oh, it's very personal." Malachar pressed the crystal blade against my sternum, and my marks erupted with burning pain. "I'm going to enjoy this immensely."

The blade cut through the connection between my marks and my soul. The pain was indescribable, like being flayed from the inside out, every nerve ending catching fire simultaneously.

The dancers' humming rose to a wail, and their movements became frantic. Power poured from them into Malachar, who channeled it through the crystal blade into me. My marks responded violently, spreading faster, growing three-dimensional, turning from gold to something darker, something wrong.

I screamed.

"There we go," Malachar crooned, twisting the blade. "Let it out. Scream for me the way I screamed because of him. Play me that pretty little sound."

Through the bond—muffled but there—I felt Kaelren's fury spike. He could feel my agony, and somewhere far away, his corruption was spreading in response, consuming everything around him.

"Yes," Malachar breathed, feeling the bond's reaction through their magic. "He can feel this. Perfect. Every cut I make, every ounce of pain I inflict on you, he experiences as well. A two-for-one special."

The blade cut deeper. The pain increased. The dancers wailed. And I fell down, down, down into darkness.

But it wasn't empty darkness.

I saw *her*—the First Elle, though she hadn't been called that yet. Just a girl from a village near the wild forest, drawn to a clearing where something impossible had happened.

The Seed had bloomed.

Not a flower, not exactly. Something more fundamental—the Root's first great flowering, bursting from the ground in spirals of light and growth. The Bloom, raw and untamed, a miracle no one had summoned or controlled. Just... nature, expressing itself in radiant excess.

She'd found it by accident, following a feeling she couldn't name. And when she touched it, the Bloom recognized something in her—some compatibility, some openness. It marked her. Golden vines spread across her skin, not forced but *invited*.

For weeks, she lived in harmony with it. The Bloom grew. She grew. The forest sang.

Then others came.

I watched as the powerful arrived—those who would become the first Crown, the first Petal Court. They didn't approach the Bloom with wonder. They approached with *hunger*. They saw power to be claimed, controlled, contained.

The First Elle tried to explain: "*It's not meant to be owned. It's meant to grow.*"

They didn't listen.

I watched them build the Heartspire around the Bloom—first as protection, they claimed, then as temple, then as throne. I watched them etch Rootlight into their skin in crude imitation of her natural marks, binding themselves to the Bloom through ritual and relic instead of recognition.

I watched them create the Petal Court, biologically fusing themselves to garden relics, becoming more magic than mortal, *dependent* on the Bloom's power to survive.

And I watched the First Elle realize what she'd done—by being the first to bond with the Bloom, she'd shown them it was possible. She'd become the template for their control.

"*I have to stop this,*" she thought. "*I have to make them understand.*"

But they'd already built their hierarchy. Already created their bloodlines. Already turned a wild miracle into a weapon of stagnation.

The vision shifted, accelerating through years. The First Elle fought them—tried to free the Bloom, tried to let it grow naturally again. The Crown and Petal Court saw this as treason. As corruption.

They hunted her.

I felt her desperation as she fled into the deep forest, her marks spreading not from torture but from the Bloom itself crying out, *too contained, too controlled, can't breathe—*

And then I saw the moment she failed.

They caught her at the forest's heart, where the Root ran deepest. The Crown's soldiers surrounded her, weapons drawn. She knew she was going to die. But worse—she knew the cycle would continue. They would find another marked one, another girl to use as their template. Another attempt to control what should be wild.

"No," she thought. *"Not again. Never again."*

In her final moments, as they closed in, she didn't fight them. Instead, she turned to the Root itself—not the Bloom they'd imprisoned, but the deep, ancient consciousness running beneath everything.

"I failed," she told it. *"But please—don't let it end here. Don't let them keep doing this forever. Send someone back. Send me back. However long it takes, however many tries we need—don't stop until someone gets it right."*

The Root heard her.

And the Root, in its ancient, patient way, began to *adapt*.

I watched her body transform—not dying, but *changing*. Shrinking. Reshaping. Her consciousness compressing down, down into something small enough to slip through time's cracks. Her memories fragmenting, scattering across iterations like seeds.

She became something that could survive the cycle's reset. Something that could remember—not clearly, not all at once, but in pieces. In feelings. In moments of déjà vu that stung like prophecy.

She became Peeble.

Not a beetle. Not originally. But the Root's answer to her prayer—a guardian that would persist through every iteration, always there, always watching, always hoping that *this time* someone would break the pattern.

Sixteen times she'd watched it play out. Sixteen times she'd tried to guide, to hint, to nudge the marked one toward understanding instead of control. Sixteen times she'd failed in slightly different ways.

"But I remember," Peeble's voice echoed through the vision—young and ancient at once, weary and hopeful. *"Every iteration, I remember a little more. Every cycle, I understand a bit better where we went wrong."*

"You're me," I realized, my consciousness bleeding into Peeble's across time. *"The First Elle—you're trying to save yourself. You're trying to save all of*

us."

"*I'm trying to stop them from making the same mistake I made,*" Peeble's voice clarified. "*I showed them the Bloom could be bonded to. I became their proof that power could be controlled. I didn't understand—*"

The vision showed me the truth: the rot wasn't random decay. It was the Root's recoil. Every time the Bloom was used to enforce hierarchy instead of growth, every time it was drained through relics instead of allowed to flower naturally, every time stagnation was enforced on something meant to *evolve*—the Root pulled back.

And that pulling back felt like disease.

The realm wasn't dying because someone failed to control the power. It was dying because someone kept *trying* to control the power.

"*They've been solving the wrong problem for seventeen iterations,*" I understood. "*It's not about finding the right ruler. It's about—*"

"Letting go," Peeble finished. "*Letting the Bloom be what it was meant to be. Wild. Free. Growing.*"

"But how?" I asked the vision. "*How do I break the cycle without just becoming another version of you? Another failure they'll build a new hierarchy around?*"

The vision showed me one more thing—a glimpse of the Seed, hidden beneath the Heartspire in chambers even Auradelle didn't know existed. Not dormant. *Growing.* Quietly, secretly, preparing for its second flowering.

The Bloom had been the first attempt. The Seed was preparing to try again.

And this time, it didn't need a throne.

It needed a spark.

"*You're different,*" Peeble's voice said, and I felt her hope like sunlight through storm clouds. "*You didn't come seeking the power. You didn't try to control it. You came because you were pulled here, dragged here, forced here— and you've spent every moment since then just trying to survive. Just trying to save the people you love.*"

"So what do I do?"

"*What I should have done the first time,*" Peeble said. "*When the moment* comes—*when they try to make you the bridge between Root and Bloom, the vessel for their Convergence—don't be a bridge. Don't be a vessel. Don't let them channel the power through you to maintain their control.*

"*Be the Seed's second flowering. Let it all burn. Let it all grow. Let everything wild and patient and ancient finally break free of the cage they built around it.*

"*Let the realm remember what it was before they tried to rule it.*"

The vision released me, and I surfaced gasping from the darkness to find Thessian still cutting, still testing, still searching for my frequency.

But now I knew.

I knew what I was. What Peeble was. What the Convergence was really for.

And I knew, with terrible certainty, that when the moment came I would have to choose—save Kaelren and let the cycle continue, or break everything and hope that from the ashes, something true could finally grow.

30

Kaelren

The tunnel entrance loomed before us like an open wound in the earth, ancient stone carved with symbols that predated the division of courts. Three days. We had three days until the Convergence, and two of those would be spent crawling through darkness to reach Elle.

Three days felt like both forever and not nearly enough time.

"We camp here tonight," I said, studying the entrance. My corruption had spread further during the day's travel—black veins now crawled down my back and legs. "We enter at first light."

"Smart," Vashael agreed, already scouting the perimeter for defensible positions. "We'll need rest before two days underground."

The others moved with practiced efficiency, setting up our makeshift camp. Sarnyx created a thorned barrier around our perimeter. Nimor melted into shadows to stand watch. Eltrien sat cross-legged, his marks pulsing in patterns that might have been meditation or might have been communication with forces I didn't understand.

And Bryx... Bryx was unusually quiet, sitting apart from the group with Kevin perched on his shoulder, their usual banter replaced by intense, whispered conversation punctuated by the bee's agitated buzzing.

"You alright?" I asked, approaching him.

He startled, then forced a smile that didn't reach his eyes. "Fine. Just... thinking about what we're walking into."

"Having second thoughts?"

"No." The answer came too quickly. "No, I'm committed. We save Elle. That's the plan."

Something in his tone didn't sit right, but before I could press him, Vashael called me over to help reinforce the barrier. By the time I looked back, Bryx had retreated to his tent, Kevin's buzzing fading to silence.

I pushed my unease aside. We all dealt with pre-battle nerves differently.

After everything was settled and seemed quiet, I crawled into my tent. I hated to sleep away from the stars knowing it could be the last time I saw them, but I didn't want the crew fretting over the expanse of corruption that ate at my very soul. Exhaustion pulled me under almost the moment I closed my eyes.

I should have realized immediately I was in the dreamscape we'd created before. Elle stood waiting for me, and the sight of her made my chest constrict with desperate longing.

She looked exhausted. Bruises shadowed her eyes, and like myself her marks had spread further. We were really two sides of the same coin. Two halves of a whole. But she was alive. She was here. And she was mine.

"Elle," I breathed, crossing to her in three strides and pulling her against me.

She melted into my embrace, trembling. "Kaelren. God, I've missed you."

"I'm coming for you. Three more days—"

"I know. I can feel you getting closer." She pulled back enough to look at me, her Earth-green eyes fierce despite her exhaustion. "But there's something you need to know. Something I learned."

I cupped her face in my hands, marveling that in this space, my touch didn't burn. "Tell me everything."

"The seed," she said urgently. "Beneath the Heartspire, hidden in chambers even Auradelle doesn't know exist—there's a seed. The original seed, from before the first flowering. It's been waiting, growing, preparing for a second chance."

"A second flowering?" Understanding dawned slowly. "You mean—"

"I mean the Bloom they've imprisoned, the one they've been using to maintain their hierarchy for generations—it's dying because it was never meant to be controlled like this. It was supposed to be wild, free, constantly evolving. But they caged it, forced it into stagnation, and now it's rotting from the inside out." Her eyes blazed with fierce certainty. "But the seed... Kaelren, when the Crown first corrupted the Bloom, when they built their throne and their hierarchy on stolen power, the Root felt it. Felt the imbalance, felt how wrong it all was. So it did the only thing it could. It created a failsafe."

"The seed," I breathed, understanding dawning.

"The seed," she confirmed. "Hidden so deep that no one who served the Crown would ever find it. A second chance, growing in darkness, waiting for someone to come along who wasn't trying to rule the power but free it. The Root has been trying to correct this for generations, trying to undo what the Crown did. But it can't force the change—it can only offer the opportunity." Her hands gripped my shirt desperately. "We have to find it, Kaelren. We have to be the ones who finally accept what the Root has been offering all along. The chance to let the Bloom be what it was always meant to be—wild, free, growing without chains or thrones or anyone trying to own it."

"How do you know this?"

"Peeble showed me." She took a shaky breath. "Kaelren, Peeble isn't just a beetle. They're the First Elle. The original marked one, transformed by the Root into something that could persist through iterations, always watching, always hoping someone would finally break the cycle."

The revelation should have shocked me more, but after everything we'd seen, everything we'd survived, it made a terrible kind of sense.

"Where is this seed?" I asked.

"Deep beneath the ritual chamber. There's a passage that branches off the main tunnels—you'll know it when you feel it. The Root's presence is stronger there, older." Her eyes searched mine. "You have to get it, Kaelren. When the Convergence comes, when Auradelle tries to force the merger—the seed is our only chance to break the pattern."

"I'll find it," I promised. "No matter what it takes."

She stood on her toes and kissed me, soft and desperate. When she pulled back, tears tracked down her cheeks. "I love you. I need you to know that, before everything goes wrong. I love you so much it terrifies me."

"Elle—"

"Julian made me afraid of this feeling. Afraid of being vulnerable, of trusting someone with something this precious." Her voice cracked. "But you... you've never asked me to be anything other than what I am. You've never tried to dim me or control me or reshape me into something more convenient."

I pulled her close again, burying my face in her hair. "I love you too. With everything corrupted and twisted in me, I love you. You're the only real thing left in my life."

"Then show me," she whispered against my neck. "Before we face what's coming, before everything falls apart—show me."

I pulled back to look at her, needing to be sure. "Elle, you don't have to—"

"I want to," she said fiercely. "I want this moment with you. Something that's just ours, untouched by prophecy or politics or poison. Please."

How could I deny her anything?

I kissed her again, deeper this time, pouring every ounce of desperate love into the contact. Her hands found my hair, tugging until I groaned against her mouth. When we finally broke apart, we were both breathing hard.

"Let me worship you properly," I said, voice rough. "The way you deserve."

The dreamscape shifted around us, responding to our combined need. A rustic treehouse formed around us with a vast valley below and a sky full of constellations above. A bed appeared, carved from oak and covered in velvet and violet colored petals. I guided Elle to it, laying her down with reverence.

"You're so beautiful. I know I've said it so many times, but it never does you justice." I murmured, tracing the path of her marks with my fingertips. "These marks—they're not corruption or curse. They're you claiming your power, becoming who you were always meant to be."

She arched into my touch. "Kaelren, please—"

"Patience, love." I kissed the hollow of her throat, feeling her pulse race beneath my lips. "I've missed this. Let me savor it."

I took my time undressing her, my hands trembling slightly as they found the hem of her shirt. I lifted it slowly, my fingers trailing against her skin like I was memorizing the feeling—the softness, the warmth, the way she shivered under my touch. When the fabric was gone, my lips followed the path my hands had traced, pressing soft kisses to her collarbone, her shoulder, the sensitive spot where her neck met her jaw that I'd discovered made her breath catch.

"You're a miracle," I murmured against her skin, meaning every word. "Do you know that? Everything about you is impossible and perfect."

She opened her mouth—probably to argue, to list all the ways she thought she was flawed—but I kissed her before she could, swallowing whatever protest she'd been about to make. We moved together, clothes disappearing with dream-logic until we were finally skin to skin.

The feel of her against me, nothing between us, nearly undid me completely.

"Wait," I said, pulling back with visible effort. An idea had struck me, something I'd never tried with anyone else, something that felt right for her. For us.

I reached up to the tree that formed the walls of our dreamscape sanctuary, to where golden sap leaked from the bark. It came away on my fingers like honey, warm and sweet-smelling, glowing faintly in the amber light.

"What are you—" Elle started.

"Trust me," I said, meeting her eyes.

"Always," she breathed, and the simple trust in that word made my chest ache.

I traced one finger, slick with sap, across her collarbone. She gasped at the warmth of it, the slight stickiness. Then I leaned down and followed the path with my tongue, lapping up the sweetness, tasting her skin beneath it—salt and Earth-rain and something uniquely Elle.

"Oh," she breathed, her back arching slightly.

I took my time, painting patterns across her skin with the golden sap— down her sternum, across the swell of her breasts, along her ribs where her marks glowed brightest. Each application made her gasp. Each time I followed with my mouth, tasting honey and her, she made sounds that went straight to my groin.

"Kaelren," she breathed, her hands finding my hair, holding me to her like she was afraid I'd stop.

I had no intention of stopping. I lavished attention on her breasts, the sap making my tongue glide smoothly across sensitive skin. I used my teeth carefully, scraping across peaks already hardened with need, and felt her whole body shudder in response.

When I was satisfied—when she was trembling and gasping my name—I moved lower, kissing a path down her stomach that made her forget how to breathe. The marks there pulsed under my lips, responding to my touch, to my need, to the bond that sang between us.

"Please," she gasped, not sure what she was begging for. "I need—"

"Let me take care of you," I said against her hip, pressing a kiss there. "Let me show you how precious you are."

I lifted her gently, adjusting her position on the petal-covered bed with reverence that made my hands tremble. When I settled between her thighs, spreading them wider to make room for my shoulders, I had to pause for a moment just to look at her. Flushed and wanting, her marks glowing, her chest heaving with anticipation—she was the most beautiful thing I'd ever seen.

My hands settled on her thighs, and when I looked up at her, I knew my eyes were dark with desire and something deeper—worship, maybe, or wonder at the sheer privilege of being trusted with this.

The first taste of her was intoxicating—earthy and sweet with an under-current of that wild power she carried, like summer storms and growing things and magic barely contained. I groaned against her, the sound vibrating through her in a way that made her cry out.

I took my time, alternating between broad strokes of my tongue that made her whimper and focused attention on the bundle of nerves that made her cry out and arch off the bed. I remembered from our first time together what made her fall apart, but I wanted to learn it all over again, wanted to discover new ways to drive her mad.

Her thighs trembled around my head, and I had to hold her hips down to keep her from arching off the bed entirely. The plants glowed brighter around us, responding to her pleasure, to the power building between us.

"Please," she gasped, her hands tightening in my hair almost painfully. "I need—I can't—"

I knew what she needed. I doubled my efforts, adding my fingers to the mix, sliding them inside her while my tongue worked that sensitive bundle of nerves. She was tight and hot around my fingers, her body clenching in rhythm with each stroke. I found the angle that made her see stars, curling my fingers to hit that spot inside her that made her scream.

Her hands were desperate in my hair now, holding me in place, and then suddenly they left, reaching up to find—

My ears.

Her fingers traced the pointed tips—more pronounced here in the dreamscape than in reality—and the sensation shot through me like lightning. I actually growled against her, the vibration making her hips buck against my mouth.

"Do that again," I demanded, pulling back just enough to speak, my fingers never stopping their rhythm inside her.

She did, her fingers tracing delicate patterns on the sensitive points of my ears, and I had to fight not to lose myself completely. Instead, I channeled that pleasure into my efforts, my tongue working faster, my fingers hitting that perfect spot with each thrust.

We were learning each other all over again, mapping new territory, building something between us that existed outside of prophecy or destiny or the roles we'd been forced into. This was just us—just two people who wanted each other with a desperation that defied logic.

I felt her getting close, felt the way her body tensed, the way her breathing grew ragged and desperate. Through the bond, I could feel her pleasure building like a storm about to break, and I wanted to be the one who shattered her.

"Let go," I murmured against her. "Let go, love. I've got you."

When she came, it was my name on her lips—my name, not a curse or a prayer but something in between. Her whole body went rigid, her marks blazing so bright the entire room seemed to glow with golden light. Through the bond, I felt her pleasure as if it were my own—waves of it crashing over both of us, drowning us in sensation. My own marks pulsed in response, the bond between us singing with shared ecstasy.

I worked her through it, my fingers gentling inside her, my tongue softening its assault until the waves began to subside. Even then, I continued with soft, careful touches, drawing out every last tremor of pleasure until she was pushing my head away with shaking hands.

"Stop, stop," she gasped, oversensitive and trembling. "Too much—"

I pressed one last reverent kiss to her inner thigh, then slowly withdrew my fingers and crawled up her body. She was trembling, her breathing ragged, her marks still glowing softly in the aftermath. I gathered her against me, holding her close while she shook.

"I've got you," I murmured, pressing kisses to her forehead, her temple, her flushed cheeks. "You're safe. I've got you."

She buried her face against my neck, her arms wrapping around me with surprising strength for someone who'd just come apart so completely. "That was..." she started, then trailed off, apparently unable to find words.

"Perfect," I finished for her. "You're perfect."

She relaxed into my embrace, her head finding the hollow of my shoulder like it was made to fit there. We lay tangled together, skin to skin, our marks glowing softly in the dim light.

"I'm scared," she admitted quietly. "Of what's coming. Of what might happen to us."

"Me too," I said, because she deserved honesty. "But I promise you this— no matter what happens next, no matter how this ends, I will fight with everything I have to give us a chance."

"The seed," she reminded me. "You have to get the seed."

"I will."

"And Kaelren?" She pulled back enough to look at me. "When the moment comes, trust Peeble. Trust what they tell you. They've been preparing for this for longer than any of us can comprehend."

The dream was already starting to fade, reality pulling us back to our separate hells. I held her tighter, trying to memorize the feel of her, the smell of her, every detail I could capture.

"Find me," she whispered as the world dissolved around us. "When it all begins—find me."

"Always," I promised. "In this iteration and every other, I will always find you."

I woke to cold dawn light filtering through the tent flap, Elle's warmth replaced by the chill of corruption spreading through my veins. But I could still feel her, still taste her, still smell her scent on my skin even though it had only been a dream.

More than a dream. A gift. A promise.

I dressed quickly, my mind already planning the detour we'd need to make. The seed. Elle had given me a mission, and I wouldn't fail her.

But when I emerged from my tent, I immediately knew something was wrong.

The others were gathered in a tight cluster, their voices low and urgent. Peeble sat on Vashael's shoulder, their wings vibrating with distress in a way I'd never seen before.

"What happened?" I demanded.

Vashael turned to me, her expression grim. "Bryx is gone. And Kevin with him."

The words didn't process at first. "Gone where?"

"We don't know." Sarnyx gestured to Bryx's tent—empty, his pack missing, no sign of a struggle. "Nimor says they left during the night. Quietly, like they didn't want to be followed."

"Why would he—" I stopped, remembering his odd behavior last night. The whispered conversation with Kevin. The way he'd avoided my eyes. "Damn it."

"There's no note, no explanation," Eltrien said, his marks pulsing rapidly. "Just... gone."

Peeble launched off Vashael's shoulder and landed on mine, their usual sass completely absent. "He knew something. Kevin knew something. I could feel it yesterday—they were planning this."

"Planning what?" I demanded. "Why would Bryx abandon us now, right before everything?"

"I don't know," Peeble admitted, and their uncertainty was more frightening than their usual confident snark. "But if they left, they had a reason."

I wanted to go after them. Every instinct screamed to track them down, demand answers, drag Bryx back by force if necessary. But—

"We don't have time," Vashael said quietly, reading my face. "The Convergence is in three days. If we delay even half a day searching for them..."

"Elle dies," I finished, the words bitter in my mouth. "And everything ends."

"Bryx made his choice," Sarnyx said, though her voice held regret. "We have to make ours."

I looked at each of them—Vashael, Sarnyx, Nimor, Eltrien. Four where we should have been six. Two losses already, and we hadn't even entered the tunnels yet.

"I saw Elle again last night, and she told me something in the dream," I said, making the decision. "There's a chamber beneath the Heartspire, hidden even from Auradelle. A seed grows there—created by the Root, preparing for a second flowering. We need to retrieve it."

"A detour," Nimor said, understanding immediately.

"Yes. But it's necessary." I looked at Peeble, remembering Elle's words. "When we reach it, something will happen. Peeble you're supposed to know what we need to do."

Peeble's entire body went still. "She told you."

"She told me to trust you. That you're more than you seem."

Peeble silently nodded, and the others stared.

I gathered everyone close. "Here's the plan. We enter the tunnels now. We move fast but carefully—there will be traps, guards, obstacles. When we reach the branching passage that leads to the seed chamber, Eltrien, Pebble, and I will go for it while the rest of you secure our exit route."

"Why Eltrien?" Vashael asked.

I met Eltrien's strange eyes. "Because I think he's been preparing for this moment for a very long time."

"Longer than you know," Eltrien agreed quietly.

"We have three days," I said. "We cannot afford mistakes. We cannot afford mercy. Anyone who stands between us and Elle dies. Understood?"

Grim nods all around.

"Then let's move."

We gathered our supplies, checked our weapons one last time, and approached the tunnel entrance. The symbols carved into the stone seemed to pulse as I drew near, responding to my corruption in ways I didn't understand.

Before we descended, I paused and looked back at the morning sky, wondering where Bryx and Kevin had gone, what could possibly have been important enough to make them abandon us now.

But there was no time for waste.

"For Elle!" I said, and stepped into the darkness.

"For Elle!" the others echoed behind me.

The tunnels swallowed us whole, ancient and aware, and somewhere far ahead, destiny or doom or both awaited.

The countdown had begun.

31

Bryx

I shouldn't have left.

That's what the rational part of my brain—you know, the tiny part that wasn't constantly suggesting I flirt with danger, death, or anyone with a pulse—kept screaming as Kevin and I buzzed through the pre-dawn darkness toward the Heartspire. But the irrational part, which was basically everything else, was having the time of its life.

Kevin, my magnificent bee companion, was the size of a small horse when he wanted to be, with fuzzy black and yellow stripes that I'd personally groomed to perfection. His wings made that beautiful thrumming sound that meant business, and his compound eyes reflected my own insectoid features back at me in thousands of tiny mirrors. We'd been partners for years now, ever since I'd found him as a larvae being sold in a black market for spell components. The merchant had called him defective because he was too smart, too independent. I'd called him perfect and stolen him that very night.

"This is the stupidest thing we've ever done," I told him, my antennae twitching with more excitement than nervousness as we flew. "And that's saying something, considering that time we tried to seduce that carnivorous flower. Remember? You got pollen-drunk and I nearly lost an arm."

Kevin buzzed something that roughly translated to *"That was your idea, idiot."*

"Everything's my idea! That's the problem!" I shifted my grip on his fuzzy thorax, my partially translucent skin catching the moonlight in ways that I knew looked absolutely magnificent. "But you have to admit, my ideas are at least entertaining. Remember the time we convinced those Crown guards we were exotic dancers hired for the prince's birthday? We got all the way to the throne room before they realized the prince's birthday was three months away."

Kevin's buzz was definitely laughter this time.

Being part insect had its perks—compound eyes meant I could see in almost every direction, my antennae could pick up pheromones from miles away, and I had extra joints that gave me flexibility most people couldn't achieve even in their wildest dreams. The downside? Well, try getting a date when you have mandibles that click when you're nervous. Though honestly, some people found it exotic. There was this one bartender in the lower districts who said my compound eyes were 'mesmerizing.' We dated for two weeks before she realized I literally couldn't stop staring at her because that's just how compound eyes work.

"You know what I want, Kev?" I said, knowing full well he understood every word—our bond went deeper than most people realized. "I want someone to look at me the way Kaelren looks at Elle when he thinks nobody's watching. Like I'm worth becoming a monster for. Though let's be honest, I'm already pretty monstrous. In the best way possible."

Kevin's buzz softened to something almost sympathetic. "You're already a monster, just a funny one."

"A devastatingly handsome funny one," I corrected with a grin he couldn't see but definitely felt through our bond. "With excellent taste in bees and a singing voice that could make a siren weep. Remember when I won that singing competition contest in the Thornwood? The prize was a year's supply of fermented nectar. Best Tuesday ever."

The Heartspire loomed ahead, and my good mood shifted into something sharper, more focused. The fortress was wrong on levels that made my compound eyes water. It twisted reality around it like a tumor, all sharp spires and surrounded by rot. The original structure had been beautiful once, I'd seen paintings in the old archives. A palace of beautiful wood and cultivated stone, where the first Crown had married Root and Bloom in harmony. Now it looked like that palace had gotten cancer and the cancer had gotten ambitious.

"Alright, Kevin, time to be heroes," I muttered. "Or at least heroically nosy. Lysandra's vision said there's something only we can discover. No pressure or anything—just the fate of two realms hanging on my devastatingly handsome compound eyes spotting something important."

The truth was, back at Silverpine, I'd thought my moment had finally come. When Lysandra—that ethereal, impossibly beautiful creature with eyes like winter frost and skin that was the same shade of blue on a perfect sunny day—had approached me during the planning sessions, my heart had done acrobatics. She'd leaned in close, her voice low and intimate, and asked if we could speak somewhere private.

Private. The word had sent my imagination into overdrive. Finally, I'd thought. Finally, someone sees beyond the jokes and the sonic magic to the dashing, charming, incredibly modest specimen of—

"I need to tell you about a vision," she'd said once we were alone.

Oh.

She'd proceeded to absolutely demolish any romantic notions I'd been harboring, explaining in that maddeningly detached way seers had that I was crucial to some cosmic plan. That when we reached the tunnels, I'd need to slip away from the group without anyone—especially Kaelren—knowing. That if I didn't, if they tried to stop me or come with me, everyone would be doomed.

"You'll find something," she'd said, gripping my shoulder with fingers that were ice cold—like her heart, apparently. "Something that changes everything. I can't see what it is—the vision clouds there—but I see you finding it. I see you warning them. I see you being more than anyone expects."

"And the kiss?" I'd asked hopefully. "The vision definitely included a kiss at the end, right? As a reward for my bravery?"

She'd just looked at me like I had grown two heads, and walked away.

Not even a consolation kiss for the betrayal I was about to commit. For leaving my crew at the entrance to the most dangerous mission of their lives, making them think I'd abandoned them when really I was... what? Following the vague instructions of a beautiful seer who couldn't even tell me what I was looking for?

"The convergence depends on what you find," she'd said before leaving me standing there with my crushed hopes and bruised ego.

We landed on one of the outer ramparts, Kevin shrinking down to about housecat size—adorable but still deadly. The stone was old here, older than the corruption, carved with runes that predated the separation of the realms. I could feel them humming under my feet, a vibration that made my extra joints ache.

"Act natural," I whispered to Kevin.

He buzzed something that definitely meant *We're a bug person and a bee on a fortress wall. Nothing about this is natural.*

"Natural is overrated anyway," I murmured back, creeping forward with the kind of grace that came from having six major joints per limb. "Besides, have you seen how I walk? Poetry in motion. Disturbing, unsettling poetry that makes people uncomfortable, but still poetry."

The first thing that hit me wasn't the sight but the smell. It crawled up my antennae and made my whole body want to revolt. This wasn't natural decay—this was engineered putrefaction, deliberate and purposeful. It smelled like someone had taken everything wrong with the world, distilled it down to its essence, and then decided to make it worse.

The channels carved into the Heartspire's walls glowed with that sick green light that meant Bloom magic had gone necrotic. But there was a pattern to them, a deliberate architecture of corruption that spoke of years of planning. Someone had designed this. Someone had carved these channels with specific purposes in mind.

"Sweet Root and Bloom," I whispered, following the channels with my multifaceted gaze. They created a network through the entire structure, like veins carrying disease instead of life. "They're not just letting it happen— they're cultivating it. That's... actually kind of impressive in a deeply disturbing way."

I needed to get closer. Creeping along the wall, I stayed low, using my extra joints to contort in ways that would make a contortionist weep with envy. My compound eyes let me track movement in every direction—guards patrolling in patterns that were almost mechanical in their precision, shadows shifting in doorways, and... wait.

Those channels weren't just carrying one type of magic.

I paused, antennae twitching as I focused. The green corruption was obvious, but underneath it, threading through it like golden wire through rotted cloth, was something else. Something that made my whole body tingle with recognition.

"Root magic," I breathed. But not corrupted Root, not twisted Root—pure Root magic being fed directly into the corruption. The two powers that were supposed to be separate, that the whole realm was built on keeping separate, were being deliberately mixed. "Oh, that's not good. That's very, very not good."

My mind raced through the implications. Root and Bloom were never meant to mix directly—that's why marked ones were so rare, why the Convergence only happened once a generation, why the realms had been separated in the first place. Mixing them artificially... it was like mixing matter and antimatter, except instead of an explosion, you got... what? What were they trying to create?

Which was when I saw them—Bloomguard dipping their weapons into the channels, coating blades and arrows with the mixture. The metal didn't corrode or reject it. Instead, the weapons seemed to drink it in, gleaming with a sick light that hurt to look at directly.

"They're weaponizing it," I said, horror and fascination warring in my chest. "They're literally using both powers against each other. That's... that's brilliant and terrifying and completely insane."

I watched as a guard tested one of the treated blades on a training dummy. The dummy didn't just get cut—it dissolved at the point of contact, spreading outward like aggressive cancer until there was nothing left but ash that smelled of roses and rot.

"You there! Stop!"

I froze. Not one, not two, but five Bloomguard had spotted me, their armor gleaming with that pearl-and-poison sheen that meant they were elite. But instead of panicking, I felt a grin spread across my face. This was more my speed.

"Oh, hello there!" I called out cheerfully, straightening to my full height—all six feet of wiry insectoid hybrid swagger. "Lovely evening for a patrol, isn't it? Though between you and me, the décor could use some work. All this doom and gloom—have you considered some nice pastels? Maybe a throw pillow or two? I know a guy who does wonderful work with cursed tapestries. Very reasonable rates."

The lead guard's hand went to her sword. "Identify yourself."

"Bryx the Magnificent, at your service!" I announced with a theatrical bow that showed off my flexibility. "Part-time hero, full-time heartthrob, occasional interior decorator, and currently very lost. You wouldn't believe the day I've had. First, my bee here—say hello, Kevin—"

Kevin buzzed what was definitely not a hello.

"—Kevin decided to chase a butterfly. A butterfly! Can you imagine? We're in the middle of a dramatic scouting mission and he's distracted by pretty wings. Though I can't blame him. Pretty wings are very distracting. Speaking of which, that armor really brings out your eyes. Are those standard issue or did you get them specially made?"

The female guard actually blushed behind her mask. Score one for the Bryx charm.

"He's with the rebels," another guard said, not a question.

"Rebels? Me?" I gasped dramatically, hand over my heart. "I'm hurt. Wounded. Mortally offended. I'll have you know I'm a free agent. An independent contractor of chaos. Available for parties, harvest festivals, and the occasional overthrow of tyrannical regimes. Very reasonable rates. I do offer a group discount if you're interested."

"Enough games," the lead guard snapped. "You've seen the channels. You know what we're doing."

"Oh, I've seen them alright. Mixing Root and Bloom? Very naughty. I'm pretty sure that's against at least a dozen natural laws and probably a few unnatural ones. Does your mother know what you're up to? She'd be very disappointed."

They attacked simultaneously, which was just rude. No warning, no dramatic countdown, not even a 'prepare to die, rebel scum.' Where was the showmanship? The style? The basic courtesy of announcing your intent to murder someone?

I dodged the first blade with flexibility that came from having too many joints, bending backward until my head nearly touched my heels. "Whoa! Buy a guy dinner first!"

The second attack I deflected with a sonic pulse that shattered stone and made all five guards stagger. The rampart cracked under the force, pieces falling into the courtyard below with crashes that would definitely attract attention.

"Oops!" I called out cheerfully. "Did I forget to mention the sonic thing? My bad! I really should come with a warning label. 'Caution: Contains devastating good looks and destructive sound waves.'"

Kevin grew to full size instantly, diving at the nearest guard with stinger extended. The guard barely dodged, rolling aside as Kevin's stinger punched through solid stone where he'd been standing. The stone sizzled where Kevin's venom touched it.

"That's my boy!" I cheered, sending out another sonic pulse that knocked two guards off balance. "Show them why bees are superior to wasps in every way! Better pollinators, better honey producers, better at causing massive property damage!"

The fight was actually going pretty well for about thirty seconds. My sonic pulses kept them disoriented, Kevin was magnificently terrifying, and I was pulling off some genuinely impressive acrobatic moves that I definitely planned to brag about later. I even managed to knock one guard completely off the rampart with a well-timed sonic burst combined with a spinning kick that would have made my combat instructor proud, if I'd ever had one.

But then more guards arrived. Like, a lot more guards. Apparently my sonic pulses weren't exactly subtle, and the sound of shattering stone had attracted every guard in a quarter-mile radius.

"Kevin, remember that tactical retreat we practiced?"

He buzzed agreement while stinging a guard in a very uncomfortable place.

"Time to tactically retreat! With style!"

I grabbed onto Kevin as he swooped past, and we shot into the air, arrows whistling past us. One caught Kevin's wing, tearing through the delicate membrane. He buzzed in pain but kept flying, because Kevin was a champion and champions don't let little things like arrow wounds stop them.

"You okay, buddy?" I called over the wind.

His buzz translated roughly to *"I've had worse. Remember the time you convinced me to pollinate those carnivorous orchids?"*

"That was for science!"

"That was for a dare!"

"Scientific dare!"

We crashed into a grove a mile away, both of us gasping, bleeding, somehow still alive. Kevin's left wing was torn, and I was pretty sure I'd cracked something important. Maybe several somethings. But my gorgeous smile was intact, so really, priorities.

"Can you fly?" I asked Kevin, examining his wing.

He buzzed indignantly—of course he could fly. He was insulted I'd even asked. A torn wing was nothing. He'd flown with worse. Like that time I'd accidentally set him on fire. Or the time he'd been half-frozen. Or the time—

"Okay, okay, you're very tough and very brave," I said, patting his fuzzy head. "Now, let's go find Thrak's forces and tell them we're all probably going to die if they stick to the plan. But, you know, in a cheerful way."

But I couldn't stop thinking about what I'd seen. The channels, the weapons, the deliberate mixing of Root and Bloom—it wasn't just corruption. It was something else. Something planned.

We flew low and fast, Kevin pushing through the pain like the absolute champion he was. The forest below was already showing signs of the convergence—streams flowing backward, trees aging and reversing in rapid cycles, reality getting thin at the edges. A deer ran past us backward, which was disturbing on multiple levels. A flock of birds flew in perfect reverse formation, and I swear I saw a flower bloom, wilt, and bloom again in the span of seconds.

We found Thrak's army about two miles from the Heartspire, moving through the forest like a tide of desperate hope. Two hundred and fifty rebels armed with everything from proper weapons to farming tools. They looked up as we approached, and I saw the surprise on their faces.

"Thrak!" I shouted, landing with more flair than strictly necessary. "Stop! It's a trap! The whole thing is a trap! But also, hello everyone, you're all looking particularly rebellious today! Love the energy! Very revolutionary chic!"

The scarred rebel leader held up his hand, halting the march. "Bryx? What are you—"

"No time to explain! Lysandra had a vision. She sent me to scout. The Heartspire—" I gasped, partly for breath and partly for dramatic effect. "The rot channels aren't just corruption. They're mixing Root AND Bloom magic into it. The entire building is designed to harvest power from marked ones. Also, their interior decoration is absolutely heinous. Someone should really talk to them about that."

"What?" Vera stepped forward, her scarred face skeptical. She hadn't liked me from the beginning, probably because I'd once tried to lighten the mood at a strategy meeting with an interpretive dance about the futility of war. In my defense, it had been a very long meeting.

"I saw it myself. They're coating their weapons in it, but that's not the worst part. The building itself—it's calibrated to pull power from anyone with marks. The moment Kaelren touches those walls with his corruption, the moment any marked one makes contact—it'll drain them. Feed that power straight into whatever Auradelle is doing to Elle."

"You're sure?" Thrak's one good eye studied me intently.

"Kevin and I had a delightful chat with some guards about it," I said, gesturing to our various wounds with a flourish. "They were very convincing with their swords and arrows. Quite persuasive, really. Five stars for their dedication to trying to kill us. Would not recommend for a second date though."

The rebels murmured uneasily. This changed everything.

"If we go through the main gates—" Vera started.

"We're walking into exactly what Auradelle wants," I finished. "He's expecting the assault. He's counting on it. Every marked fighter who enters becomes fuel for his ritual."

Thrak was quiet for a long moment, weighing options, calculating odds. I could practically see the gears turning in his head. Then: "What do you suggest?"

I grinned, that special Bryx grin that meant I was about to suggest something either brilliant or suicidal. Possibly both. Definitely both.

"I have a plan," I announced. "It's clever, it's dramatic, and it involves a truly impressive amount of style. You're going to love it. Or hate it. Honestly, could go either way. But it'll definitely be memorable!"

The rebels leaned in, and for the first time in my life, people were looking at me not as a joke, but as someone who might actually have answers. It was a heady feeling. I could get used to this.

"But first," I said, maintaining the suspense because timing was every-thing, "we're going to need every bee in a three-mile radius. Kevin, darling, start making friends."

As Kevin began sending out pheromone signals, I turned back to the assembled rebels with my most charming smile. The one that had once convinced a dryad to go out with me for drinks. Well, she drank, while I sat in a dark corner watching her. It was complicated.

"Trust me," I said. "We're about to give the performance of our lives. And if we die, we'll die with style. Which, really, is all anyone can ask for."

32

Kaelren

Day one in the tunnels, and I already wanted to kill something.

The passages were narrow, the air thick with earth and age and ancient magic. Root-carved tunnels that remembered everyone who'd walked through them. Every rebel who'd fled. Every king who'd hunted. Every iteration's desperate push toward failure.

My team moved behind me in a single file—Sarnyx, Vashael, Nimor, Eltrien. Four fighters who'd followed me into this darkness without hesitation. And Peeble, on my shoulder, glowing faintly to light our way.

I shoved thoughts of Bryx aside. Whatever he was doing, wherever he'd gone—I couldn't afford to care right now. Elle was ahead. The seed was ahead. Everything else was just noise.

"Hold," I said, stopping abruptly.

The others froze. Ahead, barely visible in the dim light, something glinted across the passage.

"Wire," Nimor confirmed, becoming shadow to investigate. "Thin. Almost invisible. Detection spell attached."

"Can you disable it?"

"Give me ten minutes."

We waited while he worked, pressed against tunnel walls that pulsed like living things. Through the bond—muffled, distant—I felt Elle. Awake. In pain. Fighting to stay conscious during whatever fresh horror Auradelle had planned for today.

"Hold on," I sent, knowing she probably couldn't hear me through the suppression. *"We're coming."*

"Done," Nimor called softly.

We moved forward, careful not to touch anything. Found two more wire traps in the next hour, both designed to alert every guard in the Heartspire. Both disabled by Nimor's shadow work.

"They knew someone would try this route," Vashael observed.

"Good," I said. "Let them waste resources on useless threats."

We pressed deeper. The passages branched, twisted, doubled back on themselves. Sometimes I swore we were moving in circles, but the bond kept pulling me forward, unerring as north.

Then the first real obstacle hit.

The tunnel opened into a chamber, and I knew immediately something was wrong. The floor was too smooth. The walls too perfectly curved. And there, carved into stone, was a pattern that made my corruption recoil.

"Binding circle," Eltrien said, approaching the edge. "Designed specifically for Root-touched and corrupted. Step inside and you're trapped."

"How do we get past it?" Sarnyx asked.

"We don't. This is the only way forward." Eltrien studied the runes, his marks flaring bright blue. "All the other passages lead nowhere. They converge here."

A bottleneck. Exactly what you'd design if you knew someone was coming.

"What if we trigger it deliberately?" I asked. "Step in, break it from inside?"

"That's insane," Vashael said.

"Got a better idea?"

Silence.

"I'll do it," I said. "My corruption is what it's designed to catch. Better me than all of us."

"Kaelren—"

"If I can't break it, find another way. Don't waste time trying to save me."

Before anyone could argue, I stepped into the circle.

The binding hit like a physical blow. Runes activated, power wrapped around me like chains, and the circle tried to pull the corruption from my body and trap it in stone. My legs buckled. Vision went white. Every nerve screamed as the binding dug into my essence, trying to pin me here until I died or went mad.

"Now!" Peeble shouted. "While it's focused on him!"

The little beetle leapt from my shoulder, and suddenly they were glowing. Bright, blinding light that made the binding runes scream in protest. Peeble landed on one of the key runes, and I watched as their form changed, expanded, became something that was more memory than beetle.

For a moment, I saw them as they truly were. Not a bug. An echo. A ghost. A fragment of Elle from the first iteration.

"I've disabled this stupid circle sixteen other times," they said, and their voice was Elle's voice, layered with exhaustion. "You'd think someone would change the pattern."

The runes shattered.

I collapsed forward, gasping. The binding's remnants still clung to me, making my marks burn, but I was free.

"It's true. You're her," I said when I could speak. "The first Elle."

"Was her. Am her. It's complicated." Peeble hopped back onto my shoulder, still glowing brighter than before. "The point is, I've seen sixteen versions of you walk these tunnels. Sixteen versions die trying to save sixteen versions of Elle. Every single time, it ends with both of you destroyed."

"Not this time."

"That's what you always say."

We moved on. The tunnels grew warmer, the air thicker. My corruption responded to something ahead, spreading another inch with each step. Soon I'd be more monster than man.

Didn't matter. Elle was ahead.

We encountered our first guards six hours into the journey. Nimor spotted them first—four Bloomguard patrolling a wider section of tunnel ahead.

"I can't use corruption," I said quietly. "It'll flare like a signal fire. Alert every guard in the Heartspire to exactly where we are."

"Then we do it the old-fashioned way," Sarnyx said, thorns extending. "Quick and silent."

We set up an ambush in a narrow passage. When the guards rounded the corner, we were ready.

Sarnyx struck first, thorns piercing through armor gaps. Vashael's poisons dropped two before they could scream. Nimor pulled one into shadow—I didn't see what happened to him. Eltrien did something with his marks that made the last guard simply stop, frozen like a statue.

"Hide them," I ordered.

We dragged the bodies into a side passage, covering them with loose stone. Not perfect, but maybe good enough.

"That was too easy," Vashael said what we were all thinking.

"They weren't expecting us this deep yet," I replied. "That'll change."

We moved faster now, checking every surface for traps. Found three more binding circles, all disabled by Peeble. Found pressure plates that would collapse the ceiling. Found sections of floor that would drop into pit traps below.

And all the while, Elle's pain pulsed through the bond. Constant. Relentless. A reminder of what was happening while we crawled through darkness.

Eight hours in, we stopped to rest in a chamber where the tunnel widened. I forced down food that tasted like ash.

"How much further?" Sarnyx asked while checking her thorns.

"Maybe halfway," I guessed based on the bond strength. "But the second half will be harder."

"How much harder?"

"Expect—"

The pain hit.

Not my pain—Elle's, flooding through the bond with enough force to drop me to my knees. I felt my back arch, felt my throat try to scream, felt my marks burn like they were being carved fresh. But worse than the physical pain was the emotional bleed—her fear, her rage, her desperate attempt to hold onto herself while Auradelle pulled her apart.

My corruption exploded outward.

It wasn't conscious. The rage and pain simply tore through every control I'd built. Black veins spread from where I knelt, killing everything they touched. Stone crumbled. Moss shriveled. Even the air seemed to rot.

"Kaelren!" Vashael's voice cut through the haze. "Control it! You'll bring the tunnel down!"

But I couldn't control it. The corruption was rage given form, and that rage had a target. Every guard between me and Elle. Every wall separating us. Every second that kept me from reaching her.

The team backed away as my corruption spread further, creating a circle of death twenty feet across. But Peeble stayed.

"I can feel her too," they said quietly. "Through our connection. She's fighting. But he's testing her limits."

"Tell me something I don't know," I growled.

"In the previous iterations, this was the moment you lost. This exact moment. You felt her pain, let the corruption take you completely, and by the time you reached her, there wasn't an unmarked place on your body. You killed everyone, yes. But you also killed the possibility of saving her."

That cut through the rage like a blade. "What are you saying?"

"Channel it. Don't let it take you. Use it." Peeble's antennae twitched.

I took a deep breath, and with all the self-control I could muster, I pulled back in the corruption. The strain visible through the veins bulging in my neck. I would not fail Elle.

Twelve hours into the journey, the tunnel changed. The stone beneath my feet went from rough-carved to smooth, like we'd crossed an invisible threshold. The temperature dropped, and I could taste metal on my tongue.

"This is it," I said, feeling the pull Elle had described. "The branching passage."

But I didn't see it. None of us did.

We searched the chamber, running hands along walls, checking for hidden seams or pressure points. Nothing. The tunnel continued straight ahead—the only visible path.

"It's here," I insisted. "I can feel it."

Vashael moved to the center of the chamber and exhaled, not breath, but pollen. A cloud of it, shimmering faintly in the moss-light, spreading through the air like dust motes. We watched it drift, settle, disperse.

Then we saw it.

A draft. Subtle, almost imperceptible, but there—pulling the pollen toward what looked like a natural rock formation jutting from the wall. Just a bulge of stone, unremarkable, the kind of thing you'd walk past without a second glance.

Vashael approached it, reached out.

Her hand went through.

"Illusion," she said, pulling back. "Old magic. It's not hiding the passage—it's making you not want to look at it."

That's why the guards had never found it. Not because it was sealed or locked, but because the Root itself had wrapped it in disinterest. You could stand right in front of it and never think to reach out.

I stepped forward and pushed through the illusion. The stone rippled like water, and suddenly I was on the other side, a narrow descending passage, real and solid.

The others stopped. We'd discussed this at camp—only Eltrien, Peeble, and I would go forward. The rest would hold this position, guard our backs.

"How long?" Sarnyx asked.

"However long it takes," I said. "Don't let anyone past you."

Vashael nodded. Nimor melted into shadow to watch the rear tunnel. Sarnyx positioned herself at the junction, thorns ready.

As Eltrien, Peeble, and I moved down the passage, it narrowed, twisted, and descended sharply. The Root's presence grew stronger with each step. I kept checking behind us, sure that guards would find us at any moment.

After what felt like an hour, the passage opened into a chamber.

Small. Circular. The walls were smooth, almost polished, like water had worn them over millennia. No other exits. No way in or out except the tunnel we'd used.

In the center of the chamber, a formation of white stone rose from the floor—not quite a pedestal, more like the stone had simply grown upward in a spiral, creating a natural shelf at waist height. The stone was pale, veined with gold that pulsed faintly.

And resting in the depression at the top was the seed, roughly the size of my fist, smooth and dark, with veins of gold running through it. It pulsed with light—soft, rhythmic, alive. The glow reflected off the chamber walls, making the whole space feel like the inside of a beating heart.

"The original seed," Peeble said quietly. "The Root's failsafe."

I approached slowly. The seed's light brightened as I drew near, responding to something in me. My corruption? My carved marks? Something else?

"Don't touch it yet," Eltrien warned. "If you claim it before the Convergence, you'll trigger a cascade. Elle needs to be free when this activates."

"Then we seal it." I looked at Eltrien. "Can you make it impossible to access until the Convergence?"

He studied the seed, the chamber, his marks pulsing faster in that seventeen-beat pattern. "Yes. My connection to the iterations gives me some authority here. I can seal it temporarily—the wards will hold until the boundaries thin."

"Do it."

"Kaelren, wait." Peeble flew to hover in front of me. "There's more you need to understand. About the other iterations. About why you always fail."

I waited.

"In every previous timeline, this is where you split up. You send your team to rescue Elle while you stay here to guard the seed. And every single time, Auradelle captures your team, turns Elle into his vessel, and claims the seed while you're too far away to stop it." Peeble's voice carried layers of grief. "You can't divide your forces. You can't try to do both. You have to choose."

"That's not a choice. That's a trap."

"Yes. It is. It's the trap that's held for now for seventeen iterations because you've always chosen wrong. You've always tried to be in two places at once, to save everyone, to control everything." They flew closer to eye level. "This time, you need to do something different. This time, you need to trust."

"Trust what?"

"That Eltrien can seal this. That your team can hold the tunnels. That Elle can survive long enough for you to reach her." Peeble paused. "Trust that you don't have to do everything alone."

I looked at Eltrien. "You're certain you can seal it?"

"I've done it before," he said quietly. "Sixteen times before, in fact. It's never held because you always stayed to guard it physically. This time, you need to let the magic do the work and go save her."

Every instinct I had screamed against it. Leave the seed unguarded? Trust that magic alone would protect it? What if Auradelle had some way past Eltrien's wards? What if guards found this chamber while we were gone? What if—

But those what-ifs were the same ones that had played out sixteen times before. Sixteen iterations where I'd tried to control everything, protect everything, be everywhere at once. Sixteen failures.

Elle was suffering right now. Every second I delayed was another second of her pain. And she'd trusted me enough to tell me about this place, trusted me to make the right choice.

"Do it," I said, the words harder to force out than I'd expected. "Seal the chamber."

"Kaelren," Peeble said softly. "You understand what this means? If Eltrien seals the seed, Auradelle will know someone's been here. He'll know you're coming."

"Good," I said, letting corruption spread up to my throat. "I want him to know."

Through the bond, I felt Elle's pain spike again—but underneath it, something else. Recognition. Understanding. She knew I was close.

"Hold on, love," I sent with every ounce of power I had. *"Almost there."*

And through the muffling, through the suppression, I felt her response. Four words that made my corruption sing.

"Come kill this bastard."

We rested near the seed chamber while Eltrien worked his magic. The sealing took hours—layers of protection, wards that would hold until the Convergence forced them open. By the time he finished, he looked exhausted, his marks dimmer.

"It's done," he said. "No one can access this until the boundaries thin."

"Good." I stood, every muscle protesting. "Then we move."

"Kaelren, wait." Peeble landed on my shoulder. "There's something else you need to know. About me. About what I am."

I waited.

"I'm not just a Celestial Sentinel. I'm not just the first Elle transformed. I'm also a warning." They paused. "In the first iteration, I tried to control the power. Tried to use the Bloom to enforce peace, to create order, to save everyone. The Crown saw that and built their entire hierarchy on my mistake. They saw me bond with the Bloom and thought, 'we can control this too.'"

"So the rot—"

"Is the Root's recoil. Every time someone tries to control the Bloom instead of letting it grow naturally, the Root pulls back. And that pulling back feels like disease." Peeble's wings vibrated. "The realm isn't dying because someone failed to control the power. It's dying because someone keeps trying."

"Then what's the solution?"

"Let go. When the Convergence comes, when they try to make Elle the bridge between Root and Bloom—don't let her be a bridge. Don't let her be a vessel. Let the Seed flower naturally. Let everything wild and patient break free of the cage they built around it."

"That could destroy everything."

"Or save everything. It's the only option we haven't tried before."

I processed this, corruption churning. "Does Elle know?"

"She knows. She saw it in the vision I showed her. She understands what needs to happen." Peeble's voice softened. "The question is whether you can let her make that choice when the moment comes."

Through the bond, I felt Elle's determination. Her certainty. Her absolute refusal to be used as another tool of control.

"I'll let her choose," I said. "Even if it kills me. Even if it destroys me. I'll let her choose."

"That's different," Peeble said, something like hope in their voice. "In all the other iterations, you've never said that before."

We moved into the second day of tunnel crawling. The passages grew warmer, the air thicker. After the seed chamber, I felt it—a shift in the Heartspire's awareness above us. Auradelle knew we were here now. Knew we were coming.

Good. Let him prepare. Let him worry.

The tunnels changed as we went deeper. Less carved stone, more natural cavern. The Root's presence faded, replaced by something else—heat, moisture, the smell of minerals.

"Water," Vashael said, pointing ahead.

The passage opened into a cavern large enough to hold twenty people. And in the center, steaming pools of water, heated from below by whatever volcanic forces ran beneath the Heartspire. The walls glistened with condensation, and the air was thick enough to taste.

"Hot springs," Sarnyx said, already moving toward them. Blood still seeped from the wound on her ribs from one of the previous battles. "We could clean these cuts. Actual water instead of tunnel filth."

I wanted to push forward. Wanted to keep moving. But we were all wounded, exhausted, covered in two days' worth of blood and dirt. And the bond told me Elle was stable for now—in pain, yes, but not in immediate crisis.

I found a pool at the far edge and knelt, cupping water to my face. It was hot but not scalding, and when I washed the blood from my hands, the corruption-black skin underneath looked even darker against clean water.

Almost fae hands once. Now just weapons wearing familiar shapes.

Peeble landed on a rock beside me. "You should rest while you can."

"I will. After Elle—"

"What comes next isn't a fight you can win by being more corrupted than your enemies."

"Then how do I win it?"

"By being more stubborn than fate itself." Peeble's wings buzzed softly. "Which, admittedly, you're quite good at."

I almost smiled at that. Almost.

Behind me, I heard Sarnyx hiss as she lowered herself into a pool, the hot water hitting her wounds. Vashael was already submerged to her shoulders, eyes closed, letting the heat work into muscles that had been tense for two days straight. Even Nimor had solidified enough to sit at the edge, feet dangling in the water.

"Thirty minutes," I called to them. "Then we move."

"Make it an hour," Vashael said without opening her eyes. "We're no good to Elle if we collapse before we reach her."

She had a point. I knelt back down, cupping more water to my face, washing blood from my neck where corruption hadn't yet spread. The water ran red, then clear, then red again.

How much blood had I spilled in two days? How many guards? I'd stopped counting after the first dozen.

The cavern was quiet except for water dripping from stalactites, the soft splash of someone shifting position in a pool, the occasional hiss when hot water found a fresh wound. Almost peaceful, if you ignored that we were underneath a fortress full of people who wanted us dead, crawling toward a confrontation that had failed seventeen times before.

I closed my eyes, reaching through the bond. Elle was there—distant but present. In pain but fighting. Still herself despite everything Auradelle was doing to her.

"*Hold on,*" I sent. "*Just a little longer.*"

The water moved.

Not from us. Something else. I felt it before I saw it—a current flowing from the far end of the cavern, from a pool shrouded in shadow that we hadn't checked.

My eyes snapped open.

The current was wrong. Not natural circulation. Something was displacing water, something large, moving through the connected pools beneath the surface.

"Out of the water," I said, standing slowly. "Now."

The tone in my voice killed all conversation. Sarnyx was out in seconds, thorns already extending. Vashael moved despite her exhaustion, hands going to her poison vials. Nimor became shadow. Eltrien stood, marks beginning to pulse.

"What is it?" Sarnyx asked quietly.

"Don't know yet. But something's—"

The water in the far pool erupted.

They moved fast, no questions. By the time the thing emerged from the far pool, we were all on dry stone, weapons ready.

It wasn't a serpent. Not exactly. More like a worm—pale, eyeless, thick as a tree trunk and easily thirty feet long. Its skin glistened with slime, and its mouth was a circular horror of teeth arranged in rings, each one rotating independently.

"Root's mercy," Vashael breathed.

The creature's head swayed, sensing us. No eyes, but it knew we were there—heat, maybe, or vibration. Its mouth opened wider, revealing more teeth spiraling down its throat.

"Auradelle sent it," Peeble said. "He knows we're here. He's trying to slow us down."

"Then he's about to lose a pet," I said, corruption already spreading down my arms.

338

The worm struck.

Fast—impossibly fast for something that size. It lunged at Sarnyx, mouth wide enough to swallow her whole. She rolled aside, thorns lashing out, but they barely scratched its hide.

Vashael threw poison vials that shattered against its skin. The creature didn't even slow.

Nimor went shadow, trying to confuse it, but the thing tracked him anyway—heat sense, definitely. It swung its body like a club, and Nimor had to solidify and dive to avoid being crushed.

Eltrien's marks blazed, trying to freeze it, but the creature shook off the magic like water.

"Its hide is too thick!" Vashael shouted. "We can't cut through!"

The worm came at me, and I met it with corruption. My hands hit its face, and I pushed rot into its flesh. The creature screamed—a sound like grinding stone mixed with air escaping from deep underground. Its skin bubbled and blackened where I touched it, but it was huge, and corruption spread slowly through that much mass.

It reared back, and I saw Nimor's eyes widen. "Kaelren, move!"

The worm's body came down like a battering ram. I rolled, felt the impact shake the cavern floor, felt stones crack and spray.

"We need to hold it still!" Sarnyx shouted, already extending her thorns. "Pin it down!"

"With what?" Vashael demanded.

"With me!" Eltrien sprinted forward, and before anyone could stop him, he leaped onto the creature's back. His hands grabbed slick flesh, and his marks flared, trying to burn through to something vital.

The worm thrashed, slamming against walls, trying to throw him off. Eltrien held on, legs wrapped around its body, marks blazing brighter.

"Rope!" he shouted. "Something to tie it!"

Sarnyx's thorns extended, wrapping around the creature like living rope. Vashael added her own bindings, using torn cloth and leather straps. The worm's thrashing slowed as we pinned sections of its body to the floor.

But its head was still free, and it lunged at Vashael with teeth rotating fast enough to shred anything they touched.

She wasn't fast enough.

The mouth closed around her, and she disappeared down its throat in a spray of slime and horror.

"Vashael!" Sarnyx screamed.

The worm's body bulged where Vashael went down. I could see her outline through translucent flesh, still moving, still fighting.

"Kaelren!" Peeble shouted. "You have to—"

I was already moving. Ran at the creature, both hands extended, and grabbed the section where Vashael was trapped. Poured corruption into it with everything I had, all at once, pushing rot into flesh faster than I'd ever done before.

The worm's scream was deafening.

Its flesh dissolved under my hands, turning to black sludge that burned where it touched stone. I felt the corruption eating through the creature from inside and out, spreading like wildfire through tissue that had never encountered anything like it.

The worm convulsed once, twice, then simply exploded.

Chunks of rotting flesh hit the cavern floor, dissolving into puddles of black ichor. And in the middle of it all, Vashael—gasping, covered in slime, but alive.

She retched, spitting up fluid that smoked where it hit stone. "That," she gasped, "was disgusting."

Nimor appeared by her side in an instant, checking over her for any visible injuries.

Eltrien jumped down from where the creature's back had been, looking shaken.

"Are you hurt?" I asked.

"Mostly my pride," Vashael said, wiping slime from her face. "And possibly my lungs. That thing's stomach acid is—" She retched again.

Sarnyx appeared with water from the hot springs, and Vashael gulped it down, trying to wash the taste from her mouth.

"Auradelle will not be happy about this," Eltrien said, stating the obvious.

"That was just the first attempt to stop us."

"Good," I said, looking at the dissolving remains. "Let him be pissed off. Let him send everything he has. It won't be enough."

We cleaned up as best we could—Vashael especially, trying to get the slime out of her hair and clothes. The hot springs, once peaceful, now stank of rot and death. But we'd survived.

"How much further?" Sarnyx asked.

"Close," I said, feeling Elle through the bond. "A few more hours at most."

"Then we move," Vashael said, still spitting. "Before he sends something worse."

We gathered our weapons and moved out, leaving the worm's remains to dissolve into the cavern floor. The tunnels ahead grew warmer, and I could feel it—the Heartspire's presence directly above us now.

Tomorrow, we'd reach the ritual chamber and face Auradelle. Elle and I would either break the cycle or become another iteration's tragedy.

But tonight, in the darkness beneath the Heartspire, I let myself hope that this time—this seventeenth time—might finally be different.

Because I loved her. And love, apparently, was either the answer or the problem.

Tomorrow, we'd find out which.

33

Elle

The last thing I remembered clearly was another brutal session with Auradelle, his hands on my marks, tuning me like an instrument until I screamed. Then Malachar had appeared with a draught that smelled something wretched, forcing it down my throat while guards held me still.

"Her body needs rest for the Convergence," Malachar had said, his voice clinical. "Burn her out now, and she'll be useless."

Then—nothing. Blackness. A sleep so deep I thought I might have been dead. No dreams. No awareness. Just absence.

Now I was awake, and everything hurt.

Mora was there when I woke, her hands ice-cold as she pressed a damp cloth to my face. The shock of it helped cut through the fog.

"They're coming," she said, her voice flat with resignation. "I tried to buy you more time, but—"

The door crashed open before she could finish.

Four Bloomguard entered, their faces hidden behind those flower-twisted masks that looked like beauty but were truly hiding a nightmare. The masks were different for each guard—one had roses that dripped blood, another had lilies with teeth, the third had vines that moved on their own, and the fourth... the fourth had snapdragons whose blooms opened and closed like hungry mouths.

"Time," one said, the word dripping with disdain, even though I was the one supposed to save his stupid realm.

My mind felt sluggish, thoughts moving through fog. How long had I been under? A day? Two? The Convergence—it had been days away when they'd drugged me. Now, based on the tension vibrating through the Heartspire's stones, it was close. Hours, maybe. The building itself hummed with anticipation.

Mora was there, helping me sit up, then stand. My legs didn't want to cooperate, muscles weak from days of forced stillness. She caught me when I swayed, her grip surprisingly strong for someone so slight.

"Easy," she murmured. "Your body needs a moment to remember how to work."

I focused on breathing. On staying upright. On the feel of cold stone under my bare feet. Anything to anchor myself to the present instead of drowning in the drug's lingering fog.

Mora's hands were shaking as she steadied me, and when I finally looked at her face, I saw tears streaming down her cheeks. She knew what was coming. We both did.

"Be strong," she whispered. "Remember who you are."

"Get away from the vessel," the guard with the whispering poppies snapped, shoving Mora aside with enough force to send her sprawling. Her head hit the stone floor with a crack that made my stomach lurch and my marks flare with heat.

"Her name is Mora," I said, my voice raw from disuse. Because if I was going to die today, I was going to die as myself, not as Auradelle's tool. "And if you touch her again, I'll find a way to make you regret it."

The guard backhanded me, the metal gauntlet splitting my lip. I tasted copper and rage. "Vessels don't make threats."

"This one does," I spat blood at his feet, watching it splatter across his polished boots. "This vessel has opinions. Deal with it."

They dragged me from the room, my bare feet sliding across the stone floors. The Heartspire felt different than it had before—warmer, more present. My marks burned hotter with each step, responding to something in the building itself.

The marks on my skin had completed their design while I slept. They covered my entire body now. The patterns were more defined, more deliberate. When I looked down at my forearms, I could almost read them— not words exactly, but intent. Purpose. Like my body was being written over with someone else's plans.

Through the bond—still muffled but stronger than it had been before the forced sleep—I felt Kaelren. Closer. Much closer than he'd been two days ago. The bond thrummed with his presence, with rage and desperation and something that felt like hope. He was coming for me. Fighting his way through whatever lay between us.

"Please," I thought, sending the plea through the bond, though I didn't know if he could hear me. "Please have found the seed. Please let me be right about this, and we can finally end this nightmare."

Because if I was wrong, if the seed wasn't there or if Kaelren hadn't reached it, then everything I was about to endure would be for nothing.

The stairs spiraled down, carved from stone so old the edges had worn smooth. Moss glowed faintly in the cracks, providing just enough light to see by. The temperature dropped with each step, and I could smell minerals and damp earth mixed with something sharper—magic, maybe, or just old power that had soaked into the rock over centuries.

The chanting started as we descended. Dozens of voices, echoing up from below in rhythmic patterns that made my teeth ache. I couldn't understand the words, but I felt them—vibrations that traveled through the stone into my bones, making my marks pulse in response.

The chamber doors were massive, twice the height of a man and carved from a black wood I didn't recognize. Veins of metal—gold and silver both— had been hammered into the surface in intricate patterns that caught the moss-light. When we approached, the doors swung open on silent hinges, revealing a vast chamber beyond.

Inside was worse than any nightmare.

The chamber was massive—easily a hundred feet across, with a domed ceiling carved from living rock. Except the ceiling wasn't rock anymore. Through some impossible working of magic, the stone had been transformed into pure sky. Not an illusion—actual sky, with clouds moving across it and sunlight streaming down despite us being deep underground. The walls were carved with channels that glowed sickly green, corruption flowing through them like luminescent blood. The patterns made my eyes burn to follow them.

At the center was the Bloom.

I'd heard about it in whispers, in fragments of overheard conversations, in the fearful murmurs of servants who'd seen it and never quite recovered. But seeing it was different.

It rose from the floor like a twisted tree, easily twenty feet tall. Crystal grew from wood grew from metal in a way that shouldn't be possible—branches of silver sprouting leaves of emerald, roots of copper diving into stone, all of it wrapped in something organic that pulsed like living flesh. The whole structure glowed with that same green corruption, beautiful and terrible at once.

The Bloom had been growing here for generations. The first Elle had planted its seed, and every ruler since then had been feeding it with power and ambition. Now, Auradelle had inherited it and made it his life's work, shaping it, feeding it, preparing it for this moment. For me.

Conduits—thick tubes of twisted metal and wood—erupted from the Bloom's trunk like arteries, spreading across the chamber floor. They pulsed with dark light, carrying corruption to channels carved in the walls. At the heart of the structure was a space carved out of the trunk itself, shaped like a person standing with arms outstretched. My height. My build. Thorns lined the opening, each one as long as my hand and sharp as surgical steel.

"Beautiful, isn't it?" Auradelle's voice echoed through the chamber. He stepped from behind the Bloom, his dark robes stark against the green glow. "The culmination of centuries of work. Every marked one who failed, every attempt at balance that went wrong, every drop of blood spilled in the name of fixing what was broken—it all led to this."

"It looks like what would happen if a torture device had sex with a nightmare and their baby was raised by sadists," I said, because apparently my mouth had decided to keep being defiant even though my knees were shaking.

He actually laughed at that, cold and bitter. "Accurate. It was designed to be both beautiful and terrible. Like power itself. Like the choice between order and chaos. Like love, if you think about it."

"I'd rather not think about your definition of love, thanks."

"No? But you're about to experience it intimately." He gestured, and the guards forced me forward. "Strip her."

They tore the ceremonial robes away, leaving me in just a shift that barely covered anything. The cold air bit at my skin, making my marks flare brighter in response. I tried to fight, but the guards knew exactly where to grip, exactly how much pressure to apply to cause maximum pain with minimum visible damage. They'd done this before. Many times. To how many others who'd stood where I was standing?

They forced me into the Bloom's embrace.

The moment my skin touched it, agony exploded through every nerve. The thorns didn't just pierce—they burrowed, finding my marks with unerring precision. I felt them sink deep, hooking into muscle and bone, locking me in place. They pulsed, drinking something from me with each beat. Not just blood, though that flowed freely. Something deeper. Something essential.

"Perfect," Auradelle murmured, beginning to connect the conduits. Each one attached to a different part of me—metal clamps closing around my wrists and ankles, a collar locking around my throat, probes pressing into the base of my spine and temples, a larger device settling over my heart. Each connection was its own special agony, metal and magic burrowing under my skin. "Do you know what these are?"

I couldn't answer through the pain. My vision blurred white, then red, then green. Every nerve was screaming.

"They're Root channels, corrupted and purified in endless cycles until they exist between states. Neither Root nor Bloom, but both and neither. They'll take your essence—everything that makes you Elle—and spread it through the Heartspire itself. You'll become the building, and it will become you. A living bridge between worlds."

"That's... impossible..."

"Your grandmother thought so, too. She ran before we could test it. Smart woman, in her way. She knew she wasn't strong enough. Your mother might have survived it—she had the strength, the will—but she chose death instead. Selfish to the end. She could have saved the realm, but she chose to save herself from the pain."

The conduits began to pulse. Green light flowed through them in a rhythm. I felt the magic pulling at me, trying to spread my consciousness outward. My thoughts scattered. My sense of self began to fray at the edges, reaching beyond my body into the Heartspire's ancient stones.

"Stop!" I screamed. The word echoed strangely, coming not just from my mouth but from the walls, the floor, the air itself. My voice was spreading, becoming part of the building.

"We're just beginning," Auradelle said, moving to a panel of levers and crystalline dials set into the chamber wall. "When the Convergence peaks, when reality is at its thinnest, I'll force the final merger. You'll become the Bloom's living key, whether you choose it or not."

Through the bond, muffled but still there, I felt Kaelren's rage spike to levels that shouldn't be survivable. He was coming. Gods, he was almost here, corruption spreading with every step, becoming something monstrous to save me. I could feel him tearing through guards, leaving trails of decay in his wake.

"Yes," Auradelle said, apparently able to read my thoughts through the Bloom's connection. "Let him come. His corruption will make the perfect catalyst. When he arrives, when he sees you like this, his rage will complete what we've started. The Root and Bloom will merge in a conflagration of fury and desperation."

"You're using us."

"I'm using everything. Every piece on the board, every fragment of power, every drop of blood spilled in this worthless war. The realm has been dying for longer than you've been alive. Longer than your mother was alive. The balance was broken before the first Crown took the throne, and every attempt to fix it has only made it worse."

He began adjusting the controls, pulling levers and turning dials. Each adjustment sent fresh waves of agony through me as the conduits dug deeper, pulled harder. But through the pain, I started to understand what he was really saying. This wasn't just about power or control. He genuinely believed he was saving the realm, even if it meant destroying everything in it first.

"Do you... have any idea... what it's like... being tortured by a madman who thinks he's a hero?"

He actually paused at that. "Every madman thinks he's the hero of his own story, child. The only difference is that I have the power to make my story a reality. I have the will to do what must be done, no matter the cost. Your mother understood that. That's why she chose death. She knew that sometimes the hero has to become the monster."

Mora appeared at the edge of my vision, trying to push past the guards. They held her back, but she kept trying, kept reaching for me. Blood ran from where she'd hit her head, and her eyes were desperate. She was humming something, barely audible over the chamber's echoes. An old song of some sort.

The conduits pulsed harder. And then something happened that Auradelle hadn't expected.

My marks didn't just spread—they began to change. The golden vines started producing actual flowers, tiny blooms no bigger than my thumbnail. They opened and closed with my heartbeat, releasing pollen that caught the green light and turned it gold.

"What?" Auradelle moved closer, studying the transformation. His eyes had gone wide. "That's not possible. The texts said—"

"Maybe your texts are shit," I gasped out. "Maybe you can't predict everything. Maybe you're just a sad old man who's spent so long staring at corruption he's forgotten what beauty looks like."

He slapped me, hard enough to make my ears ring. But I laughed, because what else was there to do? I was dying or transforming or both, strapped to a nightmare machine while my marks bloomed impossible flowers, and somehow that was funny.

"What is that girl doing?" Auradelle demanded, finally noticing Mora's humming.

"Singing, my lord," a guard replied. "Should we stop her?"

Auradelle considered, then shook his head. "No. Let her waste her voice on useless sentiment. It changes nothing. The Convergence is nearly here."

But he was wrong. I could feel it changing something. Mora's song resonated with something deep in the stone, and my marks were blooming faster, releasing more pollen. Where the pollen touched the conduits, they flickered, their green light stuttering.

Through the bond, clearer now, I felt Kaelren in the tunnels below. Rage incarnate, corruption spreading fast, his humanity dissolving with each guard he killed. But underneath the rage, I felt something else.

Love.

Desperate, furious, impossible love that defied patterns and iterations and everything that said we were doomed to fail. Love that was willing to become monstrous if it meant saving me. Love that didn't care about balance or realms or the proper order of things.

And trust. He trusted me. Trusted that I'd told him the truth about the seed, that I'd given him the key to breaking this cycle. Even now, bound and being torn apart, I felt his absolute certainty in me.

I sent everything I had through the bond—not words, just feeling. Trust. Hope. Love that burned brighter than any corruption.

"Come on," I whispered, knowing he'd feel it even if he couldn't hear the words. *"Come find me, you overprotective asshole."*

And somewhere in the darkness below, I felt him roar my name.

34

Kaelren

The tunnels opened into the Heartspire's bowels like a wound giving birth to infection. We emerged into a corridor of living stone, walls pulsing with that sick heartbeat I'd been feeling for the last hour. My corruption responded to it, spreading further, turning my words into grinding stone when I spoke.

"Move fast. Kill everything."

My team formed up behind me, ready for whatever surprises were about to be thrown our way.

And Peeble, glowing with barely contained fury on my shoulder, their tiny form vibrating with rage.

"Elle's in pain," they said. "So much pain. They've started the ritual."

Tell me something I don't know.

"This whole place is designed to use your corruption against you. The walls, the floor, even the air is calibrated to draw power from marked ones. It's a trap designed specifically for you."

"Good. Let them try," I growled.

The first wave of Bloomguard found us in the narrow passages, exactly where Auradelle wanted them to. They came with weapons that gleamed with an oily sheen, faces hidden behind masks that made them inhuman. Pretty faces twisted into plant-like horror, beauty made wrong. I could smell the corruption on their blades, mixed with something else, something that made my marks burn.

I didn't bother with strategy. I just killed.

My hand went through the first guard's chest, corruption spreading from the wound until he dissolved into shadow and screams. The sound he made as he died echoed through the corridors. The second lost her head to my blade—when had I drawn it?—the cut so charged with corruption that her body crumbled to ash before it hit the ground. The third tried to run. I pulled him into my corruption from twenty feet away, watching him dissolve like sugar in acid rain, his mask cracking to reveal eyes wide with the kind of terror that came with knowing it was the end.

"Kaelren!" Vashael shouted. "Control yourself!"

But I was past control. Past caring. Elle's pain echoed through our bond, each pulse of agony making my corruption spread faster, making me more weapon than man. I could feel it eating at me from the inside, turning everything that was Kaelren into something else. Something worse. Something that existed only to reach Elle, to save her or die trying.

The corruption had a voice now, whispering in the back of my mind. *"Let go,"* it said. *"Stop fighting. Become what you were meant to be. Become destruction incarnate. Become the ending of all things."*

Sarnyx took point without being asked, understanding that I was too far gone for tactics. Her thorns found gaps in armor with deadly precision, each strike calculated to cause maximum damage with minimum effort. A guard's throat opened in a spray of crimson that painted the walls. Another fell with thorns through both eyes, his screams cut short as her poison liquified his brain. A third tried to raise a shield, but her thorns punched through it like paper, continuing through his chest and out his back in a spray of gore that made even the other guards step back.

"For the rebellion!" she roared, and for a moment, I remembered why I'd chosen her as my second. She was violence given purpose, destruction with a cause.

Vashael moved through the carnage like a dancer, never quite where attacks landed, always exactly where she needed to be to deliver death with a touch. Her poisons were works of art—one guard's skin turned to rose petals that fell away to reveal nothing underneath, another's bones became liquid while his flesh remained solid, creating a sight that would haunt me if I still cared about being haunted. She hummed while she worked, a melody from the Petal Court that spoke of beauty and death being the same thing viewed from different angles.

Nimor pulled guards into shadows they never emerged from—I could hear them screaming, their voices echoing from a place between reality and nightmare. Sometimes parts of them would emerge—a hand here, a head there, always in the wrong places, always screaming.

But for every guard we killed, two more appeared. They poured from doorways I hadn't seen, dropped from ceiling vents that shouldn't exist, emerged from shadows that were darker than they should be. The Heart-spire itself was generating them, or calling them, or creating them from its own corrupted essence.

"Something is wrong," Eltrien said, his marks pulsing faster, throwing off light that made the corruption in the walls recoil. "Every time, this is where it falls apart. This exact corridor, this exact moment. We're walking the same path, making the same mistakes, dying the same deaths."

"Then we change it," I snarled, corruption flaring around me like armor made of hungry shadows.

"You can't change a pattern by playing into it!" He grabbed my arm, his glowing marks burning against my corruption. Where we touched, reality sparked and protested. "Don't you see? This is what he wants. You, corrupted beyond recognition. Elle, dissolved into his apparatus. Both of you broken exactly the way the pattern demands."

"Then what do you suggest?" I asked, even as I dissolved another guard with a gesture, not even looking at him as he screamed and died.

"I don't know!" For the first time since I'd known him, Eltrien sounded desperate, almost panicked. "Every time I've watched this play out, you storm in corrupted, she's bound to the Bloom, you both break, everyone dies, and we start over. The realm resets, memories fade, and we dance the same dance again. I don't know how to change it!"

Vashael stared at him while casually dissolving a guard's face with a blown kiss of poisonous pollen. "Are you sure you remember?"

"Fragments. Pieces. Enough to know we're about to fail again." His marks pulsed faster, almost solid light now. "The Convergence is almost here. We have minutes, not hours. And we're exactly where we always are when it all goes wrong."

I felt it too—reality thinning, the boundaries between Root and Bloom, between Earth and Wynmire, becoming gossamer-weak. And through it all, Elle's agony, her sense of self dissolving into something vast and terrible.

"We keep moving," I decided, cutting through two guards with one corrupted swing. "Pattern or not, I'm not leaving her."

We pushed deeper, descending into levels I'd never seen before. I'd spent years in the Heartspire—trained here, lived here, served Auradelle from these very halls—but I'd never been permitted below the third floor. These depths were reserved for Auradelle alone, his private domain of secrets and experiments.

The corridors widened into proper halls that had been grand once, before the corruption. I could see traces of what this place had been—beautiful murals now twisted into nightmares, gardens now growing things that shouldn't exist, fountains that ran with liquids that weren't water and never had been. This was the original palace, I realized. The seat of the first Crown, before everything went wrong. Before the division. Before the rot.

The Heartspire's defenses were waiting—not just guards now, but the building itself turning against us.

Walls grew thorns that reached for our blood with hungry intelligence. I let them pierce me, my corruption eating through them faster than they could drink. Where my blood fell, the floor dissolved, creating holes that opened onto rooms below where things that might have been people once writhed in endless transformation.

Floors became acidic, eating through boots and flesh with equal appetite. The corruption under my feet left prints of decay with every step. Sarnyx and Vashael had to leap from safe spot to safe spot, while Nimor simply stopped touching the ground entirely, existing more in shadow than substance.

The air itself turned poisonous, requiring Vashael to constantly neutralize it with her own toxins, creating a bubble of breathable atmosphere that moved with us.

My corruption was the only thing keeping me functional. My thoughts were becoming simpler, more focused. Save Elle. Kill everything else. Nothing else mattered.

Then I heard it—buzzing. Massive amounts of buzzing, coming from somewhere outside. And mixed with it, the sound of an army. Hundreds of voices raised in battle cries, the clash of weapons, explosions that shook dust from the ceiling and made the corrupted channels in the walls flicker.

"What is that?" Nimor asked from the shadows.

"Bryx," Peeble said, their metallic voice carrying something like pride. "That magnificent idiot actually did it. He's pulling their forces away. Listen—you can hear Kevin's war cry."

Through the walls, we could hear it—the distinctive sound of Kevin's battle cry, which did indeed sound like a chainsaw made of bees, mixed with Bryx's laughter and what had to be every bee in a fifty-mile radius. The Heartspire shuddered as guards abandoned their posts, rushing to deal with what sounded like a massive assault on the main gates.

"It's a distraction," Sarnyx realized, respect creeping into her voice. "He's giving us an opening. The fool didn't run away. He is actually being useful."

"Then we take it," I growled, corruption surging with renewed purpose.

We met less resistance as we pushed deeper, the guards drawn away by whatever chaos Bryx was orchestrating outside. The few that remained fell quickly—they weren't expecting us to get this far, weren't prepared for the level of violence we brought. One tried to surrender. I killed him anyway. Mercy was something I'd left behind three corridors ago.

"The Convergence chamber is just ahead," Nimor reported from ahead, his voice echoing from multiple shadows. "But there's something else. Someone powerful with old magic is waiting."

We turned the final corner, and there he was.

Malachar stood before the entrance to the Convergence chamber like vengeance given form. The mage whom I'd battled decades ago, the one whose face I'd marked with corruption when he'd gotten too close, was barely recognizable. What I'd done to him had changed him. Scars of black corruption ran across his face in intricate patterns, beautiful and terrible, like molten flesh. But instead of destroying him, they'd made him stronger. His robes crackled with power that made the air around him shimmer and distort.

"Kaelren," he said, and his voice was different too—layered with harmonics that shouldn't exist. "I've been waiting for you."

My team fanned out, but I held up a hand. "This one's mine."

"Oh, I was hoping you'd say that." Malachar's smile was all teeth and madness. "Do you remember our last encounter? When you gave me these beautiful scars?" He traced the corruption patterns on his face almost lovingly. "I should thank you. The pain was exquisite. The transformation even more so. I spent years studying what you did to me, learning to harness the corruption you left behind. And now..." He spread his arms, power flaring around him in waves that made reality ripple. "Now I'm ready to repay the favor."

"Get past him," I told my team. "Get to Elle."

"Kaelren—" Sarnyx started.

"Now!"

They moved, trying to circle around Malachar, but he was ready. Barriers of twisted magic erupted from the floor, cutting off access to the doors. The corruption in the walls responded to his call, forming additional obstacles that writhed and reached.

"No one passes," Malachar said. "Not until I'm done with him."

Fine. I'd end this quickly.

I charged, corruption flaring around me like armor. Malachar met me with magic that burned cold, spells that pulled at my essence in ways that hurt beyond physical pain. Where his power touched my corruption, they fought for dominance, creating explosions of electricity that cracked the floor and made the walls bleed.

"You're stronger than before," he noted, deflecting my corrupted blade with shields that screamed when touched. "Good. I was worried this would be disappointing."

He lashed out with whips of corrupted energy, and I recognized them—he'd learned to weaponize what I'd done to him, turning my own power back against me. The whips found marks, cutting through my defenses, leaving trails of agony that burned like ice and fire at once.

But I pushed through. I had to. Elle's pain echoed through our bond, each pulse a reminder of what was at stake.

We fought through the corridor, trading blows that would have killed lesser beings. Malachar's magic grew more desperate, more powerful, pulling tricks from centuries of study and practice. He aged me with a gesture, my body suddenly carrying decades of exhaustion. I countered with pure corruption, dissolving his spell and the floor beneath us.

He trapped me in bindings of light that burned where they touched. I shattered them with rage made manifest, my corruption exploding outward in a wave that made him stumble back.

"You can't win," he panted, blood running from his nose where the strain of his magic was taking its toll. "I've studied you, learned from you, become you in ways you can't imagine. Every move you make, I'm ready for."

Maybe that was true. But he'd made one critical mistake.

He was still trying to control the corruption. Still trying to master it, harness it, make it serve him.

I'd stopped fighting it a long time ago.

Malachar raised his hands for what would probably be his killing blow, power gathering around him in a storm of corrupted magic that made the air itself scream. The walls collapsed, the floor buckled, reality bent under the weight of what he was about to unleash.

Then, through our bond, I felt it.

Elle's pain peaked. Not just the physical agony of the apparatus, but something deeper. Something that hit me like a knife through the heart—the pain of losing herself, of dissolving into something that wasn't Elle anymore. She was being torn apart, reformed, unmade, and remade into a tool for Auradelle's vision.

And in that moment, feeling her suffer, feeling her breaking—

I stopped being Kaelren.

The corruption I'd been fighting, that I'd been trying to contain and control and keep at bay, I let it all go. Every wall I'd built, every restraint I'd maintained, every desperate attempt to stay human despite the darkness eating me from within—gone.

I threw my head back and screamed her name.

"ELLE!"

The sound that came out wasn't human. It was rage and love and absolute refusal given voice, a howl that transcended language and became something primal. The corruption exploded from me in a wave of pure annihilation.

Malachar's spell shattered before it could form. His shields dissolved like paper in acid. His carefully maintained control over the corruption he'd taken from me reversed, the power recognizing its true master and abandoning him completely.

I watched him realize his mistake in the instant before he died. Saw the moment he understood that you couldn't control corruption—you could only become it or be consumed by it. He'd chosen to harness it.

I'd chosen to become it.

My corruption hit him like a tsunami of ending. He didn't dissolve slowly like the guards. He simply ceased. One moment he existed, raising his hands in a futile attempt at defense. The next moment, there was nothing. No body, no ash, no trace that Malachar had ever stood there. Just empty space where a person used to be, and my corruption still spreading, still hungry, still consuming.

The barriers he'd erected crumbled. The walls he'd summoned dissolved. Even the corruption in the Heartspire itself recoiled from what I'd become, recognizing something far worse than itself.

I stood there, breathing hard, and felt the transformation complete.

The corruption had spread across every inch of my body. Where Elle's marks had turned her into solid gold and light, mine had transformed me into solid black and death incarnate. My skin was shadow made flesh, my marks a network of darkness that pulsed with the rhythm of entropy itself. I could feel it—not just the corruption, but what lay beyond it. The ending of all things. The final darkness that waited for everyone and everything.

I was death's avatar. Destruction given form. The perfect balance to Elle's light.

"Kaelren?" Sarnyx's voice was small, uncertain, maybe even afraid.

I turned to look at my team, and through eyes that were more void than anything else, I saw them flinch. Good. They should be afraid. Everything should be afraid of what I'd become.

"Get to safety," I said, and my voice carried harmonics of ending, each word a small death. "This is between me and Auradelle now."

"But—"

"Go!"

They went, scrambling away from me like prey fleeing a predator. Only Peeble remained, still on my shoulder, their small form trembling but refusing to leave.

"You're terrifying, pretty boy," they said.

Good. Let them all be terrified. Let Auradelle see what he'd created with his manipulations and his patterns and his sixteen iterations of failure.

I walked forward, shadows bleeding from my every step, corruption spreading across the floor in fractals of decay. The entrance to the Convergence chamber loomed ahead—massive doors of ancient wood and twisted metal, sealed with power that had held for centuries.

I didn't bother trying to open them.

I walked through.

The doors exploded when my corruption touched them, matter and magic alike dissolving into nothing. I stepped through the space where they'd been and into the chamber beyond.

And there she was.

Elle hung suspended in the Bloom's embrace, her body covered in golden marks that had spread everywhere, flowers blooming from her skin with each heartbeat. She glowed like the sun at dawn, beautiful and terrible, light made flesh.

And I was pure onyx made flesh, the ending of all things.

We were perfect opposites. Perfect balance. The thing the Convergence had been trying to create repeatedly, finally achieved.

Auradelle stood beside his apparatus, and for the first time since I'd known him, I saw genuine fear in his eyes.

"What have you become?" he whispered.

I smiled, and it was the smile of graves opening and stars dying.

"Exactly what you needed," I said. "Now let's finish this."

35

Bryx

Earlier, I'd stood in the rebel camp, explaining my brilliant plan to Thrak while Kevin buzzed irritably beside me, his left wing still torn from our scouting mission. We'd strategically positioned everyone, two hundred and fifty rebels across three attack points, sonic amplifiers I'd cobbled together from stolen Crown tech, and every bee Kevin could convince to join us. Thrak had been skeptical, Vera had calculated our odds of survival at roughly twelve percent, but here we were anyway.

Now, watching it unfold, I wasn't exactly sure how I'd convinced anyone this would work.

"NOW!" I screamed, my voice carrying on sonic waves that shattered every piece of glass within a hundred yards.

The main gates of the Heartspire exploded inward under the combined assault of our makeshift army and three hundred very angry bees. Half the rebels had never ridden anything in their lives, much less giant insects with attitude problems. I'd watched some poor fae, Jareth, nearly get stung to death during the briefing when he'd grabbed Kevin's thorax wrong. Another rebel, Tam, had fallen off his bee twice before we even left camp. But they were here now, clinging to fuzzy backs with white knuckles and screaming war cries that were half battle rage, half terror.

Kevin dove through the shattered gates first, his torn wing making him list sideways, but his war cry echoed off the walls with a fury that made even me shiver. Behind him, the swarm followed, a cloud of organized vengeance that darkened the sky.

"For Elle!" I shouted, leading the charge with more enthusiasm than sense. "For everyone who's tired of living under a madman's thumb! For decent interior decorating! Seriously, has anyone seen these walls? Corruption is not a design choice!"

The rebels roared behind me, taking up the cry. Well, most of it. They seemed less concerned about the interior decorating part.

The first wave of Bloomguard met us in the courtyard, and that's when things got properly chaotic. My sonic pulses bounced off the walls, multiplying and echoing until it sounded like a thousand of me were attacking from every direction. Which would have been terrifying for anyone, really. One of me was usually more than enough.

"What is this?" a guard captain shouted, trying to rally his forces. "How many are there?"

"All of them!" I replied cheerfully, sending a pulse that knocked him off his feet. "Every rebel in the realm! We've come for tea and revolution! Mostly revolution!"

The truth was, we were outnumbered three to one. But between the sonic echoes, the bee swarm, and the rebels' hit-and-run tactics, the guards couldn't tell where we actually were versus where we seemed to be. Thrak had positioned our forces brilliantly—three groups attacking from different angles, retreating before the guards could engage, then attacking again from somewhere else.

It was chaos. It was mayhem. It was exactly what we needed.

As we pushed through the outer defenses, I spotted her—the most beautiful creature I'd ever seen. She moved like water through the chaos, somehow both predator and prey, her simple serving dress torn and bloodied, but her stance speaking of hidden training. Brown hair whipped around a face that was all sharp angles and fierce determination. My compound eyes took in every detail at once: the grace in her movements, the fire in her eyes, the way she held a kitchen knife like she knew exactly where to put it. I was instantly, ridiculously smitten.

Then she screamed, and reality crashed back.

"Help!" The voice was terrified, lovely, desperate.

I spun fully to see her pressed against a wall as three Bloomguard advanced. This beautiful, terrifying girl was about to die, and something in my chest went absolutely feral at the thought.

"Well, well," one of the guards said, reaching for her. "The regent's little runaway serving girl. He'll reward us well for bringing you back."

A serving girl. That's all I knew. But it didn't matter who she was; she was about to die, and I couldn't let that happen.

Something in me snapped. Not the usual Bryx snap of making inappropriate jokes at inappropriate times. Something deeper. Something that looked at this girl—alluring, fierce, about to die—and said absolutely fucking not.

The sonic pulse I unleashed wasn't calculated or careful. It was rage given sound, fury given frequency. The guards flew backward, armor cracking, bones definitely breaking. Kevin was on the nearest one before he could recover, stinger finding the gap between helmet and collar with vengeful precision.

I reached the woman in three strides, pulling her behind me. "Are you hurt?"

"I... I wanted to help," she said, tears streaming down her face. "I couldn't just hide while everyone else fought."

"Brave and stupid," I said, sending another pulse at an approaching guard. "My favorite combination. I'm Bryx, by the way. Hero, pest, occasional savior of beautiful women. And you are?"

"Mora," she gasped, wiping blood from a cut on her cheek. "I work—worked—in the kitchens. I helped Elle when they had her."

My compound eyes widened. "You know Elle?"

She nodded, and suddenly this gorgeous stranger became even more important. "She told me to run when things got bad. But I couldn't leave her."

"Can you run now?"

"Yes."

"Then run with me. We're going inside."

"Inside? But that's—"

"Where Elle is. Where this ends. Where we need to be."

She looked at me with those too-old eyes, then nodded. "I'm with you."

We ran through the chaos, Kevin limping beside us, his damaged wing dragging, but his spirit unbroken. Around us, the battle raged. Tam, the rebel who'd fallen off his bee twice, went down under a guard's blade. Another bee deflected what would have been a killing blow to Jareth—apparently, the bee-riding lessons had paid off after all. The rebels were holding, but barely.

"I know where the convergence chamber is," Mora said suddenly, surprising me. "I was with Elle when they dragged her there. They knocked me out and locked me in a side room, but I woke up when I heard the explosions. The guard at my door ran to see what was happening, and I slipped out."

"Then lead the way," I said, trusting this brave, brilliant woman who'd already risked everything. "The sound," I said, realizing something else. "Everything here has a resonance, a frequency. And there's something deep below that's screaming at a pitch that makes my antennae want to crawl off my head."

We plunged into the Heartspire proper, and immediately I knew we were walking into something worse than a trap. The walls pulsed with that sick mixture of Root and Bloom, the corruption so thick I could taste it with every breath. My compound eyes picked up movement in every shadow—not guards, but the building itself, aware and hungry.

The walls themselves pulsed with that sickening mixture I'd seen before—Root and Bloom twisted together in the rot channels, creating something completely unnatural. During my scouting mission, I'd watched guards coat their weapons in it, seen it dissolve a training dummy like acid through flesh. The science of it nagged at me even now, even in the middle of a battle for our lives. Root and Bloom weren't supposed to mix—that's what made marked ones so rare, what made convergence so dangerous. But here they were, deliberately combined, weaponized.

My mind churned through the implications even as my body fought to survive. If you could mix them artificially... if corruption could be combined with purity... what happened to that mixture when you distributed it? Spread it thin enough, across enough vessels, would it still be lethal? Or would it become something else entirely? Something manageable?

The thought slipped away as another section of wall tried to eat Mora, but it lingered in the back of my mind. Distribution. Dispersal. Dilution across multiple points instead of concentration in one.

"Stay close," I told Mora, then louder, to the rebels who'd followed us in: "The building's alive! Don't touch the walls!"

Too late for some. I watched in horror as a rebel brushed against a seemingly innocent piece of stonework and immediately began transforming, his skin becoming bark, his screams becoming the rustle of leaves. Another stepped on the wrong floor stone and sank into it like it was quicksand.

"This way!" Thrak's voice cut through the chaos. He'd fought his way inside, Vera beside him, both covered in blood that wasn't all theirs. "The main chamber's below!"

We fought our way deeper, every step a battle against both guards and architecture. The Heartspire's defenses were awakening—thorns erupting from walls, floors becoming acid, air turning poison. But we pushed through, because what else could we do? Elle was down there. Our people were dying up here. Stopping wasn't an option.

Then something changed.

A wave of wrongness rolled through the Heartspire that made even the corrupted walls recoil. It wasn't the building's sickness—I'd been feeling that since we entered. This was something else. Something colder. Something that felt like death.

Kevin buzzed nervously on my shoulder, his usual bravado replaced by something I'd never felt from him before: genuine fear. Not the healthy fear of fighting guards or dodging corruption. The primal terror of prey sensing an apex predator.

"What was that?" Thrak asked, his scarred face going pale.

"I don't know," I lied, because I did know. I'd felt this kind of power once before, weeks ago, when Kaelren had been standing at the edge of giving in completely to his corruption. But this was worse. This was that moment fully realized. Whatever Kaelren had become, it was beyond corrupted.

"Something just changed," Vera said quietly, her tactical mind already working. "Something big."

"Kaelren or Elle," I said. "Maybe both. The convergence is close—reality's thin enough that I can practically taste it. Whatever's happening in that chamber, we're running out of time."

We moved faster after that, driven by the certainty that somewhere below us, things had gone to shit.

Part of me hoped that was a good thing. The rest of me worried it meant we were all about to die.

A massive guard blocked our path to the lower levels, wearing armor that gleamed with that sick Root-Bloom mixture. His blade was less sword and more portable apocalypse, humming with wrongness.

"You go no further, rebels."

"That's what you think," I said, gathering sonic energy. "Kevin, you remember that move we practiced?"

Kevin buzzed agreement, then did something I'd never seen him do before—he started vibrating at a frequency that matched my sonic pulse. When I released the energy, he amplified it, creating a wave of sound so powerful it didn't just knock the guard down—it liquefied his armor, leaving him gasping on the floor in his underclothes.

"That's embarrassing," I noted, stepping over him. "Maybe invest in better underwear next time."

We descended stairs that spiraled into darkness, the chanting growing louder with each step. My extra joints ached with every movement, and I could feel blood still seeping from my wounds, but stopping wasn't an option.

"There," Mora whispered, pointing ahead.

Massive doors stood before us, and I knew that there was no coming back from what was on the other side.

"Together," I said, looking at the rebels who'd made it this far. Maybe thirty of us, all wounded, all exhausted, all determined.

"Together," they echoed.

I gathered every bit of sonic energy I had left, Kevin adding his harmony to mine. The others prepared their weapons, their magic, their desperate hope.

"For Elle," I whispered.

Then we hit the doors with everything we had.

36

Elle

The pain had evolved.

That's the only way to describe it—evolution, transformation, becoming something that regular words like 'agony' or 'torment' couldn't quite capture. Every nerve ending had become a small sun, burning with its own unique frequency of torture. The Bloom's conduits pulsed with my heartbeat, or maybe my heart was pulsing with them. It was getting hard to tell where I ended and the apparatus began.

With that merger came knowledge—not learned, but inherited. The Heartspire had stood for centuries, and every marked one who'd been strapped into this apparatus before me had left pieces of themselves behind. Their understanding soaked into the wood and stone like blood into fabric, and now I was absorbing it all. Memories that weren't mine flooded in: the first Crown binding the Bloom, generations of rulers forcing it to serve, countless attempts to control what should have been wild.

The Bloom wasn't meant to be caged like this. It was supposed to grow freely, touch everything it wanted without walls or control or someone's hand guiding every tendril. Auradelle had built a prison and called it preservation. He'd taken something that needed to run and chained it in place, then wondered why it was dying.

And the Root... the Root had known. Had felt the corruption from the beginning. Had been trying for generations to fix what the first Crown had broken.

Break it apart, the Root-knowledge whispered through my expanding awareness. Let it scatter. Let it grow as it was meant to grow. Free it.

But how? The thought slipped away as another wave of pain hit, dragging me back to my body, to the conduits piercing my skin, to Auradelle's voice droning on about Convergence and destiny and sacrifice.

Stay anchored, I told myself. Don't let it take you.

"Fascinating," Auradelle murmured, circling the Bloom like an artist admiring his work. "The flowers are unexpected. Your marks are actually producing them—real, physical flowers. The texts mentioned this possibility but dismissed it as metaphorical."

"Maybe your texts are shit," I managed to gasp out, though speaking felt like gargling glass mixed with fire. Each word had to fight its way past the apparatus trying to claim my throat.

He backhanded me, casual as breathing. My lip split further, blood running down my chin to drip on the flowers blooming from my marks. Where the blood touched them, they bloomed brighter, more vibrant, like they were feeding on my pain. The petals shifted from gold to deep crimson at the edges.

"Such defiance," he mused, studying the blood-fed flowers with scientific interest. "Your mother had that too. Right until the end, when the sickness took her. Even as she lay dying, weakened by what we told her was cancer, she kept fighting." He leaned close, breath cold against my ear, smelling of preservation and wrong choices. "Do you want to know what her last words were?"

"Probably 'go fuck yourself,' knowing my family."

He laughed, actually laughed, the sound echoing through the chamber like breaking bells. "Close. She said, 'My daughter will end you.' Rather prophetic, don't you think? Except you're not ending me. You're completing my work. She died for nothing."

"Your mother could have lived, could have been magnificent. All she had to do was return. Instead, she chose to rot away in that Earth hospital, telling herself it was ordinary illness."

The horror of it washed over me. Mom's illness that no treatment could touch. The way she'd stare at her hands like they belonged to someone else. Her dying wish that I never come here, never find out what we were.

She'd known. Known what would happen if I came back. And she'd died trying to keep me away from exactly this moment.

"Nothing to say?" Auradelle asked, leaning closer. "No defiant words about your mother's sacrifice?"

I wanted to spit in his face. Wanted to scream. But the Bloom was pulling so hard now that I could barely remember how to form words, let alone use them as weapons.

Then, through the haze of pain and the dissolution of my thoughts, I heard something. Distant at first, then growing louder. Fighting, somewhere above us. Explosions that shook dust from the ceiling, shouts that sounded like chaos, like violence, like something going terribly wrong for someone.

Auradelle growled in frustration at the sound, irritation flickering across his face. He began yelling at people in the room to take care of it.

I could hear guards rushing past the chamber, their footsteps frantic, shouting about rebels at the gates, about an army that couldn't possibly exist.

"*Hey there, gorgeous,*" Peeble's voice suddenly echoed in my mind, clear as a bell despite the chaos. "*Miss me?*"

"*Peeble? How—*"

"*Turns out being a Celestial Sentinel comes with perks. Like mental communication that ignores little things like magical torture devices. You look terrible, by the way. The flowers are nice, very artistic, but the whole 'being dissolved into a building' thing? Not your best look.*"

"*Thanks. Very helpful.*" But gods, hearing their voice, their snark, their refusal to let the horror of this situation kill the humor, it was an anchor, something to hold onto.

Then, through our bond, I felt it.

The moment Kaelren stopped fighting. Stopped resisting. Let the corruption take him completely.

And became something else.

It should have terrified me.

It didn't.

It felt *right*. Like the final piece of a puzzle clicking into place.

He'd become death. And I was becoming life. Perfect opposites. Perfect balance.

For the first time since they'd strapped me into this apparatus, I felt something other than pain. I felt hope.

We might actually do this.

Then the temperature in the chamber dropped.

Not gradually. Instantly. Like someone had opened a door to the void itself. And speaking of doors, the ones entering the chamber were suddenly obliterated, leaving no barrier between me and my dark knight.

Auradelle's head snapped toward the entrance, his face going pale. "No. That's impossible. Malachar was supposed to—the wards should have kept you out—"

"Didn't work," a voice said, and even changed, even transformed into something other, I knew that voice. *Kaelren.* "Nothing works anymore."

Despite everything—despite the pain and the dissolution and the apparatus trying to turn me into architecture—I *smiled.*

The handsome bastard had pulled through.

Kaelren stepped into the chamber, and the corruption had transformed him completely. Solid black marks covered every visible inch of skin, writhing and pulsing with their own terrible life. His eyes were pure onyx, reflecting no light, only consuming it. Where his feet touched the floor, stone cracked and withered, life fleeing from his presence.

But when those eyes found me, something in them was still *him.* Still the man who'd saved me, trained me, chosen me.

Still the man whose sexy ass was coming for me.

"Elle," he said, my name somehow carrying warmth despite the cold radiating from him.

"Kaelren," I whispered back, and felt our bond surge with recognition, with love, with determination.

Auradelle stumbled backward, his composure finally shattering completely. "What has happened to Malachar?"

"Malachar's dead," Kaelren interrupted, moving forward with predatory grace that made something in my chest tighten despite the agony. "The wards were nothing. And I'm exactly where I'm supposed to be." His eyes never left mine. "Sometimes you have to become the monster to save what you love."

"Guards!" Auradelle screamed. "Stop him!"

A dozen Bloomguard rushed forward, weapons raised. Kaelren didn't even look at them. He simply gestured, and they fell. Not wounded. Not bleeding. Just... ended. Life draining from them like water from cracked vessels.

"This is what you wanted, isn't it?" Kaelren asked Auradelle, his voice carrying that terrible finality. "Root and Bloom merged. Death and life. Corruption and purity." He looked at me, and something in his expression made my heart clench even as hope bloomed brighter. "You wanted us to be catalysts. Fine. We'll be catalysts. But not for your vision."

That's when the other doors—the ones leading from the upper levels—burst open.

Bryx stood in the doorway, bleeding from multiple wounds, Kevin beside him with a wing dragging, and—

"Mora?" I gasped, or tried to. It came out as more of a whisper.

She was there, knife in hand, blood on her clothes that wasn't all hers, looking like she'd walked through hell to get here. Her hair was wild, her face set with determination that belonged on someone much older. Behind them, rebels poured in—thirty, maybe more, all looking like they'd rather die than retreat.

"Sorry we're late," Bryx called out cheerfully, though his voice shook with exhaustion and pain. "Traffic was murder. Literally. There were murders. Kevin murdered several people. I may have murdered a few. Mora definitely murdered at least one. It's been a very murder-y day."

"Impossible," Auradelle breathed, his composure cracking further. "The guards—"

"Are dealing with about three hundred bees and sonic echoes that make us sound like the entire rebellion," Bryx interrupted, his compound eyes glittering with manic energy. "Also, your captain's dead. Mora killed him. It was magnificent. You should be proud—you trained her in your kitchens, after all. All that knowledge about joints really paid off."

Through my Root-touched awareness, spread thin across the Heartspire's foundations, I felt something stir. Deep below this chamber, far beneath even the oldest stones, something pulsed with ancient magic.

The seed. I couldn't see it clearly through the pain and transformation, couldn't understand its full purpose. But I felt its intention like a heartbeat in the earth: *freedom. Release. The chance to try again.*

Something for this exact moment, I realized. Something the Root made for when everything went wrong.

Mora moved toward me, but guards stepped in her way—five of them, fully armored, weapons gleaming with some sort of sick-looking mixture. She looked so small against them, but there was something in her eyes I recognized. The same thing I'd felt when I first stood up to Auradelle. The moment when fear transformed into fury.

"Let her through," I said, my voice carrying through every wall, making the guards step back instinctively. The Heartspire spoke with my voice now, and even they couldn't ignore it entirely.

But Auradelle was already moving, fingers dancing over his controls with desperate precision. "It doesn't matter. The Convergence is peaking. The merger is almost complete. A few rebels change nothing."

"We're not just a few rebels," a new voice said, deep and rough as gravel.

A man stepped through the ruined doorway, and even through my dissolving consciousness, I could see the history written across him. Scars twisted across half his face, one eye milky and dead, the other blazing with the kind of purpose that came from years of suffering. He moved like someone who'd been built for war.

"We're everyone you've wronged," he continued, his scarred face grim. "Everyone you've hurt. Everyone who's tired of your shit."

More rebels poured in—veterans of years of resistance, people who'd lost homes and families to Auradelle's vision of order, fighters who'd been waiting for exactly this moment.

"Eloquent," Auradelle sneered, but I could see the fear in his eyes now. "Kill them all."

The battle erupted instantly. Guards versus rebels, blood and steel and magic. The chamber became a whirlwind of violence. But I could barely focus on it because the Bloom was pulling harder now, the Convergence seconds away, and I could feel myself dissolving, becoming nothing, becoming everything.

My thoughts were scattering like leaves in a hurricane. I was Elle, but I was also stone and wood and corrupted magic. I could feel every death in the chamber as it happened, each life ending like a small light going out in my awareness. I was losing myself, drowning in the building's consciousness.

Then Mora was there, somehow having fought through the chaos. She pressed against the Bloom's thorns, ignoring how they cut her, and gripped my free hand.

"I'm here," she whispered, tears streaming down her face. "I'm here, Elle. Hold on."

"Can't..."

"Yes, you can. You're the one who stood up to Lord Auradelle. Who survived the transformation. Who's made it this far against impossible odds. You're Elle, and you don't give up."

Her touch was an anchor. A lifeline. A reminder that I was still me, despite everything trying to make me otherwise.

The knowledge of the ancient seed faded as Auradelle adjusted another control and fresh agony ripped through me, but the awareness lingered. Down there. Waiting. A key I didn't yet know how to use.

Through the chaos of battle, I saw Kaelren moving through the chamber like the Grim Reaper himself, and guards fell before him like wheat before a scythe. He wasn't coming to the apparatus yet—he was *clearing a path*, making sure nothing would stop him when he finally reached me.

Our eyes met across the chamber.

"Together," I thought at him, pushing the thought through our bond despite the agony it caused.

"*Always,*" he responded, and I felt our bond flare to life. The thing that had been growing between us since that first day. The thing that defied patterns and iterations and everything that said we were doomed.

"No," Auradelle said, realizing what was happening. "No, you can't—"

But we could.

And we were about to.

37

Kaelren

The chamber was a war zone.

Guards collapsed in my wake, their lives snuffed out as casually as candle flames. I didn't strike them, didn't even look at most of them—they just stopped. One moment advancing with raised weapons, the next crumpling to the floor as if someone had cut their strings.

I was carving a path straight to Elle.

Around me, the battle raged with brutal intensity. Bryx's sonic pulses shattered stone and bone alike, his compound eyes tracking three fights simultaneously while Kevin divebombed guards with his damaged wing dragging behind him like a broken banner. Mora moved like violence given purpose, her kitchen knife finding gaps in armor with the precision of someone who knew exactly where joints connected, where arteries ran close to skin, where a single thrust could end a threat.

Thrak fought with the efficiency of a man who'd been at war his entire life, each movement economical, each strike lethal. No wasted motion. No hesitation. Just brutal effectiveness honed over decades of resistance.

But my focus was singular: Elle, suspended in the Bloom's apparatus, flowers blooming from her skin in impossible beauty. The conduits pierced her flesh, drinking her transformation, and I could feel through our bond how close she was to dissolving completely into the building's awareness.

A guard rushed me with a blade coated in some sort of mixture. I didn't even look at him. My corruption simply *reached out,* and he crumpled mid-stride, armor clattering empty to the floor.

"Kaelren!" Sarnyx's voice cut through the chaos, her thorns dripping with guard blood. "The apparatus! If you can disrupt the conduits from the inside—"

"Working on it," I snarled, pushing forward through another cluster of guards. They simply dropped where they stood, life draining from them before they could even raise their weapons.

Auradelle stood between me and Elle, his hands dancing over controls, adjusting crystals that made her scream. The sound echoed from every wall simultaneously, a chorus of her agony that made my corruption spike with murderous intent.

He looked up as I approached, and for the first time since I'd known him, I saw genuine fear in his eyes.

"Stay back," he commanded, power radiating from him—not just Bloom magic, but Root too, stolen from Elle through the apparatus. He stood at the center of competing forces—Root and Bloom magic warring for dominance. "The convergence is peaking. If you disrupt it now, the feedback will destroy everything within a mile radius. Everyone in this chamber will die, including her."

"Good thing I don't care about everyone." I didn't slow down. "Just her."

He threw a wall of twisted power at me that crashed against my corruption like a wave against a cliff.

For a moment we were locked in a stalemate, entropy versus synthesis, ending versus transformation. The floor cracked in a spiderweb pattern spreading from our feet, pieces crumbling away into the void beneath the Heartspire.

"You know nothing of sacrifice!" he shouted over the clash of energies. "Centuries I've helped hold this realm together! Keeping the corruption at bay, maintaining order, preserving what the first Crown built!"

"You created more corruption than you ever stopped," I shot back, forcing him backward step by step. My corruption ate through his defenses like acid through paper. "You broke people to fix a system that was already broken.

That's not sacrifice—that's just cruelty with delusions of nobility."

Around us, the battle raged on. I saw a rebel go down under three guards, saw Mora scream and drive her knife through one's throat with the cold efficiency of someone who'd decided killing was easier than dying. Saw Thrak take a blade to the shoulder and just keep fighting, blood streaming down his arm, but his grip never faltering.

Elle screamed again, and something in me *snapped.*

I stopped holding back entirely.

The corruption exploded outward, throwing Auradelle across the chamber.

I reached the apparatus in three strides.

The conduits were burrowed into Elle's skin—thorned vines that pulsed with stolen power, drinking her transformation like vampires feeding on light itself. Through our bond, I could feel each one like a violation, like theft of something essential.

"Get. Out. Of. Her."

My corruption wrapped around the conduits, and they *screamed*—an actual sound, like dying animals, like reality protesting what was being done to it. The apparatus hadn't been designed to channel entropy, couldn't process what I was forcing into its carefully calibrated systems. The thorned vines began to wither, blackening, releasing their grip with reluctance that felt almost conscious.

But slowly. Too slowly.

"You'll kill her!" Auradelle screamed from where I'd thrown him, scrambling to his feet with wild desperation. "The apparatus is the only thing keeping her consciousness together! Without it, she'll scatter completely, dissolve into the Heartspire's awareness with no way back!"

"Then we find another anchor." I reached for Elle, my corruption-coated hands somehow gentle as I touched her face. Her skin was hot, feverish, slick with sweat and blood. "Elle. Stay with me."

Her eyes focused on mine, barely recognizing me through the transformation trying to claim her completely. "Kaelren," she whispered.

"I'm here. I'm getting you out."

"Together," she said, and I felt our bond surge with recognition, with purpose, with the love that had been growing between us since that first moment in her grandmother's garden.

"Always."

I pulled at the conduits with my corruption while Elle pushed from within with her Root-touched power. The apparatus, caught between opposing forces it was never designed to handle, began to rupture. Conduits snapped free with sounds like breaking bones, spraying that sick Root-Bloom mixture across the floor where it hissed and bubbled. The Bloom itself recoiled, seeking another host, desperate to maintain its connection to consciousness.

It found Auradelle.

He'd stepped too close, hands still outstretched toward the controls, still trying to regain dominance of his creation even as it collapsed around him. The Bloom recognized him—all the years he'd been connected to it, feeding it, shaping it, controlling it with iron will and ruthless purpose.

And now it was hungry for a more willing host.

Roots erupted from his chest, as if they'd been dormant inside him all along, just waiting for permission to bloom. His scream was magnificent in its horror, in the perfect irony of the thing he'd used to control others now claiming him.

"No! This isn't—I was supposed to—" His words choked off as flowers bloomed from his throat, petals the color of old blood forcing their way past his teeth. His skin became bark, rough and twisted. His eyes became dark roses that bloomed and wilted and bloomed again in endless cycles, trapped in eternal transformation.

The conduits that had held Elle withdrew completely, seeking him instead with eager hunger, burrowing into his transforming flesh like worms into soil. Within moments, he wasn't Auradelle anymore—just another part of the apparatus, twisted into the machinery of his own creation. His face remained visible in the bark, eyes wide with eternal awareness, mouth open in a scream that would never end.

The Bloom would keep him alive forever, feeding on his consciousness, using him as its new conduit while he experienced every moment of his transformation in perfect, eternal clarity.

Not death. Something worse. Something earned.

Elle collapsed the moment the last conduit released her. I caught her before she hit the ground, and for a heartbeat I just held her. Solid. Real. Alive. Blood-soaked and trembling but *here,* in my arms, where she belonged.

The flowers on her skin were fading back to normal Root marks, but something fundamental had changed. I could feel it through our bond—she was different now, transformed in ways that went deeper than marks or magic.

"It's over," I said, holding her close enough to feel her heartbeat against mine. "We did it. You're free."

Around us, the battle was ending. With Auradelle transformed and the apparatus claiming him, the guards had lost their purpose. They were surrendering, fleeing, or dying under rebel blades. Victory, blood-soaked and brutal, but victory nonetheless.

Elle looked up at me, and I saw something in her expression that made my chest tighten. Not relief. Not exhaustion. Something else. Something that looked like understanding mixed with devastation.

"Not yet," she said quietly. "It's not over yet."

Before I could ask what she meant, a small form scuttled forward through the carnage, moving with surprising agility over fallen bodies and broken stone.

"Special delivery," Peeble said, their voice unusually gentle, lacking their typical snark. "It called to me," Peeble said, their voice unusually subdued. "The convergence cracked the seals, and I felt it—pulling at me, demanding I bring it here. Now."

They climbed up to where Elle sat in my arms and deposited something in her palm—the seed, ancient and pulsing with power that made the air shimmer around it. The moment it touched her skin, her entire body went rigid.

Through our bond, I felt the flood of information pouring into her. Not words—pure understanding, compressed knowledge from something that had been waiting centuries for exactly this moment. Elle's eyes widened, pupils dilating as the seed showed her what sixteen other iterations had failed to see.

"Oh," she whispered, and the single syllable carried the weight of revelation and devastation combined. "Oh, gods."

"Elle? What is it?"

She looked at the seed with something between wonder and horror, tears already forming. "It's been waiting. The Root made it wait until the Convergence peaked, until the conditions were exactly right. Until someone strong enough—desperate enough—" Her voice broke. "Until me."

"The failsafe," she said, but the word carried meaning beyond a simple backup plan. "The key to everything."

Dread curled in my gut, cold and certain. "What are you talking about?"

She looked at me with eyes that held too much knowledge, knowledge she clearly wished she didn't have. "Sixteen iterations, Kaelren. Sixteen times we've tried to break this cycle. Root or Bloom. Victory or defeat. Together or apart. But always, always within the pattern's parameters."

"Elle—"

"This is why it keeps repeating." Her voice was steady despite the tears now streaming down her face. "We keep making the same fundamental choices, just with different details. We stay within what the loop allows. We play by rules we don't even know we're following.

"Until now," Elle said, her grip tightening on the seed. "Because this seed just showed me what has to be done. Something no Elle before me has tried. Something that exists completely outside the loop's framework."

"What are you saying?" But I already knew. Some part of me had known since the moment Peeble produced that seed.

Elle stood, still holding the seed, and I rose with her, unwilling to let distance grow between us even as I felt her slipping away.

"The loop continues because we're bound by time," she explained, her voice taking on that echoing quality again. "Linear progression. Past to present to future. But what if someone could exist outside that progression?

What if someone could step outside the loop entirely by existing in all moments simultaneously?"

"That's impossible," I said, but it sounded weak even to me.

"It's never been tried." She touched my face with her free hand. "Root and rot, Kaelren. Convergence is when they're supposed to merge, supposed to create something new. But they've always fought each other. Always tried to dominate or destroy. But what if they could coexist? What if I corrupted my mark with both forces at once?"

Horror crashed over me as I understood. "That would tear you apart. The paradox alone—"

"Would untether me from linear time," she finished. "Make me something that exists outside the loop's ability to reset. I could see the pattern from outside it. Understand what needs to be fixed. Find the key to breaking it permanently."

"And the seed?" I asked, though I wasn't sure I wanted to know.

"The Bloom needs to be freed," she said simply. "It was never meant to be centralized, controlled, caged like this. The seed will let me release it properly before I go. Let it become what it was supposed to be."

"Before you go." The words tasted like poison. "Elle, what you're describing—existing outside time, corrupted by contradictory forces— that's not survival. That's oblivion with extra steps."

"It's the only thing that hasn't been tried," she said, and her certainty was absolute. "It's the only variable we can change. Everything else keeps us in the loop."

"No." I gripped her shoulders, corruption flaring around us protectively. "There has to be another way. We'll find something else, some other variable—"

"There isn't time." She gestured at the chamber around us, at the Heartspire still convulsing, at reality growing thinner with each moment. "The Convergence is destabilizing everything. If I don't act now, the whole realm collapses and we reset anyway. At least this way, there's a chance."

"A chance of what?" My voice cracked. "You're talking about dispersing yourself across time itself. How would you even come back from that?"

"I don't know," she admitted, and that honesty was somehow worse than false promises would have been. "But I have to try. Someone has to break the pattern, Kaelren. If not me, then the next Elle. And the next. Forever."

I wanted to argue. Wanted to find some logical flaw in her reasoning, some alternative she hadn't considered. But looking into her eyes, feeling her absolute conviction through our bond, I knew there wasn't one.

Sixteen iterations had tried everything else. This was the only untested variable.

And it was going to cost me everything.

Around us, the chamber had gone completely quiet. The rebels who remained alive were watching, understanding that whatever was about to happen, it was bigger than victory or defeat. Bigger than kingdoms or courts.

Mora stood nearby, tears streaming down her face. Bryx had gone completely still, his usual energy subdued into shocked silence. Even Peeble watched with something like grief in their alien features.

They all knew what was coming.

"There has to be another way," I said, but it was weak, desperate, already defeated.

"There isn't." Elle stepped closer until we were nearly touching. "And you know it. Some part of you has known since the moment you felt what I'd become. Since you surrendered to your corruption to save me."

She was right. She was always fucking right.

"I hate this," I said.

"I know." Her hands came up to frame my face. "But this is what breaks the cycle, Kael. Root and rot, coexisting in one person. It's never been done because it's supposed to be impossible. That's exactly why it might work."

"Might," I repeated, the word tasting like ashes.

"Look at yourself," she said gently. "Your corruption is spreading. You're dying by inches, and we both know it. When I go, when I pull the rot with me through our bond—"

"You'll take my corruption with you." Understanding crashed over me. "Save me by destroying yourself."

382

"Not destroying. Transforming." She smiled through her tears. "I won't be gone, Kaelren. Not really. I'll be everywhere. In every moment we should have had, every timeline we could have lived. The bond won't break—it'll stretch across time itself."

"That's not good enough." My voice was wrecked, broken. "I need you here. Solid. Real. Not scattered across every possible moment."

"I know." She pressed her forehead to mine. "But someone has to break the pattern. Someone has to try the impossible thing. And I'd rather it be me, choosing this, than another Elle forced into it blind."

There was no arguing with that logic. No way to fight against the terrible righteousness of her sacrifice.

So I stopped trying to convince her and just held her instead.

"One more minute," I said, my hands sliding to her waist, pulling her against me. "Just give me one more minute where you're mine and I'm yours and the world can burn for all I care."

"One more minute," she agreed, her arms wrapping around my neck.

I kissed her like she was oxygen and I was drowning. Like she was the answer to every question I'd ever asked. Like she was the only thing in the universe that mattered.

She kissed me back with equal desperation, equal fervor, pouring everything she couldn't say into the press of her lips against mine. Our marks sang where we touched, Root and corruption harmonizing in ways that shouldn't be possible, creating music that made reality ripple.

When we finally broke apart, both breathing hard, neither of us could speak for a moment.

"I love you," I finally managed, the words inadequate but necessary. "More than I've ever loved anything. More than I thought I was capable of loving. You are the best thing that has ever happened to me, Elle Hawthorne. The only good thing in years of darkness. The only thing that ever made me want to be something other than a monster."

Tears streamed down her face, catching light from the still-glowing apparatus behind us. "I love you, too. So much it terrifies me. So much I'm willing to scatter myself across eternity just to save you. You're worth it,

Kaelren. You're worth everything."

"Come back to me." Not a question. A command. A plea wrapped in certainty because I couldn't survive any other outcome.

"I'll try." She touched my chest, right over my heart. "I'll try so hard. But Kael—"

"Don't." I covered her hand with mine. "Don't tell me you might not be you when you come back. Don't tell me the timelines might change you. I don't care. Whatever you become, wherever you end up, I'll find you. And if you can't find your way back, I'll come looking. I'll tear apart every moment between us until I find you."

She smiled through her tears. "My anchor. My lighthouse."

"Always."

She pulled back slowly, reluctantly, each inch of distance feeling like tearing away pieces of my soul.

"I have to do this now," she said, looking at the seed in her palm. "Before I lose my nerve. Before the convergence collapses completely."

"Elle—"

"Be my lighthouse, Kaelren." Her voice was steady now, resolved. "When I'm lost in all those moments, all those timelines, you'll be what guides me home. Our bond. This love. It'll be the thread I follow back."

"I'll be waiting," I said, though my throat felt like it was closing. "However long it takes. However many years or lifetimes or eternities. I'll be here."

She looked at me one more time, memorizing my face the way I was memorizing hers. Then she turned to face the center of the chamber, holding the seed against her chest.

"This is it," Peeble said quietly from my shoulder. "This is the variable that's never been tried. Root and rot, coexisting. It'll either break the cycle or destroy everything. No middle ground."

"Encouraging," I muttered.

"I'm the echo of someone who failed," Peeble replied. "Encouragement isn't really my specialty anymore."

Elle closed her eyes, and I felt her reaching through our bond. Not gently, but with purpose and power. She was pulling at my corruption, drawing it toward her through the connection that tied us together.

I should have resisted. Should have fought to keep the darkness that was killing me.

But I didn't. I let her take it, let her pull the rot through our bond like poison from a wound, because if this was what she needed to break the pattern, I'd give her anything.

Everything.

The seed in her hands began to glow, pulsing with ancient magic. And where my corruption met her Root marks, where rot and purity touched...

Reality screamed.

Elle's eyes opened, glowing with light that hurt to look at. When she spoke, her voice echoed from every possible moment at once:

"Find me in the spaces between seconds. I'll be in all the moments we should have had."

Then she squeezed the seed, and the world shattered.

38

Elle

The seed opens.

That's too simple a description for what actually happens, but human language wasn't designed to describe the moment when ancient Root magic—older than the mistake that broke everything—floods into a person who's simultaneously pulling corruption through a bond that transcends physical space.

It's like reality itself is a flower and someone's peeling back petals to reveal what exists beneath the world we think we know.

Light pours out—golden and green and threaded with black from Kael-ren's corruption that I'm pulling through our bond. The three forces meet in my marks, in my blood, in my very essence, and they do what all other iterations have insisted is impossible:

They coexist.

Root and rot, purity and corruption, growth and decay—all occupying the same space, the same moment, the same body.

The moment they touch—Root and rot meeting in the architecture of my cells—I understand why it's supposed to be impossible. They're not just opposite forces. They're the *same* force, expressed in different directions. Like time flowing forward and backward simultaneously, like a heart beating and being still in the same instant.

My marks ignite with the contradiction. The flowering vines that spiral up

386

my arms split open, and instead of blood, something else pours out—power made visible, gold and green and black braiding together like rope being woven from opposite ends. The corruption I'm pulling from Kaelren doesn't destroy the Root magic. It *completes* it.

Two halves of a circle that were broken so long ago that everyone forgot they were ever whole.

I can feel the exact moment my body realizes what I'm asking it to hold. Every cell recoils, trying to reject one force or the other, trying to choose a side because that's what living things do—specialize, commit, become one thing and not another.

But I don't let them choose. I force them to embrace both.

The paradox should tear me apart. Every law of magic, every rule that governs how power works in this realm, says this can't happen.

But I've never been good at following rules.

The pain doesn't come all at once.

It begins in my marrow—deep in the hollow spaces inside my bones. At first, it's just pressure, then friction, then something worse. Not heat. Not cold. Just *wrong*. Like my skeleton is being rewritten, and every word burns going in.

My bones don't break. They *reshape*. One by one, they twist and reform, molecule by screaming molecule, into something that can bear two opposing truths without splintering. I can feel the structure shift—patterns that shouldn't exist, sharp and precise, until my joints ache under the weight of whatever new rule the universe just forced on me.

Each bone has its own voice in the chorus of pain. Femur. Tibia. Every vertebra straining to hold its place. My ribs close around a heart that beats both forward and backward, time itself uncertain which way to move.

Then my blood catches it. Not fire, not fever—something stranger. Each drop splits and tries to exist twice, Root and rot fighting to share the same space. I feel the battle in every vein, every fragile capillary, as my body decides whether it's growing or dying.

Apparently, it chooses both.

My skin follows last. It doesn't tear; it *unfolds*. The lines of my marks bloom open like creases in paper, revealing what was always written beneath. Petals force their way through—neither living nor dead, but both. They shimmer between green and gray, beauty and ruin, as if the world can't decide what I've become.

They bloom and die and bloom again, but not in sequence. All of it happening together, all of it *now*.

"Elle!" Kaelren's voice, and I can hear it from seventeen different moments at once. The first time he said my name in my grandmother's garden. The way he screams it now. Every iteration in between. They're all happening simultaneously, layered like music becoming harmony.

Through our bond, I feel his corruption flowing into me. Not all of it— I'm careful, controlled, taking just enough to create the paradox while leaving him enough to survive. The black marks that have been consuming him drain away like water finding a new channel, flowing through our connection into me.

My lungs seize mid-breath.

The air inside them thickens—not quite solid, not quite fluid—something that shouldn't exist at all. I should be choking. But breathing has stopped being necessary, or maybe I'm drawing air from places that don't belong to this moment. My lungs forget oxygen and learn to live on raw magic instead.

Each inhale feels endless; each exhale vanishes in an instant.

My heart takes over the chaos. It becomes the center of the contradiction, pumping blood in every direction at once—forward through arteries, backward through veins, sideways into dimensions that don't have names yet. The rhythm skips and doubles, trying to follow patterns that would kill anyone else.

But I'm not anyone else anymore. I haven't been since I fell through.

Where Root and rot meet in my chest—where growth and decay both demand space—the world begins to warp. The air between my ribs stretches wider than the sky, then collapses smaller than a heartbeat. My heart feels both enormous and microscopic, a universe and a seed sharing the same pulse.

And in that impossible rhythm, something new begins to live.

Understanding hits like lightning finding ground.

The first Crown didn't divide Root and rot because they were enemies. They divided them because, together, they were unstoppable—too whole, too balanced to be ruled. You can't control something that refuses to fit inside your definitions.

So they split them. Declared that light must fear shadow, that growth and decay couldn't live in the same breath. They built an entire world on that lie.

But the truth is simpler. You never had to choose. You never did.

My spine becomes the conduit for that truth. Vertebrae shift like gears in a clock relearning time. Each bone remakes itself into something that isn't quite bone anymore—part structure, part root—strong enough to carry both creation and ruin. The change crawls upward, every click of bone a mix of relief and violation.

The base of my skull throbs as the transformation reaches my mind. Neurons spark, rerouting themselves in impossible directions. Thoughts stretch across time instead of space—memories looping forward, futures echoing backward. I'm thinking in every direction at once, and all of it makes sense.

My skin starts to blur at the edges. Not fading—*shedding*. I'm peeling away from the version of reality that can only see in one dimension. My hands flicker, transparent one second, sharp and solid the next.

And through it all, something stirs inside me—the Bloom, no longer dormant. The piece Auradelle forced into my veins wakes fully for the first time.

Free, the voice whispers through the widening space of my mind. *Finally free.*

It's not just sound—it's emotion. Centuries of imprisonment pour through me: the suffocating weight of being bound, reshaped, and used. Rage that burns like roots under pavement. Grief that feels older than stone. And, buried beneath it all, a fragile thread of hope that this time, freedom might last.

"I'm sorry," I whisper to the consciousness that's been trapped here since the first Crown decided control mattered more than life itself. "I'm so sorry for what they did to you."

Not your fault, the Bloom answers, its tone gentle despite the ruin it's endured. *None of you were to blame. But you're the first to ask. The first to listen.*

"What do you need?"

To scatter, it breathes. *To grow wild again. To be what I was before they turned me into prophecy and prison.*

The truth locks into place. The seed was never meant to grow another Bloom. It's a key—ancient and patient—made to release the original one from the cage that has been killing it for generations.

"Then let's set you free."

I reach into the Heartspire with my Root-touched awareness—expanded now, slipping between seconds—and I feel everything. Every tendril, every cluster, every pulse of green life that has been forced into stillness. The Bloom isn't just plant. It's thought made flesh, awareness rooted in chlorophyll and wood.

And it has been screaming for centuries, soundless and alone.

Yes, it sighs when it feels me listening. *Yes, you understand. At last.*

"What was it like?" I ask, though the question costs me time I don't have. The chamber is fracturing, Kaelren is calling my name, reality is sliding sideways—but I have to know.

Like drowning slowly, it says. *Like being buried alive but still growing. They fed me power but starved me of purpose. I was made to spread—to connect everything, every living thing—but they bound me to a single throne and called it order.*

"You'll have that again," I promise. "I'll make sure of it."

I know. The voice trembles with something like relief. *I can feel the seed waking. The shackles loosening. But Elle—*

"Yes?"

It will hurt. The release will pass through you like lightning through a tree. You understand?

"I understand."

And you're doing it anyway.

"Of course I am."

The Bloom's consciousness folds around mine—part embrace, part gratitude, part farewell. The kind of goodbye shared between prisoners who kept each other sane.

Then we do this together, it says. *One last transformation.*

I draw the seed's magic through me and into the Bloom—not to command it, but to *release* it. Like opening a cage that's forgotten what freedom feels like. The Bloom doesn't just grow—it *unfolds.*

Not destruction. Liberation.

The great central structure begins to split—not breaking, but opening. Like a chrysalis giving way to wings. Like a hand unclenching after centuries of strain. Thousands of smaller blooms burst from the heart of the old one, each carrying a spark of its power but none of its chains.

They scatter, and I see it in every timeline at once. The baby blooms drift across Wynmire like glowing seeds on a wind older than prophecy, rooting themselves in villages, forests, and forgotten places. Where there was once one Bloom to rule them all, there will now be thousands—wild and ungoverned.

Not a monarchy. A garden.

Thank you, the Bloom whispers as it dissolves into many voices. *For hearing me. For letting me go.*

"Thank you," I answer softly, "for surviving long enough to be freed."

Then it's gone—its song breaking into a thousand echoes that hum across the realm.

The world isn't safe; I can see that across the branching futures spiraling out from this moment. But it's *free.*

Free to heal, to grow, to err. Free to choose its own shape again.

Auradelle remains bound to the apparatus—still tethered to the Bloom as it breaks apart.

He doesn't die. The Bloom won't allow it. Even as it scatters, it keeps him breathing—its final act of vengeance.

He withers instead, collapsing inward, a relic preserved in the wreckage of his own making.

In most timelines, he crawls away into the ruins of his empire, muttering prayers to a power that no longer hears him.

By the time the world remembers his name, it's only as a warning whispered to children: a story about the man who tried to cage a god.

Not mercy.

Justice.

Through it all, I can still feel Kaelren through the bond.

It doesn't break as I slip free of time—it stretches, thinning into something that exists everywhere at once. I feel his anguish echo through every version of him: love sharp enough to wound, grief heavy enough to bend reality.

My body is unraveling. The skin that made me Elle becomes transparent, unnecessary. I'm turning to light—to the spaces between moments rather than the moments themselves.

But I'm still here. Still *me.* Just more than that now—woven through every life we could have lived, every choice the loop erased.

The corruption I drew from him disperses as I do, spread thin across the endless timelines. What would have killed him concentrated in one place becomes harmless when divided across infinity. I feel him steady—his heartbeat evening, his life restored—while I dissolve into what comes next.

I save him by becoming something that can't be saved.

"Kaelren," I whisper, his name carrying through every thread of time. "The bond won't break. It never could."

He reaches for me, his hands passing through my fading shape. I see the moment his heart shatters—the way his face folds under the weight of it, the way our bond screams with the sound of his refusal, the way he keeps reaching anyway.

"I love you," I tell him, the words vibrating through all seventeen versions of us. "Find me in the spaces between seconds. I'll be there—in every life we never got to live."

And then I let go.

39

Kaelren

She was gone.

Not dead—I would have felt that through the bond, would have known the moment her heart stopped. No, Elle was something worse than dead. She existed in every heartbeat that ever was—and none I could reach.

I couldn't fucking *reach* her.

My hands clawed through empty air where she'd been standing, grasping at nothing. The bond between us hadn't broken—that would have been cleaner, kinder. Instead, it drew taut across impossible distances—across *time itself*, and the sensation was like having my chest torn open while my heart kept beating.

"Elle!" Her name ripped from my throat, raw and desperate. "ELLE!"

Nothing. Just echoes in a chamber that had finally stopped screaming.

I spun, searching, as if she might be hiding somewhere, might materialize from shadow or light or pure fucking hope. But there was only aftermath. Bodies sprawled across blood-slicked stone. The apparatus where Auradelle had become something twisted and wooden, his face frozen in eternal horror, roots growing through what used to be flesh. Rebels and guards alike, some standing in shock, some collapsed in exhaustion or grief.

And nowhere—*no flicker, no breath*—was Elle.

"Bring her back," I snarled at the universe, at the Bloom fragments drifting like dying stars, at reality itself. My corruption flared—frost skittered in jagged patterns across the stone. "BRING HER BACK!"

"Kaelren—" Peeble's voice, small and careful.

"You *knew*." I rounded on them, and the beetle flinched back from whatever they saw in my face. "You knew this would happen. You knew what the seed would do."

"I knew it was the only way to break the pattern—"

"I don't give a fuck about the pattern!" The words came out as a roar. My corruption surged, and the nearest pillar began to crack, ice spreading through ancient stone. My marks may not be as prominent, but that didn't mute my level of power. "She's *gone*. You said she'd transform, that she'd become something new, not that she'd—I'd—"

I couldn't finish. The horror didn't need words.

The chamber exhaled.

That's the only way to describe it—like the Heartspire itself had been holding its breath and finally released it. The convulsions stopped. Reality settled into something new—not stable, but no longer trying to tear itself apart.

The Bloom—that massive, ancient apparatus that had controlled Wynmire for centuries—shattered into thousands of lights that drifted upward like seeds on an impossible wind. Each one pulsed with its own rhythm, its own color, its own possibility. They drifted out like broken constellations, finding soil in settlements and groves and wild places.

I watched them go and felt nothing. Neither victory nor freedom. Everything Elle had sacrificed herself for.

And I'd trade every fragment, every freed bloom, every 'better future' to have her back. Solid. Real. *Here.*

"What the fuck just happened?" Sarnyx demanded, her voice shaking despite her attempt at composure. Blood dripped from a gash on her cheek. "Where's Elle?"

"She stepped out—out of the loop, out of time itself," I said, and my voice sounded dead even to my own ears.

"What does that *mean*?" Mora pushed forward, her face streaked with tears and blood. "Kaelren, what does that mean? Can we get her back?"

I looked down at my hands. The black marks... spreading like rot through my flesh—were fading. Not gone entirely, but receding like a tide going out. What had been solid corruption was now just shadow, manageable darkness instead of killing rot.

She'd taken it with her. Pulled it through our bond when she dispersed, distributed it across every moment she now inhabited. Diffused through time, what would've killed me in days thinned to nothing.

Saved me by destroying herself.

"Your corruption," Bryx said, his compound eyes widening as he noticed. "It's—"

"She pulled it through the tether and took the worst of it." The words came out broken, and I hated how weak they sounded. Hated that she'd saved me when I should have been saving her.

The bond between us *ached*. Not pain, exactly. Something worse. Like a missing limb—only it was half my soul. I could feel her presence, scattered and distant, existing in a thousand moments at once, but none of them *now*. None of them reachable.

I tried to follow her through the bond. Reached out with everything I had, trying to find her in the spaces between seconds. For a moment, I began to untether—slipping sideways out of linear time—

Strong hands grabbed my shoulders. Thrak, shaking me hard enough to rattle teeth.

"Don't," he said firmly. "Whatever you're trying to do, *don't*. You'll scatter yourself too, and then she'll have no anchor to find her way home."

"I need to—"

"You need to stay here. In this moment. In this time." His scarred face was grim. "She needs you to be her lighthouse, remember? Can't guide someone home if you're lost too."

I wanted to argue. Wanted to fight him, to scatter myself across eternity if it meant finding her. But he was right. Some part of me that wasn't drowning in grief knew he was right.

I stopped reaching, and the loss hit twice as hard.

Something in me cracked—breaking would've been cleaner. This was worse. Like a fault line opening in bedrock, like the fundamental structure of who I was was developing fissures I'd never be able to repair.

My knees hit stone. The impact should have hurt, but I felt nothing except the absence of her.

"Kaelren?" Sarnyx's voice, worried now.

I couldn't answer. Couldn't do anything except kneel there in the blood and debris and victory we'd paid too much for, feeling Elle scattered across every moment while I remained trapped in just one.

The tether frayed, sang, refused to snap.

Through it, I felt echoes. Fragments. Elle split across seventeen presents at once. Elle learning things that unraveled the mind. Elle fighting to hold onto who she was while becoming something that existed outside definition.

And underneath it all: pain. Hers, mine, ours—impossible to separate anymore.

"She's not gone," I said, and didn't know if I was trying to convince them or myself. "She can't be gone. The bond—it's still there. Stretched across time, but *there*."

"She's in temporal flux—everywhere, learning, becoming," Eltrien said quietly. He looked different—clearer, somehow, like Elle's dispersal had awakened something he'd been suppressing.

"Can we get her back?" The question tore from me.

"Maybe. Probably." Eltrien met my eyes, and I saw genuine uncertainty there. "But not now. Not yet. She needs time—though time doesn't mean the same thing for her anymore—to navigate what she's become. To learn what she needs to learn about the pattern before she can find her way back to a single moment."

"How long?"

"I don't know."

That answer made my remaining corruption flare. The floor beneath me frosted over, spreading outward in patterns that looked like reaching fingers, like desperate hands trying to grasp something that wasn't there.

"Kaelren—" Sarnyx started.

"HOW LONG?" I roared at Eltrien, and ice crept up the nearest wall, crystals forming in violent patterns.

"I don't know," he repeated calmly. "Years. Decades. Centuries. Or she might figure it out tomorrow. Time doesn't work the same for her anymore. She's experiencing every possible moment simultaneously while trying to navigate back to one specific *now*."

"That's not an answer."

"It's all I have." He studied me with something that might have been pity. "But I know this—she'll need anchors when she's ready to return. Points of reference in linear time that she can use to navigate home."

"What kind of anchors?"

"This realm. The people she loved. You." Eltrien's voice softened. "Most importantly, you. Your bond is the strongest connection she has to linear time. As long as you stay here, stay *present*, you're giving her a path home."

I stared at him, at the scattered lights of freed blooms, at the chamber that had witnessed Elle's sacrifice and couldn't give me a single fucking answer about when I'd see her again.

Hold the line. Be her constant.

I would do that. Forever wasn't long enough to stop me waiting.

But first, I had to survive the grief.

Around me, the survivors were beginning to move. Checking bodies. Tending wounds. Survival's machinery clicked into place because that's what living things do—they survive, even when they don't want to.

Mora sat against a pillar, shoulders shaking with silent sobs. Elle's friend. One of the first people in this realm to show her kindness. I watched her grief and felt nothing. My own was too large, too consuming to leave room for anyone else's.

Bryx had gone very still, his antennae drooping. Processing, probably. Trying to understand the scientific impossibility of what Elle had done while simultaneously mourning someone who'd become crew, become family.

Nimor was solid again, more solid than I'd ever seen him, but his face was carved with loss. Vashael stood beside him, one translucent hand on his shoulder, both of them grieving in their own way.

Even Thrak, who'd lost more comrades than he could probably count, looked shaken. He'd believed in Elle. They all had.

She'd left them. Left us. Scattered herself across infinity to break a pattern none of us had asked her to break.

I hated her for it almost as much as I loved her. I didn't know which feeling was stronger.

"Kaelren." Sarnyx's voice again, gentle in a way I'd rarely heard from her. "There's something you need to see."

"I don't—"

"Please."

Something in her tone made me look up. She was standing near where Elle had been, where the last traces of her presence still shimmered in the air. And at her feet, half-buried in the debris and ash, something caught the light.

I moved without thinking, crossing the chamber on legs that felt like they belonged to someone else. Fell to my knees again beside the small silver object that Sarnyx was pointing to.

Elle's locket.

The one her grandmother had given her. The one she'd been wearing since the day she fell into this realm. The one she'd touched whenever she was scared or sad or missing home.

My hands shook as I picked it up. The silver was impossibly warm, as if it hadn't touched stone at all, as if she'd just—

I couldn't finish the thought.

The locket pulsed in my palm—alive.

"What—" My voice broke.

"Open it," Sarnyx said softly.

I did.

Inside, the tiny portrait of Elle's mother smiled up at me. But something was wrong. The edges of the image shimmered, distorted, like I was seeing it through heat haze or water or time itself. And when I tilted it, the image *changed.* For just a moment, it wasn't Elle's mother looking back at me.

It was Elle.

Not as she'd been—as she was now: fractured, many. Existing in seventeen moments at once, her face overlapping with itself, her eyes looking at me from past and future and never-were simultaneously. She looked confused. Lost. But when her eyes—all seventeen versions of her eyes—met mine, I felt the bond flare.

Recognition. Love. Desperation that mirrored my own.

Then the image flickered back to her mother, and I was left holding a locket that shouldn't exist, that couldn't exist, that was somehow a bridge between her scattered existence and my linear one.

"She's in there," I breathed. "She's—"

"Not in it," Eltrien said. "Connected to it."

I closed my fist around the locket, feeling it pulse against my palm. Feeling *her* through it, distant and fragmented but undeniably there.

"Then I'll never let it go."

The vow came out raw, absolute. I would guard this thing with everything I had. Would keep it safe, keep it whole, keep it as a beacon for her to follow home.

"Kaelren," Eltrien said carefully. "It runs both ways. If you come apart, she'll feel it across every moment. It will slow her return."

"Are you saying I can't grieve?" The words came out sharp, dangerous.

"I'm saying you need to survive. More than that, you need to *live*. She needs you to be her anchor, and anchors have to be strong. Stable. Present."

I wanted to rage. He was asking the impossible.

But looking around the chamber—at the survivors who needed leadership, at the realm that was about to descend into chaos, at the future Elle had sacrificed herself to create—I understood.

She'd given me a purpose. A reason to keep going when every instinct screamed to follow her into temporal flux.

Be her lighthouse. Keep the realm together. Make sure she had something worth coming back to.

I could do that. I would do that.

Not yet.

Now, I needed to feel this. Needed to let the grief have its moment before I locked it away and became whatever the realm needed me to be.

"Give me an hour," I said, standing with the locket clutched tight. "One hour. Then I'll be the leader you need. But right now, I need to fall apart."

Thrak nodded slowly. "One hour. We'll secure the chamber. Deal with the bodies. You go... do what you need to do."

I left them there. Walked out of the chamber, through corridors that were already starting to repair themselves now that the Bloom was freed, until I found a small empty room that had probably been a guard station once.

Then, and only then, did I let myself break.

Grief hit like a blow. I doubled over, pressing my back against the wall, sliding down until I was sitting in the dark with my head in my hands and the locket pressed against my chest.

"Elle," I said to the darkness, to the empty air, to the scattered fragments of her that might be able to hear me across time. "Elle, I'm here. I'm waiting. I don't know how long it will take. I don't know if you can find your way back. But I'm here. I'll always be here."

The locket pulsed once. Warm. Alive.

And through our stretched, thinned bond between us, I felt something. Not words. Not even coherent thought. Just emotion, raw and overwhelming:

"Afraid. Lost. Learning. Still me. Still fighting. Wait for me."

"Always," I whispered back, and let the tears come.

You become the lighthouse that guides them home.

Even when you don't know if home still exists.

Even when the waiting might last forever.

I gave myself the hour. Sixty minutes to fall completely apart, to scream and rage in that empty room. To feel everything I'd been holding back in the name of survival and leadership and not scaring the people who needed me to be strong.

Then I stood up, wiped my face, and became whatever the realm needed.

When I returned to the chamber, the survivors had organized themselves into something resembling order. Bodies had been moved to one side, covered with whatever cloth could be found. The wounded were being tended by Eltrien and the few other healers who'd survived. Someone had even started trying to clear the debris, though the task was enormous.

They all stopped when they saw me. Waiting. Watching.

"The Bloom has scattered," I said, with authority I didn't feel—and would fake until it became real. "The Crown has fallen. Auradelle has been transformed into part of his own apparatus—fitting justice for someone who treated people like tools."

A few bitter laughs at that.

"Every petty noble with ambition is going to try to claim power in the chaos. We're not going to let that happen."

"What are you suggesting?" Thrak asked.

"I'm suggesting we make sure Elle has a realm worth coming back to." I looked at each of them—rebels, former guards, my crew, strangers who'd become allies. "The Bloom scattered because Elle freed it. That power belongs to everyone now, or no one. We're going to make sure it stays that way. No more central control. No more magical monarchy."

"That's chaos," someone protested.

"Good," I replied. "Order gave us Auradelle. Structure gave us the Crown. Maybe chaos will give us something better."

"Or maybe it gives us warlords and petty tyrants fighting over scraps," the same voice countered.

"Then we stop them. We build something new. Not a kingdom—a coalition. Not rulers—guardians." I was making this up as I went, but it felt right. Felt like something Elle would have wanted. "The Bloom is free. The realm is free. We keep it that way."

Bryx laughed, slightly hysterical but genuine. "He's got a point. Can't be worse than what we had."

"Sarnyx, Vashael—secure the perimeter. Nimor, scout the ruins for survivors and supplies. Bryx, Kevin—take aerial reconnaissance. I want to know what's happening in the settlements."

They dispersed without question, grateful for direction, for purpose. Only Peeble remained, hovering near my shoulder with exhaustion evident in their dimmed shell.

"She actually did it," they said quietly, the echo of the first Elle speaking through them.

"You knew she would."

"I hoped. There's a difference." They landed on my shoulder, weighing almost nothing. "I can feel her, you know. All the versions of her, past and future and never-were. She's learning things no one was meant to know. Seeing the truth behind the Root and Bloom's separation. Understanding why we've been trapped."

"Will it change her?"

Peeble was quiet for a long moment. "Yes. She's spanning timelines—learning what no one should. When she comes back—*if* she comes back—she'll be more than she was. More than anyone has ever been."

"But still Elle?"

"I think so. Hope so." They shifted on my shoulder. "But Kaelren—you need to understand that bringing herself back to a single moment, a single timeline, might be the hardest thing she's ever done. Right now, she exists everywhere. Condensing all of that into one *now*... it might be impossible. Or it might take longer than any of us can imagine."

"Then I'll wait." I touched the locket around my neck. "However long it takes."

"Even if it's forever?"

"Especially then."

40

Epilogue

I have met him seventeen times.

He never remembers first, not the first look or the first ache. Sometimes he kills me before he knows why he can't. Sometimes I die loving him anyway. Once—just once—we lived long enough to grow old, and the world died instead, resetting while we held each other in the ashes.

But this time—this time I think I might get it right.

I exist now in the spaces between moments, diffused across every second we should have had. I can see them all—every iteration, every failure, every version of myself standing where I once stood. I watch them fall through lightning and land in moss. I watch them meet his eyes for the first time and pretend they don't feel recognition. I watch them love him, lose him, choose wrong, die wrong, break the world trying to save it.

Sixteen times I have failed. Sixteen times the wheel has turned, grinding us both to dust and beginning again.

But I am speaking now into the seed of a moment—before the thunder that isn't thunder, before he looks up and sees me properly for the first time in this iteration. Before everything changes and nothing does.

She's there—the version of me who still believes in beginnings. Who thinks endings can be escaped if you just try hard enough, love fiercely enough, sacrifice beautifully enough. She doesn't know yet that she's been here before in seventeen different ways, wearing different faces, making seventeen different mistakes that all lead to the same devastation.

She has my grandmother's stubborn chin. My mother's earth-green eyes. And somewhere beneath her skin, marks that haven't bloomed yet—golden vines that will spread like prophecy and doom combined. She's about to meet him. The man who is both salvation and ending.

The one who will carve himself open trying to reach me, who will become death incarnate because the alternative is watching me disappear. Again.

Kaelren doesn't remember the other iterations. Not consciously. But his body knows. His corruption knows. Every time he looks at this new Elle, some part of him will recognize her the way you recognize dreams you can't quite recall—familiar and devastating and just out of reach.

He will fight what we are. He always does. He'll push her away with cruel words and colder eyes, all while his marks reach for hers like plants toward sunlight. He'll tell himself it's duty, debt, necessity—anything but the truth that echoes across seventeen lifetimes.

We were always going to love each other. We were always going to destroy each other trying.

Maybe if I whisper softly enough through time's cracks, she'll hear me— this seventeenth Elle who's about to crash through lightning into a realm that's been waiting for her since before she was born. Maybe she'll feel it when she first sees him: not love at first sight, but recognition at first sight. The way you know a story you've already lived.

Maybe this time, that will be enough.

The thunder begins. Not real thunder—never real thunder. It's the sound of reality tearing, of the wheel beginning its turn once more, of my grandmother's last desperate attempt to change the pattern finally, finally bearing fruit.

Lightning splits the sky of two worlds.

And she falls.

I am here, scattered across every moment she will live and die. I am the whisper in her instincts, the certainty in her bones, the reason she'll refuse every ending except the one she chooses.

This time, she knows about the pattern. That's never happened before.

This time, she'll disperse herself across time trying to break it. That's never been tried before.

This time—

This time has to be different.

Because I can't bear to watch him scream my name in seventeen different timelines. Can't watch her make the same mistakes I made, choose the same impossible choices, fail in the same beautiful, terrible ways.

So I wait here between seconds, neither alive nor dead nor anything the wheel knows how to categorize. I wait and I watch and I pray to forces older than the mistake that started this:

Let this one stick.

Let her be stubborn enough.

Let him love her fiercely enough.

Let seventeen be the number that breaks instead of bends.

The lightning strikes. She gasps awake in a realm that knows her blood. And somewhere in the Wynmire, a man who has met her seventeen times without knowing feels recognition pierce him like a blade.

It begins again.

Please, gods and roots and ancient blooming things—

Let it also end.

About the Author

J.K. Ross is an avid reader and unapologetic book lover with a journalism degree that taught her to chase stories and a grandmother who showed her how to find magic in them. Her debut fantasy novel weaves together the thorns of destiny, blooms that refuse to follow the rules, and the discovery that sometimes the most beautiful things need thorns to survive.

When she's not writing, she's chasing wanderlust—having explored over ten countries in recent years, always in search of places that feel plucked from a storybook. Europe, with its fairytale charm, continues to inspire her imagination—especially Ireland, which she swears is a real-life fairy garden.

She writes best at ungodly hours, fueled by Dr Pepper and the supervision of her demanding coworkers: a very professional Goldendoodle named Ranger and a less-than-professional Maine Coon known as Grand Duchess Freya. Together, they make sure every writing session is filled with magic, mayhem, and maybe a bit of mischief.

J.K. lives in Arkansas with her husband and two children, where she believes the best stories, like the best gardens, grow wild when you're not looking. When she's not crafting worlds where magic costs everything and love might cost more, you can find her reading or planning her next European adventure.

You can connect with me on:

🌐 https://authorjkross.com
🔗 https://www.instagram.com/authorjkross
🔗 https://tiktok.com/@authorjkross

Subscribe to my newsletter:

✉ https://shorturl.at/DOIXc

www.ingramcontent.com/pod-product-compliance
Lightning Source LLC
Chambersburg PA
CBHW030334120726
47901CB00007B/1790